Jeffrey Archer is a master storyteller, the author of ten novels which have all been worldwide bestsellers. *Not a Penny More, Not a Penny Less* was his first book, and it achieved instant success. Next came the tense and terrifying thriller *Shall We Tell the President?*, followed by his triumphant bestseller *Kane and Abel*. His first collection of short stories, *A Quiver Full of Arrows*, came next, and then *The Prodigal Daughter*, the superb sequel to *Kane and Abel*. This was followed by *First Among Equals*, considered by the *Scotsman* to be the finest novel about parliament since Trollope, the thrilling chase story *A Matter of Honour*, his second collection of stories, *A Twist in the Tale*, and the novels *As the Crow Flies* and *Honour Among Thieves*. *Twelve Red Herrings*, his third collection of stories, was followed by the novels *The Fourth Estate* and *The Eleventh Commandment*. A collected edition of his short stories was published in 1997.

Jeffrey Archer was born in 1940 and educated at Wellington School, Somerset and Brasenose College, Oxford. He represented Great Britain in the 100 metres in the early sixties, and entered the House of Commons when he won the by-election at Louth in 1969. He wrote his first novel, *Not a Penny More, Not a Penny Less*, in 1974. From September 1985 to October 1986 he was Deputy Chairman of the Conservative Party, and he was created a Life Peer in the Queen's Birthday Honours of 1992. He lives in Cambridge with his wife and two sons.

By the same author

Novels

SHALL WE TELL THE PRESIDENT?
KANE AND ABEL
THE PRODIGAL DAUGHTER
FIRST AMONG EQUALS
A MATTER OF HONOUR
AS THE CROW FLIES
HONOUR AMONG THIEVES
THE FOURTH ESTATE
THE ELEVENTH COMMANDMENT

Short Stories

A QUIVER FULL OF ARROWS
A TWIST IN THE TALE
TWELVE RED HERRINGS
THE COLLECTED SHORT STORIES

Plays

BEYOND REASONABLE DOUBT
EXCLUSIVE

JEFFREY ARCHER

NOT A PENNY MORE, NOT A PENNY LESS

SHALL WE TELL THE PRESIDENT?

Grafton

This omnibus edition published in 1998 by
HarperCollins*Publishers*

Reprinted 2003

HarperCollins*Publishers*
77-85 Fulham Palace Road,
Hammersmith, London W6 8JB

ISBN 0 007 68357 X

Printed and bound in Great Britain by
Mackays of Chatham Ltd, Chatham, Kent

**To Mary
and the fat men**

Acknowledgments

I acknowledge all the help I received from so many people in writing this book and wish to thank them: David Niven, Jr, who made me do it, Sir Noel and Lady Hall who made it possible, Adrian Metcalfe, Anthony Rentoul, Colin Emson, Ted Francis, Godfrey Barker, Willy West, Madame Tellegen, David Stein, Christian Neffe, Dr John Vance, Dr David Weeden, the Rev. Leslie Styler, Robert Gasser, Professor Jim Bolton, and Jamie Clark; Gail and Jo for putting it together; and my wife, Mary, for the hours spent correcting and editing.

Prologue

'Jörg, expect $7 million from Crédit Parisien in the No. 2 account by 6 pm tonight, Central European time, and place it with first-class banks and triple "A" commercial names. Otherwise, invest it in the overnight Euro-dollar market. Understood?'

'Yes, Harvey.'

'Place $1 million in the Banco do Minas Gerais, Rio de Janeiro, in the names of Silverman and Elliot and cancel the call loan at Barclays Bank, Lombard Street. Understood?'

'Yes, Harvey.'

'Buy gold on my commodity account until it reaches $10 million and then hold until you receive further instructions. Try and buy in the troughs and don't rush – be patient. Understood?'

'Yes, Harvey.'

Harvey Metcalfe realised that the last instruction was unnecessary. Jörg Birrer was one of the most conservative bankers in Zürich and, more important to Harvey, had over the past twenty-five years proved to be one of the shrewdest.

'Can you join me at Wimbledon on Tuesday, June 25th at 2 pm, Centre Court, my usual debenture seat?'

'Yes, Harvey.'

The telephone clicked into place. Harvey never said goodbye. He had never understood the niceties of life and it was too late to start learning now. He picked up the phone, dialled the seven digits which would give him the

Lincoln Trust in Boston, and asked for his secretary.

'Miss Fish?'

'Yes, sir.'

'Remove the file on Prospecta Oil and destroy it. Destroy any correspondence connected with it and leave absolutely no trace. Understood?'

'Yes, sir.'

The telephone clicked again. Harvey Metcalfe had given similar orders three times in the last twenty-five years and by now Miss Fish had learnt not to question him.

Harvey breathed deeply, almost a sigh, a quiet exhalation of triumph. He was now worth at least $25 million, and nothing could stop him. He opened a bottle of Krug champagne 1964, imported from Hedges & Butler of London. He sipped it slowly and lit a Romeo y Julieta Churchill, which an Italian immigrant smuggled in for him in boxes of two hundred and fifty once a month from Cuba. He settled back for a mild celebration. In Boston, Massachusetts, it was 12.20 pm – nearly time for lunch.

In Harley Street, Bond Street, the King's Road and Magdalen College, Oxford, it was 6.20 pm. Four men, unknown to each other, checked the market price of Prospecta Oil in the final edition of the London *Evening Standard*. It was £3.70. All four of them were rich men, looking forward to consolidating their already successful careers.

Tomorrow they would be penniless.

1

Making a million legally has always been difficult. Making a million illegally has always been a little easier. Keeping a million when you have made it is perhaps the most difficult of all. Henryk Metelski was one of those rare men who had managed all three. Even if the million he had made legally came after the million he had made illegally, Metelski was still a yard ahead of the others: he had managed to keep it all.

Henryk Metelski was born on the Lower East Side of New York on May 17th, 1909, in a small room that already slept four children. He grew up through the Depression, believing in God and one meal a day. His parents were from Warsaw and had emigrated from Poland at the turn of the century. Henryk's father was a baker by trade and had soon found a job in New York, where immigrant Poles specialised in baking black rye bread and running small restaurants for their countrymen. Both parents would have liked Henryk to be an academic success, but he was never destined to become an outstanding pupil at his high school. His natural gifts lay elsewhere. A cunning, smart little boy, he was far more interested in the control of the underground school market in cigarettes and liquor than in stirring tales of the American Revolution and the Liberty Bell. Little Henryk never believed for one moment that the best things in life were free, and the pursuit of money and power came as naturally to him as the pursuit of a mouse to a cat.

When Henryk was a pimply and flourishing fourteen-

11

year-old, his father died of what we now know to be cancer. His mother outlived her husband by no more than a few months, leaving the five children to fend for themselves. Henryk, like the other four, should have gone into the district orphanage for destitute children, but in the mid-1920s it was not hard for a boy to disappear in New York – though it was harder to survive. Henryk became a master of survival, a schooling which was to prove very useful to him in later life.

He knocked around the Lower East Side with his belt tightened and his eyes open, shining shoes here, washing dishes there, always looking for an entrance to the maze at the heart of which lay wealth and prestige. His first chance came when his room-mate Jan Pelnik, a messenger boy on the New York Stock Exchange, put himself temporarily out of action with a sausage garnished with salmonella. Henryk, deputed to report his friend's mishap to the Chief Messenger, upgraded food-poisoning to tuberculosis, and talked himself into the ensuing vacancy. He then changed his room, donned a new uniform, lost a friend, and gained a job.

Most of the messages Henryk delivered during the early twenties read 'Buy'. Many of them were quickly acted upon, for this was a boom era. He watched men of little ability make fortunes while he remained nothing more than an observer. His instincts directed him towards those individuals who made more money in a week on the Stock Exchange than he could hope to make in a lifetime on his salary.

He set about learning how to master the way the Stock Exchange operated, he listened to private conversations, opened sealed messages and found out which closed company reports to study. By the age of eighteen he had four years' experience of Wall Street: four years which most messenger boys would have spent simply walking across crowded floors, delivering little pink pieces of paper; four years which to Henryk Metelski were the equivalent of a Master's Degree from the Harvard Business School.

He was not to know that one day he would lecture to that august body.

One morning in July 1927 he was delivering a message from Halgarten & Co., a well-established brokerage house, making his usual detour via the washroom. He had perfected a system whereby he could lock·himself into a cubicle, study the message he was carrying, decide whether the information was of any value to him and, if it was, immediately telephone Witold Gronowich, an old Pole who managed a small insurance firm for his fellow countrymen. Henryk reckoned to pick up an extra $20 to $25 a week for the inside knowledge he supplied. Gronowich, in· no position to place large sums on the market, never let any of the leaks lead back to his young informant.

Sitting on the lavatory seat, Henryk began to realise that this time he was reading a message of considerable importance. The Governor of Texas was about to grant the Standard Oil Company permission to complete a pipeline from Chicago to Mexico, all other public bodies involved having already agreed to the proposal. The market was aware that the company had been trying to obtain this final permission for nearly a year, but the general view was that the Governor would turn it down. The message was to be passed direct to John D. Rockefeller's broker, Tucker Anthony, immediately. The granting of this permission to build a pipeline would open up the entire North to a ready supply of oil, and that could only mean increased profits. It was obvious to Henryk that Standard Oil stock must rise steadily on the market once the news had broken, especially as Standard Oil already controlled 90 per cent of the oil refineries in America.

In normal circumstances Henryk would have sent on this information direct to Mr Gronowich, and was about to do so when he noticed a rather overweight man, who was also leaving the washroom, drop a piece of paper. As there was no one else about at the time, Henryk picked it up and retreated back into his private cubicle, thinking that at best it would reveal another piece of information. In fact, it was a cheque for $50,000 made out to cash from a Mrs Rose Rennick.

Henryk thought quickly, and not on his feet. He left the washroom at speed and was soon standing outside on Wall Street itself. He made his way to a small coffee-shop on Rector Street and sat there pretending to drink a Coca-Cola while he carefully worked out his plan. He then proceeded to act on it.

First, he cashed the cheque at a branch of the Morgan Bank on the south-west side of Wall Street, knowing that in his smart uniform as a messenger at the Exchange he would easily pass as a carrier for some distinguished firm. He then returned to the Exchange and acquired from a floor broker 2,500 Standard Oil shares at $19⅞, leaving himself $126.61 change after brokerage charges. He placed the $126.61 in a Checking Account with the Morgan Bank. Then, waiting in tense anticipation for an announcement from the Governor's office, he put himself through the motions of a normal day's work, too preoccupied with Standard Oil even to make a detour via the washroom with the messages he carried.

No announcement came. Henryk could not know that the news was being held up until the Exchange had officially closed at 3 pm in order to allow the Governor himself to buy shares anywhere and everywhere he could lay his grubby hands on them. Henryk went home that night petrified that he had made a disastrous mistake. He had visions of losing his job and everything he had built up over the past four years. Perhaps he would even end up in jail.

He was unable to sleep that night and became steadily more restless in his small open-windowed but airless room. At 1 am he could stand the uncertainty no longer, so he jumped out of bed, shaved, dressed and took a subway to Grand Central Station. From there he walked to Times Square where with trembling hands he bought the first edition of the *Wall Street Journal*. For a moment he couldn't take in the news, although it was shrieking at him in banner headlines:

GOVERNOR GRANTS OIL PIPELINE RIGHTS TO ROCKEFELLER

and a secondary headline:

HEAVY TRADING EXPECTED IN STANDARD OIL SHARES

Dazed, Henryk walked to the nearest all-night café, on West 42nd Street, and ordered a large hamburger and French fries, which he covered in ketchup and nibbled at like a man eating his last breakfast before facing the electric chair, rather than his first on the way to fortune. He read the full details of Rockefeller's coup on page one, which spread over to page fourteen, and by 4 am he had bought the first three editions of the *New York Times* and the first two editions of the *Herald Tribune*. The lead story was the same in each. Henryk hurried home, giddy and elated, and changed into his uniform. He arrived at the Stock Exchange at 8 am and went through the motions of a day's work, thinking only of how to carry out the second part of his plan.

When the Stock Exchange opened officially, Henryk went over to the Morgan Bank and requested a loan of $50,000 against the security of his 2,500 Standard Oil shares, which had opened that morning at $21¼. He placed the loan in his Checking Account and instructed the bank to issue him a draft for the $50,000 to be made out to Mrs Rose Rennick. He left the bank and looked up the address and telephone number of his unwitting benefactor.

Mrs Rennick, a widow who lived off the investments left by her late husband, lived in a small apartment on 62nd Street, which Henryk knew to be one of the most fashionable parts of New York. The call from a Henryk Metelski, asking to see her on an urgent private matter, came as something of a surprise to her, but a final mention of Halgarten & Co. gave her a little more confidence and she agreed to see him at the Waldorf-Astoria at 4 pm that afteroon.

Henryk had never been inside the Waldorf-Astoria, but after four years on the Stock Exchange there were few prominent hotels or restaurants he had not heard mentioned in other people's conversations. He realised that Mrs Rennick was more likely to have tea with him there than to see a man with a name like Henryk Metelski in her own apartment, especially as his Polish accent was more pronounced over the telephone than it was face to face.

As Henryk stood in the thickly carpeted lobby of the Waldorf, he blushed at his sartorial naïveté. Imagining that everybody was staring at him, he buried his short, amply-covered frame in an elegant chair in the Jefferson Room. Some of the other patrons of the Waldorf were amply covered too, but Henryk felt that *Pommes de Terre Maître d'Hôtel* were more likely to have caused their obesity than French fries. Vainly wishing he had put a little less grease on his black wavy hair and a little more on his down-at-heel shoes, he scratched nervously at an irritating pustule on the side of his mouth and waited. His suit, in which he felt so assured and prosperous among his friends, was shiny, skimpy, cheap and loud. He did not blend in with the décor, still less with the patrons of the hotel, and, feeling inadequate for the first time in his life, he picked up a copy of the *New Yorker*, hid behind it, and prayed for his guest to arrive quickly. Waiters fluttered deferentially with instinctive superciliousness. One, he noticed, did nothing more than circle the tearoom delicately proffering lump sugar from silver tongs in a white-gloved hand: Henryk was enormously impressed.

Rose Rennick arrived a few minutes after four, accompanied by two small dogs and wearing an outrageously large hat. Henryk thought she looked over sixty, overweight, overmade-up and overdressed, but she had a warm smile and appeared to know everyone, as she moved from table to table, chatting to the regular Waldorf-Astoria set.

Eventually reaching what she had rightly assumed to be Henryk's table, she was rather taken aback, not only to find him so strangely dressed, but also looking even younger than his eighteen years.

Mrs Rennick ordered tea while Henryk recited his well-rehearsed story: there had been an unfortunate mistake with her cheque, which had been wrongly credited to his firm at the Stock Exchange on the previous day; his boss had instructed him to return the cheque immediately and to say how much they regretted the unfortunate error. Henryk then passed over the draft for $50,000, and added that he would lose his job if she insisted on taking the matter any further, as he had been entirely responsible for the mistake. Mrs Rennick had, in fact, only been informed of the missing cheque that morning and did not realise that it had been cashed, as it would have taken a few days to clear her account. Henryk's perfectly genuine anxiety as he stumbled through his tale would have convinced a far more critical observer of human nature than Mrs Rennick. Readily she agreed to let the matter drop, only too pleased to have her money returned; as it was in the form of a draft from the Morgan Bank, she had lost nothing. Henryk breathed a sigh of relief and for the first time that day began to relax and enjoy himself. He even called for the waiter with the sugar and silver tongs.

After a respectable period of time had passed, Henryk explained that he must return to work, thanked Mrs Rennick for her co-operation, paid the bill and left. Outside on the street he whistled with relief. His new shirt was soaked in sweat (Mrs Rennick would have called it perspiration), but he was out in the open and could breathe freely again. His first major operation had been a success.

He stood on Park Avenue, amused that the venue for his confrontation with Mrs Rennick had been the Waldorf, the very hotel where John D. Rockefeller, the President of Standard Oil, had a suite. Henryk had arrived on foot and used the main entrance, while Mr Rockefeller had earlier arrived by subway and taken his private lift to the

17

Waldorf Towers. Although few New Yorkers were aware of it, Rockefeller had had his own private station built fifty feet below the Waldorf-Astoria to save him travelling the eight blocks to Grand Central Station, there being no stop between there and 125th Street. (The station remains to this day, but as no Rockefellers live at the Waldorf-Astoria, the train never stops there.) While Henryk had been discussing his $50,000 with Mrs Rennick, Rockefeller had been considering an investment of $5,000,000 with Andrew W. Mellon, President Coolidge's Secretary of the Treasury, fifty-seven floors above him.

The next morning Henryk returned to work as usual. He knew he had only five days' grace to sell the shares and clear his debt with the Morgan Bank and the stockbroker, as an account on the New York Stock Exchange runs for five business days or seven calendar days. On the last day of the account the shares were standing at $23¼. He sold at $23⅛, and cleared his overdraft of $49,625 and, after expenses, realised a profit of $7,490 which he left deposited with the Morgan Bank.

Over the next three years, Henryk stopped ringing Mr Gronowich, and started dealing for himself, in small amounts to begin with, but growing larger as he gained in experience and confidence. Times were still good, and while he didn't always make a profit, he had learnt to master the occasional bear market as well as the more common bull. His system in the bear market was to sell short – not a practice considered to be entirely ethical in business. He soon mastered the art of selling shares he didn't own in expectation of a subsequent fall in their price. His instinct for market trends refined as rapidly as did his taste for clothes, and the guile learnt in the back-streets of the Lower East Side always stood him in good stead. Henryk soon discovered that the whole world was a jungle – sometimes the lions and tigers wore suits.

When the stock market collapsed in 1929 Henryk had turned his $7,490 into $51,000 of liquid assets, having sold on every share he possessed the day after the Chairman of Halgarten & Co. jumped out of one of the Stock Exchange windows. Henryk had got the message. With his newly acquired income he had moved into a smart apartment in Brooklyn and started driving a rather ostentatious red Stutz. Henryk realised at an early age that he had come into the world with three main disadvantages – his name, background and impecunity. The money problem was solving itself, and now the time had come to expunge the other two. To that end, he had made an application to change his name by court order to Harvey David Metcalfe. When the application was granted, he ceased all further contact with his friends from the Polish community, and in May 1930 he came of age with a new name, new background, and very new money.

It was later that year at a football game that he first met Roger Sharpley and discovered that the rich have their problems too. Sharpley, a young man from Boston, had inherited his father's company, which specialised in the import of whisky and the export of furs. Educated at Choate and later in Dartmouth College, Sharpley had all the assurance and charm of the Boston set, so often envied by his fellow countrymen. He was tall and fair, looked as if he came from Viking stock, and with his air of the gifted amateur, found most things came easily to him – especially women. He was in every way a total contrast to Harvey. Although they were poles apart, the contrast acted like a magnet and attracted the one to the other.

Roger's only ambition in life was to become an officer in the Navy, but after graduating from Dartmouth he had had to return to the family business because of his fater's ill-health. He had only been with the firm a few months when his father died. Roger would have liked to have sold Sharpley & Son to the first bidder, but his father had made a codicil to his will to the effect that if the firm were sold before Roger's fortieth birthday (that being the last day one can enlist for the US Navy), the money gained from the sale would be divided equally among his other relatives.

19

Harvey gave Roger's problem considerable thought, and after two lengthy sessions with a skilful New York lawyer, suggested a course of action to Roger: Harvey would purchase 49 per cent of Sharpley & Son for $100,000 and the first $20,000 profit each year. At the age of forty, Roger could relinquish the remaining 51 per cent for a further $100,000. The Board would consist of three voting members – Harvey, Roger and one nominated by Harvey, giving him overall control. As far as Harvey was concerned, Roger could join the Navy and need only attend the annual shareholders' meeting.

Roger could not believe his luck. He did not even consult anyone at Sharpley & Son, knowing only too well that they would try to talk him out of it. Harvey had counted on this and had assessed his quarry accurately. Roger gave the proposition only a few days' consideration before allowing the legal papers to be drawn up in New York, far enough away from Boston to be sure the firm did not learn what was going on. Meanwhile, Harvey returned to the Morgan Bank, where he was now looked upon as a man with a future. Since banks deal in futures, the manager agreed to help him in his new enterprise with a loan of $50,000 to add to his own $50,000, enabling Harvey to acquire 49 per cent of Sharpley & Son, and become its fifth President. The legal documents were signed in New York on October 28th, 1930.

Roger left speedily for Newport, Rhode Island, to commence his Officers Training programme in the US Navy. Harvey left for Grand Central Station to catch the train for Boston. His days as a messenger boy on the New York Stock Exchange were over. He was twenty-one years of age and the President of his own company.

What looked like disaster to most, Harvey could always turn into triumph. The American people were still suffering under Prohibition, and although Harvey could export furs, he could no longer import whisky. This had been the main reason for the fall in the company profits over the past decade. But Harvey soon found that with a little bribery, involving the Mayor of Boston, the Chief of Police and the Customs officials on the Canadian border, plus a payment to the Mafia to ensure that his products reached the restaurants and speak-easies, somehow the whisky imports went up rather than down. Sharpley & Son lost its more respectable and long-serving staff, and replaced them with animals better-suited to Harvey Metcalfe's particular jungle.

From 1930 to 1933 Harvey went from strength to strength, but when Prohibition was finally lifted by President Roosevelt after overwhelming public demand, the excitement went with it, Harvey allowed the company to continue to deal in whisky and furs while he branched out into new fields. In 1933 Sharpley & Son celebrated a hundred years in business. In three years Harvey had lost 97 years of goodwill and doubled the profits. It took him five years to reach his first million and only another four to double the sum again, which was when he decided the time had come for Harvey Metcalf and Sharpley & Son to part company. In twelve years from 1930 to 1942, he had built up the profits from $30,000 to $910,000. He sold the company in January 1944 for $7,000,000, paying $100,000 to the widow of Captain Roger Sharpley of the US Navy and keeping $6,900,000 for himself.

Harvey celebrated his thirty-fifth birthday by buying at a cost of $4 million a small, ailing bank in Boston called the Lincoln Trust. At the time it boasted a profit of approximately $500,000 a year, a prestigious building in the centre of Boston and an unblemished and somewhat boring reputation. Harvey intended to change both its reputation and its balance sheet. He enjoyed being the President of a bank – but it did nothing to improve his honesty. Every dubious deal in the Boston area seemed to emanate from the Lincoln Trust, and although Harvey increased the bank's profits to $2 million per annum during the next five years, his personal reputation was never in credit.

* * *

Harvey met Arlene Hunter in the winter of 1949. She was the only daughter of the President of the First City Bank of Boston. Until then Harvey had never taken any real interest in women. His driving force had always been making money, and although he considered the opposite sex a useful relaxation in his free time, on balance he found them an inconvenience. But having now reached what the glossy magazines referred to as middle age and having no heir to leave his fortune to, he calculated that it was time to find a wife who would present him with a son. As with everything else that he had wanted in his life, he considered the problem very carefully.

Harvey had first run into Arlene when she was thirty-one: quite literally, when she had backed her car into his new Lincoln. She could not have been a greater contrast to the short, uneducated, overweight Pole. She was nearly six feet tall, slim and although not unattractive, she lacked confidence and was beginning to think that marriage had passed her by. Most of her school friends were already on their second divorces and felt rather sorry for her. Harvey's extravagant ways came as a welcome change after her parents' prudish discipline, which she often felt was to blame for her awkwardness with men of her own age. She had only had one affair – a disastrous failure, thanks to her total innocence – and until Harvey arrived, no one had seemed to be willing to give her a second chance. Arlene's father did not approve of Harvey, and showed it, which only made him more attractive to her. Her father had not approved of any of the men she had associated with, but on this occasion he was right. Harvey on the other hand realised that to marry the First City Bank of Boston with the Lincoln Trust could only be of long-term benefit to him, and with that in mind he set out, as he always did, to conquer. Arlene didn't put up much of a battle.

Arlene and Harvey were married in 1951 at a wedding more memorable for those who were absent than those who attended. They settled into Harvey's Lincoln home outside of Boston and very shortly afterwards Arlene announced she was pregnant. She gave Harvey a daughter almost a year to the day after their marriage.

They christened her Rosalie, and she became the centre of Harvey's attention; his only disappointment came when a prolapse closely followed by a hysterectomy prevented Arlene from bearing him any more children. He sent Rosalie to Bennetts, the most expensive girls' school in Washington, and from there she was accepted at Vassar to major in English. This even pleased old man Hunter, who had grown to tolerate Harvey and adore hs granddaughter. On gaining her degree, Rosalie continued her education at the Sorbonne, after a fierce disagreement with her father concerning the type of friends she was keeping, particularly the ones with long hair who didn't want to go to Vietnam – not that Harvey had done much during the Second World War, except to cash in on every shortage. The final crunch came when Rosalie dared to suggest that morals were not to be decided only by length of hair or political views. Harvey missed her, but refused to admit the fact to Arlene.

Harvey had three loves in his life: the first was still Rosalie, the second was his paintings, and the third his orchids. The first had started the moment his daughter was born. The second was a love that had developed over many years and had been kindled in the strangest way. A client of Sharpley & Son was about to go bankrupt while still owing a fairly large sum of money to the company. Harvey got wind of it and went round to confront him, but the rot had already set in and there was no longer any hope of securing cash. Determined not to leave empty-handed, Harvey took with him the man's only tangible asset – a Renoir valued at $10,000.

Harvey's intention was to sell the picture quickly before it could be proved that he was a preferred creditor, but he became so entranced with the fine brushwork and the delicate pastel shades that his only desire was to own more. When he realised that pictures were not only a good investment, but that he actually liked them as well, his collection and his love grew hand in hand. By the early 1970s, Harvey had a Manet, two Monets, a Renoir, two Picassos, a Pissarro, a Utrillo, a Cézanne, as well as most of the recognised lesser names, and he had become quite a connoisseur of the Impressionist period. His one remaining desire was to possess a Van Gogh, and only recently he had failed to acquire *L'Hôpital de St Paul à St Remy* at the Sotheby-Parke Bernet Gallery in New York, when Dr Armand Hammer of Occidental Petroleum had outbid him – $1,200,000 had been just a little too much for Harvey.

Earlier, in 1966, he had failed to acquire Lot 49, *Mademoiselle Ravoux*, from Christie, Manson & Woods, the London art dealers; although the Rev. Theodore Pitcairn, representing the Lord's New Church in Bryn Athyn, Pennsylvania, had pushed him over the top, he had only whetted his appetite further. The Lord giveth, and on that occasion the Lord had taken away. Although it was not fully appreciated in Boston, it was already recognised in the art world that Harvey had one of the finest Impressionist collections in the world, almost as widely admired as that of Walter Annenberg, President Nixon's Ambassador to London who, like Harvey, had been one of the few people to build up a major collection since the Second World War.

Harvey's third love was his prize collection of orchids, and he had three times been a winner at the New England Spring Flower Show in Boston, twice beating old man Hunter into second place.

Harvey now travelled to Europe once a year. He had established a successful stud in Kentucky and liked to see his horses run at Longchamp and Ascot. He also enjoyed watching Wimbledon, which he considered was still the greatest tennis tournament in the world. It amused him to do a little business in Europe at the same time, giving him the opportunity to make some more money for his Swiss bank account in Zürich. He did not need a Swiss account, but somehow he got a kick out of doing Uncle Sam.

Although Harvey had mellowed over the years and cut down on his more dubious deals, he could never resist the chance to take a risk if he thought the reward was likely to be big enough. One such golden opportunity presented itself in 1964 when Her Majesty's Government invited applications for exploration and production licences in the North Sea. At that time neither the British Government nor the civil servants involved had any idea of the future significance of North Sea oil, or the role it would eventually play in British politics. If the Government had known that in 1978 the Arabs would be holding a pistol to the heads of the rest of the world, and the British House of Commons would have eleven Scottish Nationalist Members of Parliament, it would surely have reacted in a totally different way.

On May 13th, 1964, the Secretary of State for Power laid before Parliament 'Statutory Instrument – No. 708 – Continental Shelf – Petroleum'. Harvey read this particular document with great interest, thinking that it might well be a means of making an exceptional killing. He was particularly fascinated by Pargraph 4 of the document, which read:

Persons who are citizens of the United Kingdom and Colonies and are resident in the United Kingdom or who are bodies corporate incorporated in the United Kingdom may apply in accordance with these Regulations for: .

(a) a production licence; or,
(b) an exploration licence.

When he had studied the Regulations in their entirety, he had to sit back and think hard. Only a small amount of money was required to secure a production and exploration licence. As Paragraph 6 went on to point out:

(1) With every application for a production licence there shall be paid a fee of two hundred pounds with an additional fee of five pounds for every block after the first ten in respect whereof that application is made.

(2) With every application for an exploration licence there shall be paid a fee of twenty pounds.

Harvey couldn't believe it. How easy it would be to use such a licence to create an impression of a vast enterprise! For a few hundred dollars he could be alongside such names as Shell, BP, Total, Gulf and Occidental.

Harvey went over the Regulations again and again, hardly believing that the British Government could release such potential for so small an investment. Only the application form, an elaborate and exacting document, now stood in his way. Harvey was not a British subject, none of his companies was British and he realised he would have problems of presentation. He decided that his application must therefore be backed by a British bank and that he would set up a company whose directors would win the confidence of the British Government.

With this in mind, early in 1964, he registered at Companies House in England a firm called Prospecta Oil, using Malcolm, Bottnick and Davis as his solicitors and Barclays Bank, who were already the Lincoln Trust's representative in Europe, as his bankers. Lord Hunnisett became Chairman of the company and several distinguished public figures joined the Board, including two ex-Members of Parliament who had lost their seats when the Labour Party won the 1964 Election. Prospecta Oil issued 2,000,000 10-pence shares at one pound, which were all taken up for Harvey by nominees. He also deposited $500,000 in the Lombard Street branch of Barclays Bank.

Having thus created the front, Harvey then used Lord Hunnisett to apply for the licence from the British Government. The new Labour Government elected in October 1964 was no more aware of the significance of North

Sea oil than the earlier Conservative administration. The Government's requirements for a licence were a rent of £12,000 a year for the first six years, 12½ per cent revenue tax, and a further Capital Gains tax on profits; but as Harvey's plan was to reap profits for himself rather than the company that presented no problems.

On May 22nd, 1965, the Minister of Power published in the *London Gazette* the name of Prospecta Oil among the fifty-two companies granted production licences. On August 3rd, 1965, Statutory Instrument No. 1531 allocated the actual areas. Prospecta Oil's was 51° 50' 00" N: 2° 30' 20" E, a site adjacent to one of BP's holdings.

Then Harvey sat back, waiting for one of the companies which had acquired North Sea sites to strike oil. It was a longish wait but Harvey was in no hurry, and not until June 1970 did BP make a big commercial strike in their Forties Field. BP had already spent over $1 billion in the North Sea and Harvey was determined to be one of the main beneficiaries. He was now on to another winner, and immediately set the second part of his plan in motion.

Early in 1972 he hired an oil rig which, with much flourish and advance publicity, he had towed out to the Prospecta Oil site. Having hired the rig on the basis of being able to renew the contract if he made a successful strike, he engaged the minimum number of workers allowed by the Government Regulations, and then proceeded to drill to 6,000 feet. After this drilling had been completed he released from the company's employment all those involved, but told Reading & Bates, from whom he had rented the rig, that he would be requiring it again in the near future and therefore would continue to pay the rental.

Harvey then released Prospecta Oil shares on to the market at the rate of a few thousand a day for the next two months, all from his own stock, and whenever the financial journalists of the British Press rang to ask why these shares were steadily rising, the young public relations officer at Prospecta Oil's city office would say, as briefed, that he had no comment to make at present but there would be a press statement in the near future; some newspapers put two and two together and made about fifteen. The shares climbed steadily from 10 pence to nearly £2 under the guidance of Harvey's chief executive in Britain, Bernie Silverman, who, with his long experience of this kind of operation, was only too aware of what his boss was' up to. Silverman's main task was to ensure that nobody could show a direct connection between Metcalfe and Prospecta Oil.

In January 1974 the shares stood at £3. It was then that Harvey was ready to move on to the third part of his plan, using Prospecta Oil's enthusiastic new recruit, a young Harvard graduate called David Kesler, as the fall-guy.

2

David pushed his glasses back on to the bridge of his nose and read the advertisement in the Business Section of the *Boston Globe* again, to make sure he was not dreaming. It could have been tailor-made for him:

> Oil Company based in Great Britain, carrying out extensive work in the North Sea off Scotland, requires a young executive with experience in the stock market and/or financial marketing. Salary $25,000 a year. Accommodation supplied. Based in London. Apply Box No. 217A.

Knowing it could lead to other openings in an expanding industry, David thought it sounded like a challenge and wondered if they would consider him experienced enough. He recalled what his tutor in European affairs used to say: 'If you must work in Great Britain, better make it the North Sea. With their union problems, there's nothing else great about the country.'

David Kesler was a lean, clean-shaven young American, with a crew cut which would have been better suited to a lieutenant in the Marines, a fresh complexion and an unquenchable earnestness. David wanted to succeed in business with all the fervour of the new Harvard Business School graduate. He had spent six years in all at Harvard, the first four studying mathematics for his Bachelor degree, and the last two across the Charles River at the Business School. Recently graduated and armed with a BA and an

MBA, he was looking for a job that would reward him for the exceptional capacity for hard work he knew he possessed. Never a brilliant scholar, he envied those natural academics among his classmates who mastered post-Keynesian economic theories like children learning their multiplication tables. David had worked ferociously for six years, only lifting his nose far enough from the grindstone to fit in a daily workout at the gymnasium and the occasional weekend watching Harvard Jocks defending the honour of the university on the football field or on the basketball court. He would have enjoyed playing himself, but that would have meant less time for study.

He read the advertisement again, and then typed a carefully prepared letter to the box number. A few days passed before a reply came, summoning him for an interview at a local hotel on the following Wednesday at 3.00.

David arrived at 2.45 pm at the Copley Hotel on Huntingdon Avenue, the adrenalin pumping through his body. He repeated the Harvard Business School motto to himself as he was ushered into a small private room: look British, think Yiddish.

Three men, who introduced themselves as Silverman, Cooper and Elliott, interviewed him. Bernie Silverman, a short, grey-haired, check-tied New Yorker with a solid aura of success, was in charge. Cooper and Elliott sat and watched David silently.

Silverman spent a considerable time giving David an enticing description of the company's background and its future aims. Harvey had trained Silverman carefully and he had at his well-manicured fingertips all the glib expertise needed by the right-hand man in a Metcalfe coup.

'So there you have it, Mr Kesler. We're involved in one of the biggest commercial opportunities in the world, drilling for oil in the North Sea off Scotland. Our company, Prospecta Oil, has the backing of a group of banks in America. We have been granted licences from the British Government and we have the financing. But companies are made not by money, Mr Kesler, but by people – it's as simple as that. We're looking for a man who will work night and day to help put Prospecta Oil on the map, and we'll pay the right man a top salary to do just that. If we offer you the position, you'll be working in our London office under the immediate direction of our Managing Director, Mr Elliott.'

'Where are the company headquarters?'

'New York, but we have offices in Montreal, San Francisco, London, Aberdeen, Paris and Brussels.'

'Is the company looking for oil anywhere else?'

'Not at the moment,' answered Silverman. 'We're sinking millions into the North Sea after BP's successful strike, and the fields around us have so far had a one-in-five success ratio, which is very high in our business.'

'When would you want the successful applicant to start?'

'Some time in January, when he's completed a government training course on management in oil,' said Richard Elliott. The slim, sallow No. 2 sounded as if he was from Georgia. The government course was a typical Harvey Metcalfe touch – maximum credibility for minimum expense.

'And the company apartment,' said David, 'where's that?'

Cooper spoke:

'You'll have one of the company flats in the Barbican, a few hundred yards away from our London City office.'

David had no more questions – Silverman had covered everything and seemed to know exactly what he wanted.

Ten days later David received a telegram inviting him to join Silverman for lunch at the 21 Club in New York. When David arrived at the restaurant, he recognised a host of well-known faces at nearby tables and felt new confidence: his host obviously knew what he was about. Their table was in one of the small alcoves selected by businessmen who prefer their conversations to remain confidential.

Silverman was genial and relaxed. He stretched the conversation out a little, discussing irrelevancies, but finally, over a brandy, offered David the position in London. David was delighted: $25,000 a year, and the chance to be involved with a company which obviously had such an exciting future. He did not hesitate in agreeing to start his new appointment in London on January 1st.

David Kesler had never been to England before: how green the grass was, how narrow the roads, how closed in by hedges and fences were the houses! It felt like Toy Town after the vast highways and large automobiles of New York. The small flat in the Barbican was clean and impersonal and, as Mr Cooper had said, convenient for the office a few hundred yards away in Threadneedle Street.

Prospecta's offices consisted of seven rooms on one floor of a large Victorian building; Silverman's was the only office with a prestigious air about it. There was a tiny reception area, a telex room, two rooms for secretaries, a larger room for Mr Elliott and another small one for himself. It seemed very poky to David, but as Silverman was quick to point out, office rent in the City of London was $30 a square foot compared with $10 in New York.

Bernie Silverman's secetary, Judith Lampson, ushered David through to the well appointed office of the Chief Executive. Silverman sat in a large black swivel chair behind a massive desk, which made him look like a midget. By his side were positioned four telephones, three white and one red. David was later to learn that the important-looking red telephone was directly connected to a number in the States, but he never actually discovered to whom.

'Good morning, Mr Silverman. Where would you like me to start?'

'Bernie, please call me Bernie. Take a seat. Notice the change in the price of the company's shares in the last few days?'

'Oh, yes,' enthused David. 'Up a half to nearly $6. I suppose it's because of our new bank backing and the other companies' successful strikes?'

'No,' said Silverman in a low tone designed to give the impression that no one else must hear this part of the conversation, 'the truth is that we've made a big strike ourselves, but we haven't yet decided when to announce it. It's all in this geologist's report.' He threw a smart, colourful document over his desk.

David whistled under his breath. 'What are the company's plans at the moment?'

'We'll announce the strike,' said Silverman quietly, picking at his india rubber as he talked, 'in about three weeks' time, when we're certain of the full extent and capacity of the hole. We want to make some plans for coping with the publicity and the sudden inflow of money. The shares will go through the roof, of course.'

'The shares have already climbed steadily. Perhaps some people already know?'

'I guess that's right,' said Silverman. 'The trouble with that black stuff is once it comes out of the ground you can't hide it.' Silverman laughed.

'Is there any harm in getting in on the act?' asked David.

'No, as long as it doesn't harm the company in any way. Just let me know if anyone wants to invest. We don't have the problems of inside information in England – none of the restrictive laws we have in America.'

'How high do you think the shares will go?'

Silverman looked him straight in the eye and then said casually, '$20.'

Back in his own office, David carefully read the geologist's report that Silverman had given him: it certainly looked as if Prospecta Oil had made a successful strike, but the extent of the find was not, as yet, entirely certain. When he had completed the report, he glanced at his watch and cursed. The geologist's file had totally absorbed him. He threw the report into his briefcase and took a taxi to Paddington Station, only just making the 6.15 train. He was due in Oxford for dinner with an old classmate from Harvard.

33

On the train down to the university city he thought about Stephen Bradley, who had been a friend in his Harvard days and had generously helped David and other students in mathematics classes that year. Stephen, now a visiting Fellow at Magdalen College, was undoubtedly one of the most brilliant scholars of David's generation. He had won the Kennedy Memorial Scholarship to Harvard and later in 1970 the Wister Prize for Mathematics, the most sought-after award in the mathematical faculty. Although in monetary terms this award was a derisory $80 and a medal, it was the reputation and job offers it brought with it that made the competition so keen. Stephen had won it with consummate ease and nobody was surprised when he was successful in his application for a Fellowship at Oxford. He was now in his third year of research at Magdalen. His papers on Boolean algebra appeared at short intervals in the *Proceedings of the London Mathematical Society*, and it had just been announced that he had been elected to a Chair in Mathematics back at his alma mater, Harvard, to commence in the fall.

The 6.15 train from Paddington arrived in Oxford an hour later and the short taxi ride from the station down New College Lane brought him to Magdalen at 7.30. One of the College porters escorted David to Stephen's rooms, which were spacious, ancient, and comfortably cluttered with books, cushions and prints. How unlike the antiseptic walls of Harvard, thought David. Stephen was there to greet him. He didn't seem to have changed one iota. His suit seemed to hang off his tall, thin, ungainly body; no tailor would ever have employed him as a dummy. His heavy eyebrows protruded over his out-of-date round-rimmed spectacles, which he almost seemed to hide behind in his shyness. He ambled over to David and welcomed him, one minute an old man, the next younger than his thirty years. Stephen poured David a Jack Daniels and they settled down to chat. Although Stephen never looked upon David as a close friend at Harvard, he had enjoyed coaching him and always found him eager to learn; besides,

34

he always welcomed an excuse to entertain Americans at Oxford.

'It's been a memorable three years, David,' said Stephen, pouring him a second drink. 'The only sad event was the death of my father last winter. He took such an interest in my life at Oxford and gave my academic work so much support. He's left me rather well off, actually . . . Bath plugs were obviously more in demand than I realised. You might be kind enough to advise me on how to invest some of the money, because at the moment it's just sitting on deposit in the bank. I never seem to have the time to do anything about it, and when it comes to investments I haven't a clue.'

That started David off about his demanding new job with Prospecta Oil.

'Why don't you invest your money in my company, Stephen. We've had a fantastic strike in the North Sea, and when they announce it the shares are going to go through the roof. The whole operation would only take a month or so and you could make the killing of a lifetime. I only wish I had some of my own money to put into it.'

'Have you had the full details of the strike?'

'No, but I've seen the geologist's report, and that makes pretty good reading. The shares are already going up fast and I'm convinced they'll reach $20. The problem is that time is already running out.'

Stephen glanced at the geologist's report, thinking he would study it carefully later.

'How does one go about an investment of this sort?' he asked.

'Well, you find a respectable stockbroker, buy as many shares as you can afford and then wait for the strike to be announced. I'll keep you informed on how things are going and advise you when I feel is the best time to sell.'

'That would be extremely thoughtful of you, David.'

'It's the least I can do after all the help you gave me with maths at Harvard.'

'Oh, that was nothing. Let's go and have some dinner.'

Stephen led David to the college dining hall, an oblong, oak-panelled room covered in pictures of past Presidents of Magdalen, bishops and academics. The long wooden tables at which the undergraduates were eating filled the body of the hall, but Stephen shuffled up to the High Table and offered David a more comfortable seat. The students were a noisy, enthusiastic bunch – Stephen didn't notice them, but David was enjoying the whole experience.

The seven-course meal was formidable and David wondered how Stephen kept so thin with such daily temptations. When they reached the port, Stephen suggested they return to his rooms rather than join the crusty old dons in the Senior Common Room.

Late into the night, over the rubicund Magdalen port, they talked about North Sea oil and Boolean algebra, each admiring the other for his mastery of his subject. Stephen, like most academics, was fairly credulous outside the bounds of his own discipline. He began to think that an investment in Prospecta Oil would be a very astute move on his part.

In the morning, they strolled down Addison's Walk near Magdalen Bridge, where the grass grows green and lush by the Cherwell. Reluctantly, David caught a taxi at 9.45 leaving Magdalen behind him and passing New College, Trinity, Balliol and finally Worcester, where he saw scrawled across the college wall, '*c'est magnifique mais ce n'est pas la gare*'. He caught the 10.00 am train back to London. He had enjoyed his stay at Oxford and hoped he had been able to help his old Harvard friend, who had done so much for him in the past.

'Good morning, David.'

'Good morning, Bernie. I thought I ought to let you know I spent the evening with a friend at Oxford, and he may invest some money in the company. It might be as much as $250,000.'

'That's fine, David, keep up the good work. You're doing a great job.'

Silverman showed no surprise at David's news, but once back in his own office he picked up the red telephone.

'Harvey?'

'Yes.'

'Kesler seems to have been the right choice. He may have talked a friend of his into investing $250,000 in the company.'

'Good. Now listen carefully. Brief my broker to put 40,000 shares on the market at just over $6 a share. If Kesler's friend does decide to invest in the company, mine will be the only large block of shares immediately available.'

After a further day's consideration, Stephen noticed that the shares of Prospecta Oil moved from £2.75 to £3.05 and decided the time had come to invest in what he was now convinced must be a winner. He trusted David, and had been impressed by the glossy geologist's report. He rang Kitcat & Aitken, a firm of stockbrokers in the City, and instructed them to buy $250,000-worth of shares in Prospecta Oil. Harvey Metcalfe's broker released 40,000 shares when Stephen's request came on to the floor of the stock exchange and the transaction was quickly completed. Stephen's purchase price was £3.10.

After investing his father's inheritance, Stephen spent the next few days happily watching the shares climb to £3.50, even before the expected announcement. Though Stephen didn't realise it, it was his own investment that had caused the shares to rise. He began to wonder what he would spend the profit on even before he had realised it. He decided not to cash in immediately, but hold on; David thought the shares would reach $20, and in any case he had promised to tell him when to sell.

Meanwhile, Harvey Metcalfe began to release a few more shares on to the market, because of the interest created by Stephen's investment. He was beginning to agree with Silverman that David Kesler, young, honest, and with all the enthusiasm of a man in his first appointment, had been an excellent choice. It was not the first time Harvey had used this ploy, keeping himself well away from the action while placing the responsibility on inexperienced, innocent shoulders.

At the same time, Richard Elliott, acting as the company spokesman, leaked stories to the press about large buyers coming into the market, which in itself occasioned a flood of small investors and kept the price steady.

One lesson a man learns in the Harvard Business School is that an executive is only as good as his health. David never felt happy without a regular medical check-up; he rather enjoyed being told he was in good shape, but perhaps should take things a little easier. His secretary, Miss Rentoul, had therefore made an appointment for him with a Harley Street doctor.

Dr Robin Oakley was by anyone's standards a successful man. At thirty-seven he was tall and handsome, with a head of dark hair that looked as if it would never recede. He had a classic strong face and the self-assurance that came from proven success. He still played squash twice a week, which helped him look enviably younger than his contemporaries. Robin had remained fit since his Cambridge days, which he left with a Rugby Blue and an upper-second-class degree. He had gone on to complete his medical training at St Thomas's, where once again his Rugby football rather than his medical skill brought him into prominence with those who decide the future careers of young men. When he qualified, he went to work as an assistant to a highly succesful Harley Street practitioner, Dr Eugene Moffat. Dr Moffat was successful not so much in curing the sick as in charming the rich, especially middle-aged women, who came to see him again and again however little seemed to be wrong with them. At fifty guineas a visit that had to be regarded as success.

Moffat had chosen Robin Oakley as his assistant for exactly those qualities which he himself displayed, and which had made him so sought-after. Robin Oakley was unquestionably good-looking, personable, well-educated – and just clever enough. Robin settled very well into Harley Street and the Moffat system, and when the older man died suddenly in his early sixties, he took over his mantle with the ease with which a crown prince would take over a throne. Robin continued to build up the practice, losing none of Moffat's ladies other than by natural causes, and did remarkably well for himself. He had a wife and two sons, a comfortable country house a few miles outside Newbury in Berkshire, and a considerable saving in blue chip securities. He never complained at his good fortune and enjoyed life, at the same time being, he had to confess, a little bored with it all. He was beginning to find that the bland role of sympathetic doctor was almost intolerably cloying. Would the world come to an end if he admitted that he neither knew nor cared just what was causing the minute patches of dermatitis on Lady Fiona Fisher's diamond-studded hands? Would the Heavens descend if he told the dreaded Mrs Page-Stanley that she was a malodorous old woman in need of nothing more medically taxing than a new set of dentures? And would he be struck off if he personally administered to the nubile Miss Lydia de Villiers a good dose of what she so clearly indicated she desired?

David Kesler arrived on time for his appointment. He had been warned by Miss Rentoul that in England doctors and dentists cancel if you are late and still charge you.

He stripped and lay on Robin Oakley's couch. The doctor took his blood pressure, listened to his heart, and made him put out his tongue, an organ that seldom stands up well to public scrutiny. As he tapped and poked his way over David's body, they chatted.

'What brings you to work in London, Mr Kesler?'

'I'm with an oil company in the City. I expect you've heard of us – Prospecta Oil?'

'No,' said Robin. 'Can't say I have. Bend your legs up, please.' He hit David's knee-caps smartly, one after the other, with a patella hammer. The legs jumped wildly.

'Nothing wrong with those reflexes.'

'You will, Dr Oakley, you will. Things are going very well for us. Watch out for our progress in the papers.'

'Why?' said Robin, smiling, 'struck oil, have you?'

'Yes,' said David quietly, pleased with the impression he was creating, 'as a matter of fact we've done just that.'

Robin prodded David's abdomen for a few seconds. 'Good muscular wall, not fat, no sign of an enlarged liver. Young man, you're in good physical shape.'

Robin left him in the examination room to get dressed and thoughtfully wrote out a brief report on Kesler for his records, while his mind dwelt on deeper things. An oil strike.

Harley Street doctors, although they routinely keep private patients waiting for three-quarters of an hour in a gas-fired waiting-room equipped with one out-of-date copy of *Punch*, never let them feel rushed once they are in the consulting room. Robin had no intention of rushing Mr Kesler.

'There's very little wrong with you, Mr Kesler. Some signs of anaemia, which I suspect are caused by nothing more than overwork and your recent rushing about. I'm going to give you some iron tablets which should quickly take care of that. Take two a day, morning and night.' He scribbled an illegible prescription for the tablets and handed it to David.

'Many thanks. It's kind of you to give me so much of your time.'

'Not at all. How are you finding London?' asked Robin. 'Very different from America, I expect.'

'Sure – the pace is much slower. Once I've mastered how long it takes to get something done here I'll be halfway to victory.'

'Do you have many friends in London?'

'No,' replied David, 'I have one or two buddies at Oxford from my Harvard days, but I haven't yet made contact with many people in London.'

40

Good, thought Robin, here is a chance for me to find out a little more about the oil game, and spend some time with a man who makes most of his patients look as if they had both feet in the grave. It might even shake me out of my lethargy. He continued, 'Would you care to join me for lunch later in the week? You might like to see one of our antique London clubs.'

'How very kind of you.'

'Excellent. Will Friday suit you?'

'It certainly will.'

'Then let's say one o'clock at the Athenaeum Club in Pall Mall.'

David returned to his City desk, picking up his tablets on the way. He took one immediately. He was beginning to enjoy his stay in London. Silverman seemed pleased with him, Prospecta Oil was doing well and he was already meeting some interesting people. Yes, he felt this was going to be a very happy period in his life.

On Friday at 12.45 pm, David arrived at the Athenaeum, a massive white building on the corner of Pall Mall, overlooked by a statue of the Duke of York. David was amazed by the size of the rooms and his commercial mind could not help wondering what price they would fetch as office space. The place appeared to be full of moving waxworks who, Robin later assured him, were in fact distinguished generals and diplomats.

They lunched in the Coffee Room, dominated by a Rubens of Charles II, and talked about Boston, London, squash, and their shared passion for Katherine Hepburn. Over coffee, David readily told Robin the details of the geologist's findings on the Prospecta Oil site. The shares had now climbed to £3.60 on the London Stock Exchange, and were still going up.

'Sounds like a good investment,' said Robin, 'and as it's your own company, it might be worth the risk.'

'I don't think there's much of a risk,' said David, 'as long as the oil is actually there.'

41

'Well, I'll certainly consider it most seriously over the weekend.'

They parted on the steps of the Athenaeum, David to a conference on the Energy Crisis organised by the *Financial Times*, Robin to his home in Berkshire. His two young sons were back from prep school for the weekend and he was looking forward to seeing them again. How quickly they had passed from babies to toddlers, to boys; soon they would be young men, he thought. And how reassuring to know their future was secure. Perhaps he should make that future a little more secure by investing in David Kesler's company. He could always put the money back into blue chip shares once the strike had been announced.

Bernie Silverman was also pleased to hear the possibility of a further investment.

'Congratulations, my boy. We're going to need a lot of capital to finance the pipe-laying operations, you know. Pipe-laying can cost $2 million per mile. Still, you're playing your part. I've just had word from head office that we are to give you a $5,000 bonus for your efforts. Keep up the good work.'

David smiled. This was business in the proper Harvard tradition. If you bring home the results, you get the rewards.

'When will the strike be officially announced?' he asked.

'Some time in the next few days.'

David left Silverman's office with a glow of pride.

Silverman immediately contacted Harvey Metcalfe on the red phone, and he set the routine in motion once again. Metcalfe's brokers released on to the market 35,000 shares at £3.73 and approximately 5,000 each day on to the open market, always being able to feel when the market had taken enough and thus keeping the price steady. Once again, the shares climbed when Dr Oakley invested heavily in the market, this time to £3.90, keeping David, Robin and Stephen all happy. They were not to know that Harvey was releasing more shares each day because of the interest they had caused, and that this was now creating a market of its own.

42

David decided to spend some of his bonus on a painting for his little flat in the Barbican, which he felt was rather grey. About $2,000, he thought, something that was going to appreciate in value. David quite enjoyed art for art's sake, but he liked it even more for business's sake. He spent Friday afternoon tramping around Bond Street, Cork Steet and Bruton Street, the home of the London art galleries. The Wildenstein was too expensive for his pocket and the Marlborough too modern for his taste. The painting he finally picked out was at the Lamanns Gallery in Bond Street.

The gallery, just three doors away from Sotheby's, consisted of one vast room with a worn grey carpet and red faded wallpaper. As David was later to learn, the more worn the carpet, the more faded the walls, the greater the success and reputation of the gallery. There was a staircase at the far end of the room, against which some unregarded paintings were stacked, backs to the world. David sorted through them on a whim and found, to his delight, something that appealed to him.

It was an oil by Leon Underwood called *Venus in the Park*. The large, rather sombre canvas contained about six men and women sitting on metal chairs at circular tea-tables. Among them, in the foreground, was a comely naked woman with generous breasts and long hair. Nobody was paying her the slightest attention and she sat gazing out of the picture, face inscrutable, a symbol of warmth and love in indifferent surroundings. David found her utterly compelling.

The gallery proprietor, Jean-Pierre Lamanns, advanced on him, adorned in an elegantly tailored suit, as befitted a man who rarely received cheques for less than a thousand pounds. At thirty-five, he could afford the little extravagances of life, and his Gucci shoes, Yves St Laurent tie, Turnbull & Asser shirt and Piaget watch left no one, especially women, in any doubt that he knew what he was about. He was an Englishman's vision of a Frenchman, slim and neat with longish, dark wavy hair and deep brown eyes that hinted at being a little sharp. He was capable of being pernickety and demanding, with a wit that was often as cruel as it was amusing, which may have been one of the reasons why he had not married. There certainly had been no shortage of applicants. Customers, however, saw only his charming side. As David wrote out his cheque, Jean-Pierre rubbed his forefinger backwards and forwards over his fashionable moustache, only too happy to discuss the picture.

'Underwood is one of the greatest sculptors and artists in England today. He even tutored Henry Moore, you know. I believe he is underestimated because of his dislike of journalists and the press, whom he describes as nothing more than drunken scribblers.'

'Hardly the way to endear oneself to the media,' murmured David, as he handed over the cheque for £850, feeling agreeably prosperous. Although it was the most expensive purchase he had ever made, he felt the picture was a good investment and, more important, he liked it.

Jean-Pierre took David downstairs to show him the Impressionist and Modern collection he had built up over many years, continuing to enthuse about Underwood. They celebrated David's first acquisition over a whisky in Jean-Pierre's office.

'What line of business are you in, Mr Kesler?'

'I work with a small oil company called Prospecta Oil, who are exploring prospects in the North Sea.'

'Had any success?' enquired Jean-Pierre, a little too innocently.

'Well, between the two of us, we're rather excited about the future. It's no secret that the company shares have gone from £2 to nearly £4 in the last few weeks, but no one knows the real reason.'

'Would it be a good investment for a poor little art dealer like myself?' asked Jean-Pierre.

'I'll tell you how good an investment I think it is,' said David. 'I am putting $3,000 in the company on Monday, which is all I have left in the world – now that I've captured

44

Venus, that is. We'll shortly be making a rather important announcement.'

A twinkle came into Jean-Pierre's eye. To one of his Gallic subtlety, a nod was as good as a wink. He did not pursue the line of conversation any further.

'When's the strike going to be announced, Bernie?'

'I'm expecting it early next week. We've had a few problems. Nothing we can't lick, though.'

That gave David some relief, as he had taken up 500 shares himself that morning, investing the remaining $3,000 from his bonus. Like the others, he was hoping for a quick profit.

'Rowe Rudd.'

'Frank Watts, please. Jean-Pierre Lamanns.'

'Good morning, Jean-Pierre. What can we do for you?'

'I want to buy 25,000 Prospecta Oil.'

'Never heard of them. Hold on a minute . . . New company, very low capital. A bit risky, J.-P. I wouldn't recommend it.'

'It's all right, Frank, I only want them for two or three weeks, then you can sell. I've no intention of holding on to them. When did the account start?'

'Yesterday.'

'Right. Buy this morning and sell them before the end of the account, or earlier. I'm expecting an announcement next week, so once they go over £5 you can get rid of them. No need to be greedy, but buy them in my company name, I don't want the deal traced back to me – it might embarrass the informant.'

'Right, sir. Buy 25,000 Prospecta Oil at market price and sell before the last day of the account, or sooner if instructed.'

'Correct, I'll be in Paris all next week looking at pictures, so don't hesitate to sell once they go over £5.'

'Right, J.-P. Have a good trip.'

*　　*　　*

The red telephone rang.

'Rowe Rudd are looking for a substantial block of shares. Do you know anything about it?'

'No idea, Harvey. It must be David Kesler again. Do you want me to speak to him?'

'No, say nothing. I've released another 25,000 shares at £3.90. Kesler's only got to do one more big one and I'll be out. Prepare our plan for seven days before the end of this Stock Exchange account.'

'Right, boss. You know quite a few people are also buying in small amounts.'

'Yes, just as before, they all have to tell their friends they're on to a good thing. Say nothing to Kesler.'

'You know, David,' said Richard Elliott, 'you work too hard. Relax. We're going to have enough work on our hands when the announcement's made.'

'I guess so,' said David. 'Work's just a habit with me now.'

'Well, why don't you take tonight off and join me for a spot of something at Annabel's?'

David was flattered by the invitation to London's most exclusive nightclub and accepted enthusiastically.

David's hired Ford Cortina looked somewhat out of place that evening in Berkeley Square among the double-parked Rolls Royces and Mercedes. He made his way down the little iron staircase into the basement, which at one time must have been no more than the servants' quarters for the elegant town house above. Now it was a splendid club, with a restaurant, discothèque and a small elegant bar, the walls covered in old prints and pictures. The main dining-room was dimly lit and crowded with small tables, most of them already occupied. The décor was Regency and extravagant. Mark Birley, the owner, had in the short period of ten years made Annabel's the most sought-after club in London, with a waiting list for membership of well over a thousand. The discothèque was playing in the far corner of a crowded dance floor, on which you couldn't have parked two Cadillacs. Most of the couples were dancing very close to each other – they had little choice. David was somewhat surprised to observe that nearly all of the men on the floor were about twenty years older than the girls they held in their arms. The head waiter, Louis, showed David to Richard Elliott's table, realising it was David's first visit to the club by the way he stared at all the personalities of the day. Oh well, thought David, perhaps one day they'll be staring at me.

After an exceptionally good dinner Richard Elliott and his wife joined the crowd on the dance floor, while David returned to the little bar surrounded by comfortable red settees and struck up a conversation with someone who introduced himself as James Brigsley. Even if he did not treat the whole world as such, Mr Brigsley certainly treated Annabel's as a stage. Tall, blond and aristocratic, his eyes alight with good humour, he seemed at ease with everyone around him. David admired his assured manner, something he had never acquired and feared he never would. His accent, even to David's untutored ears, was resonantly upper-class.

David's new acquaintance talked of his visits to the States, flattering him by remarking how much he had always liked the Americans. After some time, David was able quietly to ask the head waiter who the Englishman was.

'He's Lord Brigsley, the eldest son of the Earl of Louth, sir.'

What do you know, thought David, lords look like anyone else, especially when they've had a few drinks. Lord Brigsley was tapping David's glass.

'Would you care for another?'

'Thank you very much, my lord,' said David.

'Don't bother with all that nonsense. The name's James. What are you doing in London?'

'I work for an oil company. You probably know my Chairman, Lord Hunnisett. I've never met him myself, to tell you the truth.'

'Sweet old buffer,' said James. 'His son and I were at Harrow together. If you're in oil, perhaps you can tell me what to do with my Shell and BP shares.'

'Hold on to them,' said David. 'It's sensible to remain in any commodities, especially oil, as long as the British Government doesn't get greedy and try to take control of the assets themselves.'

Another double whisky arrived. David was beginning to feel just slightly tipsy.

'What about your own company?' enquired James.

'We're rather small,' said David, 'but our shares have gone up more than any other oil company in the last three months. Even so, I suspect they've nowhere near reached their zenith.'

'Why?' demanded James.

David glanced round and lowered his voice to a confidential whisper.

'Well, I expect you realise that if you make an oil strike in a big company it can only put the percentage of your profits up by a tiny amount. But if you make a strike in a small company, naturally that profit will be reflected as a considerably larger percentage of the whole.'

'Are you telling me you've made a strike?'

'Perhaps I shouldn't have said that,' said David. 'I'd be obliged if you'd treat that remark in confidence.'

David could not remember how he arrived home or who put him to bed, and he appeared rather late in the office the next morning.

'I am sorry, Bernie, I overslept after a very good evening with Richard at Annabel's.'

'Doesn't matter a bit. Glad you enjoyed yourself.'

'I hope I wasn't indiscreet, but I told some lord, whose name I can't even remember, that he ought to invest in the company. I may have been a little too enthusiastic.'

'Don't worry, David, we're not going to let anyone down and you need the rest. You've been working your ass off.'

* * *

James Brigsley left his London flat in Chelsea and took a taxi to his bank, Williams & Glyn's. James was an extrovert by nature and at Harrow his only real love had been acting; but when he had left school, his father had refused to allow him to go on the stage and insisted that he complete his education at Christ Church, Oxford, where again he took a greater interest in the Dramatic Society than in gaining a degree in his chosen subjects of Politics, Philosophy and Economics. James had never mentioned to anyone since leaving Oxford the class of degree he managed to secure, but for better or worse the fourth-class Honours degree was later abolished. After Oxford he joined the Grenadier Guards, which gave him considerable scope for his histrionic talent. This was indeed to be James's introduction to society life in London, and he succeeded as well as a personable, rich young viscount might be expected to do in the circumstances.

When he had completed his two years in the Guards, the earl gave him a 250-acre farm in Hampshire to occupy his time, but James did not care for the coarser country life. He left the running of the farm to a manager and once again concentrated on his social life in London. He would dearly have liked to go on the stage, but he knew the old man still considered Mrs Worthington's daughter's ambition an improper one for a future peer of the realm. The fifth earl didn't think a great deal of his eldest son one way and another, and James did not find it easy to persuade his father that he was shrewder than he was given credit for. Perhaps the inside information David Kesler had let slip after a few drinks would give him the opportunity to prove his old dad wrong.

In Williams & Glyn's fine old building in Birchin Lane, James was ushered into the manager's office.

'I should like to borrow some money against my farm in Hampshire,' said Lord Brigsley.

Philip Izard, the manager, knew Lord Brigsley well and was also acquainted with his father. Although he had respect for the earl's judgment, he did not have a great deal of time for the young lord. Nevertheless, it was not for him to query a customer's request, especially when the customer's family was one of the longest-standing in the bank's history.

'Yes, my lord, what sum do you have in mind?'

'Well, it seems that farmland in Hampshire is worth about £1,000 an acre and is still climbing. Why don't we say £150,000? I should then like to invest the money in shares.'

'Will you agree to leave the deeds with the bank as security?' enquired Izard.

'Yes, of course. What difference does it make to me where they are?'

'Then I am sure we will find it acceptable to advance you a loan of £150,000 at 2 per cent above base rate.'

James was not at all sure what base rate was, but he knew that Williams & Glyn's were as competitive as everyone else in such matters and that their reputation was beyond dispute.

'Thank you,' said James. 'Please acquire for me 35,000 shares in a company called Prospecta Oil.'

'Have you checked carefully into this company, my lord?' enquired Izard.

'Yes, of course I have,' said Lord Brigsley, very sharply. He was not in awe of the bank-managerial class.

In Boston, Harvey Metcalfe was briefed over the telephone by Silverman of the meeting in Annabel's between David Kesler and a nameless peer who seemed to have more money than sense. Harvey released 40,000 shares on to the market at £4.80. Williams & Glyn's acquired 35,000 of them and, once again, the remainder was taken up by small investors. The shares rose a little. Harvey Metcalfe was now left with only 30,000 shares of his own, and over the next four days he was able to dispose of them all. It had taken him fourteen weeks to off-load his entire stock in Prospecta Oil at a profit of just over $6 million.

On the Friday morning, the shares stood at £4.90 and

Kesler had, in all innocence, occasioned four large investments: Harvey Metcalfe studied them in detail before
putting through a call to Jörg Birrer.

Stephen Bradley had bought 40,000 shares at $6.10
   Dr Robin Oakley had bought 35,000 shares at $7.23
   Jean-Pierre Lamanns had bought 25,000 shares at $7.80
   James Brigsley had bought 35,000 shares at $8.80
   David Kesler himself had bought 500 shares at $7.25.

Among them they had purchased 135,500 shares at a
cost of just over $1 million. They had also kept the price
rising, giving Harvey the chance to off-load all his own
stock on to a natural market.

Harvey Metalfe had done it again. His name was not on
the letterhead and now he possessed no shares. Nobody
would be able to place any blame on him. He had done
nothing illegal; even the geologist's report contained
enough ifs and buts to pass in a court of law. As for
David Kesler, Harvey could not be blamed for his youthful
over-enthusiasm. He had never even met the man. Harvey
Metcalfe opened the bottle of Krug Privée Cuvée 1964,
imported from Hedges and Butler of London. He sipped
it slowly, then lit a Romeo y Julieta Churchill, and settled
back for a mild celebration.

David, Stephen, Robin, Jean-Pierre and James celebrated
at the weekend as well. Why not? Their shares were at
£4.90 and David had assured them all that they would
reach £10. On Saturday morning David ordered his first
bespoke suit from Aquascutum, Stephen tut-tutted his way
through the end-of-vacation examination papers he had
set his freshmen students, Robin attended his sons' prep
school Sports Day, Jean-Pierre re-framed a Renoir, and
James Brigsley went shooting, convinced that at last he
had one in the eye for his father.

3

David arrived at the office at 9 am on Monday to find that the front door was locked. He could not understand it. The secretaries were supposed to be in by 8.45.

After waiting around for over an hour, he walked to the nearest telephone box and dialled Bernie Silverman's home number. There was no reply. He then rang Richard Elliott at home: the ringing tone continued. He rang the Aberdeen office with the same result. He decided to return to the office. There must be a simple explanation, he thought. Was he day-dreaming? Or was it Sunday? No – the streets were jammed with people and cars.

When he arrived back at the office a young man was nailing up a board. '2,500 sq ft to let. Apply Conrad Ritblat.'

'What do you think you are doing?' David demanded.

'The old tenants have given notice and left. We're looking for new ones. Are you interested in looking over the property?'

'No,' said David, backing away in panic. 'No, thank you.'

He raced down the street, sweat beginning to show on his forehead, praying that the telephone box would still be empty.

He flicked quickly through the L–R directory and looked up Bernie Silverman's secretary, Judith Lampson. This time there was a reply.

'Judith, in God's name, what's going on?' His voice would have left her in no doubt how anxious he was.

'No idea,' replied Judith. 'I was given my notice on Friday night with a month's pay in advance and no explanation.'

David dropped the telephone. The truth was slowly beginning to dawn on him although he still wanted to believe there was some simple explanation. Whom could he turn to? What should he do?

He returned in a daze to his flat in the Barbican. The morning post had arrived in his absence. It included a letter from the landlords of his flat:

Corporation of London,
Barbican Estate Office,
London EC2
01–628–4341

Dear Sir,

We are sorry to learn you will be leaving at the end of the month, and would like to take this opportunity of thanking you for the payment of rent in advance.

We should be pleased if you would kindly deposit the keys to this office at your earliest covenience.

Yours faithfully,

C. J. Caselton,
Estate Manager.

David stood frozen in the middle of the room, gazing at his new Underwood with sudden loathing.

Finally, fearfully, he dialled his stockbrokers.

'What price are Prospecta Oil this morning?'

'They've dipped to £3.80,' replied the broker.

'Why have they fallen?'

'I've no idea, but I'll make some enquiries and ring you back.'

'Please put my 500 shares on the market immediately.'

'500 Prospecta Oil at market price. Yes, sir.'

David put the phone down. It rang a few minutes later. It was his broker.

'They've only made £3.50 – exactly what you paid for them.'

'Would you credit the sum to my account at Lloyd's Bank, Moorgate Branch?'

'Of course, sir.'

David did not leave the flat for the rest of the day or night. He lay on his bed chain-smoking, wondering what he ought to do next, sometimes looking out of his little window over a rain-drenched City of banks, insurance companies, stockbrokers and public companies – his own world, but for how much longer? In the morning, as soon as the market opened, he rang his broker again, in the hope that they would have some new information.

'Can you give me any more news on Prospecta Oil?' His voice was tense and weary now.

'The news is bad, sir. There's been a spate of heavy selling and the shares have dropped to £2.80 on the opening of business this morning.'

'Why? What the hell's going on?' His voice rose with every word.

'I've no idea, sir,' replied a calm voice that always made one per cent, win or lose.

David replaced the receiver. All those years at Harvard were about to be blown away in a puff of smoke. An hour passed, but he did not notice it.

He ate lunch in an inconspicuous restaurant and read a disturbing report in the London *Evening Standard* by its City Editor, David Malbert, headlined 'The Mystery of Prospecta Oil'. By the close of the Stock Exchange at 4 pm the shares had fallen to £1.60.

David spent another restless night. He thought with pain and humiliation of how easily two months of good salary, a quick bonus and a good deal of smooth talk had bought his unquestioning belief in an enterprise that should have excited all business suspicion. He felt sick as he recalled his man-to-man tips on Prospecta Oil, whispered confidentially into willing ears.

On Wednesday morning, dreading what he knew he was

bound to hear, David once again rang the broker. The shares had collapsed to £1 and there was no longer a market for them. He left the flat and walked over to Lloyd's Bank where he closed his account and drew out the remaining £1,345. The cashier smiled at him as she passed over the notes, thinking what a successful young man he must be.

David picked up the final edition of the *Evening Standard* (the one marked '7RR' in the right-hand corner). Prospecta Oil had dropped again, this time to 25 pence. Numbed, he returned to his flat. The housekeeper was on the stairs.

'The police have been round enquiring after you, young man,' she said haughtily.

David climbed the stairs, trying to look unperturbed.

'Thank you, Mrs Pearson. I guess it's another parking fine I forgot to pay.'

Panic had now taken over completely: David never felt so small, so lonely and so sick in his life. He packed everything he owned into a suitcase, except the painting, which he left hanging on the wall, and booked a one-way ticket to New York.

4

Stephen Bradley was delivering a lecture on group theory at the Mathematics Institute in Oxford to a class of third-year undergraduates the morning David left. Over breakfast he had read with horror in the *Daily Telegraph* of the collapse of Prospecta Oil. He had immediately rung his broker, who was still trying to find out the full facts for him. He then phoned David Kesler, who seemed to have vanished without trace.

The lecture Stephen was delivering was not going well. He was preoccupied, to say the least. He could only hope that the undergraduates would misconstrue his absent-mindedness as brilliance, rather than recognise it for what it was – total despair. He was at least thankful that it was his final lecture of the Hilary term.

Stephen looked at the clock at the back of the lecture theatre every few minutes, until at last it pointed to the hour and he was able to return to his rooms in Magdalen College. He sat in his old leather chair wondering where to start. Why the hell had he put everything into one basket? How could he, normally so logical, so calculating, have been so recklessly stupid and greedy? He had trusted David, and still found it hard to believe that his friend was in any way involved with the collapse. Perhaps he shouldn't have taken for granted that someone he had befriended at Harvard must automatically be right. There had to be a simple explanation. Surely he must be able to get all his money back. The telephone rang. Perhaps it was his broker with more concrete news.

As he picked up the phone, he realised for the first time that the palms of his hands were slippery with sweat.

'Stephen Bradley.'

'Good morning, sir. I am sorry to bother you. My name is Detective Inspector Clifford Smith of the Fraud Squad, Scotland Yard. I was wondering if you would be kind enough to see me this afternoon?'

Stephen hesitated, thinking wildly for a minute that he might have done something criminal by investing in Prospecta Oil.

'Certainly, Inspector,' he replied uncertainly, 'would you like me to travel to London?'

'No, sir,' replied the Inspector, 'we'll come to you. We can be in Oxford by 4 pm, if that's convenient.'

'I'll expect you then. Goodbye, Inspector.'

Stephen replaced the receiver. What could they want? He knew little of English law and hoped he was not going to be involved with the police as well. All this just six months before he was due to return to Harvard as a professor. Stephen was even beginning to wonder if that would materialise.

The Detective Inspector was about 5 ft 11 in in height, and somewhere between forty-five and fifty. His hair was turning grey at the sides, but brilliantine toned it in with the original black. His shabby suit, Stephen suspected, was more indicative of a policeman's pay than of the Inspector's personal taste. His heavy frame would have fooled most people into thinking he was rather slow. In fact, Stephen was in the presence of one of the few men in England who fully understood the criminal mind. Time and time again he had been the man behind the arrest of international defrauders. He had a tired look that came from years of putting men behind bars for major crimes, only to see them freed again shortly after and living comfortably off the spoils of their shady transactions. In his opinion, crime did pay. The department was so understaffed that some of the smaller fry even got away scot-free; often the office of the Director of Public Prosecutions would decide it would be too expensive to follow the case through to a proper conclusion. On other occasions, the Fraud Squad simply did not have the back-up staff to finish the job properly.

The Detective Inspector was accompanied by Detective Sergeant Ryder, a considerably younger man – 6 ft 1 in thin in body and face. His large brown eyes had a more innocent look against his sallow skin. He was at least a little better dressed than the Inspector, but then, thought Stephen, he probably wasn't married.

'I'm sorry about this intrusion, sir,' began the Inspector, after he had settled himself comfortably in the large arm-chair usually occupied by Stephen, 'but I'm making enquiries into a company called Prospecta Oil. Now before you say anything, sir, we realise that you had no personal involvement in the running of this company or indeed its subsequent collapse. But we do need your help, and I would prefer to ask you a series of questions which will bring out the points I need answered, rather than have you just give me a general assessment. I must tell you, sir, you don't have to answer any of my questions if you don't want to.'

Stephen nodded.

'First, sir, what made you invest such a large amount in Prospecta Oil?'

The Inspector had in front of him a sheet of paper with a list of all the investments made in the company over the past four months.

'The advice of a friend,' replied Stephen.

'Mr David Kesler, no doubt?'

'Yes.'

'How do you know Mr Kesler?'

'We were students at Harvard together and when he took up his appointment in England to work for an oil company, I invited him down to Oxford for old times' sake.'

Stephen went on to detail the full background of his association with David, and the reason he had been willing

58

to invest such a large amount. He ended his explanation by asking if the Inspector thought that David was criminally involved in the rise and fall of Prospecta Oil.

'No, sir. My own view is that Kesler, who incidentally has made a run for it and left the country, is no more than the dupe of bigger men. But we would still like to question him, so if he contacts you, please let me know immediately. Now, sir,' the Inspector continued, 'I'm going to read you a list of names and I would be obliged if you could tell me whether you have ever met, spoken to or heard of any of them . . . Harvey Metcalfe?'

'No,' said Stephen.

'Bernie Silverman?'

'I've never met or spoken to him, but David did mention his name in conversation when he dined with me here in college.'

The Detective Sergeant was writing down everything Stephen said, slowly and methodically.

'Richard Elliott?'

'The same applies to him as Silverman.'

'Alvin Cooper?'

'No,' said Stephen.

'Have you had any contact with anyone else who was involved in the company?'

'No.'

For well over an hour the Inspector quizzed Stephen on minor points, but he was unable to give him very much help, although he had kept a copy of the geologist's report.

'Yes, we are in possession of one of those documents, sir,' said the Inspector, 'but it's cleverly worded. I doubt if we'll be able to rely much on that for evidence.'

Stephen sighed and offered the two men some whisky and poured himself a donnish dry sherry.

'Evidence against whom or for what, Inspector?' he said as he returned to his chair. 'It's clear to me that I've been taken for a sucker. I probably don't need to tell you what a fool I've made of myself. I put my shirt on Prospecta Oil because it sounded like a sure-fire winner, and ended up losing everything I had without having a clue what to do about it. What in heaven's name has been going on in Prospecta Oil?'

'Well, sir,' said the Inspector, 'you'll appreciate there are aspects of the case I'm not at liberty to discuss with you. Indeed, there are some things that aren't very clear to us yet. But the game isn't a new one, and this time it's been played by an old pro, a very cunning old pro. It works something like this: a company is set up or taken over by a bunch of villains who acquire the majority of the shares. They invent a plausible story about a new discovery or super product that will send the shares up, whisper it in a few willing ears, release their own shares on to the market and let them be snapped up by the likes of you, sir, at a higher price. Then they clear off with the profit they have made, after which the shares collapse because the company has no real substance. As often as not, it ends with dealings in the shares being suspended on the stock market, and finally in the compulsory liquidation of the company. That hasn't happened yet in this case, and it may not. The London Stock Exchange is only just recovering from the Caplan fiasco and they don't want another scandal on their hands. I'm sorry to say that we can hardly ever recover the money, even if we produce enough evidence to nail the villains. They have it all stashed away all over the world before you can say Dow-Jones Index.'

Stephen groaned. 'My God, you make it all sound so appallingly simple, Inspector. The geologist's report was a fake, then?'

'Not exactly, sir. Very impressively worded and well presented, but with plenty of ifs and buts; and one thing is for certain; the DPP's office is hardly likely to spend millions finding out if there *is* any oil in that part of the North Sea.'

Stephen buried his head in his hands and mentally cursed the day he met David Kesler.

'Tell me, Inspector, who put Kesler up to this? Who was the real brains behind it all?'

The Inspector realised only too well the terrible agony Stephen was going through. During his career he had faced many men in the same position, and he was grateful for Stephen's co-operation.

'I'll answer any questions I feel cannot harm my own enquiry,' said the Inspector. 'But it's no secret that the man we'd like to nail is Harvey Metcalfe.'

'Who's Harvey Metcalfe, for God's sake?'

'He's a first-generation American who's had his fingers in more dubious deals in Boston than you've had hot dinners. Made himself a multi-millionaire and a lot of other people bankrupt on the way. His style is so professional and predictable now we can smell the man a mile off. It will not amuse you to learn that he is a great benefactor of Harvard – does it to ease his conscience, no doubt. We've never been able to pin anything on him in the past, and I doubt if we'll be able to this time either. He was never a director of Prospecta Oil, and he only bought and sold shares on the open market. He never, as far as we know, even met David Kesler. He hired Silverman, Cooper and Elliott to do the dirty work, and they found a bright enthusiastic young man all freshly washed behind the ears to sell their story for them. I'm afraid it was a bit unlucky for you, sir, that the young man in question was your friend, David Kesler.'

'Never mind him, poor sod,' said Stephen. 'What about Harvey Metcalfe? Is he going to get away with it again?'

'I fear so,' said the Inspector. 'We have warrants out for the arrest of Silverman, Elliott and Cooper. They all beat it off to South America. After the Ronald Biggs fiasco I doubt if we'll ever get an extradition order to bring them back, even though the American and Canadian police also have warrants out for them. They were fairly cunning too. They closed the London office of Prospecta Oil, surrendered the lease and returned it to Conrad Ritblat, the estate agents, and gave notice to both secretaries with one month's pay in advance. They cleared the bill on the oil rig with Reading & Bates. They paid off their hired hands, Mark Stewart in Aberdeen, and took the Sunday morning flight to Rio de Janeiro, where there was $1 million in a private account waiting for them. Another two or three years, after they've spent all the money, and they'll undoubtedly turn up again with different names and a different company. Harvey Metcalfe rewarded them well and left David Kesler holding the baby.'

'Clever boys,' said Stephen.

'Oh, yes,' said the Inspector, 'it was a neat little operation. Worthy of the talents of Harvey Metcalfe.'

'Are you trying to arrest David Kesler?'

'No, but as I said we would like to question him. He bought and sold 500 shares, but we think that was only because he believed in the oil strike story himself. In fact, if he was wise, he would return to England and help the police with their enquiries, but I fear the poor man has panicked under pressure and made a bolt for it. The American police are keeping an eye out for him.'

'One last question,' said Stephen. 'Are there any other people who made such fools of themselves as I did!'

The Inspector gave this question long consideration. He had not had as much success with the other big investors as he had had with Stephen. They had all been evasive about their involvement with Kesler and Prospecta Oil. Perhaps if he released their names it might bring them out in some way.

'Yes, sir, but . . . you must understand that you never heard about them from me.'

Stephen nodded.

'For your own interest you could find out what you need to know by making some discreet enquiries through the Stock Exchange. There were four main punters, of whom you were one. Between the four of you you lost approximately $1 million. The others were a Harley Street doctor, Robin Oakley, a London art dealer called Jean-Pierre Lamanns, and a farmer, the unluckiest of all, really. As far as I can gather, he mortgaged his farm to put up the money. Titled young gentleman: Viscount Brigsley.

Metcalfe's snatched the silver spoon out of his mouth, all right.'

'No other big investors?'

'Two or three banks burnt their fingers badly, but there were no other private investors above £10,000. What you, the banks and the other big investors did was to keep the market buoyant long enough for Metcalfe to off-load his entire holding.'

'I know, and worse, I foolishly advised some of my friends to invest in the company as well.'

'Er . . . there are two or three small investors from Oxford, yes sir,' said the Inspector, looking down at the sheet of paper in front of him, 'but don't worry – we won't be approaching them. Well, that seems to be all. It only leaves me to thank you for your co-operation and say we may be in touch again some time in the future. In any case, we'll keep you informed of developments, and I hope you'll do the same for us.'

'Of course, Inspector. I do hope you have a safe journey back to town.' The two policemen downed their drinks and left.

Stephen could never recall if it was while sitting in his armchair looking out at the Cloisters, or later in bed that night, that he decided to employ his academic mind to carry out a little research on Harvey Metcalfe and his fellow dupers. His grandfather's advice to him, when as a small child he failed to win their nightly game of chess, floated across his mind: Stevie, don't get cross, get even. He was pleased he had given his final lecture and finished work for the term, and as he fell asleep at 3 am only one name was on his lips: Harvey Metcalfe.

5

Stephen awoke at about 5.30 am. He seemed to have been heavily, dreamlessly asleep, but as soon as he came to, the nightmare started again. He forced himself to use his mind constructively, to put the past firmly behind him and see what could be done about the future. He washed, shaved, dressed and missed college breakfast, occasionally murmuring to himself 'Harvey Metcalfe'. He then pedalled to Oxford station on an ancient bicycle, his preferred mode of transport in a city blocked solid with juggernaut lorries and full of unintelligible one-way systems. He left Ethelred the Unsteady padlocked to the station railings. There were as many bicycles standing in the ranks as there are cars in other railway stations.

He caught the 8.17 train so favoured by those who commute from Oxford to London every day. All the people at breakfast seemed to know each other and Stephen felt like an uninvited guest at someone else's party. The ticket collector bustled through the buffet car and clipped Stephen's first-class ticket. The man opposite Stephen produced a second-class ticket from behind his copy of the *Financial Times*. The collector clipped it grudgingly.

'You'll have to return to a second-class compartment when you've finished your breakfast, sir. The restaurant car is first-class, you know.'

Stephen considered the implication of these remarks as he watched the flat Berkshire countryside jolt past, and his coffee cup lurched unsampled in its saucer before he turned his mind to the morning papers. *The Times* carried no news of Prospecta Oil that morning. It was, he supposed, an insignificant story, even a dull one. Not kidnap, not arson, not even rage; just another shady business enterprise collapsing – nothing there to hold the attention of the front page for more than one day. Not a story he would have given a second thought to himself but for his own involvement, which gave it all the makings of a personal tragedy.

At Paddington he pushed through the ants rushing round the forecourt, glad that he had chosen the closeted life of a university or, more accurately, that it had chosen him. Stephen had never come to terms with London – he found the city large and impersonal, and he always took a taxi everywhere for fear of getting lost on the buses or the underground. Why didn't the English number their streets so Americans would know where they were?

'*The Times* office, Printing House Square.'

The cabby nodded and moved his black Austin deftly down the Bayswater Road, alongside a rain-sodden Hyde Park. The crocuses at Marble Arch looked sullen and battered, splayed wetly on the close grass. Stephen was impressed by London cabs: they never had a scrape or mark on them. He had once been told that cab-drivers are not allowed to pick up fares unless their vehicles are in perfect condition. How different from New York's battered yellow monsters, he thought. The cabby proceeded to swing down Park Lane to Hyde Park Corner, past the House of Commons and along the Embankment. The flags were out in Parliament Square. Stephen frowned. What was the lead story he had read over so inattentively in the train? Ah yes, a meeting of Commonwealth leaders. He supposed he must allow the world to go about its daily business as usual.

Stephen was unsure how to tackle the problem of checking Harvey Metcalfe out. Back at Harvard he would have had no trouble, first making a bee-line for his father's old friend Hank Swaltz, the business correspondent of the *Herald American*. Hank would be sure to have supplied

65

him with the inside dope. The diary correspondent of *The Times*, Richard Compton-Miller, was by no means as appropriate a contact, but he was the only British press man Stephen had ever met. Compton-Miller had been visiting Magdalen the previous spring to write a feature on the time-honoured observance of May Day in Oxford. The choristers on the top of the College tower had sung the Miltonian salute as the sun peeped over the horizon on May 1st:

> Hail, bounteous May, that doth inspire
> Mirth and youth and warm desire.

On the banks of the river beneath Magdalen bridge where Compton-Miller and Stephen had stood, several couples had clearly been inspired.

Later, Stephen had been more embarrassed than flattered by his appearance in the resulting piece written by Compton-Miller for *The Times* diary: academics are sparing with the word brilliant, but journalists are not. The more self-important of Stephen's Senior Common Room colleagues had not been amused to see him described as the brightest star in a firmament of moderate luminescence.

The taxi pulled into the forecourt and came to a stop by the side of a massive hunk of sculpture by Henry Moore. *The Times* and the *Observer* shared a building with separate entrances, *The Times*'s by far the more prestigious. Stephen asked the sergeant behind the desk for Richard Compton-Miller, and was directed to the fifth floor and then to his little private cubicle at the end of the corridor.

It was only a little after 10 am when Stephen arrived, and the building was practically deserted. Compton-Miller later explained that a national newspaper does not begin to wake up until 11 am and generally indulges itself in a long lunch hour until about 3. Between then and putting the paper to bed, about 8.30 pm for all but the front page, the real work is done. There is usually a complete change of staff, staggered from 5 pm onwards, whose job it is to watch for major news stories breaking during the night. They always have to keep a wary eye on what is happening in America, because if the President makes an important statement in the afternoon in Washington they are already going to press in London. Sometimes the front page can change as often as five times during the night; in the case of the assassination of President Kennedy, news of which first reached England about 7 pm on the evening of November 22nd, 1963, the entire front page had to be scrapped to make way for the tragedy.

'Richard, it was kind of you to come in early for me. I didn't realise that you started work so late. I rather take my daily paper for granted.'

Richard laughed. 'That's OK. We must seem a lazy bunch to you, but this place will be buzzing at midnight when you're tucked up in bed and sound asleep. Now, how can I help you?'

'I'm trying to do a little research on a fellow countryman of mine called Harvey Metcalfe. He's a substantial benefactor of Harvard, and I want to flatter the old boy by knowing all about him when I return.' Stephen didn't care very much for the lie, but these were strange circumstances he now found himself in.

'Hang on here and I'll go and see if we have anything in the cutting room on him.'

Stephen amused himself by reading the headlines pinned up on Compton-Miller's board – obviously stories he had taken some pride in: 'Prime Minister to Conduct Orchestra at Royal Festival Hall', 'Miss World loves Tom Jones', 'Muhammad Ali says "I will be Champion Again"'.

Richard returned fifteen minutes later, carrying a thickish file.

'Have a go at that, Descartes. I'll be back in an hour and we can have some coffee.'

Stephen nodded and smiled gratefully. Descartes never had to solve the problems he was facing.

Everything Harvey Metcalfe wanted the world to know was in that file, and a little bit he didn't want the world to know. Stephen learned of his yearly trips to Europe to visit Wimbledon, of the success of his horses at Ascot and of his pursuit of Impressionist pictures for his private art collection. William Hickey of the *Daily Express* had on one occasion titillated his readers with a plump Harvey clad in Bermuda shorts and a report that he spent two or three weeks a year on his private yacht at Monte Carlo, gambling at the Casino. The Metcalfe fortune was in his opinion too new to be respectable. Stephen wrote down meticulously all the facts he thought relevant and was studying the photographs when Richard returned.

He took Stephen off to have some coffee in the canteen on the same floor. Cigarette smoke swirled mistily round the girl at the cashier's desk at the end of the self-service counter.

'Richard, I don't quite have all the information I might need. Harvard want to touch this man for quite a large sum: I believe they are thinking in terms of about $1 million. Where could I find out some more about him?'

'*New York Times*, I should imagine,' said Compton-Miller. 'Come on, we'll give Terry Robards a visit.'

The *New York Times* office in London was also on the fifth floor of *The Times* building in Printing House Square. Stephen thought of the vast *New York Times* building on 43rd Street and wondered if the London *Times* had a reciprocal arrangement, and was secreted away in their basement. Terry Robards turned out to be a wiry American wearing a perpetual smile. Terry immediately made Stephen feel at ease, a knack he had developed almost subconsciously over the years and which was a great asset when digging a little deeper for stories.

Stephen repeated his piece about Metcalfe. Terry laughed.

'Harvard aren't too fussy where they get their money from, are they? That guy has discovered more legal ways of stealing money than the Internal Revenue Service.'

'You don't say,' said Stephen innocently.

The *New York Times* file on Harvey was voluminous.

'Metcalfe's rise from Messenger Boy to Millionaire', as one headline put it, was documented admirably. Stephen took further careful notes. The details of Sharpley & Son fascinated him, as did the facts on some war-time arms dealing and the background of his wife Arlene and their daughter Rosalie. There was a picture of both of them, but the daughter was only fifteen at the time. There were also long reports of two court cases some twenty-five years past, in which Harvey had been charged with fraud but never convicted, and a more recent case in 1956 concerning a share transfer scheme in Boston. Again Harvey had escaped the law, but the District Attorney had left the jury in little doubt of his views on Mr Metcalfe. The most recent press stories were all in the gossip columns: Metcalfe's paintings, his horses, his orchids, his daughter's success at Vassar and his trips to Europe. Of Prospecta Oil there was not a word. Stephen had to admire Harvey's ability to conceal his more dubious activities from the press.

Terry invited his fellow expatriate to lunch. Newsmen always like new contacts and Stephen looked like a promising one. He asked the cabby to go to Whitfield Street. As they inched their way out of the City into the West End, Stephen hoped that the meal would be worth the journey. He was not disappointed.

Lacy's restaurant was airy and bedecked with clean linen and young daffodils. Terry said it was greatly favoured by press men. Margaret Costa, the cookery writer and her chef husband, Bill Lacy, certainly knew their onions. Over delicious watercress soup followed by *Médaillons de veau à la crème au calvados* and a bottle of *Château de Péronne 1972*, Terry became quite expansive on the subject of Harvey Metcalfe. He had interviewed him once at Harvard on the occasion of the opening of Metcalfe Hall, which included a gymnasium and four indoor tennis courts.

'Hoping to get himself an honorary degree one day,' said Terry cynically, 'but not much hope, even if he gives a billion.'

Stephen noted the words thoughtfully.

'I guess you could get some more facts on the guy at the American Embassy,' said Terry. He glanced at his watch. 'No, hell, the library closes at 4 pm. Too late today. Time I got back to the office now America's awake.'

Stephen wondered if press men ate and drank like that every day. They made University dons look positively celibate – and however did they manage to get a paper out?

Stephen fought his way on to the 5.15 train to return with the Oxford-bound commuters, and only when he was alone in his room did he begin to study the results of his day's work. Though exhausted, he forced himself to sit at his desk until he had prepared the first neat draft of a dossier on Harvey Metcalfe.

Next day Stephen again caught the 8.17 to London, this time buying a second-class ticket. The ticket collector repeated his piece about leaving the restaurant car after he had finished his meal.

'Sure,' said Stephen, as he toyed with the remains of his coffee for the rest of the hour-long journey, never shifting from first-class. He was pleased with himself: he had saved £2, and that was exactly how Harvey Metcalfe would have behaved.

At Paddington he followed Terry Robard's advice and took a taxi to the American Embassy, a vast monolithic building which sprawls over 250,000 square feet and is nine storeys high, stretching the entire length of one side of Grosvenor Square. It was not, however, as elegant as the American Ambassador's magnificent official residence, Winfield House in Regents Park, where Stephen had been summoned to drinks last year, which was once the private home of Barbara Hutton before it was sold to the American government in 1946. Certainly, either of them was large enough for seven husbands, thought Stephen.

The entrance to the Embassy Reference Library on the ground floor was firmly shut. Stephen was reduced to a close study of the plaques on the wall in the corridor outside, honouring recent Ambassadors to the Court of St

James. Reading backwards from Walter Annenberg, he had reached Joseph Kennedy when the doors of the library swung open, not unlike a bank. The prim girl behind a sign marked 'Enquiries' was not immediately forthcoming on the subject of Harvey Metcalfe.

'Why do you require this information?' she asked sharply.

This threw Stephen for a moment, but he quickly recovered. 'I'm returning to Harvard in the fall as a professor and I feel I should know more about his involvement with the university. I'm at present a Visiting Fellow at Magdalen College, Oxford.'

Stephen's answer motivated the girl to immediate action and she produced a file within a few minutes. Though by no means as racy as the *New York Times*'s, it did put figures on the amounts Harvey Metcalfe had donated to charity and gave precise details of his gifts to the Democratic Party. Most people do not divulge the exact amount they give to political parties, but Harvey only knew about lights – no one seemed to have told him about bushels.

Having finished his research at the Embassy, Stephen took a taxi to the Cunard offices in St James's Square and spoke to a booking clerk and from there on to Claridge's in Brook Street, where he spent a few minutes with the duty manager. A telephone call to Monte Carlo completed his research. He travelled back to Oxford on the 5.15.

Stephen returned to his college rooms. He felt he now knew as much about Harvey Metcalfe as anyone, except perhaps for Arlene and Detective Inspector Clifford Smith of the Fraud Squad. Once again he stayed up into the early hours completing his dossier, which now ran to over forty typewritten pages.

When the dossier was finally completed he went to bed and fell into a deep sleep. He rose again early in the morning, strolled across the Cloisters to a Common Room breakfast and helped himself to eggs, bacon, coffee and toast. He then took his dossier to the Bursar's office where he made four copies of every document, ending up with five dossiers in all. He strolled back across Magdalen Bridge, admiring as always the trim flower beds of the University Botanic Gardens beneath him on his right, and called in at Maxwell's Bookshop on the other side of the bridge.

Stephen returned to his rooms with five smart files all of different colours. He then placed the five dossiers in the separate files and put them in a drawer of his desk which he kept locked. Stephen had a tidy and methodical mind, as a mathematician must: a mind the like of which Harvey Metcalfe had never yet come up against.

Stephen then referred to the notes he had written after his interview with Detective Inspector Smith and rang Directory Enquiries, asking for the London addresses and telephone numbers of Dr Robin Oakley, Jean-Pierre Lamanns and Lord Brigsley. Directory Enquiries refused to give him more than two numbers at any one time. Stephen wondered how the GPO expected to make a profit. In the States the Bell Telephone Company would happily have given him a dozen telephone numbers and still ended with the inevitable 'You're welcome'.

The two he managed to wheedle out of his reluctant informant were Dr Robin Oakley at 122 Harley Street, London W1, and Jean-Pierre Lamanns at the Lamanns Gallery, 40 New Bond Street, W1. Stephen then dialled Directory Enquiries a second time and requested the number and address of Lord Brigsley.

'No one under Brigsley in Central London,' said the operator. 'Maybe he's ex-Directory. That is, if he really is a lord,' she sniffed.

Stephen left his study for the Senior Common Room, where he thumbed through the latest copy of *Who's Who* and found the noble lord:

BRIGSLEY, Viscount; James Clarence Spencer; b. 11 Oct. 1942; Farmer; *s* and *heir* of 5th Earl of Louth, *cr* 1764, *qv*. *Educ*: Harrow; Christ Church, Oxford (BA). Pres.

Oxford University Dramatic Society. Lt Grenadier Guards 1966–68. *Recreations*: polo (not water), shooting. *Address*: Tathwell Hall, Louth, Lincs. *Clubs*: Garrick, Guards.

Stephen then strolled over to Christ Church and asked the secretary in the Treasurer's office if she had in her records a London address for James Brigsley, matriculated 1963. It was duly supplied as 119 King's Road, London SW3.

Stephen was beginning to warm to the challenge of Harvey Metcalfe. He left Christ Church by Peckwater and the Canterbury Gate, out into the High and back to Magdalen, hands in pockets, composing a brief letter in his mind. Oxford's nocturnal slogan-writers had been at work on a college wall again: 'Deanz meanz feinz' said one neatly painted graffito. Stephen, the reluctant Junior Dean of Magdalen, responsible for undergraduate discipline, smiled. If they were funny enough he would allow them to remain for one term, if not, he would have the porter scrub them out immediately. Back at his desk, he wrote down what had been in his mind.

Magdalen College,
Oxford.
April 15th

Dear Dr Oakley,

I am holding a small dinner party in my rooms next Thursday evening for a few carefully selected people.

I would be delighted if you could spare the time to join me, and I think you would find it worth your while to be present.

Yours sincerely,
Stephen Bradley

PS: I am sorry David Kesler is unable to join us.
Black Tie: 7.30 for 8 pm.

Stephen changed the sheet of letter paper in his old Remington typewriter and addressed similar letters to Jean-Pierre Lamanns and Lord Brigsley. Then he sat thinking for a little while before picking up the internal telephone.

'Harry?' he said to the head porter. 'If anyone rings the lodge to ask if the college has a fellow called Stephen Bradley, I want you to say, "Yes, sir, a new Mathematics Fellow from Harvard, already famous for his dinner parties." Is that clear, Harry?'

'Yes, sir,' said Harry Woodley, the head porter. He had never understood Americans – Dr Bradley was no exception.

All three men did ring and enquire, as Stephen had anticipated they might. He himself would have done the same in the circumstances. Harry remembered his message and repeated it carefully, although the callers still seemed a little baffled.

'No more than me, or is it I?' muttered the head porter.

Stephen received acceptances from all three during the next week, James Brigsley's arriving last, on the Friday. The crest on his letter paper announced a promising motto: *ex nihilo omnia*.

The butler to the Senior Common Room and the college chef were consulted, and a meal to loosen the tongues of the most taciturn was planned:

Coquilles St Jacques	Pouilly Fuissé 1969
Carrée d'agneau en croûte	Feux St Jean 1970
Casserôle d'artichauds et champignons	
Pommes de terre boulangère	
Griestorte with raspberries	Barsac Ch. d'Yquem 1927
Camembert frappé	Port Taylor 1947
Café	

Everything was ready; all Stephen could do now was wait for the appointed hour.

* * *

On the stroke of 7.30 pm on the appointed Thursday Jean-Pierre arrived. Stephen admired the elegant dinner-jacket and large floppy bow-tie that his guest wore, while he fingered his own little clip-on, surprised that Jean-Pierre Lamanns, who had such obvious savoir-faire, could also have fallen victim to Prospecta Oil. Stephen plunged into a monologue on the significance of the isosceles triangle in modern art while Jean-Pierre stroked his moustache. It was not a subject Stephen would normally have chosen to speak on without a break for five minutes, and he was only saved from the inevitability of more direct questions from Jean-Pierre by the arrival of Dr Robin Oakley. Robin had lost a few pounds in the past month, but Stephen could see why his practice in Harley Street was a success. He was, in the words of H. H. Munro, a man whose looks made it possible for women to forgive any other trifling inadequacies. Robin studied his shambling host, wondering whether he dared to ask immediately if they had ever met before. No, he decided; he would leave it a little and hope perhaps some clue as to why he had been invited would materialise during dinner. The David Kesler P.S. worried him.

Stephen introduced him to Jean-Pierre and they chatted while their host checked the dinner-table. Once again the door opened, and with a little more respect than previously displayed, the porter announced, 'Lord Brigsley'. Stephen walked forward to greet him, suddenly unsure whether he should bow or shake hands. Although James did not know anyone present at the strange gathering, he showed no signs of discomfort and entered easily into the conversation. Even Stephen was impressed by James's relaxed line of small talk, although he couldn't help recalling his academic results when at Christ Church and wondered whether the noble lord would in fact be an asset to his plans.

The culinary efforts of the chef worked their intended magic. No guest could possibly have asked his host why the dinner party was taking place while such delicately garlic-flavoured lamb, such tender almond pastry, such excellent wine, were still to hand.

Finally, when the servants had cleared the table and the port was on its way round for the second time, Robin could stand it no longer:

'If it's not a rude question, Dr Bradley.'

'Do call me Stephen.'

'Stephen, may I ask what is the purpose of this select little gathering?'

Six eyes bored into him demanding an answer to the same question.

Stephen rose and surveyed his guests. He walked around the table twice before speaking and then started his discourse by recalling the entire history of the past few weeks. He told them of his meeting in that very room with David Kesler, his investment in Prospecta Oil, followed soon afterwards by the visit of the Fraud Squad, and their disclosure about Harvey Metcalfe. He ended his carefully prepared speech with the words, 'Gentlemen, the truth is that the four of us are in the same bloody mess.' He felt that sounded suitably British.

Jean-Pierre reacted even before Stephen could finish what he was saying.

'Count me out. I couldn't be involved in anything quite so ridiculous as that. I am a humble art dealer, not a speculator.'

Robin Oakley also jumped in before Stephen was given the chance to reply:

'I've never heard anything so preposterous. You must have contacted the wrong man. I'm a Harley Street doctor – I don't know the first thing about oil.'

Stephen could see why the Fraud Squad had had trouble with these two and why they had been so thankful for his co-operation. They all looked at Lord Brigsley, who raised his eyes and said very quietly:

'Absolutely right on every detail, Dr Bradley, and I'm in more of a pickle than you. I borrowed £150,000 to buy the shares against the security of my small farm in

Hampshire and I don't think it will be long before the bank insists that I dispose of it. When they do and my dear old pa, the fifth earl, finds out, it's curtains for me unless I become the sixth earl overnight.'

'Thank you,' said Stephen. As he sat down, he turned to Robin and raised his eyebrows interrogatively.

'What the hell,' said Robin. 'You're quite right – I was involved. David Kesler was a patient of mine and in a rash moment I invested £100,000 in Prospecta Oil as a temporary advance against my securities. God only knows what made me do it. As the shares are only worth 50 pence I'm stuck with them. I have a shortfall at my bank which they're beginning to fuss about. I also have a large mortgage on my country home in Berkshire and a heavy rent on my Harley Street consulting-room, a wife with expensive tastes and two boys at the best private prep school in England. I've hardly slept a wink since Detective Inspector Smith visited me two weeks ago.' He looked up. His face had drained of colour and the suave self-confidence of Harley Street had gone. Slowly, they all turned and stared at Jean-Pierre.

'All right, all right,' he admitted, 'me too. I was in Paris when the damned thing folded under me, so now, I'm stuck with the useless shares. £80,000 borrowed against my stock at the gallery. And what's worse, I advised some of my friends to invest in the bloody company too.'

Silence enveloped the room. It was Jean-Pierre who broke it again:

'So what do you suggest, Professor,' he said sarcastically. 'Do we hold an annual dinner to remind us what fools we've been?'

'No, that was not what I had in mind.' Stephen hesitated, realising that what he was about to suggest was bound to cause even more commotion. Once again he rose to his feet, and said quietly and deliberately:

'We have had our money stolen by a very clever man who has proved to be an expert in share fraud. None of us is knowledgeable about stocks and shares, but we are all experts in our own fields. Gentlemen, I therefore suggest we steal it back.

    – NOT A PENNY MORE AND NOT A PENNY LESS.'

A few seconds' silence was followed by uproar.

'Just walk up and take it I suppose?' said Robin.

'Kidnap him,' mused James.

'Why don't we just kill him and claim the life insurance?' said Jean-Pierre.

Several moments passed. Stephen waited until he had complete silence again, and then he handed round the four dossiers marked 'Harvey Metcalfe' with each of their names below. A green dossier for Robin, a blue one for James and a yellow for Jean-Pierre. The red master copy Stephen kept for himself. They were all impressed. While they had been wringing their hands in unproductive dismay, it was obvious that Stephen Bradley had been hard at work.

Stephen continued:

'Please read your dossier carefully. It will brief you on everything that is known about Harvey Metcalfe. Each of you must take the document away and study the information, and then return with a plan of how we are, between us, to extract $1,000,000 from him without his ever being aware of it. All four of us must come up with a separate plan. Each may involve the other three in his own operation. We will return here in fourteen days' time and present our conclusions. Each member of the team will put $10,000 into the kitty as a float and I, as the mathematician, will keep a running account. All expenses incurred in retrieving our money will be added to Mr Metcalfe's bill, starting with your journey down here this evening and the cost of the dinner tonight.'

Jean-Pierre and Robin began to protest again, but it was James who stopped the proceedings, by simply saying:

'I agree. What have we got to lose? On our own we've no chance at all: together we might just tweak the bastard.'

Robin and Jean-Pierre looked at each other, shrugged and nodded.

The four of them settled down to discuss in detail the material Stephen had acquired over the past few days. They left the college a little after midnight, each agreeing to have a plan ready for the Team's consideration in fourteen days' time. None of them was quite sure where it all might end, but each was relieved to know he was no longer on his own.

Stephen decided that the first part of the Team versus Harvey Metcalfe had gone as well as he could have wished. He only hoped his co-conspirators would now get down to work. He sat in his armchair, stared at the ceiling and continued thinking.

6

Robin retrieved his car from the High Street, not for the first time in his life being thankful for the 'Doctor on Call' sticker which always gave him an extra degree of freedom when parking. He headed back towards his home in Berkshire. There was no doubt about it, Stephen Bradley was a very impressive man; Robin was determined to come up with something that would ensure that he played his full part.

Robin let his mind linger a little on the delightful prospect of recovering the money he had so ill-advisedly entrusted to Prospecta Oil and Harvey Metcalfe. It must be worth a try: after all, he might as well be struck off the register of the General Medical Council for attempted robbery as for bankruptcy. He wound the window of the car down a little way to dispel the last delicious effects of the claret and considered Stephen's challenge more carefully.

The journey between Oxford and his country house passed very quickly. His mind was so preoccupied with Harvey Metcalfe that when he arrived home to his wife there were large sections of the journey that he could not even remember. Robin had only one talent to offer, apart from his natural charm, and he hoped that he was right in thinking that particular talent was the strength in his armour and a weakness in Harvey Metcalfe's. He began to repeat aloud something that was written on page 16 of Stephen's dossier, 'One of Harvey Metcalfe's recurrent worries is . . .'

'What was it all about, darling?'

His wife's voice brought Robin quickly to his senses and he locked the briefcase containing the green Metcalfe dossier.

'You still awake, Mary?'

'Well, I'm not talking in my sleep, love.'

Robin had to think quickly. He had not yet steeled himself to tell Mary the details of his foolish investment, but he had let her know about the dinner in Oxford, not at that time realising it was in any way connected with Prospecta Oil.

'It was a tease, sweetheart. An old friend of mine from Cambridge has been appointed a lecturer at Oxford, so he dragged a few of his contemporaries down for dinner and we had a damn good evening. Jim and Fred from my old college were there, but I don't expect you remember them.'

A bit weak, thought Robin, but the best he could do at 1.15 in the morning.

'Sure it wasn't some beautiful girl?' said Mary.

'I'm afraid Jim and Fred could hardly be described as beautiful, even by their loving wives.'

'Do lower your voice, Robin, or you'll wake the children.'

'I'm going down again in two weeks time to . . .'

'Oh, come to bed and tell me about it at breakfast.'

Robin was relieved to be let off the hook until the morning. He clambered in beside his fragrant silk-clad wife and ran his finger hopefully down her vertebral column to her coccyx.,

'You'll be lucky, at this time of night,' she mumbled.

They both slept.

Jean-Pierre had booked himself in at the Eastgate Hotel in the High. There was to be an undergraduate exhibition the next day at the Christ Church Art Gallery. Jean-Pierre was always on the look-out for new young talent which he could contract to the Lamanns Gallery. It was the Marlborough Gallery, a few doors away from him in Bond

Street, that had taught the London art world the astuteness of buying up young artists and being closely identified with their careers. But for the moment, the artistic future of his gallery was not uppermost in Jean-Pierre's mind: its very survival was threatened, and the quiet American don from Magdalen had offered him the chance of redress. He settled down in his comfortable hotel bedroom, oblivious of the late hour, reading his dossier and working out where he could fit into the jig-saw. He was not going to allow two Englishmen and a Yank to beat him. His father had been relieved at Rochefort by the British in 1918 and released from a prisoner-of-war camp near Frankfurt by the Americans in 1945. Nothing was going to stop him being a full participant in this operation. He read his yellow dossier late into the night: the germ of an idea was beginning to form in his mind.

James made the last train from Oxford and looked for an empty carriage where he could settle down to study the blue dossier. He was a worried man: he was sure the other three would each come up with a brilliant plan and, as had always seemed to be the case in the past, he would be found lacking. He had never been under any real pressure before – everything had come to him so easily; now it had all gone just as easily. A foolproof scheme for relieving Harvey Metcalfe of some of his excess profits was not James' idea of an amusing pastime. Still, the awful vision of his father discovering that the Hampshire farm was mortgaged up to the hilt was always there to keep his mind on the job. But fourteen days was such a short time: where on earth should he begin? He was not a professional man like the other three and had no particular skills to offer. He could only hope that his stage experience might come in useful at some point.

He bumped into the ticket collector, who was not sur-prised to find James was the holder of a first-class ticket. The quest for an empty compartment was in vain. James concluded that Richard Marsh must be trying to run the railways at a profit. Whatever next? Still more aggravating, they would probably give him a knighthood for his pains.

The next best thing to an empty compartment, James always thought, was one containing a beautiful girl – and this time his luck was in. One of the compartments was occupied by a truly stunning creature who looked as if she was alone. The only other person in the carriage was a middle-aged lady reading *Vogue*, who showed no signs of knowing her travelling companion. James settled down in the corner with his back to the engine, realising he could not study the Metcalfe dossier on the train. They had all been sworn to total secrecy, and Stephen had cautioned them against reading the dossiers in anyone else's company. James feared that of the four of them he was going to find it the most difficult to remain silent: a companionable man, he found secrets rather burdensome. He touched his overcoat pocket, the one holding the dossier in the envelope supplied by Stephen Bradley. What an efficient man he was, thought James. Alarmingly brainy, too. He was bound to have a dozen clever plans ready for consideration by the next meeting. James frowned and stared out of the window hoping some serendipitous idea would strike him. Instead he found himself studying the reflection of the profile of the girl sitting opposite him.

She had a shiny nob of dark brown hair, a slim straight nose and her large hazel eyes seemed fixed on the book she held in her lap. James wondered if she was as entirely oblivious of his presence as she appeared to be, and reluctantly decided that she was. His eyes slipped down to the gentle curve of her breast, softly encased in angora. He craned his neck slightly to see what sort of legs the reflection had. Damn it, she was wearing boots. He looked back at the face again. It was now looking back at him, faintly amused. Embarrassed, he switched his attention to the third occupant of the carriage, the unofficial chaperone in front of whom James lacked the courage even to strike up a conversation with the beautiful profile.

In desperation he stared at the cover of the middle-aged

lady's *Vogue*. Another beautiful girl. And then he looked more carefully. It wasn't another girl, it was the same girl. To begin with, he could hardly believe his eyes, but a quick check against the genuine article left him in no doubt. As soon as *Vogue* was relinquished in favour of *Queen*, James leant across and asked the chaperone if he might be allowed to read it.

'Station bookstalls are closing earlier and earlier,' he said idiotically. 'I couldn't get anything to read.'

The chaperone agreed reluctantly.

He turned to the second page. 'Cover: Picture yourself like this . . . black silk georgette dress with chiffon handkerchief points. Ostrich-feather boa. Turban with flower, matching dress. Made to measure by Zandra Rhodes. Anne's hair by Jason at Vidal Sassoon. Photograph by Lichfield. Camera: Hasselblad.'

James was quite unable to picture himself like that. But at least he now knew the girl's name, Anne. The next time the real-life version looked up, he showed her by sign language that he had spotted the photograph. She smiled briefly at James and then returned to her book.

At Reading station the middle-aged lady left, taking *Vogue* with her. Couldn't be better, mused James. Anne looked up, faintly embarrassed, and smiled hopefully at the few passers-by walking up and down the corridor looking for a seat. James glared at them as they passed. No one entered the carriage. James had won the first round. As the train gathered speed he tried his opening gambit, which was quite good by his normal standards:

'What a super picture on the front of *Vogue* taken by my old friend Patrick Lichfield.'

Anne Summerton looked up. She was even more beautiful than the picture James had referred to. Her dark hair, cut softly in the latest Vidal Sassoon style, her big hazel eyes and faultless skin gave her a gentle look that James found irresistible. She had that slim, graceful body that all leading models need to earn their living, but Anne also had a presence that most of them would never have. James was quite stunned and wished she would say something.

Anne was used to men trying to pick her up but she was rather taken aback by the remarks about Lord Lichfield. If he was a friend, it would be offhand not to be at least polite. On a second glance she found James's diffidence rather charming. He had used the self-deprecating approach many times with great success, but this time it was perfectly genuine. He tried again.

'It must be a hell of a job being a model.'

What a bloody silly line, he thought. Why couldn't he just say to her, I think you're absolutely fantastic? Can we talk a little and if I still think you're fantastic perhaps we can take it from there? But it never worked that way. He knew he would have to go through the usual routine.

'It's bearable if the contracts are good,' she replied, 'but today's been particularly tiring.' Her voice was gentle, and the faint transatlantic accent appealed to James. 'I've been smiling my head off all day, modelling an advertisement for Close-Up toothpaste: the photographer never seemed to be satisfied. The only good thing about it was that it ended a day earlier than expected. How do you know Patrick?'

'We were fags together at Harrow in our first year. He was rather better than me at getting out of work.'

Anne laughed – a gentle, warm laugh. It was obvious he knew Lord Lichfield.

'Do you see much of him now?'

'Occasionally at dinner parties, but not regularly. Does he photograph you a lot?'

'No,' said Anne, 'the cover picture for *Vogue* was the only time.'

As they chatted on, the thirty-five minute journey between Reading and London seemed to pass in a flash. Walking down the platform of Paddington Station with Anne, James ventured:

'Can I give you a lift home? My car is parked round the corner in Craven Street.'

Anne accepted, relieved not to have to search for a taxi at that late hour.

James drove her home in his Alfa Romeo. He had already decided that he could not hold on to that particular luxury for much longer with petrol going up and cash flow going down. He chattered merrily all the way to her destination, which turned out to be a block of flats in Cheyne Row overlooking the Thames; much to Anne's surprise he just dropped her off at the front door and said goodnight. He did not even ask for her telephone number and he only knew her Christian name. In fact, she did not have any idea what his name was. Pity, she thought as she closed the front door; he had been a rather pleasant change from the men who worked on the fringe of the advertising media, who imagined they had an automatic right to a girl's compliance just because she posed in a bra.

James knew exactly what he was doing. He had always found a girl was more flattered if he called her when she least expected it. His tactics were to leave the impression that she had seen the last of him, especially when the first meeting had gone well. He returned to his home in the King's Road and considered the situation. Unlike Stephen, Robin and Jean-Pierre, with thirteen days to go, he still had no ideas for defeating Harvey Metcalfe. But he was hatching plans for Anne.

On waking in the morning, Stephen began to do a little more research. He started with a close study of the way the university was administered. He visited the Vice-Chancellor's office in the Clarendon Building, where he spent some time asking strange questions of his personal secretary, Miss Smallwood. She was most intrigued. He then left for the office of the University Registrar, where he was equally inquisitive. He ended the day by visiting the Bodleian Library, and copying out some of the University Statutes. Among other outings during the next fourteen days was a trip to the Oxford tailors, Shepherd and Woodward, and a full day at the Sheldonian Theatre to watch the brief ceremony as a batch of students took their Bachelor of Arts degrees. Stephen also studied the layout of the Randolph, the largest hotel in Oxford. This he took some considerable time over, so much so that the manager became inquisitive and Stephen had to leave before he became suspicious. His final trip was a return journey to the Clarendon to meet the Secretary of the University Chest, and to be taken on a guided tour of the building by the porter. Stephen warned him that he anticipated showing an American around the building on the day of Encaenia, but remained vague.

'Well, that won't be easy . . .' began the porter. Stephen carefully and deliberately folded a pound note and passed it to the porter '. . . though I'm sure we'll be able to work something out, sir.'

In between his trips all over the university city, Stephen did a lot of thinking in the big leather chair and a lot more writing at his desk. By the fourteenth day his plan was perfected and ready for presentation to the other three. He had put the show on the road, as Harvey Metcalfe might have said, and he intended to see it had a long run.

Robin rose early on the morning after the Oxford dinner, and avoided awkward questions from his wife at breakfast about his experience the night before. He travelled up to London as soon as he could get away, and on arrival in Harley Street was greeted by his efficient secretary-cum-receptionist, Miss Meikle.

Elspeth Meikle was a dedicated, dour Scot who looked upon her work as nothing less than a vocation. Her devotion to Robin, not that she ever called him that even in her own mind, was obvious for all to see.

'I want as few appointments as possible over the next fourteen days, Miss Meikle.'

'I understand, Dr Oakley,' she said.

'I have some research to carry out and I don't want to be interrupted when I'm alone in my study.'

Miss Meikle was somewhat surprised. She had always

thought of Dr Oakley as a good physician, but had never known him in the past to over-indulge in research work. She padded off noiselessly in her white-shod feet to admit the first of a bunch of admirably healthy ladies to Dr Oakley's clinic.

Robin disposed of his patients with less than dignified speed. He went without lunch and began the afternoon by making several telephone calls to the Boston Infirmary and several to a leading gastroenterologist for whom he had been a houseman at Cambridge. Then he pressed the buzzer to summon Miss Meikle.

'Could you pop round to H. K. Lewis for me, Miss Meikle, and put two books on my account. I want the latest edition of Polson and Tattersall's *Clinical Toxicology* and Harding Rain's book on the bladder and abdomen.'

'Yes, sir,' she said, quite unperturbed at the thought of interrupting her lunchtime sandwich to fetch them.

They were on his desk before he had completed his calls, and he immediately started reading long sections of them carefully. The following day he cancelled his morning clinic and went to St Thomas's Hospital to watch two of his old colleagues at work. His confidence in the plan he had formulated was growing. He returned to Harley Street and wrote some notes on the techniques he had observed that morning, much as he had done in his student days. He paused to remember the words Stephen had used:

'Think as Harvey Metcalfe would. Think for the first time in your life, not as a cautious professional man, but as a risk-taker, as an entrepreneur.'

Robin was tuning in to Harvey Metcalfe's wavelength, and when the time came he would be ready for the American, the Frenchman and the lord. But would they be willing to fall in with his plan? He looked forward to their meeting.

Jean-Pierre returned from Oxford the next day. None of the youthful artists had greatly impressed him, though he had felt that Brian Davis's still life showed considerable promise and had made a mental note to keep an eye on his future work. When he arrived back in London he started, like Robin and Stephen, on his research. A tentative idea that had come to him in the Eastgate Hotel was beginning to germinate. Through his numerous contacts in the art world he checked all the buying and selling of major Impressionist paintings over the previous twenty years and made a list of the pictures which were currently thought to be on the market. He then contacted the person who held it in his power to set his plan in motion. Fortunately the man whose help he most needed, David Stein, was in England and free to visit him: but would he fall in with the plan?

Stein arrived late the following afternoon and spent two hours with Jean-Pierre privately in his little room in the basement of the Lamanns Gallery. When he left Jean-Pierre was smiling to himself. A final afternoon spent at the German Embassy in Belgrave Square, followed by a call to Dr Wormit of the Preussischer Kulturbesitz in Berlin and a further one to Mme Tellegen at the Rijksbureau in The Hague, gave him all the information he required. Even Metcalfe would have praised him for the final touch. There would be no relieving the French this time. The American and the Englishman had better be up to scratch when he presented his plan.

On waking in the morning the last thing James had on his mind was an idea for outwitting Harvey Metcalfe. His thoughts were fully occupied with more important things. He telephoned Patrick Lichfield at home.

'Patrick?'

'Yes,' mumbled a voice.

'James Brigsley.'

'Oh, hello James. Haven't seen you for some time. What are you doing waking a fellow up at this filthy hour?'

'It's 10 am Patrick.'

'Is it? It was the Berkeley Square Ball last night and I didn't get to bed until four. What can I do for you?'

'You took a picture for *Vogue* of a girl whose first name was Anne.'

'Summerton,' said Patrick without hesitation. 'Got her from the Stacpoole Agency.'

'What's she like?'

'No idea,' said Patrick. 'I thought she was awfully nice. She just thought I wasn't her type.'

'Obviously a woman of taste, Patrick. Now go back to sleep.' James put the phone down.

Anne Summerton was not listed in the telephone directory – so that ploy had failed. James remained in bed, scratching the stubble on his chin, when a triumphant look came into his eye. A quick flip through the S–Z directory revealed the number he required. He dialled it.

'The Stacpoole Agency.'

'Can I speak to the manager?'

'Who's calling?'

'Lord Brigsley.'

'I'll put you through, my lord.'

James heard the phone click and the voice of the manager.

'Good morning, my lord. Michael Stacpoole speaking. Can I help you?'

'I hope so, Mr Stacpoole. I have been let down at the last moment and I'm looking for a model for the opening of an antique shop and I'll need a classy sort of bird. You know the kind of girl.'

James then described Anne as if he had never met her.

'We have two models on our books who I think would suit you, my lord,' offered Stacpoole. 'Pauline Stone and Anne Summerton. Unfortunately, Pauline is in Birmingham today for the launching of the new Allegro car and Anne is completing a toothpaste session in Oxford.'

'I need a girl today,' James said. How he would have liked to have informed Stacpoole that Anne was back in town. 'If you find either of them are free for any reason, perhaps you would ring me at 735–7227.'

James rang off, a little disappointed. At least, he

thought, if nothing comes of it today he could start planning his part in the Team versus Harvey Metcalfe. He was just resigning himself to that when the phone rang. A shrill, high-pitched voice announced:

'This is the Stacpoole Agency. Mr Stacpoole would like to speak to Lord Brigsley.'

'Speaking,' said James.

'I'll put you through, my lord.'

'Lord Brigsley?'

'Yes.'

'Stacpoole here, my lord. It seems Anne Summerton is free today. When would you like her to come to your shop?'

'Oh,' said James, taken aback for a second. 'The shop is in Berkeley Street, next to the Empress Restaurant. It's called Albemarle Antiques. Perhaps we could meet outside at 12.45?'

'I'm sure that will be acceptable, my lord. If I don't ring you back in the next ten minutes, you can assume the meeting is on. Perhaps you'd be kind enough to let us know if she's suitable. We normally prefer you to come to the office, but I'm sure we can make an exception in your case.'

'Thank you,' said James and put the phone down, pleased with himself.

James stood on the west side of Berkeley Street in the doorway of the Mayfair Hotel so that he could catch Anne arriving. When it came to work, Anne was always on time, and at 12.40 pm she appeared from the Piccadilly end of the street. Her skirt was of the latest elegant length, but this time James could see that her legs were as slim and shapely as the rest of her. She stopped outside the Empress Restaurant and looked in bewilderment at the Brazilian Trade Centre on her right and the Rolls Royce showrooms of H. R. Owen on her left.

James strode across the road, a large grin on his face.

'Good morning,' he said casually.

'Oh hello,' said Anne, 'what a coincidence.'

'What are you doing here all alone and looking lost?' said James.

'I'm trying to find a shop called Albemarle Antiques. You don't know it by any chance? I must have the wrong street. As you go in for knowing lords, you might know the owner, Lord Brigsley?'

James smiled:

'I am Lord Brigsley.'

Anne looked surprised and then burst out laughing. She realised what James had done and was flattered by the compliment.

They lunched together at the Empress, James's favourite eating place in town. He explained to Anne why it had been Lord Clarendon's favourite restaurant as well – 'Ah,' he had once declared, 'the millionaires are just a little fatter, and the mistresses are just a little thinner, than in any other restaurant in town.'

The meal was a triumph and James had to admit that Anne was the best thing that had happened to him for a long time. After lunch she asked where the agency should send their account.

'With what I have in mind for the future,' replied James, 'they'd better be prepared for a large bad debt.'

7

Stephen wrung James warmly by the hand the way the
Americans will and presented him with a large whisky on
the rocks. Impressive memory, thought James, as he took
a gulp to give himself a little Dutch courage, and then
joined Robin and Jean-Pierre. By unspoken mutual con-
sent, the name of Harvey Metcalfe was not mentioned.
They chattered inconsequentially of nothing in particular,
each clutching his own dossier, until Stephen summoned
them to the table. Stephen had not, on this occasion,
exercised the talents of the college chef and the butler to
the Senior Common Room. Instead, sandwiches, beer and
coffee were stacked neatly on the table, and the college
servants were not in evidence.

'This is a working supper,' said Stephen firmly, 'and as
Harvey Metcalfe will eventually be footing the bill, I've
cut down considerably on the hospitality. We don't want
to make our task unnecessarily harder by eating our way
through hundreds of dollars per meeting.'

The other three sat down quietly as Stephen took out
some closely-typed sheets of paper.

'I'll begin,' he said, 'with a general comment. I've been
doing some further research into Harvey Metcalfe's movements over the next few months. He seems to spend
every summer doing the same round of social and sporting
events. Most of the details are already well documented
in your files. My latest findings are summarised on this
separate sheet which should be added as page 38A of your
dossiers. It reads:

Harvey Metcalfe will arrive in England on the morning of June 21st on board the QE2, docking at Southampton. He has already reserved the Trafalgar Suite for his crossing and booked a Rolls Royce from Guy Salmon to take him to Claridge's. He will stay there for two weeks in the Royal Suite and he has his own debenture tickets for every day of the Wimbledon Championships. When they are over he flies to Monte Carlo to stay on his yacht *Messenger Boy* for another two weeks. He then returns to London and Claridge's to see his filly, Rosalie, run in the King George VI and Queen Elizabeth Stakes. He has a private box at Ascot for all five days of Ascot Week. He returns to America on a Pan American jumbo jet from London Heathrow on July 29th, flight no. 009 at 11.15 to Logan International Airport, Boston.'

The others attached page 38A to their dossiers, aware once again how much detailed research Stephen had undertaken. James was beginning to feel ill, and it certainly was not the excellent salmon sandwiches that were causing his discomfort.

'The next decision to be taken,' said Stephen, 'is to allocate the times during Metcalfe's trip to Europe when each plan will be put into operation. Robin, which section would you prefer?'

'Monte Carlo,' said Robin without hesitation. 'I need to catch the bastard off his home ground.'

'Anyone else want Monte Carlo?'

Nobody spoke.

'Which would you prefer, Jean-Pierre?'

'I'd like Wimbledon fortnight.'

'Any other takers?'

Again, nobody spoke. Stephen continued:

'I'm keen to have the Ascot slot myself and the short time before he returns to America. What about you, James?'

'It won't make any difference what period I have,' said James rather sheepishly.

'Right,' said Stephen.

Everybody, except James, seemed to be warming to the exercise.

'Now expenses. Have all of you brought your cheques for $10,000? I think it's wise to think in dollars as that was the currency Harvey Metcalfe worked in.'

Each member of the Team passed over a cheque to Stephen. At least, thought James, this is something I can do as well as the others.

'Expenses to date?'

Each passed a chit to Stephen again and he began to work out figures on his stylish little HP 65 calculator, the digits glowing red in the dimly-lit room.

'The shares cost us $1 million. Expenses to date $142, so Mr Metcalfe is in debt to us to the tune of $1,000,142. Not a penny more and not a penny less,' he repeated. 'Now to our individual plans. We will take them in the order of execution.' Stephen was pleased with that word. 'Jean-Pierre, Robin, myself and finally James. The floor is yours, Jean-Pierre.'

Jean-Pierre opened a large envelope and took out four sets of documents. He was determined to show that he had the measure of Stephen as well as of Harvey Metcalfe. He handed round photographs and road maps of the West End and Mayfair. Each street was marked with a number, indicating how many minutes it took to walk. Jean-Pierre explained his plan in great detail, starting with the crucial meeting he had had with David Stein, and ending with the roles the others would have to carry out.

'All of you will be needed on the day. Robin will be the journalist, James the representative from Sotheby's, and Stephen, you will act as the purchaser. You must practise speaking English with a German accent. I shall also require two tickets for the whole of Wimbledon fortnight on the Centre Court opposite Harvey Metcalfe's debenture box.'

Jean-Pierre consulted his notes.

'That is to say, opposite box No. 17. Can you arrange that, James?'

'No problem. I'll have a word with Mike Gibson, the Club referee, in the morning.'

'Good. Finally, then, you must all learn to operate these little boxes of tricks. They are called Pye Pocketfones and don't forget that the use and ownership of them are illegal.'

Jean-Pierre produced four miniature sets and handed three to Stephen.

'Any questions?'

There was a general murmur of approval. There were going to be no loose ends in Jean-Pierre's plan.

'My congratulations,' said Stephen. 'That should get us off to a good start. Now, how about you, Robin?'

Robin relayed the story of his fourteen days. He reported on his meeting with the specialist, and explained the toxic effects of anticholinesterase drugs.

'This one will be hard to pull off; we'll have to be patient and wait for the right opportunity. But, we must stay prepared every moment Metcalfe is in Monte Carlo.'

'Where will we be staying in Monte Carlo?' asked James. 'I usually go to the Metropole. Better not make it there.'

'No, it's all right, James, I have provisional reservations at the Hôtel de Paris from June 29th to July 4th. However, before that you are all to attend several working sessions at St Thomas's Hospital.'

Diaries were consulted, and a series of meetings agreed upon.

'Here is a copy of Houston's *Short Textbook of Medicine* for each of you. You must all read the chapter on severe cuts and bruises. I don't want any of you to stick out like sore thumbs when we're all dressed in white. You, Stephen, will come to Harley Street the week after next for an intensive medical course, as you must be totally convincing as a doctor.'

Robin had chosen Stephen because he felt that with his academic mind he would pick up the most in the short time available.

'Jean-Pierre, you must attend a gaming club every evening for the next month and learn exactly how baccarat and blackjack are played, and how to continue playing for several hours at a time without losing money. It'll help if you get hold of Peter Arnold's *The Encyclopedia of Gambling* from Hatchards. James, you will learn to drive a small van through the rush hour traffic, and you are also to report to Harley Street next week so that we can try a dry run together.'

All eyes were wide open. If they pulled that one off they could do anything. Robin could see the anxiety in their faces.

'Don't worry,' he said, 'my profession has been carried on by witch-doctors for a thousand years. People never argue when they're confronted with a trained man, and you, Stephen, are going to be a trained man.'

Stephen nodded. Academics could be equally naïve. Hadn't that been exactly what had happened to all of them with Prospecta Oil?

'Remember,' said Robin, 'Stephen's comment at the bottom of page 33 of the dossier . . . "At all times we must think like Harvey Metcalfe".'

Robin gave a few more details of how certain procedures were to be carried out. He then answered demanding questions for twenty-eight minutes. Finally, Jean-Pierre softened:

'I thought none of you would beat me, but Robin's plan is brilliant. If we get the timing right we'll only need an ounce of luck.'

James was beginning to feel distinctly uneasy as his time drew nearer. He rather wished he had never accepted the invitation to dinner in the first place and regretted being the one to urge the others to take up Stephen's challenge. At least the duties he had been given in the first two operations were well within his scope.

'Well, gentlemen,' said Stephen, 'you've both risen admirably to the occasion, but my proposals will make more demands on you.'

Stephen began to reveal the fruits of his research during the past two weeks and the substance of his plan. They all felt rather like students in the presence of a professor. Stephen's lecturing tone was not intentional; it was a manner he had developed, and like so many academics, he was unable to switch it off in private company. He produced a calendar for Trinity Term and outlined how the university weeks worked, the role of its Chancellor, Vice-Chancellor, the Registrar and the Secretary of the University Chest. Like Jean-Pierre, he supplied maps to each member of the Team, this time of Oxford. He had carefully marked a route from the Sheldonian Theatre to Lincoln College, and from Lincoln to the Randolph Hotel, and had drawn up a contingency plan if Harvey Metcalfe insisted on using his car, despite the one-way system.

'Robin, you must study what the Vice-Chancellor does at Encaenia. It won't be like Cambridge; the two universities do everything similarly but not identically. You must know the route he's likely to take on that day and his habits backwards. I've arranged for a room at Lincoln to be at your disposal on the final day. Jean-Pierre, you will study and master the duties of the Registrar at Oxford and know the alternative route marked on your map so that you never come face to face with Robin. James, you must know how the Secretary of the University Chest goes about his work – the location of his office, which banks he deals with and how the cheques are cashed. You must also know the routes he's likely to take on the day of Encaenia as if they were part of your father's estate. I have the easiest role on the day, because I will be myself in everything but name. You must all learn how to address each other correctly and we'll have a dress rehearsal in the ninth week of term, on a Tuesday when the university is fairly quiet. Any questions?'

Silence reigned, but it was a silence of respect. All could see that Stephen's operation would demand split-second timing and that they would have to run through it several times to cover all contingencies. But if they were convincing they could hardly fail.

'Now, the Ascot part of my plan is simple. I will only

want Jean-Pierre and James inside the Members' Enclosure. I shall need two Enclosure tickets which I'm hoping you can acquire, James.'

'You mean badges, Stephen,' corrected James.

'Oh, do I?' said Stephen. 'I also require someone in London to send the necessary telegram. That'll have to be you, Robin.'

'Agreed,' said Robin.

For nearly an hour the others asked several questions of detail in order to be as familiar with the plan as Stephen was.

James asked no questions and his mind began to drift, hoping the earth would swallow him up. He even began to wish that he had never met Anne, although she was hardly to blame. In fact, he could not wait to see her again. What was he going to say when they . . .

'James, wake up,' said Stephen sharply. 'We're all waiting.'

Six eyes were now fixed on him. They had produced the ace of hearts, diamonds and spades. But had he the ace of trumps? James was flustered and poured himself another drink.

'You bloody upper-class twit,' said Jean-Pierre, 'you haven't got an idea, have you?'

'Well, actually, I've given the problem a lot of thought, but nothing seemed to come.'

'Useless – worse than useless,' said Robin.

James was stammering helplessly. Stephen cut him short.

'Now listen, James, and listen carefully. We meet here again in twenty-one days' time. By then we must know each other's plans backwards. One error could blow the whole thing. Do you understand?'

James nodded – he was determined not to let them down in that.

'And what's more,' said Stephen firmly, 'you must have your own plan ready for scrutiny. Is that also clear?'

'Yes,' mumbled James unhappily.

'Any other questions?' said Stephen.

There were none.

'Right. We go through the three individual operations again in full.'

Stephen ignored the muttered protests.

'Remember, we're up against a man who isn't used to being beaten. We won't get a second chance.'

For an hour and a half they went through the details of each operation in the order of action. First, Jean-Pierre during Wimbledon fortnight: second, Robin in Monte Carlo: third, Stephen during and after Ascot.

It was late and they were all weary when they finally rose from the table. They departed sleepily, each with several tasks to carry out before their next meeting. Each went his separate way, but all were due to meet again the following Friday in the Jericho Theatre of St Thomas's Hospital.

8

The next twenty days turned out to be an exacting time for all four of them. Each had to master the other plans as well as organising his own. Friday brought them all together for the first of many sessions at St Thomas's Hospital, which would have been entirely successful if James had managed to stay on his feet. It was not the sight of blood that daunted him – the sight of the knife was enough. The only virtue from James's standpoint was that he once again avoided having to explain why he had not come up with any ideas of his own.

The next week was almost full time, with Stephen in Harley Street taking a potted course in one particular field of medicine at a fairly high level.

James spent several hours driving an old van through the heavy traffic from St Thomas's to Harley Street, preparing for his final test in Monte Carlo, which he felt could only be considerably easier. He also returned to Oxford for a week, learning how the Secretary of the University Chest's office operated, and also studying the movements of the Secretary himself, Mr Caston.

Jean-Pierre, at a cost to Mr Metcalfe of $25 and a 48-hour wait, became an overseas member of The Claremont, London's most distinguished gaming club, and passed his evenings watching the wealthy and lazy play baccarat and blackjack, their stakes often reaching $1,000. After three weeks of watching he ventured to join the Golden Nugget casino in Soho, where the stakes rarely exceeded £5. By the end of the month he had played for 56 hours, but so conservatively that he was only showing a small loss.

James's overriding worry was still his personal contribution. The more he grappled with the problem, the less he came to grips with it. He turned it over and over in his mind, even when he was travelling through London at high speed. One night after returning the van to Carnie's in Lots Road, Chelsea, he drove his Alfa Romeo over to Anne's flat by the river, wondering if he dared confide in her.

Anne was preparing a special meal for James. She was aware that he not only appreciated good food, but had taken it for granted all his life. The homemade gazpacho was smelling good and the *Coq au vin* was all but ready. Lately she had found herself avoiding modelling assignments out of London as she did not care to be away from James for any length of time. She was also conscious that he was the first man for some time that she would have been willing to go to bed with – and to date he had made no efforts to leave the dining-room.

James arrived carrying a bottle of Beaune Montée Rouge 1971 – even his wine cellar was fast diminishing. He only hoped it would last long enough for the plans to come to fruition. Not that he felt an automatic right to a part of the bounty while he failed to contribute his own plan.

Anne looked stunning. She was wearing a long black dress of some soft material that tantalised James with the reticence with which it outlined her shape. She wore no makeup or jewellery, and her heavy nob of hair gleamed in the candlelight. The meal was a triumph for Anne, and James started wanting her badly. She seemed nervous, spilling a little ground coffee as she filtered two strong tiny cups. What was in her mind? He did not want to blunder with unwanted attentions. James had had much more practice at being loved than at being in love. He was used to adulation, to ending up in bed with girls who made him shudder in the cold clear light of morning. Anne affected him in an entirely different way. He wanted to be close to her, to hold her and to love her. Above all, he wanted her to be there in the morning.

Anne cleared away the supper, avoiding James's eye, and they settled down to brandy and Lena Horne singing 'I get Along Without You Very Well'. She sat, hands clasped round her knees on the floor at James's feet, staring into the fire. Tentatively, he put out a hand and stroked her hair. She sat unresponsive for a moment and then bent her head back and stretched out her arm to bring his face down to hers. He responded, leaning forward and stroking her cheek and nose with his mouth, holding her head in his hands, his fingers gently exploring her ears and neck. Her skin smelled faintly of jasmine and her open mouth glinted in the firelight as she smiled up at him. He kissed her and slid his hands down on to her body. She felt soft and slight under his hands. He caressed her breasts gently, and moved down beside her, his body pressing against hers. Wordlessly, he reached behind her and unzipped her dress and watched it fall to the ground. He stood up, his eyes never leaving hers, and undressed quickly. She glanced at his body and smiled shyly.

'Darling James,' she said softly.

After they had made love, like two people in love and not as lovers, Anne settled her head on James's shoulder and stroked the hair on his chest with a fingertip.

'What's the matter, James? I know I'm rather shy. But it will . . .'

'You were beautiful. God knows, you were perfect. That's not the problem . . . Anne, I have to tell you something, so just lie back and listen.'

'You're married.'

'No, it's far worse than that.' James lay silent for a moment, lit a cigarette and inhaled deeply. There are occasions in life when revelation is made easier by circumstance; it all came out in an unco-ordinated jumble. 'Anne darling, I've made a bloody fool of myself by investing a vast sum of money with a bunch of crooks who've stolen

103

it. I haven't even told my family – they'd be terribly distressed if they ever found out. To make matters better or worse, I've got myself involved with three other chaps who found themselves in the same predicament, and now we're all trying to get our money back. They're nice fellows, full of bright ideas, but I haven't a clue how to begin to keep my part of the bargain. What with the worry of being £150,000 down the drain and having to keep racking my brain for a good idea, I'm half frantic. You're the only thing that's kept me sane the last month.'

'James, start again, but slower this time,' said Anne.

Thus James revealed the entire history of Prospecta Oil, from his meeting with David Kesler at Annabel's to his invitation to dine with Stephen Bradley at Magdalen, finally explaining why he had been driving a hired van like a maniac through the rush hour. The only detail James left out was the name of their intended victim, as he felt that by withholding that he was not completely violating his bond of secrecy with the rest of the Team.

Anne inhaled very deeply.

'I hardly know what to say. It's incredible. It's so unbelievable that I believe every word.'

'I feel better just for telling someone, but it would be terrible if the others ever found out.'

'James, you know I won't say a word to anyone. I'm just so very sorry you're in such a mess. You must let me see if I can come up with an idea. Why don't we work together without letting the others know?'

James felt better already.

She began stroking the inside of his leg. Twenty minutes later, they sank into a blissful sleep, dreaming up plans to defeat Harvey Metcalfe.

9

In Lincoln, Massachusetts, Harvey Metcalfe began to prepare for his annual trip to England. He intended to enjoy himself thoroughly and expensively. He had plans for transferring some more money from his numbered accounts in Zürich to Barclays Bank, Lombard Street, ready to buy yet another stallion from one of the Irish stables to join his stud in Kentucky. Arlene had decided not to accompany him on this trip: she did not care too much for Ascot and even less for Monte Carlo. In any case, it gave her the chance to spend some time with her ailing mother in Vermont, who still had little respect for her prosperous son-in-law.

Harvey checked with his secretary that all the arrangements for the holiday had been completed. There was never any need to check up on Miss Fish, it was simply a habit on Harvey's part. Miss Fish had been with him for twenty-five years, from the days when he had first taken over the Lincoln Trust. Most of the respectable staff had walked out on Harvey's arrival, or shortly afterwards, but Miss Fish had remained, nursing in her unalluring bosom ever fainter hopes of eventual marriage to Harvey. By the time Arlene appeared on the scene, Miss Fish was an able and completely discreet accomplice without whom Harvey could hardly have operated. He paid her accordingly, so she swallowed her chagrin at the thought of another Mrs Metcalfe, and stayed put.

Miss Fish had already booked the short flight to New York and the Trafalgar Suite on the QE2. The trip across the Atlantic was almost the only total break Harvey ever had from the telephone or telex. The bank staff were instructed to contact the great liner only in dire emergency. On arrival at Southampton it would be the usual Rolls Royce to London and the private suite at Claridge's, which Harvey judged to be one of the last English hotels, along with the Connaught and Browns, where his money allowed him to mix with what he called 'class'.

Harvey flew to New York in high good humour, relaxing and drinking a couple of Manhattans on the way. The arrangements on board ship were as impeccable as ever. The Captain, Peter Jackson, always invited the occupant of the Trafalgar Suite or the Queen Anne Suite to join him on the first night out at the Captain's table. At $1,250 a day for the suites it could hardly be described as an extravagant gesture on Cunard's part. On such occasions, Harvey was always on his best behaviour, although even that struck most onlookers as somewhat brash.

One of the Italian stewards was detailed to arrange a little diversion for Harvey, preferably in the shape of a tall blonde with a large bosum. The going rate for the night was $200, but the Italian could charge Harvey $250 and still get away with it. At 5ft 7in and 227lb, Harvey's chances of picking up a young thing in the discothèque were slender, and by the time he had lashed out on drinks and dinner, he could have spent almost as much money and achieved absolutely nothing. Men in Harvey's position do not have time for that sort of failure and expect everything in life to have its price. As the voyage was only five nights, the steward was able to keep Harvey fully occupied, although he felt it was just as well that Harvey had not booked a three-week Mediterranean cruise.

Harvey spent his days catching up with the latest novels he had been told he must read and also taking a little exercise, a swim in the morning and a painful session in the gymnasium during the afternoon. He reckoned to lose 10lb during the crossing, which was pleasing, but somehow Claridge's always managed to put it back on again before he returned to the States. Fortunately, his suits were tailored by Bernard Weatherill of Dover Street, Mayfair, who by dint of near-genius and impeccable skill made him look well-built rather than distinctly fat. At £300 per suit it was the least he could expect.

When the five days were drawing to a close, Harvey was more than ready for land again. The women, the exercise and the fresh air had quite revived him and he had lost all of 11lb on the crossing. He felt a good deal of this must have come off the night before, which he had spent with a young Indian girl who had made the *Kama Sutra* look like a Boy Scout's handbook.

One of the advantages of real wealth is that menial tasks can always be left to someone else. Harvey could no longer remember when he last packed or unpacked a suitcase, and when the ship docked at the Ocean Terminal it came as no surprise to him to discover everything packed and ready for Customs – a $100 bill for the head steward seemed to bring men in little white coats from every direction.

Harvey always enjoyed disembarking at Southampton. The English were a race he liked, though he feared he would never understand them. He found them always so willing to be trodden on by the rest of the world. Since the Second World War, they had relinquished their colonial power in a way no American business man would have ever considered for an exit from his own boardroom. Harvey had finally given up trying to understand the British way of business during the 1967 devaluation of the pound. Every jumped-up speculator on the face of the globe had taken advantage of the inside knowledge. Harvey knew on the Tuesday morning that Harold Wilson was going to devalue any time after Friday, 5 pm Greenwich Mean Time, when the Bank of England closed for the weekend. On the Thursday even the junior clerk at the Lincoln Trust knew. It was no wonder that the Old Lady of Threadneedle Street was raped and despoiled of an estimated £1½ billion over the next few days. Harvey had often thought that if only the British could liven up their boardrooms and get their tax structure right, they might end up being the richest nation in the world, instead of a nation which, as *The Economist* had stated, could now be taken over by the Arabs with ninety days of oil revenue. While the British flirted with socialism and still retained a *folie de grandeur*, they seemed doomed to sink into insignificance. But still Harvey adored them.

He strode down the gangplank like a man with a purpose. Harvey had never learnt to relax completely, even when he was on vacation. He could spend just about four days away from the world, but if he had been left on the QE2 any longer he would have been negotiating to buy the Cunard Steamship Company. Harvey had once met the Chairman of Cunard, Vic Matthews, at Ascot and had been baffled to hear him harking on the prestige and reputation of the company. Harvey had expected him to brag about the balance sheet. Prestige interested Harvey, of course, but he always let people know how much he was worth first.

Customs clearance was given with the usual speed. Harvey never had anything of consequence to declare on his European trips, and after they had checked two of his Gucci suitcases, the other seven were allowed through without inspection. The chauffeur opened the door of the white Rolls Royce Corniche. The vehicle sped through Hampshire and into London in a little over two hours, which gave Harvey time for a rest before dinner.

Albert, the head doorman at Claridge's, stood smartly to attention and saluted as the car drew up. He knew Harvey of old and was aware that he had come, as usual, for Wimbledon and Ascot. Albert would undoubtedly receive a 50 pence tip every time he opened the white Rolls door. Harvey didn't know the difference between a 50 pence and 10 pence piece – a difference which Albert had welcomed since the introduction of decimilisation in Britain. Moreover, Harvey always gave Albert £5 at the end of Wimbledon fortnight if an American won the singles title. An American invariably reached the finals, so Albert always placed a bet with Ladbrokes on the other finalist and won either way. Gambling appealed to both Harvey and Albert; only the sums involved were different.

Albert arranged for the luggage to be sent up to the Royal Suite, which during the year had already been occupied by King Constantine of Greece, Princess Grace of Monaco and Emperor Hailé Selassié of Ethiopia, all with considerably more conviction than Harvey. But Harvey still considered that his annual holiday at Claridge's was more assured than theirs.

The Royal Suite is on the first floor at Claridge's and can be reached by an elegant sweeping staircase from the ground floor, or by a commodious lift with its own seat. Harvey always took the lift up and walked down. At least that way he convinced himself he was taking some exercise. The suite itself consists of four rooms: a small dressing-room, a bedroom, a bathroom, and an elegant drawing-room overlooking Brook Street. The furniture and pictures make it possible for you to believe that you are still in Victorian England. Only the telephone and television dispel the illusion. The room is large enough to be used for cocktail parties or by visiting heads of state to entertain large parties. Henry Kissinger had received Harold Wilson there only the week before. Harvey enjoyed the thought of that. It was about as close as he was going to get to either man.

After a shower and change of clothes, Harvey glanced through his waiting mail and telexes from the bank, which were all routine. He took a short nap before going down to dine in the main restaurant.

There in the large foyer was the usual string quartet, looking like out-of-work refugees from Hungary. Harvey even recognised the four musicians. He had reached that time in life when he did not like change; the management of Claridge's, aware that the average age of their customers was over fifty, catered accordingly. François, the head waiter, showed Harvey to his usual table.

109

Harvey managed a little shrimp cocktail and a medium fillet steak with a bottle of Mouton Cadet. As he leaned forward to study the sweets trolley, he did not notice the four young men eating in the alcove on the far side of the room.

Stephen, Robin, Jean-Pierre and James all had an excellent view of Harvey Metcalfe. He would have had to bend double and move slightly backwards to have any sight of them.

'Not exactly what I expected,' commented Stephen.

'Put on a bit of weight since those photographs you supplied,' said Jean-Pierre.

'Hard to believe he's real after all this preparation,' remarked Robin.

'The bastard's real enough,' said Jean-Pierre, 'and a million dollars richer because of our stupidity.'

James said nothing. He was still in disgrace after his futile efforts and excuses at the last full briefing, although the other three had to admit that they did receive good service wherever they went with him. Claridge's was proving to be no exception.

'Wimbledon tomorrow,' said Jean-Pierre. 'I wonder who'll win the first round?'

'You will of course,' chipped in James, hoping to soften Jean-Pierre's acid comments about his own feeble efforts.

'We can only win your round, James, if we ever fill in an entry form.'

James sank back into silence.

'I must say, looking at the size of Metcalfe we ought to get away with your plan, Robin,' said Stephen,

'If he doesn't die of cirrhosis of the liver before we're given the chance,' replied Robin. 'How do you feel about Oxford now you've seen him, Stephen?'

'I don't know yet. I'll feel better when I've belled the cat at Ascot. I want to hear him speak, watch him in his normal environment, get the feel of the man. You can't do all that from the other side of the dining-room.'

'You may not have to wait too long. This time tomorrow we may know everything we need to know – or all be in West End Central Police Station,' said Robin. 'Maybe we won't even pass Go, let alone collect £200.'

'We have to – I can't afford bail,' said Jean-Pierre.

When Harvey had downed a large snifter of Rémy Martin VSOP he left his table, slipping the head waiter a crisp new pound note.

'The bastard,' said Jean-Pierre with great feeling. 'It's bad enough knowing he's stolen our money, but it's humiliating having to watch him spend it.'

The four of them prepared to leave, the object of their outing achieved. Stephen paid the bill and carefully added the sum to the list of expenses against Harvey Metcalfe. Then they left the hotel separately and as inconspicuously as possible. Only James found this difficult as all the waiters and porters insisted on saying 'Good night, my lord.'

Harvey took a stroll round Berkeley Square and did not even notice the tall young man slip into the doorway of Moyses Stevens, the florists, for fear of being spotted by him. Harvey could never resist asking a policeman the way to Buckingham Palace, just to compare his reaction with that of a New York cop, leaning on a lamp post, chewing gum, holster on hip. As Lenny Bruce had said on being deported from England, 'Your pigs is so much better than our pigs'. Yes, Harvey liked England.

He arrived back at Claridge's at about 11.15 pm, showered and went to bed – a large double bed with that glorious feel of clean sheets. There would be no women for him at Claridge's or, if there were, it would be the last time he would find the Royal Suite available to him during Wimbledon or Ascot. The room moved just a little, but then after five days on an ocean liner it was unlikely to be still for a couple of nights. He slept well in spite of it, without a worry on his mind.

10

Harvey rose at 7.30 am, a habit he could not break, but he did allow himself the holiday luxury of breakfast in bed. Ten minutes after he had called room service, the waiter arrived with a trolley laden with half a grapefruit, bacon and eggs, toast, steaming black coffee, a copy of the previous day's *Wall Street Journal*, and the morning edition of *The Times*, *Financial Times* and *International Herald Tribune*.

Harvey was not sure how he would have survived on a European trip without the *International Herald Tribune*, known in the trade as the 'Trib'. This unique paper, published in Paris, is jointly owned by the *New York Times* and the *Washington Post*. Although only one edition of 120,000 copies is printed, it does not go to press until the New York Stock Exchange is closed. Therefore, no American need wake up in Europe out of touch. When the *New York Herald Tribune* folded in 1966, Harvey had been among those who advised John H. Whitney to keep the *International Herald Tribune* going in Europe. Once again, Harvey's judgment had been proved sound. The *International Herald Tribune* went on to absorb its faltering rival, the *New York Times*, which had never been a success in Europe. From then on the paper went from strength to strength.

Harvey ran an experienced eye down the Stock Exchange lists in the *Wall Street Journal* and the *Financial Times*. His bank now held very few shares as he, like Jim Slater in England, had suspected that the Dow-Jones Index would collapse and had therefore gone almost entirely liquid, holding only some South African gold shares and a few well-chosen stocks about which he had inside information. The only monetary transaction he cared to undertake with the market so shaky was to sell the dollar short and buy gold, so that he caught the dollar on the way down and gold on the way up. There were already rumours in Washington that the President of the United States had been advised by his Secretary of the Treasury, George Schultz, to allow the American people to buy gold on the open market later that year or early the following year. Harvey had been buying gold for the past fifteen years: all the President was going to do was to stop him from breaking the law. Harvey was of the opinion that the moment the Americans were able to buy gold, the bubble would burst and the price of gold would recede – the real money would be made while the speculators anticipated the rise, and Harvey intended to be out of gold well before it came on to the American market. Once the President made it legal, Harvey couldn't see a profit in it.

Harvey checked the commodity market in Chicago. He had made a killing in copper a year before. Inside information from an African ambassador had made this possible – information the ambassador had imparted to too many people. Harvey had not been surprised to read that he had later been recalled to his homeland and shot.

He could never resist checking the price of Prospecta Oil, now at an all-time low of $1/8: there could be no trading in the stock, simply because there would only be sellers and no buyers. The shares were virtually worthless. He smiled sardonically and turned to the sports page of *The Times*.

Rex Bellamy's article on the forthcoming Wimbledon Championships tipped John Newcombe as favourite and Jimmy Connors, the new American star who had just won the Italian Open, as the best outside bet. The British press wanted the 39-year-old Ken Rosewall to win. Harvey could well remember the epic final between Rosewall and

Drobny in 1954, which had run to 58 games. Like most of the crowd, he had supported the 33-year-old Drobny, who had finally won after three hours of play, 13–11, 4–6, 6–2, 9–7. This time, Harvey wanted history to repeat itself and Rosewall to win, though he felt the popular Australian's chance had slipped by during the ten years when the professionals were barred from Wimbledon. Still, he saw no reason why the fortnight should not be a pleasant break, and perhaps there might be an American victor even if Rosewall couldn't manage it.

Harvey had time for a quick glance at the art reviews before finishing his breakfast, leaving the papers strewn over the floor. The quiet Regency furniture, the elegant service and the Royal Suite did nothing for Harvey's habits. He padded into the bathroom for a shave and a shower. Arlene told him that most people did it the other way round – showered and then ate breakfast. But, as Harvey pointed out to her, most people did things the other way round from him, and look where it got them.

Harvey habitually spent the first morning of Wimbledon fortnight visiting the Summer Exhibition at the Royal Academy in Piccadilly. He would then follow this with visits to most of the West End's major galleries – Agnew's, Tooths, the Marlborough, Wildenstein – all within easy walking distance of Claridge's. This morning would be no exception. If Harvey was anything, he was a creature of habit, which was something the Team were quickly learning.

After he had dressed and bawled out room service for not leaving enough whisky in his cabinet, he headed down the staircase, emerged through the swing door on to Davies Street and strode off towards Berkeley Square. Harvey did not observe a studious young man with a two-way radio on the other side of the road.

'He's left the hotel by the Davies Street entrance,' said Stephen quietly to his little Pye Pocketfone, 'and he's heading towards you, James.'

'I'll pick him up as he comes into Berkeley Square, Stephen. Robin can you hear me?'

114

'Yes.'

'I'll let you know as soon as I spot him. You stay put at the Royal Academy.'

'Right you are,' said Robin.

Harvey strolled round Berkeley Square, down into Piccadilly and through the Palladian arches of Burlington House. With a bad grace, he stood and queued with the assorted humanity in the forecourt, shuffling past the Astronomical Society and the Society of Antiquaries. He did not see another young man opposite standing in the entrance of the Chemical Society, deep in a copy of *Chemistry in Britain*. Finally, Harvey made it up the red-carpeted ramp into the Royal Academy itself. He handed the cashier £5.00 for a season ticket, realising that he would probably want to return at least three or four times. He spent the rest of the morning studying the 1,182 pictures, none of which had been exhibited anywhere else in the world before the opening day, in accordance with the stringent rules of the Academy. Despite that ruling, the Hanging Committee had still had over 5,000 pictures to choose from.

On the opening day of the exhibition the month before, Harvey had acquired, through his agent, a watercolour by Alfred Daniels of the House of Commons for £350 and two oils by Bernard Dunstan of English provincial scenes for £125 each. The Summer Exhibition was still, in Harvey's estimation, the best value in the world. Even if he did not want to keep all the pictures himself, they made wonderful presents when he returned to the States. The Daniels reminded him of a Lowry he had bought some twenty years before at the Academy for £80: that had turned out to be another shrewd investment.

Harvey made a special point of looking at the Bernard Dunstans in the Exhibition. Of course, they were all sold. Dunstan was one of the artists whose pictures always sold in the first minutes of the opening day. Although Harvey had not been in London on that day, he had had no difficulty in buying what he wanted. He had planted a man

115

at the front of the queue, who had obtained a catalogue and marked those artists he knew Harvey could resell easily if he made a mistake and keep if his judgment were right. When the exhibition opened on the dot of 10 am, the agent had gone straight to the purchasing desk and acquired the five or six pictures he had marked in the catalogue before he or anyone other than the Academicians had seen them. Harvey studied his vicarious purchases with care. On this occasion he was happy to keep them all. If there had been one that did not quite fit in with his collection, he would have returned the picture for resale, undertaking to purchase it if nobody else showed any interest. In twenty years he had acquired over a hundred pictures by this method and returned a mere dozen, never once failing to secure a resale. Harvey had a system for everything.

At 1 pm, after a thoroughly satisfactory morning, he left the Royal Academy. The white Rolls Royce was waiting for him in the forecourt.

'Wimbledon.'

'Shit.'

'What did you say?' queried Stephen.

'S.H.I.T. He's gone to Wimbledon, so today's down the drain,' said Robin.

That meant Harvey would not return to Claridge's until at least seven or eight that evening. A rota had been fixed for watching him, and Robin accordingly picked up his Rover 3500 V8 from a parking meter in St James's Square and headed off to Wimbledon. James had obtained two tickets for every day of the Championships opposite Harvey Metcalfe's debenture box.

Robin arrived at Wimbledon a few minutes after Harvey and took his seat in the Centre Court, far enough back in the sea of faces to remain inconspicuous. The atmosphere was already building up for the opening match. Wimbledon seemed to be getting more popular every year and the Centre Court was packed to capacity. Princess Alexandra and the Prime Minister were in the Royal Box awaiting

116

the entrance of the gladiators. The little green scoreboards at the southern end of the court were flashing up the names of Kodeš and Stewart as the umpire took his seat on the high chair in the middle of the court directly overlooking the net. The crowd began to applaud as the two athletes, both dressed in white, entered the court carrying four rackets each. Wimbledon does not allow its competitors to dress in any colour other than white, although they had relaxed a little by permitting the trimming of the ladies' dresses to be coloured.

Robin enjoyed the opening match between Kodeš and an unseeded player from the United States, who gave the champion a hard time before losing to the Czech 6–3, 6–4, 9–7. Robin was sorry when Harvey decided to leave in the middle of an exciting doubles match. Back to duty, he told himself, and followed the white Rolls at a safe distance to Claridge's. On arriving, he telephoned James's flat, which was being used as the Team's headquarters in London, and briefed Stephen.

'May as well call it a day,' said Stephen. 'We'll try again tomorrow. Poor old Jean-Pierre's heart-beat reached 150 this morning. He may not last many days of false alarms.'

When Harvey left Claridge's the following morning he went through Berkeley Square into Bruton Street and then on into Bond Street, stopping only 50 yards from Jean-Pierre's gallery. But he turned east instead of west and slipped into Agnew's, where he had an appointment with Sir Geoffrey Agnew, the head of the family firm, for news of Impressionist pictures on the market. Sir Geoffrey was anxious to get away to another meeting and could only spend a few minutes with Harvey. He had nothing worthwhile to offer him.

Harvey left Agnew's soon afterwards clutching a small consolation prize of a maquette by Rodin, a mere bagatelle at £800.

'He's coming out,' said Robin, 'and heading in the right direction.' Jean-Pierre held his breath, but Harvey stopped once again, this time at the Marlborough Gallery to study their latest exhibition of Barbara Hepworth. He spent over an hour appreciating her beautiful work, but decided the prices were now outrageous. He had bought two Hepworths only ten years before for £800. The Marlborough was now asking between £7,000 and £10,000 for her work. So he left and continued up Bond Street.

'Jean-Pierre?'

'Yes,' replied a nervous voice.

'He's reached the corner of Conduit Street and he's about 50 yards away from your front door.'

Jean-Pierre prepared his window, removing the Graham Sutherland watercolour of the Thames and the Boatman.

'He's turned left, the bastard,' said James, who was stationed opposite the gallery. 'He's walking down Bruton Street on the right-hand side.'

Jean-Pierre put the Sutherland back on the easel in the window and retired to the lavatory, muttering to himself:

'I can't cope with two shits at once.'

Harvey meanwhile stepped into an inconspicuous entrance on Bruton Street and climbed the stairs to Tooths, more hopeful of finding something in a gallery which had become famous for its Impressionists. A Klee, a Picasso and two Salvador Dalis – not what Harvey was looking for. Though very well executed, the Klee was not as good as the one in his dining-room in Lincoln, Massachusetts. Besides, it might not fit in with any of Arlene's decorative schemes. Nicholas Tooth, the managing director, promised to keep his eyes open and ring Harvey at Claridge's should anything of interest turn up.

'He's on the move again, but I think he's heading back to Claridge's.'

James willed him to turn round and return in the direction of Jean-Pierre's gallery, but Harvey strode purposefully towards Berkeley Square, only making a detour to the O'Hana Gallery. Albert, the head doorman, had told him there was a Renoir in the window, and indeed there was. But it was only a half-finished canvas which Renoir had obviously used for a practice run or had disliked enough to leave unfinished. Harvey was curious as to the price and entered the gallery.

'£30,000,' said the assistant, as if it was $10 and a snip at that.

Harvey whistled through the gap between his front teeth. It never ceased to amaze him that an inferior picture by a first-rank name could fetch £30,000 and an outstanding picture by an artist with no established reputation could only bring a few hundred dollars. He thanked the assistant and left.

'A pleasure, Mr Metcalfe.'

Harvey was always flattered by people who remembered his name. But hell, they ought to remember – he had purchased a Monet from them last year for £62,000.

'He's definitely on his way back to the hotel,' said James.

Harvey spent only a few minutes in Claridge's, picking up one of their famous specially prepared luncheon hampers of caviar, beef, ham and cheese sandwiches and chocolate cake for later consumption at Wimbledon.

James was next on the rota for the Championships and decided to take Anne with him. Why not – she knew the truth. It was Ladies' Day and the turn of Billie Jean King, the vivacious American champion, to take the court. She was up against the unseeded American, Kathy May, who looked as if she was in for a rough time. The applause Billie Jean received was unworthy of her abilities, but for some reason she had never become a Wimbledon favourite. Harvey was accompanied by a guest who James thought had a faintly mid-European look.

'Which one is your victim?' asked Anne.

'He's almost exactly opposite us talking to the man in a light grey suit who looks like a government official from the EEC.'

'The short fat one?' asked Anne.

'Yes,' said James.

Whatever comments Anne made were interrupted by the umpire's call of 'Play' and everyone's attention focused on Billie Jean. It was exactly 2 pm.

*   *   *

119

'Kind of you to invite me to Wimbledon, Harvey,' said Jörg Birrer. 'I never seem to get the chance for much relaxation nowadays. You can't leave the market for more than a few hours without some panic breaking out somewhere in the world.'

'If you feel that way it's time for you to retire,' said Harvey.

'No one to take my place,' said Birrer. 'I've been chairman of the bank for ten years now and finding a successor is turning out to be my hardest task.'

'First game to Mrs King. Mrs King leads by one game to love in the first set.'

'Now, Harvey, I know you too well to expect this invitation to have been just for pleasure.'

'What an evil mind you have, Jörg.'

'In my profession I need it.'

'I just wanted to check how my three accounts stand and brief you on my plans for the next few months.'

'Game to Mrs King. Mrs King leads by two games to love in the first set.'

'Your No. 1 official account is a few thousand dollars in credit. Your numbered commodity account' – at this point Birrer unfolded a small piece of unidentifiable paper with a set of neat figures printed on it – 'is short by $3,726,000, but you are holding 37,000 ounces of gold at today's selling price of $135 an ounce.'

'What's your advice on that?'

'Hold on, Harvey. I still think your President is either going to announce a new gold standard or allow your fellow-countrymen to buy gold on the open market some time next year.'

'That's my view too, but I'm still convinced we want to sell a few weeks before the masses come in. I have a theory about that.'

'I expect you're right, as usual, Harvey.'

'Game to Mrs King. Mrs King leads by three games to love in the first set.'

'What are your charges on my overdraft?'

'1½ per cent above inter-bank rate, which at present is 13.25, and therefore we're charging you 14.75 per cent per annum, while gold is rising in price at nearly 70 per cent per annum. It can't go on that way; but there are still a few months left in it.'

'OK,' said Harvey, 'hold on until November 1st and we'll review the position again then. Coded telex as usual. I don't know what the world would do without the Swiss.'

'Just take care, Harvey. Do you know there are more specialists in our police force on fraud than there are for homicide?'

'You worry about your end, Jörg, and I'll worry about mine. The day I get uptight about a few underpaid bureaucrats from Zürich who haven't got any balls, I'll let you know. Now, enjoy your lunch and watch the game. We'll have a talk about the other account later.'

'Game to Mrs King. Mrs King leads by four games to love in the first set.'

'They're very deep in conversation,' said Anne. 'I can't believe they're enjoying the match.'

'He's probably trying to buy Wimbledon at cost price,' laughed James. 'The trouble with seeing the man every day is that one begins to have a certain respect for him. He's the most organised man I've ever come across. If he's like this on holiday, what the hell is he like at work?'

'I can't imagine,' said Anne.

'Game to Miss May. Mrs King leads by four games to one in the first set.'

'No wonder he's so overweight. Just look at him stuffing that cake down.' James lifted his Zeiss binoculars. 'Which reminds me to ask, darling, what have you brought for lunch?'

Anne dug into her hamper and unpacked a crisp salad in French bread for James. She contented herself with nibbling a stick of celery.

'Getting far too fat,' she explained. 'I'll never get into those winter clothes I'm supposed to be modelling next week.' She touched James's knee and smiled. 'It must be because I'm so happy.'

'Well, don't get too happy. I prefer you thin.'

'Game to Mrs King. Mrs King leads by five games to one in the first set.'

'This is going to be a walkover,' said James. 'It so often is in the opening match. People only come to see if the champion's in good form, and I think she'll be very hard to beat this year now she's after Helen Moody's record of eight Wimbledon championships.'

'Game and first set to Mrs King by six games to one. Mrs King leads one set to love. New balls, please. Miss May to serve.'

'Do we have to watch him all day?' asked Anne.

'No, we must make sure he returns to the hotel and doesn't change his plans suddenly or anything silly like that. If we miss our chance when he walks past Jean-Pierre's gallery, we may not get another one.'

'What do you do if he does decide to change his plans?'

'God knows, or to be more accurate, Stephen knows – he's the mastermind.'

'Game to Mrs King. Mrs King leads by one game to love in the second set.'

'Poor Miss May, she's about as successful as you are, James. How is the Jean-Pierre operation looking?'

'Awful. Metcalfe hasn't been anywhere near the gallery. He was within 30 yards of the window today and marched off in the opposite direction. Poor Jean-Pierre nearly had heart failure. But we're more hopeful of tomorrow. So far he seems to have covered Piccadilly and the top end of Bond Street, and the one thing we can be sure of with Harvey Metcalfe is that he's thorough. So he's almost bound to cover our bit of territory at one time or another.'

'You should all have taken out life insurance for $1 million, naming the other three as beneficiaries,' said Anne, 'and then if one of you had a heart attack, the others would all get their money back.'

'It's no laughing matter, Anne. It's bloody nerve-racking

while you're hanging around, especially when you have to wait for him to make all the moves.'

'Game to Mrs King. Mrs King leads by two games to love in the second set and by one set to love.'

'How about your own plan?'

'Nothing. Useless. And now we've started on the others I seem to have less time to concentrate on my own.'

'Why don't I seduce him?'

'Not a bad idea, but you'd have to be pretty special to get £100,000 out of him, when he can hang around outside the Hilton or in Shepherd Market and get it for £30. If there's one thing we've learnt about that gentleman it's that he expects value for money. At £30 a night it would take you just under fifteen years to repay my share, and I'm not sure the other three would be willing to wait that long. In fact, I'm not sure they'll wait another fifteen days.'

'We'll think of something, don't worry,' said Anne.

'Game to Miss May. Mrs King leads by two games to one and by one set to love.'

'Well, well. Miss May has managed another game. Excellent lunch, Harvey.'

'A Claridge's special,' said Harvey, 'so much better than getting caught up with the crowds in the restaurant where you can't even watch the tennis.'

'Billie Jean is making mincemeat of the poor girl.'

'No more than I expected,' said Harvey. 'Now, Jörg, to my second numbered account.'

Once again the unidentifiable piece of paper that bore a few numbers appeared. It is this discretion of the Swiss that leads half the world, from heads of state to Arab sheiks, to trust them with their money. In return the Swiss maintain one of the healthiest economies in the world. The system works, so why go elsewhere? Birrer spent a few seconds studying the figures.

'On April 1st – only you could have chosen that day, Harvey – you transferred $7,486,000 to your No. 2 account, which was already in credit $2,791,428. On April 2nd, on your instructions, we placed $1 million in the Banco do

Minas Gerais in the names of Mr Silverman and Mr Elliott. We covered the bill with Reading & Bates for the hire of the rig for $420,000 and several other bills amounting to $104,112, leaving your present No. 2 account standing at $8,753,316.'

'Game to Mrs King. Mrs King leads three games to one in the second set and by one set to love.'

'Very good,' said Harvey.

'The tennis or the money?' said Birrer.

'Both. Now, Jörg, I anticipated needing about $2 million over the next six weeks. I want to purchase one or two pictures in London. I have seen a Klee that I quite like and there are still a few galleries I want to visit. If I'd known the Prospecta Oil venture was going to be such a success, I'd have outbid Armand Hammer at the Sotheby-Parke Bernet for that Van Gogh last year. I shall also need some ready cash for some new horses at the Ascot Blood Stock Auctions. My stud's running down and it's still one of my greatest ambitions to win the King George and Elizabeth Stakes.' (James would have winced if he could have heard Harvey describe the race so inaccurately.) 'My best result so far, as you know, was third place, and that's not good enough. This year I've entered Rosalie, my best filly for years. If I lose I'll have to build up the stud again, but I'm damn well going to win this year.'

'Game to Mrs King. Mrs King leads four games to one and by one set to love.'

'So is Mrs King, it seems,' said Birrer. 'I'll brief my senior cashier that you're likely to be drawing large amounts over the next few weeks.'

'Now I don't wish the remainder to lie idle, so I want you to purchase more gold carefully over the next few months, with a view to off-loading it in the New Year. If the market does take a downward turn, I'll phone you in Zürich. At the close of business each day you are to loan the outstanding balance on an overnight basis to first-class banks and triple "A" commercial names.'

'What are you going to do with it all, Harvey, if those cigars don't get you first?'

'Oh, lay off, Jörg. You sound like my doctor. I've told you a hundred times, next year I retire, I quit, finito.'

'I can't see you dropping out of the rat race voluntarily, Harvey. It pains me to think how much you're worth now.'

Harvey laughed.

'I can't tell you that, Jörg. It's like Aristotle Onassis said – if you can count it, you haven't got any.'

'Game to Mrs King. Mrs King leads by five games to one and by one set to love.'

'How's Rosalie? We still have your instructions to pass the accounts on to her in Boston if anything should happen to you.'

'She's well. Phoned me this morning to tell me she won't be able to join me at Wimbledon because she's tied up with her work. I expect she'll end up marrying some rich American and won't need it. Enough of them have asked her. Can't be easy for her to decide if they like her or my money. I'm afraid we had a row about that a couple of years back and she still hasn't forgiven me.'

'Game, set and match to Mrs King: 6–1, 6–1.'

Harvey, Jörg, James and Anne joined in the applause while the two women left the court, curtseying in front of the Royal Box to the President of the All England Club, His Royal Highness, The Duke of Kent. Harvey and Jörg Birrer stayed for the next match, a doubles, and then returned to Claridge's together for dinner.

James and Anne had enjoyed their afternoon at Wimbledon and when they had seen Harvey safely back to Claridge's, accompanied by his mid-European friend, they returned to James's flat.

'Stephen, I'm back. Metcalfe is settled in for the night. On parade at 8.30 tomorrow morning.'

'Well done, James. Maybe he'll bite then.'

'Let's hope so.'

The sound of running water led James to the kitchen in

search of Anne. She was elbow-deep in suds, attacking a soufflé dish with a scourer. She turned and brandished it at him.

'Darling, I don't want to be offensive about your daily, but this is the only kitchen I've ever been in where you have to do the washing up before you make the dinner.'

'I know. She only ever cleans the clean bits of the flat. Her work load's getting lighter by the week.'

He sat on the kitchen table, admiring her slim body.

'Will you scrub my back like that if I go and have a bath before dinner?'

'Yes, with a scourer.'

The water was deep and comfortably hot. James lay back in it luxuriously, letting Anne wash him. Then he stepped dripping out of the bath.

'You're a bit overdressed for a bathroom attendant, darling,' he said. 'Why don't we do something about it?'

Anne slipped out of her clothes while James dried himself. When he went into the bedroom, Anne was already huddled under the sheets.

'I'm cold,' she said.

'Fear not,' said James. 'You're about to be presented with your very own six-foot hot water bottle.'

She took him in her arms.

'Liar, you're freezing.'

'And you're lovely,' said James, trying to hold on to every part of her at once.

'How's your plan going, James?'

'I don't know yet, I'll tell you in about twenty minutes.'

She didn't speak again for nearly half an hour, when she said:

'Out you get. The baked cheese will be ready by now and in any case I want to remake the bed.'

'No need to bother about that, you silly woman.'

'Yes, there is. Last night I didn't sleep at all. You pulled all the blankets over to your side and I just watched you huddled up like a self-satisfied cat while I froze to death.

126

Making love to you isn't at all what Harold Robbins promised it would be.'

'When you've finished chattering, woman, set the alarm for 7 am.'

'7 am? You don't have to be at Claridge's until 8.30.'

'I know, but I want to go to work on an egg.'

'James, you really must give up your undergraduate sense of humour.'

'Oh, I thought it was rather funny.'

'Yes, darling. Why don't you get dressed before the dinner is burnt to a cinder?'

James arrived at Claridge's at 8.29 am. Whatever his own inadequacies, he was determined not to fail the others in their plans. He tuned in to check that Stephen was in Berkeley Square and Robin in Bond Street.

'Morning,' said Stephen. 'Had a good night?'

'Bloody good,' said James.

'Sleep well, did you?' asked Stephen.

'Hardly a wink.'

'Stop making us jealous,' said Robin, 'and concentrate on Harvey Metcalfe.'

James stood in the doorway of Slater's, the furriers, watching the early morning cleaners leave for home and the first of the office staff arriving.

Harvey Metcalfe was going through his normal routine of breakfast and the papers. Just before he had gone to bed he had a telephone call from his wife in Boston and another from his daughter during breakfast the next morning, which started his day well. He decided to continue his pursuit of an Impressionist picture in some of the other galleries in Cork Street and Bond Street. Perhaps Sotheby's would be able to help him.

He left the hotel at 9.47 am at his usual brisk pace.

'Action stations.'

Stephen and Robin snapped out of their day-dreaming.

'He's just entered Bruton Street. Now he's heading for Bond Street.'

Harvey walked briskly down Bond Street, past the territory he had already covered.

'Only 50 yards off now, Jean-Pierre,' said James. '40 yards, 30 yards, 20 yards . . . Oh no, damn it, he's gone into Sotheby's. There's only a sale of medieval painted panels on there today. Hell, I didn't know he was interested in them.'

He glanced up the road at Stephen, padded out and aged to the condition of a wealthy, middle-class business man for the third day in a row. The cut of the collar and the rimless glasses proclaimed him as West German. Stephen's voice came over the speaker:

'I am going into Jean-Pierre's gallery. James, you stay north of Sotheby's on the far side of the street and report in every fifteen minutes. Robin, you go inside and dangle the bait under Harvey's nose.'

'But that's not in the plan, Stephen,' stammered Robin.

'Use your initiative and get on with it, otherwise all you'll be doing is taking care of Jean-Pierre's heart condition and receiving no fees. Right?'

'Right,' said Robin nervously.

Robin walked into Sotheby's and made a surreptitious bee-line for the nearest mirror. Yes, he was still unrecognisable. Upstairs, he spotted Harvey near the back of the sale room, and planted himself on a nearby seat in the row behind him.

The sale of medieval painted panels was well under way. Harvey knew he ought to like them, but could not bring himself to condone the Gothic partiality for jewellery and bright, gilded colours. Behind him, Robin hesitated but then struck up a quiet-voiced conversation with his neighbour.

'Looks all very fine to me, but I've no knowledge of the period. I'm so much happier with the modern era. Still, I must think of something appropriate to say for my readers.'

Robin's neighbour smiled politely.

'Do you have to cover all the auctions?'

'Almost all – especially when there may be surprises. In

any case, at Sotheby's you can always find out what's going on everywhere else. Only this morning one of the assistants gave me a tip that the Lamanns Gallery may have something special in the Impressionist field.'

Robin beamed the whispered information carefully at Harvey's right ear and then sat back and waited to see if it had created any effect. Shortly afterwards, he was rewarded by the sight of Harvey squeezing out of his row to leave. Robin waited for three more lots to be auctioned, then followed him, fingers crossed.

Outside, James had been keeping a patient vigil.

'10.30 – no sign of him.'

'Roger.'

'10.45 – still no sign of him.'

'Roger.'

'11.00 – he's still inside.'

'Roger.'

'11.12 action stations, action stations.'

James slipped quickly into the Lamanns Gallery as Jean-Pierre once again removed from his window the Sutherland watercolour of the Thames and the Boatman, and replaced it with an oil by Van Gogh, as magnificent an example of the master's work as a London gallery had ever seen. Now came the acid test: the litmus paper was walking purposefully down Bond Street towards it.

The picture had been painted by David Stein, who had achieved notoriety in the art world for faking 300 paintings and drawings by well-known Impressionists, for which he had received a total of $864,000 and, later, four years. He was only exposed when he put on a Chagall exhibition at the Niveaie Gallery in Madison Avenue in 1969. Unknown to Stein, Chagall himself was in New York at the time for an exhibition at the museum in Lincoln Center where two of his most famous works were on display. On being informed of the Niveaie exhibition, Chagall furiously reported the pictures to the District Attorney's office as fakes. Stein had already sold one of the imitation Chagalls to Louis D. Cohen at a price of nearly $100,000, and to this day there is a Stein Chagall and a Stein Picasso at the Galleria d'Arte Moderna in Milan. Jean-Pierre was confident that what Stein had achieved in the past in New York and Milan he could now repeat in London.

Stein had continued to paint Impressionist pictures, but now signed them with his own name; thanks to his indubitable talent he was still making a handsome living. He had known and admired Jean-Pierre for several years and when he heard the story of Metcalfe and Prospecta Oil, he agreed to produce a Van Gogh for $10,000 and to sign the painting with the master's famous 'Vincent'.

Jean-Pierre had gone to considerable lengths to identify a Van Gogh that had vanished in mysterious circumstances, so that Stein could resurrect it to tempt Harvey. He had started with de la Faille's comprehensive *oeuvres* catalogue, *The Works of Vincent Van Gogh*, and selected from it three pictures that had hung in the National Gallery in Berlin prior to the Second World War. In de la Faille, they were entered under Nos. 485, *Les Amoureux* (*The Lovers*), 628, *La Moisson* (*The Harvest*), and 766, *Le Jardin de Daubigny* (*The Garden of Daubigny*). The last two were known to have been bought in 1929 by the Berlin Gallery, and *Les Amoureux* probably bought around the same time. At the start of the war, all three had disappeared.

Jean-Pierre then contacted Professor Wormit of the Preussischer Kulturbesitz. The Professor, a world authority on missing works of art, was able to rule out one of the possibilities, *Le Jardin de Daubigny*; soon after the war it apparently had reappeared in the collection of Siegfried Kramarsky in New York, though how it got there remains a mystery. Kramarsky had subsequently sold the painting to the Nichido Gallery in Tokyo, where it now hangs. The Professor confirmed that the fate of the other two Van Goghs remained unknown.

Next Jean-Pierre turned to Madame Tellegen-Hoogendoorm of the Dutch Rijksbureau voor Kunsthistorische Documentatie. Madame Tellegen was the acknowledged authority on Van Gogh and gradually, with her expert help, Jean-Pierre pieced together the story of the missing paintings. They had been removed, along with many others, from the Berlin National Gallery in 1937 by the Nazis, despite vigorous protests from the Director, Dr Hanfstaengl, and the Keeper of Paintings, Dr Hentzen. The paintings, stigmatised by the philistinism of the National Socialists as degenerate art, were stored in a depot in the Kopenickerstrasse in Berlin. Hitler himself visited the depot in January 1938, and legalised the proceedings as an official confiscation.

What happened to the two Van Goghs after that, nobody knows. Many of the Nazi-confiscated works were quietly sold abroad by Joseph Angerer, an agent of Hermann Goering, to obtain much-needed foreign currency for the Führer. Some were disposed of in a sale organised by the Fischer Art Gallery in Lucerne on June 30th, 1939. But many of the works in the depot in the Kopenickerstrasse were simply burned, stolen, or are still missing.

Jean-Pierre managed to obtain black-and-white reproductions of *Les Amoureux* and *La Moisson*: no colour positives survive, if they were ever made. It seemed to Jean-Pierre unlikely that any colour reproductions of two paintings last seen in 1938 would exist anywhere. He therefore settled down to choose between the two.

Les Amoureux was the larger of the two, at 76 × 91 cm. However, Van Gogh did not seem to have been satisfied with it. In October 1889 (letter No. 556) he referred to 'a very poor sketch of my last canvas'. Moreover, it was impossible to guess the colour of the background. *La Moisson*, in contrast, had pleased Van Gogh. He had painted the oil in September 1889 and written of it, 'I feel very much inclined to do the reaper once more for my mother' (letter No. 604). He had in fact already painted three other very similar pictures of a reaper at harvest time. Jean-Pierre was able to obtain colour transparencies of two of them, one from the Louvre and the other from the Rijksmuseum, where they now hang. He studied the

131

sequence. The position of the sun, and the play of light on the scene, were practically the only points of difference. Jean-Pierre was therefore able to see in his mind's eye what *La Moisson* must have looked like in colour.

Stein agreed with Jean-Pierre's final choice and he studied the black-and-white reproduction of *La Moisson* and the colour transparencies of its sister paintings long and minutely before he set to work. He then found an insignificant late-nineteenth-century French work, and skilfully removed the paint from it, leaving a clean canvas except for a vital stamp on the back which even Stein could not have reproduced. He marked on the canvas the exact size of the picture, 48.5 × 53 cm and selected a palette knife and brush of the type that Van Gogh had favoured. Six weeks later *La Moisson* was finished. Stein varnished it, and baked it for four days in an oven at a gentle 85°F to age it. Jean-Pierre provided a heavy gilt Impressionist frame and it was well ready for Harvey Metcalfe's scrutiny.

Harvey, acting on his overheard tip, could see no harm in dropping into the Lamanns Gallery. He was about five paces away when he first caught sight of the picture being taken out of the window. He could not believe his eyes. A Van Gogh, without a doubt, and a superlative one at that. *La Moisson* had actually been on display for only two minutes.

Harvey almost ran into the gallery, only to discover Jean-Pierre deep in conversation with Stephen and James. None of them took any notice of him. Stephen was addressing Jean-Pierre in a guttural accent.

'170,000 guineas seems high, but it is a fine example. Can you be sure it is the picture that disappeared from Berlin in 1937?'

'You can never be sure of anything, but you can see on the back of the canvas the stamp of the Berlin National Gallery, and the Bernheim Jeune have confirmed they sold it to the Germans in 1927. The rest of its history is well chronicled back to 1890. It seems certain that it was looted from the museum in the upheaval of the war.'

'How did you come into possession of the painting?'

'From the private collection of a member of the British aristocracy who wishes to remain anonymous.'

'Excellent,' said Stephen. 'I would like to reserve it until 4 pm when I will bring round a cheque for 170,000 guineas from the Dresdner Bank AG. Will that be acceptable?'

'Of course, sir,' replied Jean-Pierre. 'I will place a red dot on it.'

James, in the sharpest of suits and a dashing trilby, hovered knowledgeably behind Stephen.

'It certainly is a marvellous example of the master's work,' he remarked ingratiatingly.

'Yes. I took it round to Julian Barron at Sotheby's and he seemed to like it.'

James retreated mincingly to the end of the gallery, relishing his role as a connoisseur. At that moment Robin walked in, a copy of the *Guardian* sticking out of his pocket.

'Good morning, Mr Lamanns. I heard a rumour at Sotheby's about a Van Gogh which I'd always thought must be in Russia. I'd like to write a few paragraphs about the history of the painting and how you came into possession of it for tomorrow's paper. Is that OK by you?'

'I should be delighted,' said Jean-Pierre, 'although actually I have just reserved the picture for Herr Drosser, the distinguished German dealer, at 170,000 guineas.'

'Very reasonable,' said James knowingly from the end of the gallery. 'I think it's the best Van Gogh I have seen in London since *Mademoiselle Revoux* and I'm only sorry my house won't be auctioning it. You're a lucky man, Mr Drosser. If you ever decide to sell it, don't hesitate to contact me.' James handed Stephen a card and smiled at Jean-Pierre.

Jean-Pierre watched James. It was a fine performance. Robin began to take notes in what he hoped looked like shorthand and again addressed Jean-Pierre.

133

'Do you have a photograph of the picture?'

'Of course.'

Jean-Pierre opened a drawer and took out a colour photograph of the picture with a typewritten description attached. He handed it to Robin.

'Do watch the spelling of Lamanns, won't you? I get so bored with being confused with a French motor car race.'

He turned to Stephen.

'So sorry to keep you waiting, Herr Drosser. How would you like us to despatch the picture?'

'You can send it to me at the Dorchester tomorrow morning, room 120.'

'Certainly, sir.'

Stephen started to leave.

'Excuse me, sir,' said Robin, 'can I take the spelling of your name?'

'D.R.O.S.S.E.R.'

'And may I have permission to quote you in my article?'

'You may. I am with my purchase very pleased. Good day, gentlemen.'

Stephen bowed his head smartly, and departed. He stepped out into Bond Street and to the horror of Jean-Pierre, Robin and James, Harvey, without a moment's hesitation, also walked out.

Jean-Pierre collapsed heavily on his Georgian mahogany desk and looked despairingly at Robin and James.

'God Almighty, the whole thing's a fiasco. Six weeks of preparation, three days of agony, and then he walked out on us.' Jean-Pierre looked at *La Moisson* angrily.

'I thought Stephen assured us that Harvey would stay and bargain with Jean-Pierre. It's in his character,' mimicked James plaintively. 'He'd never let the picture out of his sight.'

'Who the hell thought up this bloody silly enterprise?' muttered Robin.

'Stephen,' they all cried together, and rushed to the window.

'What an interesting maquette by Henry Moore,' said

134

an impeccably corsetted middle-aged lady, her hand firmly placed on the bronze loin of a naked acrobat. She had slipped unnoticed into the gallery while the three had been grumbling. 'How much are you asking for it?'

'I will be with you in a minute, madam,' said Jean-Pierre. 'Oh hell, I think Metcalfe's following Stephen. Get him on the pocket radio, Robin.'

'Stephen, can you hear me? Whatever you do, don't look back. We think Harvey's only a few yards behind you.'

'What the hell do you mean he's only a few yards behind me? He's meant to be in the gallery with you buying the Van Gogh. What are you playing at?'

'Harvey didn't give us a chance. He walked straight out after you before any of us could continue as planned.'

'Very clever. Now what am I meant to do?'

Jean-Pierre took over:

'You'd better go to the Dorchester just in case he is actually following you.'

'I don't even know where the Dorchester is,' yelped Stephen.

Robin came to his rescue:

'Take the first right, Stephen, and that'll bring you into Bruton Street, keep walking as straight as you can until you reach Berkeley Square. Stay on the line, but don't look back or you may turn into a pillar of salt.'

'James,' said Jean-Pierre, thinking on his feet for the first time in his life. 'You take a taxi immediately to the Dorchester and book room 120 in the name of Drosser. Have the key ready for Stephen the moment he walks through the door, then make yourself scarce. Stephen, are you still there?'

'Yes.'

'Did you hear all that?'

'Yes. Tell James to book 119 or 121 if 120 is not available.'

'Roger,' replied Jean-Pierre. 'Get going, James.'

James bolted out of the gallery and barged in front of a

woman who had just hailed a taxi, a thing he had never done before.

'The Dorchester,' he hollered, 'as fast as you can go.'

The taxi shot off.

'Stephen, James has gone and I'm sending Robin to follow Harvey so he can keep you briefed and guide you to the Dorchester. I'm staying put. Everything else OK?'

'No,' said Stephen, 'start praying. I've reached Berkeley Square. Where now?'

'Across the garden then continue down Hill Street.'

Robin left the gallery and ran all the way to Bruton Street until he was only 50 yards behind Harvey.

'Now about the Henry Moore,' said the well-corsetted lady.

'Screw Henry Moore,' said Jean-Pierre, not even looking around.

The steel-reinforced bosom heaved.

'Young man, I have never been spoken to in . . .'

But Jean-Pierre had already reached the lavatory, and closed the door.

'You're crossing South Audley Street now, then continue into Deanery Street. Keep going, don't turn right or left and don't whatever you do look back. Harvey is still about 50 yards behind you. I'm a little more than 50 yards behind him,' said Robin. Passers-by stared at the man talking into his little instrument.

'Is Room 120 free?'

'Yes, sir, they checked out this morning, but I'm not sure if it's ready for occupancy yet. I think the maid may still be clearing the room. I'll have to check, sir,' said the tall receptionist in the morning suit, which indicated that he was a senior member of the floor staff.

'Oh, don't worry about that,' said James, his German accent far better than Stephen's. 'I always have that room. Can you book me in for one night? Name's Drosser, Herr – um – Helmut Drosser.'

He slipped a pound over the counter.

'Certainly, sir.'

'That's Park Lane, Stephen. Look right – the big hotel on the corner straight in front of you is the Dorchester. The semi-circle facing you is the main entrance. Go up the steps, past the big man in the green overcoat, and through the revolving door and you'll find reception on your right. James ought to be there waiting for you.'

Robin was grateful that the annual dinner of the Royal Society for Medicine had been held at the Dorchester last year.

'Where's Harvey?' bleated Stephen.

'Only 40 yards behind you.'

Stephen quickened his pace, ran up the steps of the Dorchester and pushed through the revolving door so hard that the other residents coming out found themselves on the street faster than they had planned. Thank God, James was standing there holding a key.

'The lift's over there,' said James, pointing. 'You've only chosen one of the most expensive suites in the hotel.'

Stephen glanced in the direction James had indicated and turned back to thank him. But James was already heading off to the American Bar to be sure he was well out of sight when Harvey arrived.

Stephen left the lift at the first floor and found that the Dorchester, which he had never entered before, was as traditional as Claridge's, its thick royal blue and golden carpets leading to a magnificently appointed corner suite which overlooked Hyde Park. He collapsed into an easy chair, not quite sure what to expect next. Nothing had gone as planned.

Jean-Pierre waited at the gallery, James sat in the American Bar and Robin loitered by the side of Barclays Bank, Park Lane, a mock-tudor building 50 yards from the entrance of the Dorchester.

*   *   *

'Have you a Mr Drosser staying at this hotel? I think it's room 120,' barked Harvey.

The receptionist looked through the card index.

'Yes, sir. Is he expecting you?'

'No, but I'll have a word with him on the house phone.'

'Of course, sir. If you'd be kind enough to go through the small archway on your left you will find five telephones. One of them is a house phone.'

Harvey marched through the archway as directed.

'Room 120,' he instructed the operator, who sat in his own little section, wearing the green Dorchester uniform with golden castles on the lapels.

'Cubicle No. 1, please, sir.'

'Mr Drosser?'

'Speaking,' said Stephen, summoning up his German accent for a sustained effort.

'My name is Harvey Metcalfe. I wonder if I could come up and have a word with you? It's about the Van Gogh you bought this morning.'

'Well, it's a little inconvenient at the moment. I am about to take a shower and I do have a lunch appointment.'

'I won't keep you more than a few minutes.'

Before Stephen could reply, the telephone clicked. A few moments later there was a knock on the door. Stephen's legs wobbled. He answered it nervously. He had changed into a white Dorchester dressing-gown and his brown hair was somewhat dishevelled and darker than normal. It was the only disguise he could think of at such short notice as the original plan had not allowed for a face-to-face meeting with Harvey.

'Sorry to intrude, Mr Drosser, but I had to see you immediately. I know you have just purchased a Van Gogh from the Lamanns Gallery and I was hoping that, as you are a dealer, you might be willing to sell it on for a quick profit.'

'No, thank you,' said Stephen, relaxing for the first time. 'I've wanted a Van Gogh for my gallery in Munich for many years. I'm sorry, Mr Metcalfe, it's not for sale.'

'Listen, you paid 170,000 guineas for it. What's that in dollars?'

Stephen paused.

'Oh, about $435,000.'

'I'll give you $15,000 if you release the picture to me. All you have to do is ring the gallery and tell them that the picture is now mine and that I will cover the bill.'

Stephen sat silent, not sure how to handle the situation without blowing it. Think like Harvey Metcalfe, he told himself.

'$20,000 in cash and you've got a deal.'

Harvey hesitated. Stephen's legs wobbled again.

'Done,' said Harvey. 'Ring the gallery immediately.'

Stephen picked up the telephone.

'Can you get me the Lamanns Gallery in Bond Street as quickly as possible, please – I have a lunch appointment.'

A few seconds later the call came through.

'Lamanns Gallery.'

'I would like to speak to Mr Lamanns.'

'At last, Stephen. What the hell is happening your end?'

'Ah, Mr Lamanns, this is Herr Drosser. You remember, I was in your gallery earlier this morning.'

'Of course I remember, you fool. What are you going on about Stephen? It's me – Jean-Pierre.'

'I have a Mr Metcalfe with me.'

'Christ, I'm sorry, Stephen. I didn't . . .'

'And you can expect him in the next few minutes.'

Stephen looked towards Harvey who nodded his assent.

'You are to release the Van Gogh I purchased this morning to Mr Metcalfe and he will give you a cheque for the full amount, 170,000 guineas.'

'Out of disaster, triumph,' said Jean-Pierre quietly.

'I'm very sorry I shall not be the owner of the picture myself, but I have, as the Americans would say, had an offer I can't refuse. Thank you for the part you played,' said Stephen and put the telephone down.

Harvey was writing out a cheque to cash for $20,000.

'Thank you, Mr Drosser. You have made me a happy man.'

'I am not complaining myself,' said Stephen honestly. He escorted Harvey to the door and they shook hands.

'Goodbye, sir.'

'Good day, Mr Metcalfe.'

Stephen closed the door and tottered to the chair, almost too weak to move.

Robin and James saw Harvey leave the Dorchester. Robin followed him in the direction of the gallery, his hopes rising with each stride. James took the lift to the first floor and nearly ran to Room 120. He banged on the door. Stephen jumped at the noise. He didn't feel he could face Harvey again. He opened the door.

'James, it's you. Cancel the room, pay for one night and then join me in the cocktail bar.'

'Why? What for?'

'A bottle of Krug 1964 Privée Cuvée.'

One down and three to go.

11

Jean-Pierre was the last to arrive at Lord Brigsley's King's Road flat. He felt he had earned the right to make an entrance. Harvey's cheque had been cleared and the Lamanns Gallery account was for the moment $447,560 in credit. The painting was in Harvey's possession and the heavens had not yet fallen in. Jean-Pierre had cleared more money in two months of crime than he had in ten years of legitimate trading.

The other three greeted him with the acclaim normally reserved for a sporting hero, and a glass of James's last bottle of Veuve Clicquot 1959.

'We were lucky to pull it off,' said Robin.

'We weren't lucky,' said Stephen. 'We kept our nerve under pressure, and the one thing we've learned from the exercise is that Harvey can change the rules in the middle of the game.'

'He almost changed the game, Stephen.'

'Agreed. So we must always remember that we shall fail unless we can be as successful, not once, but four times. We must not underestimate our opponent just because we've won the first round.'

'Relax, Professor,' said James. 'We can get down to business again after dinner. Anne came in this afternoon especially to make the salmon mousse, and it won't go down well with Harvey Metcalfe.'

'When am I going to meet this fabulous creature!' asked Jean-Pierre.

'When this is all over and behind us.'

'Don't marry her, James. She's only after our money.'

They all laughed. James hoped the day would come when he could tell them she had known all along. He produced the *boeuf en croûte* and two bottles of Echezeaux 1970. Jean-Pierre sniffed the sauce appreciatively.

'On second thoughts she ought to be seriously considered if her touch in bed is half as deft as it is in the kitchen.'

'You're not going to get the chance to be the judge of that, Jean-Pierre. Content yourself with admiring her French dressing.'

'You were quite outstanding this morning, James,' said Stephen, steering the conversation away from Jean-Pierre's pet subject. 'You should go on the stage. As a member of the British aristocracy, your talent's simply wasted.'

'I've always wanted to, but my old pa is against it. Those who live in expectation of a large inheritance must expect to have to toe the filial line.'

'Why don't we let him play all four parts in Monte Carlo?' suggested Robin.

The mention of Monte Carlo sobered them up.

'Back to work,' said Stephen. 'We have so far received $447,560. Expenses with the picture and an unexpected night at the Dorchester were $11,142 so Metcalfe still owes us $563,582. Think of what we've still lost, not of what we've gained. Now for the Monte Carlo operation, which depends upon split-second timing and our ability to sustain our roles for several hours. Robin will bring us up to date.'

Robin retrieved the green dossier from the briefcase by his side and studied his notes for a few moments.

'Jean-Pierre, you must grow a beard, starting today, so that in three weeks' time you'll be unrecognisable. You must also cut your hair very short.' Robin grinned unsympathetically at Jean-Pierre's grimace. 'Yes, you'll look absolutely revolting.'

'That,' said Jean-Pierre, 'will not be possible.'

'How are the baccarat and blackjack coming on?' continued Robin.

'I have lost $37 in five weeks, which includes my member's fee at the Claremont and the Golden Nugget.'

'It all goes on expenses,' said Stephen. 'That puts the bill up to $563,619.'

The others laughed. Only Stephen's lips did not move. He was in sober earnest.

'James, how is your handling of the van going?'

'I can reach Harley Street from St Thomas's in 14 minutes. I should be able to do the actual run in Monte Carlo in about 11 minutes, though naturally I shall want to do some practice runs the day before. To start with I'll have to master driving on the wrong side of the road.'

'Strange how everybody except the British drives on the wrong side of the road,' observed Jean-Pierre.

James ignored him.

'I'm not sure of all the continental road signs either.'

'They are detailed in the Michelin guide that I gave you as part of my dossier,'

'I know, but I'll still feel easier when I've experienced the actual run and not just studied maps. There are quite a few one-way streets in Monaco and I don't want to be stopped going down the wrong one with Harvey Metcalfe unconscious in the back.'

'Don't worry. You'll have ample time when we're there. So, that only leaves Stephen, who's about the most competent medical student I've ever had. You're confident of your newly acquired knowledge, I hope?'

'About as confident as I am with your American accent, Robin. Anyway, I trust that Harvey Metcalfe will be in no state of mind to worry about such trivialities by the time we meet up.'

'Don't worry, Stephen. Believe me, he wouldn't even register who you were if you introduced yourself as Herr Drosser with a Van Gogh under both arms.'

Robin handed round the final schedule of rehearsals for

Harley Street and St Thomas's, and once again consulted the green file.

'I've booked four single rooms on different floors at the Hôtel de Paris and confirmed all the arrangements with the Centre Hospitalier Princesse Grace. The hotel is reputed to be one of the best in the world – it's certainly expensive enough – but it's convenient for the Casino. We fly to Nice on Monday, the day Harvey is due to arrive on his yacht.'

'What do we do for the rest of the week?' enquired James innocently.

Stephen resumed control:

'We master the green dossier backwards, frontwards and sideways for a full dress rehearsal on Friday. The most important thing for you, James, is to get a grip of yourself and let us know what you intend to do.'

James sank back into gloom.

Stephen closed his file briskly.

'That seems to be all we can cover tonight.'

'Hang on, Stephen,' said Robin. 'Let's strip you off once more. I'd like to see if we can do it in 90 seconds.'

Stephen lay down slightly reluctantly in the middle of the room, and James and Jean-Pierre swiftly and carefully removed all his clothes.

'87 seconds. Excellent,' said Robin, looking down at Stephen, naked except for his watch. 'Hell, look at the time. I must get back to Newbury. My wife will think I have a mistress and I don't fancy any of you.'

Stephen dressed himself quickly while the others prepared to leave. A few minutes later, James stood by the front door, watching them depart one by one. As soon as Stephen was out of sight, he bounded downstairs into the kitchen.

'Did you listen?'

'Yes, darling. They're all rather nice and I don't blame them for being cross with you. They're being very professional about the whole venture, while you sounded like the only amateur. We'll have to think up something good

144

for you to match them. We've over a week before Mr Metcalfe goes to Monte Carlo and we must use the time constructively.'

James sighed: 'Well, let's enjoy tonight. At least this morning was a triumph.'

'Yes, but not yours. Tomorrow we work.'

12

'Passengers for flight 017 to Nice are now requested to board the aircraft at gate No. 7,' boomed the loudspeaker at Heathrow's No. 1 terminal.

'That's us,' said Stephen.

The four of them took the escalator to the first floor, and walked down the long corridor. After being searched for guns, bombs, and whatever else terrorists are searched for, they proceeded down the ramp.

They sat separately, never speaking or even looking at each other. Stephen had warned them that the flight could well be sprinkled with Harvey's friends, and each imagined himself to be sitting next to the closest of them.

James gazed moodily at the cloudless sky and brooded. He and Anne had read every book they could lay their hands on that even hinted at stolen money or successful duplicity, but they had found nothing they could plagiarise. Even Stephen, in between being undressed and practised upon at St Thomas's, was becoming daunted by the task of finding a winning plan for James.

The Trident touched down at Nice at 13.40, and the train journey from Nice to Monte Carlo took them a further twenty minutes. Each member of the team made his own way to the elegant Hôtel de Paris in the Place du Casino. At 7 pm they were all present in room 217.

'All settled into your rooms?'

The other three nodded. 'So far, so good,' said Robin. 'Right, let's go over the timing. Jean-Pierre, you will go to the Casino tonight and play a few hands of baccarat and blackjack. Try to acclimatise to the place and learn your way around. In particular, master any variations in the rules there might be from the Claremont, and be sure you never speak in English. Do you foresee any problems?'

'No, can't say I do, Robin. In fact I may as well go now and start rehearsing.'

'Don't lose too much of our money,' said Stephen.

Jean-Pierre, resplendent in beard and dinner-jacket, grinned and slipped out of room 217 and down the staircase, avoiding the lift. He walked the short distance from the hotel to the famous Casino.

Robin continued:

'James, you take a taxi from the Casino to the hospital. On arrival you will leave the meter running for a few minutes and then return to the Casino. You can normally rely on a taxi to take the shortest route, but to be sure, tell the driver it's an emergency. That'll give you the opportunity of seeing which traffic lanes he uses under pressure. When he's returned you to the Casino, walk the route from there to the hospital and back. Then you can assimilate it in your own time. After you've mastered that, repeat the same procedure for the route between the hospital and Harvey's yacht. Never enter the Casino or even get close enough to the boat to be seen. Being seen now means being recognised later.'

'What about my knowledge of the Casino on the night of the operation?'

'Jean-Pierre will take care of that. He'll meet you at the door because Stephen won't be able to leave Harvey. I don't think they will charge you the 12 franc entrance fee if you're wearing a white coat and carrying a stretcher, but have it ready to be sure. When you've completed the walk, go to your room and stay there until our meeting at 11 am tomorrow. Stephen and I will also be going to the hospital to check that all the arrangements have been carried out as cabled from London. If at any time you see us, ignore us.'

As James left room 217, Jean-Pierre arrived at the Casino.

The Casino stands in the heart of Monte Carlo overlooking the sea, surrounded by the most beautiful gardens. The present building has several wings, the oldest of which was designed by Charles Garnier, the architect of the Paris Opera House. The gambling rooms, which were added in 1910, are linked by an atrium to the Salle Garnier in which operas and ballets are performed.

Jean-Pierre marched up the marble staircase to the entrance and paid his 12 francs. The gambling rooms are vast, full of the decadence and grandeur of Europe at the turn of the century. Massive red carpets, statues, paintings and tapestries give the building an almost regal appearance and the portraits lend an air of a country home still lived in. Jean-Pierre found the clientèle were of all nationalities: Arabs and Jews played next to each other at the roulette wheel and chatted away with an ease that would have been unthinkable at the United Nations. Jean-Pierre felt totally relaxed in the unreal world of the wealthy. Robin had assessed his character accurately and given him a role he could master with aplomb.

Jean-Pierre spent over three hours studying the layout of the Casino – its gambling rooms, bars and restaurants, the telephones, the entrances and exits. Then he turned his attention to the gambling itself. He discovered that two shoes of baccarat were played in the Salons Privés at 3 pm and 11 pm, and learned from Pierre Cattalano, the head of the public relations department of the Casino, which of the private rooms Harvey Metcalfe preferred to play in.

Blackjack is played in the Salon des Amériques from 11 am daily. There are three tables, and Jean-Pierre's informant told him that Harvey always played on table No. 2, seat No. 3. Jean-Pierre played a little blackjack and baccarat, to discover any slight variations in rules there might be from the Claremont. In fact there were none, as the Claremont still adheres to French rules.

Harvey Metcalfe arrived noisily at the Casino just after

11 pm, leaving a trail of cigar ash leading to his baccarat table. Jean-Pierre, inconspicuous at the bar, watched as the head croupier first showed Harvey politely to a reserved seat, and then walked through to the Salon des Amériques to the No. 2 blackjack table and placed a discreet white card marked '*Réservé*' on one of the chairs. Harvey was clearly a favoured client. The management knew as well as Jean-Pierre which games Harvey Metcalfe played. At 11.27 pm Jean-Pierre left quietly and returned to the solitude of his hotel room where he remained until 11 am the next day. He phoned no one and did not use room service.

James's evening also went well. The taxi-driver was superb. The word 'emergency' brought out the Walter Mitty in him: he travelled through Monte Carlo as if it were nothing less than the Rally itself. When James arrived at the hospital in 8 minutes 44 seconds, he genuinely felt a little sick and had to rest for a few minutes in the Entrée des Patients before returning to the taxi.

'Back to the Casino, but much slower, please.'

The journey back along the Rue Grimaldi took just over eleven minutes and James decided he would settle for trying to cover it in about ten. He paid off the taxi-driver and carried out the second part of his instructions.

Walking to the hospital and back took just over an hour. The night air was gentle on his face, and the streets crowded with lively chattering people. Tourism is the chief source of income for the Principality, and the Monégasques take the welfare of their visitors very seriously. James passed innumerable little pavement restaurants and souvenir shops stocked with expensive trinkets of no significance that once bought would be forgotten or lost within a week. Noisy groups of holiday-makers strolled along the pavements, their multilingual babel forming a meaningless chorus to James's thoughts of Anne. On arrival back at the Casino, James then took a taxi to the harbour to locate *Messenger Boy*, Harvey's yacht, and from there once more to the hospital. He then walked the same route and, like

Jean-Pierre, he was safely in his room before midnight, having completed his first task.

Robin and Stephen found the walk to the hospital from their hotel took a little over 40 minutes. On arrival Robin asked the receptionist if he could see the superintendent.

'The night superintendent is now on duty,' said a freshly starched French nurse. 'Who shall I say is asking him for?'

Her English pronunciation was excellent and they both avoided a smile at her slight mistake.

'Doctor Wiley Barker of the University of California.'

Robin began to pray that the French superintendent would not happen to know that Wiley Barker, President Nixon's physician and one of the most respected surgeons in the world, was actually touring Australia at the time lecturing to the major universities.

'Bon soir, Docteur Barker. Monsieur Bartise à votre service. Votre visite fait grand honneur à notre hôpital humble.'

Robin's newly acquired American accent stopped any further conversation in French.

'I would like to check the layout of the theatre,' said Robin, 'and confirm that we have it provisionally booked for tomorrow from 11 pm to 4 am for the next five days.'

'That is quite correct, *Docteur Barker*,' said the superintendent, looking down at a clip-board. 'The theatre is off the next corridor. Will you follow me, please?'

The theatre was not dissimilar to the one the four of them had been practising in at St Thomas's – two rooms with a rubber swing door dividing them. The main theatre was well equipped and a nod from Robin showed Stephen that it had all the instruments he required. Robin was impressed. Although the hospital had only some 200 beds, the theatre itself was of the highest standard. Rich men had obviously been ill there before.

'Will you be requiring an anaesthetist or any nurses to assist you, *Docteur Barker*?'

'No,' said Robin. 'I have my own anaesthetist and staff but I will require a tray of laparotomy instruments to be

150

laid out every night. However, I will be able to give you at least an hour's warning before you need make any final preparations.'

'That's plenty of time. Will there be anything else, sir?'

'Yes, the special vehicle I ordered. Can it be ready for my driver at 12 pm tomorrow?'

'Yes, *Docteur Barker*. It will be in the small car park behind the hospital and your driver can pick up the keys from the reception.'

'Can you recommend an agency from which I can hire an experienced nurse for post-operative care?'

'*Bien sûr*, the Auxiliaire Médical of Nice will be only too happy to oblige – at a certain price, of course.'

'Of course,' said Robin. 'And that reminds me to ask, have all your expenses been dealt with?'

'Yes, *Docteur*. We received a cheque from California last Thursday for $7,000.'

Robin had been very pleased with that touch. It had been so simple. Stephen had contacted his bank at Harvard and asked them to send a draft from the First National City Bank in San Francisco to the hospital secretary at Monte Carlo.

'Thank you all for your help, Monsieur Bartise. You have been most obliging. Now you do understand that I am not quite sure which night I shall be bringing my patient in. He's a sick man, although he doesn't know it, and I have to prepare him for the operation.'

'Of course, *mon cher Docteur*.'

'Finally, I would appreciate it if you would tell as few people as possible that I am in Monte Carlo. I am trying to snatch a holiday at the same time as working.'

'I understand, Docteur Barker. You can be assured of my discretion.'

Robin and Stephen bade farewell to Monsieur Bartise and took a taxi back to the hotel.

'I'm always slightly humiliated by how well the French speak our language compared with our grasp of theirs,' said Stephen.

'It's all the fault of you bloody Americans,' said Robin.

'No, it isn't. If France had conquered America, your French would be excellent. Blame it on the Pilgrim Fathers.'

Robin laughed. Neither of them spoke again until they reached room 217 for fear of being overheard. Stephen had no doubts about the responsibility and risk they were taking with Robin's plan.

Harvey Metcalfe was on the deck of his yacht, sunbathing and reading the morning papers. *Nice-Matin*, irritatingly enough, was in French. He read it laboriously, with the aid of a dictionary, to see if there were any social events to which he ought to get himself invited. He had gambled late into the night, and was enjoying the sun's rays on his fleshy back. If money could have obtained it, he would have been 6 ft and 170 lb with a handsome head of hair, but no amount of suntan oil would stop his balding dome from burning, so he covered it with a cap inscribed with the words 'I'm sexy'. If Miss Fish could see him now . . .

At 11 am, as Harvey turned over and allowed the sun to see his massive stomach, James strolled into room 217 where the rest of the Team were waiting for him.

Jean-Pierre reported on the layout of the Casino and Harvey Metcalfe's habits. James brought them up to date on the result of his race through the city the night before and confirmed that he thought he could cover the distance in just under eleven minutes.

'Perfect,' said Robin. 'Stephen and I took 15 minutes by taxi from the hospital to the hotel so if Jean-Pierre warns me immediately the balloon goes up in the Casino, I should have enough time to see that everything is ready before you all arrive.'

'I do hope the balloon will be going down, not up, in the Casino,' remarked Jean-Pierre.

'I have booked an agency nurse to be on call from tomorrow night. The hospital has all the facilities I require. It'll take about two minutes to walk a stretcher from the front door to the theatre, so from the moment James leaves the car park I should have at least 16 minutes to prepare myself. James, you'll be able to pick up the vehicle from the hospital car park at 12 pm. The keys have been left in reception in the name of Dr Barker. Do a couple of practice runs and no more. I don't want you causing interest by looking conspicuous. And could you leave this parcel in the back, please.'

'What is it?'

'Three long white laboratory coats and a stethoscope for Stephen. While you're at it, better check that you can unfold the stretcher easily. When you've finished the two runs, put the vehicle back in the car park and return to your room until 11 pm. From then through to 4 am you'll have to wait in the car park until you get the "action stations" or "all clear" signal from Jean-Pierre. Everybody buy new batteries for your transmitters. I don't want the whole plan to collapse for the sake of a ten-penny battery. I'm afraid there's nothing much for you to do, Jean-Pierre, until this evening, except relax. I hope you have some good books in your room.'

'Can't I go to the Princess Cinema and see François Truffaut's *La Nuit Américaine*? I just adore Jacqueline Bisset. *Vive la France*.'

'My dear Jean-Pierre, Miss Bisset's from Reading,' said James.

'I don't care. I still want to see her.'

'A frog he would a-wooing go,' said James mockingly.

'But why not?' said Robin. 'The last thing Harvey will do is take in an intellectual French film with no sub-titles. Hope you enjoy it – and good luck tonight, Jean-Pierre.'

Jean-Pierre left for his room as quietly as he had come, leaving the rest of them together in room 217.

'Right, James. You can do your practice runs any time that suits you. Just make sure you're wide awake tonight.'

'Fine. I'll go and pick up the keys from the hospital reception. Let's just hope nobody stops me for a real emergency.'

'Now, Stephen, let's go over the details again. There's more than money to lose if we get this wrong. We'll start from the top. What do you do if the nitrous oxide falls below five litres . . .'

'Station check – station check – operation Metcalfe. This is Jean-Pierre. I am on the steps of the Casino. Can you hear me, James?'

'Yes. I am in the car park of the hospital. Out.'

'Robin here. I am on the balcony of room 217. Is Stephen with you, Jean-Pierre?'

'Yes. He's drinking on his own at the bar.'

'Good luck and out.'

Jean-Pierre carried out a station check every hour on the hour from 7 pm until 11 pm, merely to inform Robin and James that Harvey had not arrived.

Eventually, at 11.16, he did show up, and took his reserved place at the baccarat table. Stephen stopped sipping his tomato juice and Jean-Pierre moved over and waited patiently by the table for one of the men seated on the left or right of Harvey to leave. An hour passed by. Harvey was losing a little, but continued to play. So did the tall thin American on his right and the Frenchman on his left. Another hour and still no movement. Then suddenly the Frenchman on the left of Metcalfe had a particularly bad run, gathered his few remaining chips and left the table. Jean-Pierre moved forward.

'I am afraid, Monsieur, that that seat is reserved for another gentleman,' said the banker. 'We do have an unreserved place on the other side of the table.'

'It's not important,' said Jean-Pierre, who backed away, not wanting to be remembered, cursing the deference with which the Monégasques treat the wealthy. Stephen could see from the bar what had happened and made furtive signs to leave. They were all back in room 217 just after 2 am.

* * *

'What a bloody silly mistake. *Merde, merde, merde*. I should have thought of reservations the moment I knew Harvey had one.'

'No, it was my fault. I don't know anything about how casinos work and I should have queried it during rehearsals,' said Robin, stroking his newly acquired moustache.

'No one is to blame,' chipped in Stephen. 'We still have three more nights, so no need to panic. We'll just have to work out how to overcome the seating problem, but for now we'll all get some sleep and meet again in this room at 10 am.'

They left, a little depressed. Robin had sat waiting in the hotel on edge for four hours. James was cold and bored in the hospital car park, Stephen was sick of tomato juice and Jean-Pierre had been on his feet by the baccarat table waiting for a seat that wasn't even available.

Once again Harvey lounged in the sun. He was now a light pink and was hoping to be a better colour towards the end of the week. According to his copy of the *New York Times*, gold was still climbing and the Deutschmark and the Swiss franc remained firm, while the dollar was on the retreat against every currency except sterling. Sterling stood at $2.42. Harvey thought a more realistic price was $1.80 and the sooner it reached that the better.

Nothing new, he thought, when the sharp ring of a French telephone roused him. He never could get used to the sound of foreign telephones. The attentive steward bustled out on deck with the instrument on an extension lead.

'Hi, Lloyd. Didn't know you were in Monte . . . why don't we get together? . . . 8 pm? . . . Me too . . . I'm even getting brown . . . Must be getting old . . . What? . . . Great, I'll see you then.'

Harvey replaced the receiver and asked the steward for a large whisky on the rocks. He once again settled down happily to the morning's financial bad news.

*   *   *

'That seems to be the obvious solution,' said Stephen.

They all nodded their approval.

'Jean-Pierre will give up the baccarat table and book a place next to Harvey Metcalfe on his blackjack table in the Salon des Amériques and wait for him to change games. We know both the seat numbers Harvey plays at and we'll alter our own plans accordingly.'

Jean-Pierre dialled the number of the Casino and asked to speak to Pierre Cattalano:

'Réservez-moi la deuxième place à la table 2 pour le vingt-et-un ce soir et demain soir, s'il vous plaît.'

'Je pense que cette place est déjà réservée, Monsieur. Un instant, s'il vous plaît, je vais vérifier.'

'Peut-être que 100 francs la rendra libre,' replied Jean-Pierre.

'Mais certainement, Monsieur. Présentez-vous à moi dès votre arrivée, et le nécessaire sera fait.'

'Merçi,' said Jean-Pierre and replaced the receiver. 'That's under control.'

Jean-Pierre was visibly sweating, though had his call had no other outcome than to secure him a reserved seat, not a drop of perspiration would have appeared. They all returned to their rooms.

When the clock in the town square struck twelve, Robin was waiting quietly in room 217, James stood in the car park humming 'I Get Along Without You Very Well', Stephen was at the bar of the Salon des Amériques toying with yet another tomato juice and Jean-Pierre was at seat No. 2 on table No. 2, playing blackjack. Both Stephen and Jean-Pierre saw Harvey come through the door, chatting to a man in a loud-checked jacket which only a Texan could have worn outside his own back yard. Harvey and his friend sat down together at the baccarat table. Jean-Pierre beat a hasty retreat to the bar.

'Oh, no. I give up.'

'No, you don't,' whispered Stephen. 'Back to the hotel.'

* * *

Spirits were very low when they were all assembled in room 217, but it was agreed that Stephen had made the right decision. They could not risk the entire exercise being carefully observed by a friend of Harvey's.

'The first operation is beginning to look a bit too good to be true,' said Robin.

'Don't be silly,' said Stephen. 'We had two false alarms then, and the entire plan had to be changed at the last minute. We can't expect him just to walk in and hand over his money. Now snap out of it, all of you, and go and get some sleep.'

They returned to their separate rooms, but not to much sleep. The strain was beginning to tell.

'That's enough I think, Lloyd. A goodish evening.'

'For you, you mean, Harvey, not for me. You are one of nature's winners.'

Harvey patted the checked shoulder expansively. If anything pleased him more than his own success, it was other people's failure.

'Do you want to spend the night on my yacht, Lloyd?'

'No thanks. I must get back to Nice. I have a meeting in Paris, France, tomorrow lunch. See you soon, Harvey – take care of yourself.' He dug Harvey in the ribs jocularly. 'That's a fair-sized job.'

'Goodnight, Lloyd,' said Harvey, a little stiffly.

The next evening Jean-Pierre did not arrive at the Casino until 11 pm. Harvey Metcalfe was already at the baccarat table minus Lloyd. Stephen was at the bar looking angry, and Jean-Pierre glanced at him apologetically as he took his seat at the blackjack table. He played a few hands to get the feel, trying to keep his losses fairly limited without drawing attention to the modesty of his stakes. Suddenly Harvey left the baccarat table and stalked into the Salon des Amériques, glancing at the roulette tables as he passed more out of curiosity than interest. He detested games of pure chance, and considered baccarat and blackjack games of skill. He headed to table No. 2 seat No. 3, on Jean-Pierre's left. Jean-Pierre felt his adrenalin start pumping round and his heart-beat rise up to 120 again. Stephen left the Casino for a few minutes to warn James and Robin that Harvey had moved to the blackjack table and was now sitting next to Jean-Pierre. He then returned to the bar and waited.

There were seven punters at the blackjack table. On box No. 1, a middle-aged lady smothered in diamonds, who looked as if she might be passing time while her husband played roulette or perhaps baccarat. On box No. 2, Jean-Pierre. On Box No. 3, Harvey. On Box No. 4, a dissipated young man with the world-weariness that usually goes with a large unearned income. On box No. 5, an Arab in full robes. On box No. 6, a not-unattractive actress who was clearly resting, Jean Pierre suspected, with the occupant of box No. 5; and on box No. 7, an elderly, straight-backed aristocratic Frenchman in evening dress.

'A large black coffee,' Harvey drawled to the slim waiter in his smart brown jacket.

Monte Carlo does not allow hard liquor to be sold at the tables or girls to serve the customers. In direct contrast to Las Vegas, the Casino's business is gambling, not booze or women. Harvey had enjoyed Vegas when he was younger, but the older he became the more he appreciated the sophistication of the French. He had grown to prefer the formal atmosphere and decorum of this particular Casino. Although at the No. 3 table only he, the aristocratic Frenchman and Jean-Pierre wore dinner-jackets, it was frowned upon by the management to be dressed in any way that might be described as casual.

A moment later, piping hot coffee in a large golden cup arrived at Harvey's side. Jean-Pierre eyed it nervously while Harvey placed 100 francs on the table next to Jean-Pierre's 3-franc chip, the minimum and maximum stake allowed. The dealer, a tall young man of not more than thirty, who was proud of the fact that he could deal a hundred hands in an hour, slipped the cards deftly out of the shoe. A king for Jean-Pierre, a four for Harvey, a five for the young man on Harvey's left and a six for the dealer. Jean-Pierre's second card was a seven. He stuck. Harvey drew a ten and also stuck. The young man on Harvey's left also drew ten and asked the dealer to twist again. It was an eight – bust.

Harvey despised amateurs in any field and even fools know you don't twist if you have twelve or more when the dealer's card face up is a three, four, five or six. He grimaced slightly. The dealer dealt himself a ten and a six. Harvey and Jean-Pierre were winners. Jean-Pierre ignored the fate of the other players.

The next round was unwinnable. Jean-Pierre stuck at eighteen, two nines which he chose not to split as the dealer had an ace. Harvey stuck on eighteen, an eight and a jack, and the young man on the left bust again. The bank drew a queen – 'Black Jack' – and took the table.

The next hand gave Jean-Pierre a three, Harvey a seven and the young man a ten. The dealer drew himself a seven. Jean-Pierre drew an eight and doubled his stake to 6 francs and then drew a ten – vingt-et-un. Jean-Pierre did not blink. He realised he was playing well and that he must not draw attention to himself, but let Harvey take it for granted. In fact Harvey hadn't even noticed him: his attention was riveted on the young man on his left, who seemed anxious to make a gift to the management on every hand. The dealer continued, giving Harvey a ten and the young man an eight, leaving them both no choice but to stick. The dealer drew a ten, giving himself seventeen. He paid Jean-Pierre, left Harvey's stake and paid the young man. The management was happy to pay the young man occasionally, if only to keep him sitting there all night.

There were no more cards left in the shoe. The dealer made a great show of re-shuffling the four packs and invited Harvey to cut the cards before replacing them in the shoe. They slipped out again: a ten for Jean-Pierre, a five for Harvey, a six for the young man and a four for the dealer. Jean-Pierre drew an eight. The cards were running well.

159

Harvey drew a ten and stuck at fifteen. The young man drew a ten and asked for another card. Harvey could not believe his eyes and whistled through the gap in his front teeth. Sure enough, the next card was a king. The young man was bust. The dealer dealt himself a jack and then an eight, making twenty-two, but the young man had learned nothing from it. Harvey stared at him. When would he discover that, of the fifty-two cards in the pack, no less than sixteen have a face value of ten?

Harvey's distraction gave Jean-Pierre the opportunity he had been waiting for. He slipped his hand into his pocket and took the prostigmin tablet Robin had given him into the palm of his left hand. He sneezed, pulling his handkerchief from his breast pocket in a well-rehearsed gesture with his right hand. At the same time, he quickly and unobtrusively dropped the tablet into Harvey's coffee. It would, Robin had assured him, be an hour before it took effect. To begin with Harvey would only feel a little sick; then he would get rapidly worse until the pain was too much to bear, before finally collapsing in absolute agony.

Jean-Pierre turned to the bar, gripped his right-hand fist three times and then placed it in his pocket. Stephen left immediately and warned Robin and James from the steps of the Casino that the prostigmin tablet was in Metcalfe's drink. It was now Robin's turn to be tested under pressure. First he rang the hospital and asked the sister on duty to have the theatre in full preparation. Then he rang the nursing agency and asked for the nurse he had booked to be waiting in the hospital reception in exactly ninety minutes' time. He sat alone, nervously waiting for another call from the Casino.

Stephen returned to the bar. Harvey had started to feel a little sick, but was loath to leave. Despite the growing pain, his greed was forcing him to play on. He drank the rest of this coffee and ordered another one, hoping it would clear his head. The coffee did not help and Harvey began to feel steadily worse. An ace and a king followed by a seven, a four and a ten, and then two queens helped him to stay at the table. Jean-Pierre forced himself not to look at his watch. The dealer gave Jean-Pierre a seven, Harvey another ace and the young man a two. Quite suddenly, almost exactly on the hour, Harvey could bear the pain no longer. He tried to stand up to leave the table.

'*Le jeu a commencé, Monsieur*,' the dealer said formally.

'Go stuff yourself,' said Harvey and collapsed to the ground, gripping his stomach in agony. Jean-Pierre sat motionless while the croupiers and gamblers milled around helplessly. Stephen fought his way through the circle which had gathered round Harvey.

'Stand back, please. I am a doctor.'

The crowd moved back quickly, relieved to have a professional man on the scene.

'What is it, Doctor?' gasped Harvey, who felt the end of the world was about to come.

'I don't know yet,' replied Stephen. Robin had warned him that from collapse to passing out might be as short a time as ten minutes, so he set to work fast. He loosened Harvey's tie and took his pulse. He then undid his shirt and started feeling his abdomen.

'Have you a pain in the stomach?'

'Yes,' groaned Harvey.

'Did it come on suddenly?'

'Yes.'

'Can you try and describe the quality of the pain? Is it stabbing, burning or gripping?'

'Gripping.'

'Where is it most painful?'

Harvey touched the right side of his stomach. Stephen pressed down the tip of the ninth rib, making Harvey bellow with pain.

'Ah,' said Stephen, 'a positive Murphy's sign. You probably have an acutely inflamed gall-bladder. I'm afraid that may mean gallstones.' He continued to palpate the massive abdomen gently. 'It looks as if a stone has come out of your gall-bladder and is passing down the tube to your

161

intestine – it's the squeezing of that tube that's giving you such a dreadful pain. I'm afraid your gall-bladder and the stone must be removed at once. I can only hope there is someone at the hospital who can perform an emergency operation.'

Jean-Pierre came in bang on cue:

'Doctor Wiley Barker is staying at my hotel.'

'Wiley Barker, the American surgeon?'

'Yes, yes,' said Jean-Pierre. 'The chap who's been taking care of Nixon.'

'My God, what a piece of luck. We couldn't have anyone better, but he might turn out to be very expensive.'

'I don't give a damn about expense,' wailed Harvey.

'Well, it might be as high as $50,000.'

'I don't care if it's $100,000,' screamed Harvey. At that moment he would have been willing to part with his entire fortune.

'Right,' said Stephen. 'You, sir,' looking at Jean-Pierre, 'ring for an ambulance and then contact Doctor Barker and ask if he can get to the hospital immediately. Tell him it's an emergency. This gentleman requires a surgeon of the highest qualifications.'

'You're damn right I do,' said Harvey, and passed out.

Jean-Pierre left the Casino and called over his transmitter:

'Action stations. Action stations.'

Robin left the Hôtel de Paris and took a taxi. He would have given $100,000 to change places with the driver, but the car was already moving relentlessly towards the hospital. It was too late to turn back now.

James smashed the ambulance into first gear and rushed to the Casino, siren blaring. He was luckier than Robin. With so much to concentrate on he didn't have time to consider the consequences of what he was doing.

Eleven minutes and forty-one seconds later he arrived, leapt out of the driver's seat, opened the back door, gathered the stretcher and rushed up the Casino steps in his long white coat. Jean-Pierre was standing expectantly on the top step waiting for him. No words passed between them as he guided James quickly through the Salon des Amériques where Stephen was bending over Harvey. The stretcher was placed on the floor. It took all three of them to lift Harvey Metcalfe's 227 lb on to the canvas. Stephen and James picked up the stretcher and took him quickly through to the waiting ambulance, followed by Jean-Pierre.

'Where are you going with my boss?' demanded a voice.

Startled, the three of them turned round. It was Harvey Metcalfe's chauffeur, standing by the white Rolls Royce. After a moment's hesitation, Jean-Pierre took over.

'Mr Metcalfe has collapsed and has to go to hospital for an emergency operation. You must return to the yacht immediately, tell the staff to have his cabin ready and await further instructions.'

The chauffeur touched his cap and ran to the Rolls Royce. James leapt behind the wheel, while Stephen and Jean-Pierre joined Harvey in the back of the vehicle.

'Hell, that was close. Well done, Jean-Pierre. I was speechless,' admitted Stephen.

'It was nothing,' said Jean-Pierre, sweat pouring down his face.

The ambulance shot off like a scalded cat. Stephen and Jean-Pierre both replaced their jackets with the long white laboratory coats left on the seat and Stephen put the stethoscope round his neck.

'It looks to me as if he's dead,' said Jean-Pierre.

'Robin says he isn't,' said Stephen.

'How can he tell from four miles away?'

'I don't know. We'll just have to take his word for it.'

James screeched to a halt outside the entrance to the hospital. Stephen and Jean-Pierre hurried their patient through to the operating theatre. James returned the ambulance to the car park and quickly joined the others in the theatre.

Robin, scrubbed up and gowned, was there to meet

them at the door and while they were strapping Harvey Metcalfe to the operating table in the small room next to the theatre, he spoke for the first time:

'All of you, change your clothes. And Jean-Pierre, you scrub up as instructed.'

All three of them changed and Jean-Pierre started to wash immediately – a long, laborious process which Robin had firmly taught him must never be cut short. Post-operative septicaemia formed no part of his plan. Jean-Pierre appeared from the scrubbing-up room ready for action.

'Now, relax. We've done this nine times already. Just carry on exactly as if we were still in St Thomas's.'

Stephen moved behind the mobile Boyles machine. For four weeks he had been training as an anaesthetist: he had rendered James and a faintly protesting Jean-Pierre unconscious twice each in practice runs at St Thomas's. Now was his chance to exercise his new powers over Harvey Metcalfe.

Robin removed a syringe from a plastic packet and injected 250 mg of thiopentone into Harvey's arm. The patient sank back into a deep sleep. Quickly and efficiently Jean-Pierre and James undressed Harvey and then covered him in a sheet. Stephen placed the mask from the Boyles machine over Metcalfe's nose. The two flow-meters on the back of the machine showed 5 litres of nitrous oxide and 3 litres of oxygen.

'Take his pulse,' said Robin.

Stephen placed a finger in front of the ear just above the lobe to check the pre-auricular pulse. It was 70.

'Wheel him through into the theatre,' instructed Robin.

James pushed the trolley into the next room until it was just under the operating lights. Stephen trundled the Boyles machine along behind them.

The operating theatre was windowless and coldly sterile. Gleaming white tiles covered every wall from floor to ceiling, and it contained only the equipment needed for one operation. Jean-Pierre had covered Harvey with a sterile green sheet, leaving only his head and left arm exposed. One trolley of sterile instruments, drapes and towels had been carefully laid out by the theatre nurse, and stood covered with a sterile sheet. Robin hung the bottle of intravenous fluid from a standard near the head of the table and taped the end of the tubing to Harvey's left arm to complete the preparation. Stephen sat at the head of the table with the Boyles machine and adjusted the face-mask over Harvey's mouth and nose. Only one of the three massive operating lights hanging directly over Harvey had been turned on, causing a spotlight effect on the protruding bulge of his abdomen.

Eight eyes stared down on their victim. Robin continued:

'I shall give exactly the same instructions as I did in all our rehearsals, so just concentrate. First, I shall clean the abdomen with a skin preparation of iodine.'

Robin had all the instruments ready on the side of the table next to Harvey's feet. James lifted the sheet and folded it back over Harvey's legs, then he carefully removed the sterile sheet covering the trolley of instruments and poured iodine into one of the small basins. Robin picked up a swab in a pair of forceps and dipped it in the iodine solution. With a swift action up, down, and over the abdomen, he cleaned about 1 square foot of Harvey's massive body, throwing the swab into a bin and repeating the action with a fresh one. Next he placed a sterile towel below Harvey's chin, covering his chest, and another over his hips and thighs. A third one he placed lengthways along the left-side of his body and a final one along the right-hand side, leaving a 9 inch square of flabby belly exposed. He put a towel clip on each corner to secure them safely and then placed the laparotomy drapes over the prepared site. Robin was now ready.

'Scalpel.'

Jean-Pierre placed what he would have called a knife firmly in Robin's outstretched palm, as a runner might when passing a baton. James's apprehensive eyes met

Jean-Pierre's across the operating table, while Stephen concentrated on Harvey's breathing. Robin hesitated only for a second and then made a 10 cm paramedian incision, reaching about 3 cm into the fat. Robin had rarely seen a larger stomach: he could probably have gone as far as 8 cm deep without reaching the muscle. Blood started flowing everywhere, which Robin stopped with diathermy. No sooner had he finished the incision and stanched the flow of blood than he began to stitch up the patient's wound with a 3/0 interrupted plain catgut for ten stitches.

'That will dissolve within a week,' he explained.

He then closed the skin with a 2/0 interrupted plain silk, using an atraumatic needle. Then he cleaned the wound, removing the patches of blood that still remained. Finally, he placed a medium self-adhesive wound dressing over his handiwork.

James took off the drapes and sterile towels and placed them in the bin while Robin and Jean-Pierre put Metcalfe into a hospital gown and carefully packed his clothes in a grey plastic bag.

'He's coming round,' said Stephen.

Robin took another syringe and injected 10 mg of diazepan.

'That will keep him asleep for at least 30 minutes,' he said, 'and in any case, he'll be ga-ga for about three hours and won't remember much of what has happened. James, fetch the ambulance immediately and bring it round to the front of the hospital.'

James left the theatre and changed back into his clothes, a procedure which he could now perform in 90 seconds. He disappeared to the car park.

'Now, you two, get changed and then place Harvey very carefully in the ambulance and Jean-Pierre, wait in the back with him. Stephen, you carry out your next assignment.'

Stephen and Jean-Pierre changed quickly, back into their long white coats and wheeled the slumbering Harvey Metcalfe gently towards the ambulance. Once safely in,

Stephen ran to the public telephone by the hospital entrance, checked a piece of paper in his wallet and dialled.

'Hello, *Nice-Matin*? My name's Terry Robards of the *New York Times*. I'm here on holiday, and I have a great little story for you . . .'

Robin returned to the operating theatre and wheeled the trolley of instruments he had used to the sterilising room, and left them there to be dealt with by the hospital theatre staff in the morning. He picked up the plastic bag containing Harvey's clothes and, going through to the changing room, quickly removed his operating gown, cap and mask and put on his own clothes. He went in search of the theatre sister, and smiled charmingly at her.

'All finished, *ma soeur*. I have left the instruments by the steriliser. Please thank Monsieur Bartise for me once again.'

'*Oui, Monsieur. Notre plaisir. Je suis heureuse d'être à même de vous aider. Votre infirmière de l'Auxiliaire Médicale est arrivée.*'

A few moments later, Robin walked to the ambulance, accompanied by the agency nurse. He helped her into the back.

'Drive very slowly and carefully to the harbour.'

James nodded and set off at funeral pace.

'Nurse Faubert.'

'Yes, Docteur Barker.' Her hands were tucked primly under her blue cape, and her French accent was enchanting. Robin thought Harvey would not find her ministrations unwelcome.

'My patient has just had an operation for the removal of a gall stone and will need plenty of rest.'

With that Robin took out of his pocket a gall stone the size of an orange with a hospital tag on it which read 'Harvey Metcalfe'. Robin had in fact acquired the huge stone from St Thomas's Hospital, the original owner being a 6 ft 6 in West Indian bus conductor on the No. 14 route. Stephen and Jean-Pierre stared at it in disbelief. The nurse checked her new charge's pulse and respiration.

'If I were your patient, Nurse Faubert,' said Jean-Pierre, 'I should take good care never to recover.'

By the time they arrived at the yacht, Robin had briefed the nurse on diet and rest, and told her that he would be round to see his patient at 11 am the next day. They left Harvey sleeping soundly in his large cabin, stewards and staff clucking attentively.

James drove the other three back to the hospital, deposited the ambulance in the car park and left the keys with reception. The four of them then headed back to the hotel by separate routes. Robin was the last to arrive at room 217, just after 3.30 am. He collapsed into an armchair.

'Will you allow me a whisky, Stephen?'

'Yes, of course.'

'Good God, he meant it,' said Robin, and downed a large Johnny Walker before handing the bottle over to Jean-Pierre.

'He will be all right, won't he?' said James.

'You sound quite concerned for him. Yes, he can have his ten stitches out in a week's time and all he'll have is a nasty scar to brag about to his friends. I must get some sleep. I have to see our victim at 11 tomorrow morning and the confrontation may well be harder than the operation. You were all great tonight. My God, am I glad we had all those sessions at St Thomas's. If you're ever out of work and I need a croupier, a driver and an anaesthetist, I'll know who to ring.'

The others left and Robin collapsed on to his bed, exhausted. He fell into a deep sleep and woke just after 8 the next morning, to discover he was still fully dressed. That had not happened to him since his days as a young houseman, when he had been on night duty after a fourteen-hour day without a break. Robin had a long soothing bath in very hot water. He dressed and put on a clean shirt and suit, ready for his face-to-face meeting with Harvey Metcalfe. His newly acquired moustache and rimless glasses and the success of the operation made him feel a little like the famous surgeon he was impersonating.

The other three all appeared during the next hour to wish him luck and elected to wait in room 217 for his return. Stephen had checked them all out of the hotel and booked a flight to London for late that afternoon. Robin left, again taking the staircase rather than the lift. Once outside the hotel, he walked a little way before hailing a taxi to drive him to the harbour.

It was not hard to find the *Messenger Boy*. She was a gleaming, newly painted 100-footer lying at the east end of the harbour. She sported a massive Panamanian flag on her stern mast, which Robin assumed must be for tax purposes. He ascended the gangplank and was met by Nurse Faubert.

'*Bonjour, Docteur Barker.*'

'Good morning, Nurse. How is Mr Metcalfe?'

'He has had a very peaceful night and is having a light breakfast and making a few telephone calls. Would you like to see him now?'

'Yes, please.'

Robin entered the magnificent cabin and faced the man he had spent eight weeks plotting and planning against. He was talking into the telephone:

'Yes, I'm fine, dear. But it was an A-1 emergency at the time. Don't worry, I'll live,' and he put the telephone down. 'Doctor Barker, I have just spoken to my wife in Massachusetts and told her that I owe you my life. Even at 5 am she seemed pleased. I understand that I had private surgery, a private ambulance and that you saved my life. Or that's what it says in *Nice-Matin*.'

There was the old picture of Harvey in Bermuda shorts on the deck of the *Messenger Boy*, familiar to Robin from his dossier. The headline read '*Millionaire s'évanouit au Casino*' over '*La Vie d'un Millionnaire Américain a été sauvée par une Opération Urgente Dramatique!*' Stephen would be pleased.

'Tell me, Doctor,' said Harvey with relish, 'was I really in danger?'

169

'Well, you were on the critical list, and the consequences might have been fairly serious if we hadn't removed this from your stomach.' Robin took out the inscribed gall stone from his pocket with a flourish.

Harvey's eye grew large as saucers.

'Gee, have I really been walking round with that inside me all this time? Isn't that something? I can't thank you enough. If ever I can do anything for you, Doctor, don't hesitate to call on me.' He offered Robin a grape. 'Look, you're going to see me through this thing, aren't you? I don't think the nurse fully appreciates the gravity of my case.'

Robin thought fast.

'I'm afraid I'm not free to do that, Mr Metcalfe. My holiday finishes today and I have to return to California. Nothing urgent: just a few elective surgeries and a rather heavy lecture schedule.' He shrugged deprecatingly. 'Not exactly earth-shattering but it helps me keep up a way of life I have grown accustomed to.'

Harvey sat bolt upright, tenderly holding his stomach.

'Now you listen to me, Doctor Barker. I don't give a damn about a few students. I'm a sick man and I need you here until I've fully recovered. I'll make it worth your while to stay, don't you worry. I never grudge the money where my health is concerned, and what's more if it will persuade you, I'll make the cheque out to cash. The last thing I want Uncle Sam to know is how much I'm worth.'

Robin coughed delicately, wondering how American doctors approached the ticklish subject of fees with their patients.

'The cost could be rather high if I'm not to be out of pocket by staying. It might be as much as $80,000.' Robin drew a deep breath.

Harvey didn't blink.

'Sure. You're the best. That's not a lot of money to stay alive.'

'Very well. I'll get back to my hotel and see if it's possible to rearrange my schedule for you.'

Robin retreated from the sick-room and the white Rolls

Royce took him back to the hotel. In room 217 they all sat staring at Robin in disbelief as he completed his story.

'Stephen, for Christ's sake, the man's a raving hypochondriac. He wants me to stay on here while he convalesces. None of us planned for that.'

Stephen looked up coolly:

'You'll stay here and play ball. Why not give him value for money – at his own expense, of course. Go on, get on the blower and tell him you'll be round to hold his hand every day at 11 am. We'll just have to go back without you. And keep the hotel bill down, won't you?'

Robin picked up the telephone . . .

Three young men left the Hôtel de Paris after a long lunch in room 217, allowing themselves another bottle of Krug '64, and then returned to Nice Airport in a taxi, catching BA flight 012 at 16.10 to London Heathrow. They were once again in separate seats. One sentence remained on Stephen's mind from Robin's reported conversation with Harvey Metcalfe.

'If ever I can do anything for you, don't hesitate to call me at any time.'

Robin visited his patient once a day, borne in the white Corniche with white-walled tyres and a chauffeur in a white uniform. Only Harvey could be quite so brash, he thought. On the third, Nurse Faubert asked for a private word with him.

'My patient,' she said plaintively, 'is making improper advances when I change his dressing.'

Robin allowed Dr Wiley Barker the liberty of an unprofessional remark.

'Can't say I altogether blame him. Still, be firm, Nurse. I'm sure you must have encountered that sort of thing before.'

'*Naturellement*, but never from a patient only three days after major surgery. His constitution, it must be *formidable*.'

'I tell you what, let's catheterise him for a couple of days. That'll cramp his style.' She smiled. 'It must be pretty boring for you cooped up here all day,' Robin continued. 'Why don't you come and have a spot of supper with me after Mr Metcalfe has gone to sleep tonight?'

'I should love to, *Docteur*. Where shall I meet you?'

'Room 217, Hôtel de Paris,' said Robin unblushingly. 'Say 9 pm.'

'I'll look forward to it, *Docteur*.'

'A little more Chablis, Angeline?'

'No more, thank you, Wiley. That was a meal to remember. I think, maybe, you have not yet had everything you want?'

She got up, lit two cigarettes and put one in his mouth. Then she moved away, her long skirt swinging slightly from the hips. She wore no bra under her pink shirt. She exhaled smokily and watched him.

Robin thought of the blameless Doctor Barker in Australia, of his wife and children in Newbury, and the rest of the Team in London. Then he put them all out of his mind.

'Will you complain to Mr Metcalfe if I make improper advances to you?'

'From you, Wiley,' she smiled, 'they will not be improper.'

Harvey made a talkative recovery, and Robin removed the stitches gravely on the sixth day.

'That seems to have healed very cleanly, Mr Metcalfe. Take it easy, and you should be back to normal by the middle of next week.'

'Great. I have to get over to England right away for Ascot week. You know, my horse Rosalie is favourite this year. I suppose you can't join me as my guest? What if I have a relapse.'

Robin suppressed a smile.

'Don't worry. You're getting along fine. Sorry I can't stay to see how Rosalie performs at Ascot.'

'So am I, Doc. Thanks again, anyway. I've never met a surgeon like you before.'

And you're not likely to again, thought Robin, his American accent beginning to fray at the edges. He bid his adieus to Harvey with relief and to Angeline with regret, and sent the chauffeur back from the hotel with a copper-plate bill:

> *Dr Wiley Franklin Barker*
> *presents his Compliments to*
> *Mr Harvey Metcalfe*
> *and begs to inform him that the Bill for*
> *Professional Services rendered is*
> *$80,000*
> *in respect of surgery and post-operative treatment.*

The chauffeur was back within the hour with a cash cheque for $80,000. Robin bore it back to London in triumph.

Two down and two to go.

13

The following day, Friday, Stephen sat on Robin's examination couch in Harley Street and addressed the troops.

'The Monte Carlo operation was a total success in every way, thanks to Robin keeping his cool. The expenses were fairly high, though. The hospital and hotel bills totalled $11,351, while we received $80,000. Therefore, we've had $527,560 returned to us, and expenses so far have come to $22,530, which leaves Mr Metcalfe still in debt to the tune of $494,970. Does everyone agree with that?'

There was a general murmur of approval. Their confidence in Stephen's arithmetic was unbounded, although in fact, like all algebraists, he found working with figures somewhat tedious.

'Incidentally, Robin, however did you manage to spend $73.50 on dinner last Wednesday night? What did you have, caviar and champagne?'

'Something a little out of the ordinary,' admitted Robin. 'It seemed to be called for at the time.'

'I'd bet more than I laid out in Monte Carlo that I know who joined you for dinner, and I bet she shared more than a table with you too,' said Jean-Pierre, taking his wallet out of his pocket. 'Here you are Stephen, 219 francs – my winnings from the Casino on Wednesday night. If you'd left me alone in peace, we needn't have bothered with Robin's butchery. I could have won the whole amount back on my own. I think the least I deserve is Nurse Faubert's telephone number.'

Jean-Pierre's remarks went straight over Stephen's head.

'Well done, Jean-Pierre, it'll all come off expenses. At today's exchange rate, your 219 francs,' he paused for a moment and tapped out on his calculator, 'is worth $46.76. That brings the expenses down to $22,483.24.

'Now, my plans for Ascot are simple. James has acquired two badges for the Members' Enclosure at a cost of $10. We know that Harvey Metcalfe also has a badge, as all owners do, so as long as we get our timing right and make it look natural, he should once again fall into our trap. James will keep us briefed on the walkie-talkie and will follow the movements of Metcalfe from his arrival to his leaving. Jean-Pierre will wait by the entrance of the Members' Enclosure and follow him in. Robin will send the telegram from Heathrow Airport at 1 pm, so Harvey ought to receive it during lunch in his private box. That part of the plan is easy. It's if we manage to lure him to Oxford that we all have to be on our toes. I must confess, it'd make a pleasant change if Ascot were to work first time.'

Stephen grinned widely.

'That would give us much needed extra time to go over the Oxford plan again. Any questions?'

'You don't need us for part (*a*) of the Oxford plan, only (*b*)?' asked Robin, checking Stephen's notes.

'That's right. I can manage part (*a*) on my own. In fact, it will be better if you all remain in London on that night, well out of the way. Our next priority must be to think up some ideas for James or he might, heaven preserve us, even think up something for himself. I'm becoming very concerned about this,' continued Stephen, 'because once Harvey returns to America we'll have to deal with him on his own ground. To date he's always been at the venue of our choosing. James would stick out like a sore thumb in Boston, even though he's the best actor of the four of us. In Harvey's words, "It would be a whole different ball game".'

James sighed lugubriously and studied the Axminster carpet.

'Poor old James – don't worry, you drove that ambulance like a trooper,' said Robin.

'Perhaps you could learn to learn to fly a plane and then we could hijack him,' suggested Jean-Pierre.

Miss Meikle did not approve of the laughter coming from Doctor Oakley's room and she was glad to see the oddly assorted trio leave. When she had closed the door finally on James she returned to Robin's room.

'Will you see your patients now, Doctor Oakley?'

'Yes, if I must, Miss Meikle.'

Miss Meikle pursed her lips. Whatever had come over him? It must be those dreadful types he had started mixing with lately. He had become so unreliable.

'Mrs Wentworth-Brewster – Doctor Oakley will see you now, and I'll have the pills for your trip to Italy ready for you when you come out.'

Stephen returned for a few days' recuperation to Magdalen College. He had started the entire exercise eight weeks before and two of the Team had succeeded far beyond his expectations. He was conscious that he must crown their efforts with something that would live on in the legends of Oxford long after his departure.

Jean-Pierre returned to work in his gallery in Bond Street. Since he only had to deliver one sentence at Ascot he was not going to be overtaxed, although part (b) of Stephen's Oxford plan kept him nightly in front of a mirror rehearsing his role.

James took Anne down to Stratford-upon-Avon for the weekend. The Royal Shakespeare Company obliged with a sparkling performance of *Much Ado about Nothing* and afterwards, walking along the banks of the Avon, James proposed. Only the royal swans could have heard her reply. The diamond ring James had noticed in the window of Cartier while he had been waiting for Harvey Metcalfe to join Jean-Pierre in the gallery, looked even more beautiful on her slender finger. James's happiness seemed complete. If only he could come up with a plan and shock them all, he would want for nothing. He discussed it with Anne again that night, considering new ideas and old ones, still getting nowhere.

But an idea was beginning to formulate in her mind.

14

On Monday morning James drove Anne back to London and changed into the most debonair of his suits. Anne had to return to work, despite James's suggestion that she should accompany him to Ascot. She felt the others would not approve of her presence and would suspect that James had confided in her.

Although James had not told her the details of the Monte Carlo exercise, Anne knew every step of the planned proceedings at Ascot and she could tell that James was nervous. Still, she would be seeing him that night and would know the worst by then. James looked lost. Anne was only thankful that Stephen, Robin and Jean-Pierre held the baton most of the time in this relay team – but the idea that was taking shape in her mind just might surprise them all.

Stephen rose early and admired his grey hair in the mirror. The result had been expensively achieved the previous day in the hairdressing salon of Debenhams. He dressed carefully, putting on his one respectable grey suit and blue checked tie. These were brought out for all special occasions, ranging from a talk to students at Sussex University to a dinner with the American Ambassador. No one had told him the colours clashed and the suit sagged unfashionably at the elbow and knees, because by Stephen's standards it was elegance itself. He travelled from Oxford to Ascot by train, while Jean-Pierre came from London by car. They met up with James at the Belvedere Arms at 11 am, almost a mile from the course.

Stephen immediately telephoned Robin to confirm that all three of them had arrived and asked for the telegram to be read over to him.

'That's perfect, Robin. Now travel to Heathrow and send it at exactly 1 pm.'

'Good luck, Stephen. Grind the bastard into the dust.'

Stephen returned to the others and confirmed that Robin had the London end under control.

'Off you go, James, and let us know the minute Harvey arrives.'

James downed a bottle of Carlsberg and departed. The problem was that he kept bumping into friends and he could hardly explain why he was prevented from joining them.

Harvey arrived at the members' car park just after midday, his white Rolls Royce shining like a Persil advertisement. The car was being stared at by all the racegoers with an English disdain which Harvey mistook for admiration. He led his party to the private box. His newly tailored suit had taxed the ingenuity of Bernard Weatherill to the utmost. A red carnation in his buttonhole and a hat to cover his bald head left him nearly unrecognisable, and James might have missed him had it not been for the white Rolls Royce. James followed the little group at a careful distance until he saw Harvey enter a door marked 'Mr Harvey Metcalfe and Guests'.

'He's in his private box,' said James.

'Where are you?' asked Jean-Pierre.

'Directly below him on the ground level by a course bookmaker called Sam O'Flaherty.'

'No need to be rude about the Irish, James,' said Jean-Pierre. 'We'll be with you in a few minutes.'

James stared up at the vast white stand, which accommodated 10,000 spectators in comfort and gave an excellent view of the racecourse. He was finding it hard to concentrate on the job in hand as once again he had to avoid relations and friends. First was the Earl of Halifax, and then that frightful girl he had so unwisely agreed to take to

Queen Charlotte's Ball last spring. What was the creature's name? Ah yes. The Hon. Selina Wallop. How appropriate. She was wearing a mini-skirt that was a good four years out of fashion and a hat which looked as if it could never come into fashion. James jammed his trilby over his ears, looked the other way and passed the time by chatting to Sam O'Flaherty about the 3.20, the King George VI and Queen Elizabeth Stakes. O'Flaherty quoted the latest odds on the favourite at the top of his voice:

'Rosalie at 6:4, owned by that American, Harvey Metcalfe, and ridden by Pat Eddery.'

Eddery was on the way to becoming the youngest-ever champion jockey – and Harvey always backed winners.

Stephen and Jean-Pierre joined James at the side of Sam O'Flaherty's bag. His tick-tack man was standing on an upturned orange box beside him and swinging his arms like a semaphore sailor aboard a sinking ship.

'What's your fancy, gentlemen?' Sam asked the three of them.

James ignored Stephen's slight frown of disapproval.

'£5 each way on Rosalie,' he said, and handed over a crisp £10 note, receiving in return a little green card with the series number and 'Sam O'Flaherty' stamped right across the middle.

'I must presume, James, this is an integral part of your as yet undisclosed plan,' said Jean-Pierre. 'What I should like to know is, if it works, how much do we stand to make?'

'£9.10 after tax if Rosalie wins,' chipped in Sam O'Flaherty, his stub cigar bobbing up and down in his mouth as he spoke.

'Hardly a great contribution towards $1 million, James. Well, we're off to the Members' Enclosure. Let us know the moment Harvey leaves his box. My guess is that around 1.45 he'll come and look at the runners and riders for the two o'clock, so that gives us a clear hour.'

* * *

The waiter opened another bottle of Krug 1964 and began pouring it for Harvey's guests; three bankers, two economists, a couple of ship-owners and a distinguished City journalist.

Preferring his guests to be famous and influential, Harvey always invited people who would find it almost impossible to refuse because of the business he might put their way. He was delighted with the company he had assembled for his big day. Senior among them was Sir Howard Dodd, the ageing chairman of the merchant bank that bore his name, but which actually referred to his great-grandfather. Sir Howard was 6 ft 2 in, as straight as a ramrod, and looked more like a Grenadier Guard than a respectable banker. The only thing he had in common with Harvey was the hair, or lack of hair, on his balding head. His young assistant, Jamie Clark, accompanied him. Just over thirty and extremely bright, he was there to be sure his chairman did not commit the bank to anything he might later regret. Although he had a sneaking admiration for Harvey, Clark did not think him the sort of customer the bank should do business with. Nevertheless, he was far from averse to a day at the races.

The two economists, Mr Colin Emson and Dr Michael Hogan from the Hudson Institute, were there to brief Harvey on the parlous state of the British economy. They could not have been more different. Emson was a totally self-made man who had left school at fifteen and educated himself. Using his social contacts, he had built up a company specialising in taxation, which had been remarkably successful thanks to the British Government's habit of putting through a new Finance Act every few weeks. Emson was 6 ft tall, solid and genial, game to help the party along whether Harvey lost or won. Hogan, in contrast, had been to all the right places, – Winchester, Trinity College, Oxford, and the Wharton Business School in Pennsylvania. A spell with McKinsey, the management consultants, in London had made him one of the best-informed economists in Europe. Those who observed his slim, sinewy body would

181

not have been surprised to learn that he had been an international squash player. Dark-haired, with brown eyes that rarely left Harvey, he found it hard not to show his contempt; this was his fifth invitation to Ascot – Harvey, it seemed, was never going to take no for an answer.

The Kundas brothers, second-generation Greeks who loved racing almost as much as ships, could hardly be told apart, with their black hair, swarthy skins and heavy dark eyebrows. It was difficult to guess how old they were, and nobody knew how much they were worth. They probably did not know themselves. Harvey's final guest, Nick Lloyd of the *News of the World*, had come along to pick up any dirt he could about his host. He had come near to exposing Metcalfe in the mid-sixties, but another scandal had kept less juicy stories off the front page for several weeks, and by then Harvey had escaped. Lloyd, hunched over the inevitable triple gin with a faint suggestion of tonic, watched the motley bunch with interest.

'Telegram for you, sir.'

Harvey ripped it open. He was never neat about anything.

'It's from my daughter Rosalie. It's cute of her to remember, but damn it all, I named the horse after her. Come on everybody, let's eat.'

They all took their seats for lunch – cold vichyssoise, pheasant and strawberries. Harvey was even more loquacious than usual, but his guests took no notice, aware he was nervous before the race and knowing that he would rather be a winner of this trophy than any he could be offered in America. Harvey himself could never understand why he felt that way. Perhaps it was the special atmosphere of Ascot which appealed to him so strongly – the combination of lush green grass and gracious surroundings, of elegant crowds and an efficiency of organisation which made Ascot the envy of the racing world.

'You must have a better chance this year than ever before, Harvey,' said the senior banker.

'Well, you know, Sir Howard, Lester Piggott is riding the Duke of Devonshire's horse, Crown Princess, and the Queen's Horse, Highclere, is the joint favourite, so I can't afford to over-estimate my chances. When you've been third twice before, and then favourite and not placed, you begin to wonder if one of your horses is going to make it.'

'Another telegram, sir.'

Once again Harvey's fat little finger ripped it open.

'"All the best wishes and good luck for the King George VI and Queen Elizabeth Stakes". It's from the staff of your bank, Sir Howard. Jolly good show.'

Harvey's Polish-American accent made the English expression slightly ridiculous.

'More champagne, everybody.'

Another telegram arrived.

'At this rate, Harvey, you'll need a special room at the Post Office.' There was laughter all round at Sir Howard's feeble joke. Once again Harvey read it out aloud:

'"Regret unable to join you Ascot. Heading soonest California. Grateful look out for old friend Professor Rodney Porter, Oxford Nobel Prize Winner. Don't let English bookies stitch you up. Wiley B., Heathrow Airport". It's from Wiley Barker. He's the guy who did stitch me up in Monte Carlo. He saved my life. He took out a gall stone the size of that bread roll you're eating, Dr Hogan. Now how the hell am I supposed to find this Professor Porter?' Harvey turned to the head waiter. 'Find my chauffeur.'

A few seconds later the smartly-clad Guy Salmon flunkey appeared.

'There's a Professor Rodney Porter of Oxford here today. Go find him.'

'What does he look like, sir?'

'How the hell do I know,' said Harvey. 'Like a professor.'

The chauffeur regretfully abandoned his plans for an afternoon at the railings and departed, leaving Harvey and his guests to enjoy the strawberries, the champagne and the string of telegrams that were still arriving.

'You know if you win, the cup will be presented by the Queen,' said Nick Lloyd.

'You bet. It'll be the crowning moment of my life to win the King George and Elizabeth Stakes and meet Her Majesty The Queen. If Rosalie wins, I'll suggest my daughter marries Prince Charles – they're about the same age.'

'I don't think even you will be able to fix that, Harvey.'

'What'll you do with the odd £81,000 prize money, Mr Metcalfe?' asked Jamie Clark.

'Give it to some charity,' said Harvey, pleased with the impression the remark made on his guests.

'Very generous, Harvey. Typical of your reputation.' Nick Lloyd gave Michael Hogan a knowing look. Even if the others didn't, they both knew what was typical of his reputation.

The chauffeur returned to report that there was no trace of a solitary professor anywhere in the champagne bar, balcony luncheon room or the paddock buffet, and that he'd been unable to gain access to the Members' Enclosure.

'Naturally not,' said Harvey rather pompously. 'I shall have to find him myself. Drink up and enjoy yourselves.'

Harvey rose and walked to the door with the chauffeur. Once he was out of earshot of his guests, he said: 'Get your ass out of here and don't give me any crap about not being able to find him or you can find something for yourself – another job.'

The chauffeur bolted. Harvey turned to his guests and smiled.

'I'm going to look at the runners and riders for the 2 o'clock.'

'He's leaving the box now,' said James.

'What's that you're saying?' asked an authoritative voice he recognised. 'Talking to yourself, James?'

James stared at the noble Lord Somerset, 6 ft 1 in and still able to stand his full height, an MC and a DSO in the First World War. He still exuded enthusiastic energy although the lines on his face suggested that he had passed the age at which the Maker had fulfilled his contract.

'Oh hell. No, sir, I was just . . . em . . . coughing.'

'What do you fancy in the King George VI and Queen Elizabeth Stakes?' asked the peer of the realm.

'Well, I have put £5 each way on Rosalie, sir.'

'He seems to have cut himself off,' said Stephen.

'Well, buzz him again,' said Jean-Pierre.

'What's that noise, James? Have you taken to a hearing-aid or something?'

'No, sir. It's . . . it's . . . it's a transistor radio.'

'Those things ought to be banned. Bloody invasion of privacy.'

'Absolutely right, sir.'

'What's he playing at, Stephen?'

'I don't know – I think something must have happened.'

'Oh my god, it's Harvey heading straight for us. You go into the Members' Enclosure, Stephen, and I'll follow you. Take a deep breath and relax. He hasn't seen us.'

Harvey marched up to the official blocking the entrance to the Members' Enclosure.

'I'm Harvey Metcalfe, the owner of Rosalie, and this is my badge.'

The official let Harvey through. Thirty years ago, he thought, they would not have let him into the Members' Enclosure if he'd owned every horse in the race. Then racing at Ascot was only held on four days a year, jolly social occasions. Now it was twenty-four days a year and big business. Times had changed. Jean-Pierre followed closely, showing his pass without speaking to the official.

A photographer broke away from stalking the outrageous hats for which Ascot has such a reputation, and took a picture of Harvey just in case Rosalie won the King George VI Stakes. As soon as his bulb flashed he rushed over to the other entrance, where Linda Lovelace, the star of *Deep Throat*, the film running to packed houses in New

185

York but banned in England, was trying to enter the Members' Enclosure. In spite of being introduced to a well-known London banker, Richard Szpiro, just as he was entering the Enclosure, she was not succeeding. She was wearing a top hat and morning suit with nothing under the top coat, and no one was going to bother with Harvey while she was around. When Miss Lovelace was quite certain that every photographer had taken a picture of her attempting to enter the Enclosure she left, swearing at the top of her voice, her publicity stunt completed.

Harvey returned to studying the horses as Stephen moved up to within a few feet of him.

'Here we go again,' said Jean-Pierre in French and went smartly over to Stephen and, standing directly between the two of them, shook Stephen's hand warmly, declaring in a voice that was intended to carry:

'How are you, Professor Porter? I didn't know you were interested in racing.'

'I'm not really, but I was on my way back from a seminar in London and thought it a good opportunity to see how . . .'

'Professor Porter,' cried Harvey. 'I'm honoured to make your acquaintance, sir, my name is Harvey Metcalfe from Boston, Massachusetts. My good friend, Dr Wiley Barker, who saved my life, told me you'd be here today on your own, and I'm going to make sure you have a wonderful afternoon.'

Jean-Pierre slipped away unnoticed. He could not believe how easy it had been. The telegram had worked like a charm.

'Her Majesty The Queen; His Royal Highness The Duke of Edinburgh; Her Majesty Queen Elizabeth The Queen Mother; and her Royal Highness The Princess Anne are now entering the Royal Box.'

The massed bands of the Brigade of Guards struck up the National Anthem:

'God Save the Queen.'

The crowd of 25,000 rose and sang loyally out of tune.

'We should have someone like that in America,' said Harvey to Stephen, 'to take the place of Richard Nixon. We wouldn't have any Watergate problems then.'

Stephen thought his fellow American was being just a little unfair. Richard Nixon was almost a saint by Harvey Metcalfe's standards.

'Come and join me in my box, Professor, and meet my other guests. The damned box cost me £750, we may as well fill it. Have you had some lunch?'

'Yes, I've had an excellent lunch, thank you,' Stephen lied – something else Harvey had taught him. He had stood by the Members' Enclosure for an hour, nervous and pensive, unable even to manage a sandwich, and now he was starving.

'Well, come and enjoy the champagne,' roared Harvey. On an empty stomach, thought Stephen.

'Thank you, Mr Metcalfe. I am a little lost. This is my first Royal Ascot.'

'This isn't Royal Ascot, Professor. It's the last day of Ascot Week, but the Royal Family always comes to see the King George and Elizabeth Stakes, so everybody dresses up.'

'I see,' said Stephen timidly, pleased with his deliberate error.

Harvey collared his find and took him back to the box.

'Everybody, I want you to meet my distinguished friend, Rodney Porter. He's a Nobel Prize Winner, you know. By the way, what's your subject, Rod?'

'Biochemistry.'

Stephen was getting the measure of Harvey. As long as he played it straight, the bankers and shippers, and even the journalists, would never doubt that he was the cleverest thing since Einstein. He relaxed a little and even found time to fill himself with smoked salmon sandwiches when the others were not looking.

Lester Piggott won the 2 o'clock on Olympic Casino and the 2.30 on Roussalka, achieving his 3,000th win. Harvey

187

was getting steadily more nervous. He talked incessantly without making much sense. He had sat through the 2.30 without showing any interest in the result and consumed more and more champagne. At 2.50 he called for them all to join him in the Members' Enclosure to look at his famous filly. Stephen, like the others, trailed behind him in a little pseudo-royal entourage.

Jean-Pierre and James watched the procession from a distance.

'He's too deep in to climb out now,' said Jean-Pierre.

'He looks relaxed enough to me,' replied James. 'Let's make ourselves scarce. We can only get under his feet.'

They headed into the champagne bar, which was filled with red-faced men who looked as if they spent more time drinking than they did watching the racing.

'Isn't she beautiful, Professor? Almost as beautiful as my daughter. If she doesn't win today I don't think I'm ever going to make it.'

Harvey left his little clique to have a word with the jockey, Pat Eddery, to wish him luck. Peter Walwyn, the trainer, was giving final instructions before the jockey mounted and left the Enclosure. The ten horses were then paraded in front of the stand before the race, a custom only carried out at Ascot for the King George VI and Queen Elizabeth Stakes. The gold, purple and scarlet colours of Her Majesty The Queen's horse Highclere led the procession, followed by Crown Princess, who was giving Lester Piggott a little trouble. Directly behind her came Rosalie, looking very relaxed, fresh and ready to go. Buoy and Dankaro trotted behind Rosalie, with the outsiders Mesopotamia, Ropey and Minnow bringing up the rear. The crowd rose to cheer the horses and Harvey beamed with pride, as if he owned every horse in the race.

'. . . and I have with me today the distinguished American owner, Harvey Metcalfe,' said Julian Wilson into the BBC TV outside-broadcast camera. 'I'm going to ask him if he'd be kind enough to give me his views on the King George VI and Queen Elizabeth Stakes, for which he has the joint favourite, Rosalie. Welcome to England, Mr Metcalfe. How do you feel about the big race?'

'It's a thrill to be here, just to participate in the race once again. Rosalie's got a great chance. Still, it's not winning that matters. It's taking part.'

Stephen flinched. Baron de Coubertin, who had first made that remark when opening the 1896 Olympics, must have turned in his grave.

'The latest betting shows Rosalie to be the joint favourite with Her Majesty The Queen's Horse, Highclere. How do you feel about that?'

'I'm just as worried about the Duke of Devonshire's Crown Princess. Lester Piggott is always hard to beat on a great occasion. He won the first two races and he'll be all set for this one – Crown Princess is a fine little filly.'

'Is a mile and a half a good distance for Rosalie?'

'Results this season show it's definitely her best distance.'

'What will you do with the £81,240 prize money?'

'The money is not important, it hasn't even entered my mind.'

It had certainly entered Stephen's mind.

'Thank you, Mr Metcalfe, and the best of luck. And now over for the latest news of the betting.'

Harvey moved back to his group of admirers and suggested that they return to watch the race from the balcony just outside his box.

Stephen was fascinated to observe Harvey at such close quarters. He had become nervous and even more mendacious than usual under pressure – not at all the icy, cool operator they had all feared him to be. This man was human, susceptible and could be beaten.

They all leant over the rails watching the horses being put into the stalls. Crown Princess was still giving a little trouble while all the others waited. The tension was becoming unbearable.

'They're off,' boomed the loudspeaker.

As twenty-five thousand people raised glasses to their eyes, Harvey said, 'She's got a good start – she's well placed,' continuing to give everybody a running commentary until the last mile, when he became silent. The others also waited in silence, intent on the loudspeaker.

'They're into the straight mile – Minnow leads the field around the bend – with Buoy and Dankaro, looking relaxed, just tucked in behind him – followed by Crown Princess, Rosalie and Highclere . . .

'As they approach the six-furlong marker – Rosalie and Crown Princess come up on the stand side with Highclere making a bid . . .

'Five furlongs to go – Minnow still sets the pace, but is beginning to tire as Crown Princess and Buoy make up ground . . .

'Half a mile to go – Minnow still just ahead of Buoy, who has moved up into second place, perhaps making her move too early . . .

'Three furlongs from home – they're quickening up just a little – Minnow sets the pace on the rails – Buoy and Dankaro are now about a length behind – followed by Rosalie, Lester Piggott on Crown Princess and the Queen's filly Highclere all making ground . . .

'Inside the two-furlong marker – Highclere and Rosalie move up to challenge Buoy – Crown Princess is right out of it now . . .

'A furlong to go . . .'

The commentator's voice rose in pitch and volume.

'It's Joe Mercer riding Highclere who hits the front, just ahead of Pat Eddery on Rosalie – two hundred yards to go – they're neck and neck – one hundred yards to go – it's anybody's race and on the line it's a photo finish between the gold, purple and scarlet colours of Her Majesty the Queen and the black-and-green check colours of the American owner, Harvey Metcalfe – M. Moussac's Dankaro was third.'

Harvey stood paralysed, waiting for the result. Even Stephen felt a little sympathy for him. None of Harvey's guests dared to speak for fear they might be wrong.

'The result of The King George VI and The Queen

Elizabeth Stakes.' Once again the loudspeaker boomed out and silence fell over the whole course:

'The winner is No. 5, Rosalie.'

The rest of the result was lost in the roar of the crowd and the bellow of triumph from Harvey. Pursued by his guests, he raced to the nearest lift, pressed a pound note into the lift-girl's hand and shouted 'Get this thing moving.' Only half of his guests managed to jump in with him. Stephen was among them. Once they reached the ground floor, the lift gates opened and Harvey came out like a thoroughbred, past the champagne bar, through the rear of the Members' Enclosure into the Winners' Enclosure, and flung his arms round the horse's neck, almost unseating the jockey. A few minutes later he triumphantly led Rosalie to the little white post marked 'FIRST'. The crowd thronged around him, offering their congratulations.

The Clerk of the Course, Captain Beaumont, stood by Harvey's side, briefing him on the procedure that would be followed when he was presented. Lord Abergavenny, the Queen's Representative at Ascot, accompanied Her Majesty to the Winners' Enclosure.

'The winner of The King George VI and The Queen Elizabeth Stakes – Mr Harvey Metcalfe's Rosalie.'

Harvey was in a dream world. Flash-bulbs popped and film cameras followed him as he walked towards the Queen. He bowed and received his trophy. The Queen, resplendent in a turquoise silk suit and matching turban that could only have been designed by Norman Hartnell, said a few words, but for the first time in his life Harvey was speechless. Taking a pace backwards, he bowed again and returned to his place accompanied by loud applause.

Back in his box the champagne flowed and everybody was Harvey's friend. Stephen realised this was not the moment to try anything clever. He must bide his time and watch his quarry's reaction to these changed circumstances. He stayed quietly in a corner, letting the excitement subside, and observed Harvey carefully.

It took another race before Harvey was half back to

normal and Stephen decided the time had now come to act. He made as if to leave.

'Are you going already, Professor?'

'Yes, Mr Metcalfe. I must return to Oxford and mark some scripts before tomorrow morning.'

'I always admire the work you boys put in. I hope you enjoyed yourself?' Stephen avoided Shaw's famous riposte, 'I had to, there was nothing else to enjoy'.

'Yes, thank you, Mr Metcalfe. An amazing achievement. You must be a very proud man.'

'Well, I guess so. It's been a long time coming, but it all seems worthwhile now . . . Rod, it's too bad you have to leave us. Can't you stay on a little longer and join my party at Claridge's tonight?'

'I should have liked that, Mr Metcalfe, but you must visit me at my college at Oxford and allow me to show you the university.'

'That's swell. I have a couple of days after Ascot and I've always wanted to see Oxford, but I never seem to have found the time.'

'It's the university Garden Party next Wednesday. Why don't you join me for dinner at my college on Tuesday evening and then we can spend the following day looking at the university and go on to the Garden Party?' Stephen scribbled a few directions on a card.

'Fantastic. This is turning out to be the best vacation I've ever had in Europe. How are you getting back to Oxford, Professor?'

'By train.'

'No, no,' said Harvey. 'My Rolls Royce will take you. It'll be back well in time for the last race.'

And before Stephen could protest, the chauffeur was called for.

'Take Professor Porter back to Oxford and then return here. Have a good trip, Professor. I'll look forward to seeing you next Tuesday at 8 pm. Great meeting you.'

'Thank you for a wonderful day, Mr Metcalfe, and congratulations on your splendid victory.'

Seated in the back of the white Rolls Royce on his way to Oxford, the car which Robin had boasted he and he alone would travel in, Stephen relaxed and smiled to himself. Taking a small notebook from his pocket he made an entry:

'Deduct 98 pence from expenses, the price of a single second-class ticket from Ascot to Oxford.'

15

'Bradley,' said the Senior Tutor. 'You're going a bit grey at the edges, dear boy. Is the office of Junior Dean proving too much for you?'

Stephen had wondered whether any of the Senior Common Room would think the change in the colour of his hair worthy of comment. Dons are seldom surprised by anything their colleagues do.

'My father went grey at an early age, Senior Tutor, and there seems to be no way of defying heredity . . .'

'Ah well, dear boy, you'll look all the more distinguished at next week's Garden Party.'

'Oh yes,' replied Stephen, who had been thinking of nothing else. 'I'd quite forgotten about that.'

He returned to his rooms where the rest of the Team were assembled and waiting for their next briefing.

'Wednesday is the day of the Encaenia and the Garden Party,' began Stephen without as much as a 'Good morning, gentlemen'. His students made no protest. 'Now the one thing we've learnt about our millionaire friend is that when we take him away from his own environment he still continues to assume he knows everything. We've now shown that his bluff can be called, as long as we know what's going to happen next week and he doesn't. It's only the same skill he used when promoting Prospecta Oil – always keeping one step ahead of us. Now, we're going to keep two steps ahead of him by having a rehearsal today and a full dress-rehearsal tomorrow.'

'Time spent on reconnaissance is seldom wasted,' muttered James. It was about the only sentiment he could recall from his Army Cadet days at Harrow.

'Haven't had to spend much time on reconnaissance for your plan, have we?' chipped in Jean-Pierre.

Stephen ignored the interruptions.

'Now, the whole process on the day will take about seven hours for me and four hours for you, which includes the time required for make-up; we'll need an extra session on that from James the day before.'

'How often will you need my two sons?' asked Robin.

'Only once, on the Wednesday. Too many runs at it will make them look stiff and awkard.'

'When do you imagine Harvey will want to return to London?' enquired Jean-Pierre.

'I rang Guy Salmon to check their timetable and they've been instructed to have him back at Claridge's by 7 pm, so I've assumed we have only until 5.30.'

'Clever,' said Robin.

'It's awful,' said Stephen. 'I even think like the man now. Right, let's go over the whole plan once again. We'll take it from the red dossier, halfway down page 16. When I leave All Souls . . .'

On Sunday and Monday they carried out full rehearsals. By the Tuesday they knew every route Harvey could take and where he would be at any given moment of the day from 9 am to 5.30 pm. Stephen hoped he had covered every eventuality. He had little choice. They were only going to be allowed one crack at this one. Any mistakes like Monte Carlo and there would be no second chance. The dress-rehearsal went to a second.

'I haven't worn clothes like this since I was six years old and attending a fancy-dress party,' said Jean-Pierre. 'We're going to be anything but inconspicuous.'

'There'll be red and blue and black all round you on the day,' said Stephen. 'It's like a circus for peacocks. No one will give us a second look, not even you, Jean-Pierre.'

They were all nervous again, waiting for the curtain to

go up. Stephen was glad they were on edge: he had no doubt that the moment they relaxed with Harvey Metcalfe, they would be found out.

The Team spent a quiet weekend. Stephen watched the College Dramatic Society's annual effort in Magdalen gardens, Robin took his wife to Glyndebourne and was uncommonly attentive, Jean-Pierre read *Goodbye Picasso* by David Douglas Duncan, and James took Anne to Tathwell Hall in Lincolnshire, to meet his father, the fifth earl.

Even Anne was nervous that weekend.

'Harry?'

'Doctor Bradley.'

'I have an American guest dining with me in my rooms tonight. His name is Harvey Metcalfe. When he arrives will you see he is brought over to my rooms, please.'

'Certainly, sir.'

'And one small thing. He seems to have mistaken me for Professor Porter of Trinity College. Don't correct the mistake, will you? Just humour him.'

'Certainly, sir.'

Harry retreated into the Porter's Lodge shaking his head sadly. Of course, all academics went dotty in the end, but Dr Bradley had been afflicted at an unusually tender age.

Harvey arrived at eight. He was always on time in England. The head porter guided him through the cloisters and up the old stone staircase to Stephen's rooms.

'Mr Metcalfe, sir.'

'How are you, Professor?'

'I'm well, Mr Metcalfe. Good of you to be so punctual.'

'Punctuality is the politeness of princes.'

'I think you'll find it is the politeness of kings, and, in this particular instance, of Louis XVIII.' For a moment Stephen forgot that Harvey wasn't a pupil.

'I'm sure you're right, Professor.'

Stephen mixed him a large whisky. His guest's eyes took in the room and settled on the desk.

'Gee – what a wonderful set of photographs. You with the late President Kennedy, another with the Queen and even the Pope.'

That touch was due to Jean-Pierre, who had put Stephen in contact with a photographer who had been in jail with his artist friend David Stein. Stephen was already looking forward to burning the photographs and pretending they had never existed.

'Let me give you another to add to your collection.'

Harvey pulled out of his inside coat pocket a large photograph of himself receiving the trophy for the King George VI and Queen Elizabeth Stakes from the Queen.

'I'll sign it for you, if you like.'

Without waiting for a reply, he scribbled an exuberant signature diagonally across the Queen.

'Thank you,' said Stephen. 'I can assure you I will treasure it with the same affection as I do my other photographs. I certainly appreciate you sparing the time to visit me here, Mr Metcalfe.'

'It's an honour for me to come to Oxford, and this is such a lovely old college.'

Stephen really believed he meant it, and he suppressed the inclination to tell Harvey the story of the late Lord Nuffield's dinner at Magdalen. For all Nuffield's munificence to the university, the two were never on entirely easy terms. When a manservant assisted the guest's departure after a college feast, Nuffield took the proffered hat ungraciously. 'Is this mine?' he said, disdainfully. 'I wouldn't know, my lord,' was the rejoinder, 'but it's the one you came with.'

Harvey was gazing a little blankly at the books on Stephen's shelves. The disparity between their subject matter, pure mathematics, and the putative Professor Porter's discipline, biochemistry, happily failed to arrest him.

'Do brief me on tomorrow.'

'Surely,' said Stephen. Why not? He had briefed every-one else. 'Let me first call for dinner and I'll go through what I've planned for you and see if it meets with your approval.'

'I'm game for anything. I feel ten years younger since this trip to Europe – it must've been the operation – and I'm thrilled about being here at Oxford University.'

Stephen wondered if he really could stand seven hours of Harvey Metcalfe, but for another $250,000 and his reputation with the rest of the Team . . .

The college servants brought him shrimp cocktail.

'My favourite,' said Harvey. 'How did you know?'

Stephen would have liked to say, 'There's very little I don't know about you,' but he satisfied himself with, 'A fortunate guess. Now, if we meet up at 10 tomorrow morning we can take part in what is thought to be the most interesting day in the university calendar. It's called Encaenia.'

'What's that?'

'Well, once a year at the end of Trinity Term, which is the equivalent of the summer term in an American university, we celebrate the ending of the university year. There are several ceremonies followed by a magnificent Garden Party, which will be attended by the Chancellor and Vice-Chancellor of the University. The Chancellor is the former British Prime Minister, Harold Macmillan, and the Vice-Chancellor is Mr Habakkuk. I'm hoping it will be possible for you to meet them both, and we should manage to cover everything in time for you to be back in London by 7 pm.'

'How did you know I had to be back by 7?'

'You warned me at Ascot.' Stephen could lie very quickly now. He was afraid that if they did not get their miliion soon he would end up a hardened criminal.

Harvey enjoyed his meal, which Stephen had planned almost too cleverly, each course featuring one of Harvey's favourite dishes. After Harvey had drunk a good deal of after-dinner brandy (price £7.25 per bottle, thought Stephen) they strolled through the quiet Magdalen Cloisters past the Song School. The sound of the choristers rehearsing a Gabrieli mass hung gently in the air.

'Gee, I'm surprised you allow record players on that loud,' said Harvey.

Stephen escorted his guest to the Randolph Hotel, pointing out the iron cross set in Broad Street outside Balliol College, said to mark the spot on which Archbishop Cranmer was burnt at the stake for heresy in 1556. Harvey forbore to say that he had never even heard of the reverend gentleman.

Stephen and Harvey parted on the steps of the Randolph.

'See you in the morning, Professor. Thanks for a great evening.'

'My pleasure. I'll pick you up at 10 am. Sleep well – you have a full day ahead of you tomorrow.'

Stephen returned to Magdalen and immediately called Robin.

'All's well, but I nearly went too far. The meal was altogether too carefully chosen – I even had his favourite brandy. Still, it'll keep me on my toes tomorrow. We must remember to avoid overkill. See you then, Robin.'

Stephen reported the same message to Jean-Pierre and James before falling gratefully into bed. The same time tomorrow he would be a wiser man, but would he be a richer one?

16

At 5 am the sun rose over the Cherwell, and those few Oxonians who were about that early would have been left in no doubt as to why the connoisseurs consider Magdalen to be the most beautiful college at either Oxford or Cambridge. Nestling on the banks of the river, its perpendicular architecture is easy on the eye. King Edward VII, Prince Henry, Cardinal Wolsey, Edward Gibbon and Oscar Wilde had all passed through its portals. But the only thing that was passing through Stephen's mind as he lay awake that morning was the education of Harvey Metcalfe.

He could hear his own heartbeat, and for the first time he knew what Robin and Jean-Pierre had been through. It seemed a lifetime since their first meeting only three months before. He smiled to himself at the thought of how close they had all become in their common aim of defeating Harvey Metcalfe. Although Stephen, like James, was beginning to have a sneaking admiration for the man, he was now even more convinced that Metcalfe could be outmanoeuvred when he was not on home ground. For over two hours Stephen lay motionless in bed, deep in thought, going over his plan again and again. When the sun had climbed over the tallest tree, he rose, showered, shaved and dressed slowly and deliberately, his mind still on the day ahead.

He made his face up carefully to age himself by fifteen years. It took him a considerable time, and he wondered whether women had to struggle as long in front of the mirror to achieve the opposite effect. He donned his gown, a magnificent scarlet, proclaiming him a Doctor of Philosophy of the University of Oxford. It amused him that Oxford had to be different. Every other university abbreviated this universal award for research work, to Ph.D. In Oxford, it was D.Phil. He studied himself in the mirror.

'If that doesn't impress Harvey Metcalfe, nothing ever will.'

And what's more, he had the right to wear it. He sat down to study his red dossier for the last time. He had read the closely typewritten pages so often that he practically knew them by heart.

He avoided breakfast. Looking nearly fifty, he would undoubtedly have caused a stir amongst his colleagues, though probably the older dons would have failed to observe anything unusual in his appearance.

Stephen headed out of the college into the High, unnoticed among the thousand or so other graduates all dressed like fourteenth-century archbishops. Anonymity on that particular day was going to be easy. That, and the fact that Harvey would be bemused by the strange traditions of the ancient university, were the two reasons why Stephen had chosen Encaenia for his day of battle.

He arrived at the Randolph at 9.55 am and informed one of the younger bell-boys that his name was Professor Porter and that he had come to pick up Mr Metcalfe. Stephen took a seat in the lounge. The young man scurried away and returned moments later with Harvey.

'Mr Metcalfe – Professor Porter.'

'Thank you,' said Stephen. He made a mental note to return and tip the bell-boy. That touch had been useful, even if it was only part of his job.

'Good morning, Professor,' said Harvey, taking a seat. 'So tell me, what have I let myself in for?'

'Well,' said· Stephen, 'Encaenia begins officially when all the notables of the university take a breakfast of champagne, strawberries and cream at Jesus College, which is known as Lord Nathaniel Crewe's Benefaction.'

'Who's this Lord Crewe guy? Will he be at the breakfast?'

'Only in spirit; the great man died some three hundred years ago. Lord Nathaniel Crewe was a doctor of the university and the Bishop of Durham, and he left £200 a year to the university as a Benefaction to provide the breakfast and an oration which we shall hear later. Of course, the money he willed no longer covers expenses nowadays, with rising prices and inflation, so the university has to dip into its own pocket to continue the tradition. When breakfast is over there is a procession and parade to the Sheldonian Theatre.'

'What happens then?'

'The parade is followed by the most exciting event of the day. The presentation of the Honorands for degrees.'

'The what?' said Harvey.

'The Honorands,' said Stephen. 'They are the distinguished men and women who have been chosen by the senior members of the university to be awarded Oxford honorary degrees.' Stephen looked at his watch. 'In fact, we must leave now to be sure of having a good position on the route from which to watch the procession.'

Stephen rose and guided his guest out of the Randolph Hotel. They strolled down the Broad and found an excellent spot just in front of the Sheldonian Theatre, where the police cleared a little space for Stephen because of his scarlet gown. A few minutes later the procession wound into sight round the corner from the Turl. The police held up all the traffic and kept the public on the pavement.

'Who are the guys in front carrying those clubs?' enquired Harvey.

'They are the University Marshal and the Bedels. They are carrying maces to safeguard the Chancellor's procession.'

'Jesus, of course it's safe. This isn't Central Park, New York.'

'I agree,' said Stephen, 'but it hasn't always been so over

202

the past three hundred years, and tradition dies hard in England.'

'And who's that behind the Bedel fellows?'

'The one wearing the black gown with gold trimmings is the Chancellor of the university, accompanied by his page. The Chancellor is the Right Honourable Harold Macmillan, who was Prime Minister of Great Britain in the late '50's and early '60's.'

'Oh yes, I remember the guy. Tried to get the British into Europe but De Gaulle wouldn't have it.'

'Well, I suppose that's one way of remembering him. Now, he's followed by the Vice-Chancellor, Mr Habakkuk, who is also the Principal of Jesus College.'

'You're losing me, Professor.'

'Well, the Chancellor is always a distinguished Englishman who was educated at Oxford; but the Vice-Chancellor is a leading member of the university itself and is usually chosen from the heads of one of the colleges.'

'Got it, I think.'

'Now, after him, we have the University Registrar, Mr Caston, who is a fellow of Merton College. He is the senior administrator of the university, or you might look on him as the university's top civil servant. He's directly responsible to the Vice-Chancellor and Hebdomadal Council, who are the sort of cabinet for the university. Behind them we have the Senior Proctor, Mr Campbell of Worcester College, and the Junior Proctor, the Reverend Doctor Bennett of New College.'

'What's a Proctor?'

'For over 700 years the Proctors have been responsible for decency and discipline in the university.'

'What? Those two old men take care of 9,000 rowdy youths?'

'Well, they are helped by the bulldogs,' said Stephen.

'Ah, that's better, I suppose. A couple of bites from an old English bulldog would keep anyone in order.'

'No, no,' protested Stephen, trying desperately not to laugh. 'The name bulldog is given to the men who help the Proctors keep order. Now, finally in the procession you can observe that tiny crocodile of colour: it consists of heads of colleges who are doctors of the university, doctors of the university who are not heads of colleges and the heads of colleges who are not doctors of the university, in that order.'

'Listen, Rod, all doctors mean to me is pain and money.'

'They are not that sort of doctor,' replied Stephen.

'Forget it. I love everything but don't expect me to understand what it's all about.'

Stephen watched Harvey's face carefully. He was drinking the scene in and had already become quieter.

'The long line will now proceed into the Sheldonian Theatre and all the people in the procession will take their places in the hemicycle.'

'Excuse me, sir, what type of cycle is that?'

'The hemicycle is a round bank of seats inside the theatre, distinguished only by being the most uncomfortable in Europe. But don't you worry. Thanks to your well-known interest in education at Harvard I've managed to arrange special seats for us and there will just be time for us to secure them ahead of the procession.'

'Well, lead the way, Rod. Do they really know what goes on at Harvard here?'

'Why yes, Mr Metcalfe. You have a reputation in university circles as a generous man interested in financing the pursuit of academic excellence.'

'Well, what do you know.'

Very little, thought Stephen.

He guided Harvey to his reserved seat in the balcony, not wanting his guest to be able to see the individual men and women too clearly. The truth of the matter was that the senior members of the university in the hemicycle were so covered from head to toe in gowns and caps and bow-ties and bands, that even their mothers would not have recognised them. The organist played his final chord and the guests settled.

'The organist,' said Stephen, 'is from my own college.

He's the Choragus, the leader of the chorus, and Deputy Professor of Music.'

Harvey could not take his eyes off the hemicycle and the scarlet-clad figures. He had never seen a sight like it in his life. The music stopped and the Chancellor rose to address the assembled company in vernacular Latin.

'*Causa hujus convocationis est ut . . .*'

'What the hell's he saying?'

'He's telling us why we're here,' explained Stephen. 'I'll try and guide you through it.'

'*Ite Bedelli,*' declared the Chancellor, and the great doors opened for the Bedels to go and fetch the Honorands from the Divinity School. There was a hush as they were led in by the Public Orator, Mr J. G. Griffith, who presented them one by one to the Chancellor, enshrining the careers and achievements of each in polished and witty Latin prose.

Stephen's translation, however, followed a rather more liberal line and was embellished with suggestions that their doctorates were as much the result of financial generosity as of academic prowess.

'That's Lord Amory. They're praising him for all the work he has done in the field of education.'

'How much did he give?'

'Well, he *was* Chancellor of the Exchequer. And there's Lord Hailsham. He has held eight Cabinet positions, including Secretary of State for Education and finally Lord Chancellor. Both he and Lord Amory are receiving the degree of Doctor of Civil Law.'

Harvey recognised Dame Flora Robson, the actress, who was being honoured for a distinguished lifetime in the theatre; Stephen explained that she was receiving the degree of Doctor of Letters, as was the Poet Laureate, Sir John Betjeman. Each was presented with his scroll by the Chancellor, shaken by the hand and then shown to a seat in the front row of the hemicycle.

The final Honorand was Sir George Porter, Director of

the Royal Institution and Nobel Laureate. He received his honorary degree of Doctor of Science.

'My namesake, but no relation. Oh well, nearly through,' said Stephen. 'Just a little prose from John Wain, the Professor of Poetry, about the benefactors of the university.'

Mr Wain delivered the Crewian Oration, which took him some twelve minutes, and Stephen was grateful for something so lively in a language they could both understand. He was only vaguely aware of the recitations of undergraduate prize winners which concluded the proceedings.

The Chancellor of the university rose and led the procession out of the hall.

'Where are they all off to now?' asked Harvey.

'They are going to have lunch at All Souls, where they will be joined by other distinguished guests.'

'God, what I would give to be able to attend that.'

'I have arranged it,' replied Stephen.

Harvey was quite overwhelmed.

'How did you fix that, Professor?'

'The Registrar was most impressed by the interest you have shown in Harvard and I think they hope you might find it possible to assist Oxford in some small way, especially after your wonderful win at Ascot.'

'What a great idea. Why didn't I think of that?'

Stephen tried to show little interest, hoping that by the end of the day he would have thought of it. He had learnt his lesson on overkill. The truth was that the Registrar had never heard of Harvey Metcalfe, but because it was Stephen's last term at Oxford he had been put on the list of invitations by a friend who was a Fellow of All Souls.

They walked over to All Souls, just across the road from the Sheldonian Theatre. Stephen attempted, without much success, to explain the nature of All Souls to Harvey. Indeed, many Oxonians themselves find the college something of an enigma.

'Its corporate name,' Stephen began, 'is the College

of All Souls of the Faithful Departed of Oxford, and it resonantly commemorates the victors of Agincourt. It was intended that masses should forever be said there for the repose of their souls. Its modern role is unique in academic life. All Souls is a society of graduates distinguished either by promise or achievement, mostly academic, from home and abroad, with a sprinkling of men who have made their mark in other fields. The college has no undergraduates, and generally appears to the outside world to do much as it pleases with its massive financial and intellectual resources.'

Stephen and Harvey took their places among the hundred or more guests at the long table in the noble Codrington Library. Stephen spent the entire time ensuring that Harvey was kept fully occupied and was not too obvious. He was thankfully aware that on such occasions people never remember whom they meet or what they say, and happily introduced Harvey to everyone around as a distinguished American philanthropist. He was fortunately placed some way from the Vice-Chancellor, the Registrar and the Secretary of the University Chest.

Harvey was quite overcome by the new experience and was content just to listen to the distinguished men around him – which surprised Stephen, who had feared he would never stop talking. When the meal was over and the guests had risen, Stephen drew a deep breath and played one of his riskier cards. He deliberately marched Harvey up to the Chancellor.

'Chancellor,' he said to Harold Macmillan.

'Yes, young man.'

'May I introduce Mr Harvey Metcalfe from Boston. Mr Metcalfe, as you will know, Chancellor, is a great benefactor of Harvard.'

'Yes, of course. Capital, capital. What brings you to England, Mr Metcalfe?'

Harvey was nearly speechless.

'Well, sir, I mean Chancellor, I came to see my horse Rosalie run in the King George and Elizabeth Stakes.'

Stephen was now standing behind Harvey and made signs to the Chancellor that Harvey's horse had won the race. Harold Macmillan, as game as ever and never one to miss a trick, replied:

'Well, you must have been very pleased with the result, Mr Metcalfe.'

'Well, sir, I guess I was lucky.

'You don't look to me the type of man who depends on luck.'

Stephen took his career firmly in both hands.

'I am trying to interest Mr Metcalfe in supporting some research we are doing at Oxford, Chancellor.'

'What a good idea.' No one knew better than Harold Macmillan, after seven years of leading a political party, how to use flattery on such occasions. 'Keep in touch, young man. Boston was it, Mr Metcalfe? Do give my regards to the Kennedys.'

Macmillan swept off, resplendent in his academic dress. Harvey stood dumbfounded.

'What a great man. What an occasion. I feel I'm part of history. I just wish I deserved to be here.'

Having completed his task, Stephen was determined to escape before any mistakes could be made. He knew Harold Macmillan would shake hands with and talk to over a thousand people that day and the chances of his remembering Harvey were minimal. In any case, it would not much matter if he did. Harvey was, after all, a genuine benefactor of Harvard.

'We ought to leave before the senior members, Mr Metcalfe.'

'Of course, Rod. You're the boss.'

'I think that would be courtesy.'

Once they were out on the street Harvey glanced at his large Jaeger le Coultre watch. It was 2.30 pm.

'Excellent,' said Stephen, who was running three minutes late for the next rendezvous. 'We have just over an hour before the Garden Party. Why don't we take a look at one or two of the colleges.'

They walked slowly up past Brasenose College and Stephen explained that the name really meant 'brass nose' and that the famous original brass nose, a sanctuary knocker of the thirteenth century, was still mounted in the hall. A hundred yards further on, Stephen directed Harvey to the right.

'He's turned right, Robin, and he's heading towards Lincoln College,' said James, well hidden in the entrance of Jesus College.

'Fine,' said Robin and checked his two sons. Aged seven and nine, they stood awkwardly, in unfamiliar Eton suits, ready to play their part as pages, unable to understand what Daddy was up to.

'Are you both ready?'

'Yes, Daddy,' they replied in unison.

Stephen continued walking slowly towards Lincoln, and they were no more than a few paces away when Robin appeared from the main entrance of the college in the official dress of the Vice-Chancellor, bands, collars, white tie and all. He looked fifteen years older and as much like Mr Habakkuk as possible. Perhaps not quite so bald, thought Stephen.

'Would you like to be presented to the Vice-Chancellor?' asked Stephen.

'That would be something,' said Harvey.

'Good afternoon, Vice-Chancellor, may I introduce Mr Harvey Metcalfe.'

Robin doffed his academic cap and bowed. Stephen returned the compliment in like manner. Robin spoke before Stephen could continue:

'Not the benefactor of Harvard University?'

Harvey blushed and smiled at the two little boys who were holding the Vice-Chancellor's train. Robin continued:

'This is a pleasure, Mr Metcalfe. I do hope you are enjoying your visit to Oxford. Mind you, it's not everybody

209

who's fortunate enough to be shown around by a Nobel Laureate.'

'I've enjoyed it immensely, Vice-Chancellor, and I'd like to feel I could help this university in some way.'

'Well, that is excellent news.'

'Look, gentlemen, I'm staying here at the Randolph Hotel. It would be my great pleasure if you could all have tea with me later this afternoon.'

Robin and Stephen were thrown for a moment. He'd done it again – the unexpected. Surely the man realised that on the day of Encaenia the Vice-Chancellor did not have a moment free to attend private tea parties.

Robin recovered first.

'I'm afraid that would be difficult. One has so many responsibilities on a day like this, you understand. Perhaps you could join me in my rooms at the Clarendon Building? That would give us a chance to have a more private discussion?'

Stephen immediately picked up the lead:

'How kind of you, Vice-Chancellor. Will 4.30 be convenient?'

'Yes, yes, that will be fine, Professor.'

Robin tried not to look as if he wanted to run a mile. Although they had only been standing there for about five minutes, to him it seemed a lifetime. He had not objected to being a journalist, or an American surgeon, but he genuinely hated being a Vice-Chancellor. Surely someone would appear at any moment and recognise him for the fraud he was. Thank God most of the undergraduates had gone home the week before. He began to feel even worse when a tourist started taking photos of him.

Now Harvey had turned all their plans upside down. Stephen could only think of Jean-Pierre and of James, the finest string to their dramatic bow, loitering uselessly in fancy dress behind the tea tent at the Garden Party in the grounds of Trinity College, waiting for them.

'Perhaps it might be wise, Vice-Chancellor, if we were to invite the Registrar and the Secretary of the University Chest to join us?'

'First-class idea, Professor. I'll ask them to be there. It isn't every day we're visited by such a distinguished philanthropist. I must take my leave of you now, sir, and proceed to my Garden Party. An honour to have made your acquaintance, Mr Metcalfe, and I look forward to seeing you again at 4.30.'

They shook hands warmly, and Stephen guided Harvey towards Exeter College while Robin darted back into the little room in Lincoln that had been arranged for him. He sank heavily into a seat.

'Are you all right, Daddy?' asked his elder son, William.

'Yes, I'm fine.'

'Do we get the ice cream and Coca-Cola you promised us if we didn't say a word?'

'You certainly do,' said Robin.

Robin slipped off all the paraphernalia – the gown, hood, bow-tie and bands – and placed them back in the suitcase. He returned to the street just in time to watch the real Vice-Chancellor, Mr Habakkuk, leave Jesus College on the opposite side of the road, obviously making his way towards the Garden Party. Robin glanced at his watch. If they had run five minutes late the whole plan would have struck disaster.

Meanwhile, Stephen had done a full circle and was now heading towards Shepherd & Woodward, the tailor's shop which supplies academic dress for the university. He was, however, preoccupied with the thought of getting a message through to James. Stephen and Harvey came to a halt in front of the shop window.

'What magnificent robes.'

'That's the gown of a Doctor of Letters. Would you like to try it on and see how you look?'

'That would be great. But would they allow it?' said Harvey.

'I'm sure they won't object.'

211

They entered the shop, Stephen still in his full academic dress as a Doctor of Philosophy.

'My distinguished guest would like to see the gown of a Doctor of Letters.'

'Certainly, sir,' said the young assistant, who was not going to argue with a Fellow of the University.

He vanished to the back of the shop and returned with a magnificent red gown with grey facing and a black, floppy velvet cap. Stephen forged on, brazen-faced.

'Why don't you try them on, Mr Metcalfe? Let's see what you would look like as an academic.'

The assistant was somewhat surprised. He wished Mr Venables would return from his lunch break.

'Would you care to come through to the fitting-room, sir?'

Harvey disappeared. Stephen slipped out on to the road.

'James, can you hear me? Oh hell, for God's sake answer, James.'

'Cool down, old fellow. I'm having a deuce of a time putting on this ridiculous gown, and in any case, our rendezvous isn't for another seventeen minutes.'

'Cancel it.'

'Cancel it?'

'Yes, and tell Jean-Pierre as well. Both of you report to Robin and meet up as quickly as possible. He will fill you in on the new plans.'

'New plans. Is everything all right, Stephen?'

'Yes, better than I could have hoped for.'

Stephen clicked off his speaker and rushed back into the tailor's shop.

Harvey reappeared as a Doctor of Letters; a more unlikely sight Stephen had not seen for many years.

'You look magnificent.'

'What do they cost?'

'About £100, I think.'

'No, no. How much would I have to give . . .?'

'I have no idea. You would have to discuss that with the Vice-Chancellor after the Garden Party.'

Harvey took a long look at himself in the mirror, and then returned to the dressing-room while Stephen thanked the assistant, asked him to wrap up the gown and cap and send them to the Clarendon building to be left with the porter in the name of Sir John Betjeman. He paid cash. The assistant looked even more bewildered.

'Yes, sir.'

He was not sure what to do, except continue praying for Mr Venables' arrival. His prayers were answered some ten minutes later, but by then Stephen and Harvey were well on their way to Trinity College and the Garden Party.

'Mr Venables, I've just been asked to send the full D.Litt. dress to Sir John Betjeman at the Clarendon Building.'

'Strange. We kitted him out for this morning's ceremony weeks ago. I wonder why he wants a second outfit.'

'He paid cash.'

'Well, send it round to the Clarendon, but be sure it's in his name.'

When Stephen and Harvey arrived at Trinity College shortly after 3.30, the elegant green lawns, the croquet hoops having been removed, were already crowded with over a thousand people. The members of the university wore an odd hybrid dress: best lounge suits or silk dresses topped with gowns, hoods and caps. Cups of tea and crates of strawberries and cucumber sandwiches were disappearing rapidly.

'What a swell party this is,' said Harvey unintentionally mimicking Frank Sinatra. 'You certainly do things in style here, Professor.'

'Yes, the Garden Party is always rather fun. It's the main social event of the university year, which as I explained, is just ending. Half the senior members here will be snatching an afternoon off from reading examination scripts. Exams for the final-year undergraduates have only just ended.'

Stephen observed the Vice-Chancellor, the Registrar and the Secretary of the University Chest carefully, and steered Harvey well away from them, introducing him to as many of the older members of the university as possible, hoping they would not find the encounter too memorable. They spent just over three-quarters of an hour moving from person to person, Stephen feeling rather like an aide-de-camp to an incompetent dignitary whose mouth must be kept shut for fear of a diplomatic incident. Despite Stephen's anxious approach, Harvey was clearly having the time of his life.

'Robin, Robin, can you hear me?'

'Yes, James.'

'Where are you?'

'I'm in the Eastgate Restaurant: come and join me here and bring Jean-Pierre.'

'Fine. We'll be there in five minutes. No, make it ten. With my disguise, I'd better go slowly.'

Robin paid his bill. The children had finished their reward, so he took them out of the Eastgate to a waiting car and instructed the driver, who had been hired especially for the day, to return them to Newbury. They had played their part and now could only get in the way.

'Aren't you coming home with us, Dad?' demanded Jamie.

'No, I'll be back later tonight. Tell your mother to expect me about seven.'

Robin returned to the Eastgate to find Jean-Pierre and James hobbling towards him.

'Why the change of plan?' asked Jean-Pierre. 'It's taken me over an hour to get dressed and ready.'

'Never mind. You're still in the right gear. We had a stroke of luck. I chatted up Harvey in the street and the cocky bastard invited me to tea with him at the Randolph Hotel. I said that would be impossible, but asked him to join me at the Clarendon. Stephen suggested that you two should be invited along as well.'

'Clever,' said James. 'No need for the deception at the Garden Party.'

'Let's hope it's not too clever,' said Jean-Pierre.

'Well, at least we can do the whole damn charade behind closed doors,' said Robin, 'which ought to make it easier. I never did like the idea of walking through the streets with him.'

'With Harvey Metcalfe nothing is ever going to be easy,' said Jean-Pierre.

'I'll get myself into the Clarendon Building by 4.15,' continued Robin. 'You will appear a few minutes after 4.20, Jean-Pierre, and then you, James, about 4.25 pm. But keep exactly to the same routine, act as if the meeting had taken place, as originally planned, at the Garden Party and we had all walked over to the Clarendon together.'

Stephen suggested to Harvey that they should return to the Clarendon Building, as it would be discourteous to be late for the Vice-Chancellor.

'Sure.' Harvey glanced at his watch. 'Jesus, it's 4.30 already.'

They left the Garden Party and walked quickly down towards the Clarendon Building at the bottom of the Broad, Stephen explaining en route that the Clarendon was a sort of Oxford White House where all the officers and officials of the university had their rooms.

The Clarendon is a large, imposing eighteenth-century building which could be mistaken by a visitor for another college. A few steps lead up to an impressive hallway, and on entering you realise you are in a magnificent old building which has been converted for use as offices, with as few changes as possible.

When they arrived the porter greeted them.

'The Vice-Chancellor is expecting us,' said Stephen.

The porter had been somewhat surprised when Robin had arrived fifteen minutes earlier and told him that Mr Habakkuk had asked him to wait in his room; even though Robin was in full academic dress, the porter kept a beady eye on him, not expecting the Vice-Chancellor or any of his staff to return from the Garden Party for at least

215

another hour. The arrival of Stephen gave him a little more confidence. He well remembered the pound he had received for his guided tour of the building.

The porter ushered Stephen and Harvey through to the Vice-Chancellor's rooms and left them alone, tucking another pound note into his pocket.

The Vice-Chancellor's room was in no way pretentious and its beige carpet and pale walls would have given it the look of any middle-ranking civil servant's office, had it not been for the magnificent picture of a village square in France by Wilson Steer which hung over the marble fireplace.

Robin was staring out of the vast windows overlooking the Bodleian Library.

'Good afternoon, Vice-Chancellor.'

Robin spun round. 'Oh, welcome, Professor.'

'You remember Mr Metcalfe?'

'Yes, indeed. How nice to see you again.' Robin shuddered. All he wanted to do was to go home. They chatted for a few minutes. Another knock and Jean-Pierre entered.

'Good afternoon, Registrar.'

'Good afternoon, Vice-Chancellor, Professor Porter.'

'May I introduce Mr Harvey Metcalfe.'

'Good afternoon, sir.'

'Registrar, would you like some . . .'

'Where's this man Metcalfe?'

The three of them stood, stunned, as a man looking ninety entered the room on sticks. He hobbled over to Robin, winked, bowed and said:

'Good afternoon, Vice-Chancellor,' in a loud, crotchety voice.

'Good afternoon, Horsley.'

James went over to Harvey and prodded him with his sticks as if to make sure he was real.

'I have read about you, young man.'

Harvey had not been called young man for thirty years. The others stared at James in admiration. None of them knew that in his last year at university James had played

L'Avare to great acclaim. His Secretary of the Chest was simply a repeat performance, and even Molière would have been pleased with it. James continued:

'You have been most generous to Harvard.'

'That's very kind of you to mention it, sir,' said Harvey respectfully.

'Don't call me sir, young man. I like the look of you – call me Horsley.'

'Yes, Horsley, sir,' blurted Harvey.

The others were only just able to keep a straight face.

'Well, Vice-Chancellor,' continued James. 'You can't have dragged me halfway across the city for my health. What's going on? Where's my sherry?'

Stephen wondered if James was overdoing it, but looking at Harvey saw that he was evidently captivated by the scene. How could a man so mature in one field be so immature in another, he thought. He was beginning to see how Westminster Bridge had been sold to at least four Americans in the past twenty years.

'Well, we were hoping to interest Mr Metcalfe in the work of the university and I felt that the Secretary of the University Chest should be present.'

'What's this chest?' asked Harvey.

'Sort of treasury for the university,' replied James, his voice loud, old and very convincing. 'Why don't you read this?' and he thrust into Harvey's hand an Oxford University Calendar, which Harvey could have obtained at Blackwell's bookshop for £2 as indeed James had.

Stephen was not sure what move to make next when, happily for him, Harvey took over.

'Gentlemen, I would like to say how proud I am to be here today. This has been a wonderful year for me. I was present when an American won Wimbledon, I finally obtained a Van Gogh. My life was saved by a wonderful, wonderful surgeon in Monte Carlo and now here I am in Oxford surrounded by all this history. Gentlemen, it would give me a great deal of pleasure to be associated with this famous university.'

James took the lead again:

'What have you in mind?' he shouted at Harvey, adjusting his hearing-aid.

'Well, sir, I achieved my life's ambition when I received the King George and Elizabeth trophy from your Queen, but the prize money, well, I would like to use that to make a benefaction to your university.'

'But that's over £80,000,' gasped Stephen.

'£81,240 to be exact, sir. But why don't I call it $250,000.'

Stephen, Robin and Jean-Pierre were speechless. James alone was left to command the day. This was the opportunity he had needed to show why his great-grandfather had been one of Wellington's most respected generals.

'We accept. But it would have to be anonymous,' said James. 'I think I can safely say in the circumstances that the Vice-Chancellor would inform Mr Harold Macmillan and Hebdomadal Council, but we would not want a fuss made of it. Of course, Vice-Chancellor, I would ask you to consider an honorary degree.'

Robin was so conscious of James's obvious control of the entire situation that he could only add:

'How would you recommend we go about it, Horsley?'

'Cash cheque, so nobody can trace the money back to Mr Metcalfe. We can't have those bloody men from Cambridge chasing him for the rest of his life. Same way as we did for Sir David – no fuss.'

'I agree,' said Jean-Pierre, not having the vaguest idea what James was talking about. Neither, for that matter, had Harvey.

James nodded to Stephen, who left the Vice-Chancellor's office and made his way to the porter's room to enquire if a parcel had been left for Sir John Betjeman.

'Yes, sir. I don't know why they left it here. I'm not expecting Sir John.'

'Don't worry,' said Stephen. 'He's asked me to pick it up for him.'

Stephen returned to find James holding forth to Harvey

218

on the importance of keeping his donation as a bond between himself and the university.

Stephen undid the box and took out the magnificent gown of a Doctor of Letters. Harvey turned red with embarrassment and pride as Robin placed it on his shoulders, chanting '*De mortuis nil nisi bonum. Dulce et decorum est pro patria mori. Per ardua ad astra. Nil desperandum.*'

'Many congratulations,' bellowed James. 'A pity we could not have organised this to be part of today's ceremony, but for such a munificent gesture as yours we could hardly wait another year.'

Brilliant, thought Stephen, Laurence Olivier could not have done better.

'That's fine by me,' said Harvey, as he sat down and made out a cheque to cash. 'You have my word that this matter will never be mentioned to anyone.'

None of them believed that.

They stood in silence as Harvey rose and passed the cheque to James.

'No, sir.' James transfixed him with a glare.

The others looked dumbfounded.

'The Vice-Chancellor.'

'Of course,' said Harvey. 'Excuse me, sir.'

'Thank you,' said Robin, his hand trembling as he received the cheque. 'A most gracious gift, and you may be sure we shall put it to good use.'

There was a loud knock on the door. They all looked round terrified except for James, who was now ready for anything. It was Harvey's chauffeur. James had always hated the pretentious white uniform with the white hat.

'Ah, the efficient Mr Mellor,' said Harvey. 'Gentlemen, I guarantee he's been watching every move we've made today.'

The four froze, but the chauffeur had clearly made no sinister deductions from his observations.

'Your car is ready, sir. You wanted to be back at

Claridge's by 7 pm to be in good time for your dinner appointment.'

'Young man,' bellowed James.

'Yes, sir,' whimpered the chauffeur.

'Do you realise you are in the presence of the Vice-Chancellor of this university?'

'No, sir. I'm very sorry, sir.'

'Take your hat off immediately.'

'Yes, sir.'

The chauffeur removed his hat and retreated to the car, swearing under his breath.

'Vice-Chancellor, I sure hate to break up our party, but as you've heard I do have an appointment . . .'

'Of course, of course, we understand you're a busy man. May I once again officially thank you for your most generous donation, which will be used to benefit many deserving people.'

'We all hope you have a safe journey back to the States and will remember us as warmly as we shall remember you,' added Jean-Pierre.

Harvey moved towards the door.

'I will take my leave of you now, sir,' shouted James. 'It will take me twenty minutes to get down those damned steps. You are a fine man and you have been most generous.'

'It was nothing,' said Harvey expansively.

True enough, thought James, nothing to you, but everything to us.

Stephen, Robin and Jean-Pierre accompanied Harvey from the Clarendon to the waiting Rolls.

'Professor,' said Harvey, 'I didn't quite understand everything the old guy was saying.' As he spoke he shifted the weight of his heavy robes on his shoulders self-consciously.

'Well, he's very deaf and very old, but his heart's in the right place. He wanted you to know that this has to be an anonymous donation as far as the university is concerned, though, of course, the Oxford hierarchy will be informed

220

of the truth. If it were to be made public all sorts of undesirables who have never done anything for education in the past would come trooping along on the day of Encaenia wanting to buy an honorary degree.'

'Of course, of course. I understand. That's fine by me,' said Harvey. 'I want to thank you for a swell day, Rod, and I wish you all the luck for the future. What a shame our friend Wiley Barker wasn't here to share it all.'

Robin blushed.

Harvey climbed into the Rolls Royce and waved enthusiastically to the three of them as they watched the car start effortlessly on its journey back to London.

Three down and one to go.

'James was brilliant,' said Jean-Pierre. 'When he first came in I didn't know who the hell it was.'

'I agree,' said Robin. 'Let's go and rescue him – he's truly the hero of the day.'

They all three ran up the steps, forgetting that they looked somewhere between the ages of fifty and sixty, and rushed back into the Vice-Chancellor's room to congratulate James, who lay silent in the middle of the floor. He had passed out.

In Magdalen an hour later, with the help of Robin and two large whiskies, James was back to his normal health.

'You were fantastic,' said Stephen, 'just at the point when I was beginning to lose my nerve.'

'You would have received an Academy Award if we could have put it on screen,' said Robin. 'Your father will have to let you go on the stage after that performance.'

James basked in his first moment of glory for three months. He could not wait to tell Anne.

'Anne.' He quickly looked at his watch. '6.30. Oh hell, I must leave at once. I'm meant to be meeting Anne at eight. See you all next Monday in Stephen's rooms for dinner. By then I'll try to have my plan ready.'

James rushed out of the room.

'James.'

His face reappeared round the door. They all said in chorus: 'Fantastic.'

He grinned, ran down the stairs and leapt into his Alfa Romeo, which he now felt they might allow him to keep, and headed towards London at top speed.

It took him 59 minutes from Oxford to the King's Road. The new motorway had made a considerable difference since his undergraduate days. Then the journey had taken anything from an hour and a half to two hours through High Wycombe or Henley.

The reason for his haste was that the meeting with Anne was most important and under no circumstances must he be late; tonight he was due to meet her father. All James knew about him was that he was a senior member of the Diplomatic Corps in Washington. Diplomats always expect you to be on time. He was determined to make a good impression on her father, particularly after Anne's successful weekend at Tathwell Hall. The old man had taken to her at once and never left her side. They had even managed to agree on a wedding date, subject, of course, to the approval of Anne's parents.

James had a quick cold shower and removed all his make-up, losing some sixty years in the process. He had arranged to meet Anne for a drink at Les Ambassadeurs in Mayfair before dinner, and as he put on his dinner-jacket he wondered if he could make it from the King's Road to Hyde Park Corner in 12 minutes: it would require another Monte Carlo. He leapt into his car, revving it quickly through the gears, shot along to Sloane Square, through Eaton Square, up past St George's Hospital, round Hyde Park Corner into Park Lane, and arrived at 7.58 pm.

'Good evening, my lord,' said Mr Mills, the club owner.

'Good evening. I'm dining with Miss Summerton and I've had to leave my car double-parked. Can you take care of it?' said James, dropping the keys and a pound note into the doorman's white-gloved hand.

'Delighted, my lord. Show Lord Brigsley to the private rooms.'

James followed the head porter up the red staircase and into a small Regency room where dinner had been laid for three. He could hear Anne's voice in the next room. She came through, looking even more beautiful than usual in a floating mint-green dress.

'Hello, darling. Come on, I want you to meet Daddy.'

James followed Anne into the next room.

'Daddy, this is James. James, this is my father.'

James went red and then white, and then he felt green.

'How are you, my boy. I've heard so much about you from Rosalie that I can't wait to get acquainted.'

17

'Call me Harvey.'

James stood aghast and speechless. Anne jumped into the silence.

'Would you like a whisky, James?'

James found his voice with difficulty.

'Thank you.'

'I want to know all about you, young man,' continued Harvey, 'what you get up to and why I've seen so little of my daughter in the past few weeks, though I think I can guess the answer to that.'

James drank the whisky in one gulp and Anne quickly refilled his glass.

'You see so little of your daughter because I'm always modelling, which means that I'm very rarely in London.'

'I know, Rosalie . . .'

'James knows me as Anne, Daddy.'

'We christened you Rosalie. It was a good enough name for your mother and me and it ought to be good enough for you.'

'Daddy, whoever heard of a top European model calling herself Rosalie Metcalfe? All my friends know me as Anne Summerton.'

'What do you think, James?'

'I was beginning to think I didn't know her at all,' replied James, recovering slowly. It was obvious that Harvey did not suspect a thing. He had not seen James face to face at the gallery, he had never seen him at Monte Carlo or Ascot, and James had looked ninety years of age at Oxford earlier in the day. He was beginning to believe he had got away with it. But how the hell could he tell the others at their Monday meeting that the final plan, his plan, would be to outwit not Harvey Metcalfe, but his future father-in-law?

'Shall we go through to dinner?'

Harvey did not wait for a reply. He marched on into the adjoining room.

'Rosalie Metcalfe,' whispered James fiercely. 'You've got some explaining to do.'

Anne kissed him gently on the cheek.

'You're the first person who's given me the chance to beat my father at anything. Can't you forgive me? . . . I do love you . . .'

'Come on, you two. Anyone would think you'd never met before.'

Anne and James joined Harvey for dinner. James was amused by the sight of the shrimp cocktail and remembered how Stephen had regretted that touch at Harvey's Magdalen dinner.

'Well, James, I understand you and Anne have fixed a date for the wedding.'

'Yes, sir, if it meets with your approval.'

'Of course I approve. I was hoping Anne would marry Prince Charles after I'd won the King George and Elizabeth Stakes, but an earl will have to do for my only daughter.'

They both laughed, neither of them thinking it was remotely funny.

'I wish you'd come to Wimbledon this year, Rosalie. Imagine, me there on Ladies' Day and the only company I had was a boring old Swiss banker.'

Anne looked at James and grinned.

The waiters cleared the table and wheeled in a trolley bearing a crown of lamb in immaculate cutlet frills, which Harvey studied with great interest.

'Still,' said Harvey, chattering on, 'it was thoughtful of you to ring me at Monte Carlo, my dear. I really thought

I was going to die, you know. James, you wouldn't have believed it. They removed a gall stone the size of a baseball from my stomach. Thank God, the operation was performed by one of the greatest surgeons in the world, Wiley Barker, the President's surgeon. He saved my life.'

Harvey promptly undid his shirt and revealed a 4 inch scar across his vast stomach.

'What do you think of that, James?'

'Remarkable.'

'Daddy, really. We're having dinner.'

'Stop fussing, honey. It won't be the first time James has seen a man's stomach.'

It's not the first time I've seen that one, thought James.

Harvey pushed his shirt back into his trousers and continued:

'Anyway, it was really kind of you to phone me.' He leant over and patted her hand. 'I was a good boy too. I took your advice and kept that nice Doctor Barker on for another week in case any complications arose. Mind you, the price these doctors . . .'

James dropped his wine glass. The claret covered the tablecloth with a red stain.

'I'm so sorry.'

'You all right, James?'

'Yes, sir.'

James looked at Anne in silent outrage. Harvey was quite unperturbed.

'Bring a fresh tablecloth and some more wine for Lord Brigsley.'

The waiter opened a fresh bottle of claret and James decided it was his turn to have a little fun. Anne had been laughing at him for three months. Why shouldn't he tease her a little, if Harvey gave him the chance? Harvey was still talking.

'You a racing man, James?'

'Yes, sir, and I was delighted by your victory in the King George VI and Queen Elizabeth Stakes – for more reasons than you realise.'

226

In the diversion caused by the waiters clearing the table, Anne whispered *sotto voce*:

'Don't try to be too clever, darling – he's not as stupid as he sounds.'

'Well, what do you think of her?'

'I beg your pardon, sir?'

'Rosalie.'

'Magnificent. I put £5 each way on her.'

'Yes, it was a great occasion for me and I was sorry you missed it, Rosalie, because you would have met the Queen and a nice guy from Oxford University called Professor Porter.'

'Professor Porter?' enquired James, burying his face in his wine glass.

'Yes, Professor Porter, James. Do you know him?'

'No, sir, I can't say I do, but didn't he win a Nobel Prize?'

'He sure did and he gave me a wonderful time at Oxford. I enjoyed myself so much I ended up presenting the university with a cheque for $250,000 to be used for research of some kind, so he should be happy.'

'Daddy, you know you're not meant to tell anybody about that.'

'Sure, but James is family now.'

'Why can't you tell anyone else, sir?'

'Well, it's a long story, James, but it was quite an honour for me. You do understand this is highly confidential, but I was Professor Porter's guest at Encaenia. I lunched at All Souls with Mr Harry Macmillan, your dear old Prime Minister, and then I attended the Garden Party, and afterwards I had a meeting with the Vice-Chancellor in his private rooms along with the Registrar and the Secretary of the University Chest. Were you at Oxford, James?'

'Yes, sir. The House.'

'The House?' queried Harvey.

'Christ Church, sir.'

'I'll never understand Oxford.'

'No, sir.'

'You must call me Harvey. Well, as I was saying, we all met at the Clarendon and they stammered and stuttered and they were totally lost for words, except for one funny old guy, who was ninety if he was a day. The truth is that those people just don't know how to approach millionaires for money, so I put them out of their embarrassment and took over. They'd have gone on all day about their beloved Oxford, so eventually I had to shut them up and simply wrote out a cheque for $250,000.'

'That was very generous, Harvey.'

'I'd have given them $500,000 if the old boy had asked. James, you've gone quite white. Do you feel all right?'

'I'm sorry. Yes, I'm fine. I was quite carried away with your description of Oxford.'

Anne joined in:

'Daddy, you made an agreement with the Vice-Chancellor that you would keep your gift as a bond between the university and yourself, and you must promise never to repeat that story again.'

'I think I shall wear the robes for the first time when I open the new Metcalfe library at Harvard in the fall.'

'Oh, no sir,' stammered James a little too quickly, 'that wouldn't be quite the thing. You should only wear full robes in Oxford on ceremonial occasions.'

'Gee, what a shame. Still, I know what sticklers you English are for etiquette. Which reminds me, we ought to discuss your wedding. I suppose you two will want to live in England?'

'Yes, Daddy, but we'll visit you every year and when you make your annual trip to Europe you can come and stay with us.'

The waiters cleared the table again and reappeared with Harvey's favourite strawberries. Anne tried to steer the conversation to domestic issues and stop her father returning to what he'd been up to during the past two months, while James did everything to get him back on the subject.

'Coffee or liqueur, sir?'

'No, thank you,' said Harvey. 'Just the check. I thought

we'd have a drink in my suite at Claridge's, Rosalie. I have something to show you both. It's a bit of a surprise.'

'I can't wait, Daddy. I love surprises. Don't you, James?'

'Normally yes, but I think I've had enough for one day.'

James left them and drove the Alfa Romeo to Claridge's garage so that Anne could have a few moments alone with her father. They strolled along Curzon Street, arm in arm.

'Isn't he wonderful, Daddy?'

'Yeah, great guy. Didn't seem too bright to begin with, but he cheered up as the meal went on. And fancy my little girl turning out to be a genuine English lady. Your Momma's tickled pink and I'm pleased that we've patched up our silly quarrel.'

'Oh, you helped a lot, Daddy.'

'I did?' queried Harvey.

'Yes, I managed to get things back into perspective during the last few weeks. Now tell me, what is your little surprise?'

'Wait and see, honey. It's your wedding present.'

James rejoined them at the entrance to Claridge's. He could tell from Anne's look that Harvey had given him the seal of parental approval.

'Good evening, sir. Good evening, my lord.'

'Hi there, Albert. Could you fix some coffee and a bottle of Rémy Martin to be sent up to my suite?'

'Right away, sir.'

James had never seen the Royal Suite before. Off the small entrance room, there is a master bedroom on the right and a sitting-room on the left. Harvey took them straight to the sitting-room.

'Children, you are about to see your wedding present.'

He threw the door open in dramatic style and there on the far wall, facing them, was the Van Gogh. They both stared, quite unable to speak.

'That's exactly how it left me,' said Harvey. 'Speechless.'

'Daddy.' Anne swallowed. 'A Van Gogh. But you've always wanted a Van Gogh. You've dreamed of possessing one for years. I couldn't possibly deprive you of it now, and anyway I couldn't think of having anything as valuable as that in my house. Think of the security risk – we don't have the protection you have.' Anne stammered on. 'We couldn't let you sacrifice the pride of your collection, could we, James?'

'Absolutely not,' said James with great feeling. 'I wouldn't have a moment's peace with that on the premises.'

'Keep the painting in Boston, Daddy, in a setting worthy of it.'

'But I thought you'd love the idea, Rosalie.'

'I do, I do, Daddy, I just don't want the responsibility, and in any case Mother must have the chance to enjoy it too. You can always leave it to James and me if you like.'

'What a great idea, Rosalie. That way we can both enjoy the painting. Now I shall have to think of another wedding present. She nearly got the better of me then, James, and she hasn't done that in twenty-four years.'

'Well, I've managed it two or three times lately, Daddy, and I'm still hoping I shall do it once more.'

Harvey ignored Anne's remark and went on talking.

'That's the King George and Elizabeth trophy,' he said, pointing to a magnificent bronze sculpture of a horse and jockey with his hoop and quartered cap studded with diamonds. 'The race is so important they present a new trophy every year – so it's mine for life.'

James was thankful that the trophy at least was genuine.

The coffee and brandy arrived and they settled down to discuss the wedding in detail.

'Now, Rosalie, you must fly over to Lincoln next week and help your mother with the arrangements, otherwise she'll panic and nothing will get done. And, James, you let me know how many people you'll have coming over and I'll put them up at the Ritz. The wedding will be in Trinity Church, Copley Square, and we'll have a real English-style reception afterwards back in my home in Lincoln. Does all that make sense, James?'

'Sounds wonderful. You're a very well organised man, Harvey.'

'Always have been, James. Find it pays in the long run. Now, you and Rosalie must get the details sewn up before she comes over next week; you may not have realised it, but I'm returning to America tomorrow.'

Page 38A of the blue dossier, thought James.

James and Anne spent another hour chatting about the wedding arrangements and left Harvey just before midnight.

'I'll see you first thing in the morning, Daddy.'

'Goodnight, sir.'

James shook hands and left.

'I told you he was super.'

'He's a fine young man and your mother will be very pleased.'

James said nothing to Anne in the lift on the way down because two other men stood beside them in silence, also intent on reaching the ground floor. But once they were in the Alfa Romeo he took Anne by the scruff of her neck, threw her across his legs, and spanked her so hard that she didn't know whether to laugh or cry.

'What's that for?'

'Just in case you ever forget after we're married who's the head of this household.'

'You male chauvinist pig, I was only trying to help.'

James drove at furious speed to Anne's flat.

'What about all your so-called background – "My parents live in Washington and Daddy's in the Diplomatic Corps",' James mimicked. 'Some diplomat.'

'I know, darling, but I had to think of something once I'd realised who it was you were up against.'

'What in hell's name am I going to tell the others?'

'Nothing. You invite them to the wedding, explain that my mother is American and that's why we're getting married in Boston. I'd give the earth to see their faces when they discover who your father-in-law is. In any case, you

231

still have a plan to think of and you can't possibly let them down.'

'But the circumstances have changed.'

'No, they haven't. The truth of the matter is that they've all succeeded and you've failed, so you be sure you think of a plan by the time you reach America.'

'It's obvious now that we wouldn't have succeeded without your help.'

'Nonsense, darling. I had nothing to do with Jean-Pierre's scheme. I just added some background colour here and there – Promise you'll never spank me again?'

'Certainly I will, every time I think of that picture, but now, darling . . .'

'James, you're a sex maniac.'

'I know, darling. How do you think we Brigsleys have reared tribes of little lords for generations?'

Anne left James early the next morning to spend some time with her father, and they both saw him off at the airport on the midday flight to Boston. Anne could not resist asking in the car on the way back what James had decided to tell the others. She could get no response other than:

'Wait and see. I'm not having it changed behind my back. I'm only too glad you're off to America on Monday.'

18

Monday was a double hell for James. First, he had to see Anne off on the morning TWA flight for Boston, and then he had to spend the rest of the day preparing for the Team meeting in the evening. The other three had now completed their operations and would be waiting to hear what he had come up with. It was twice as hard now he knew that the victim was to be his father-in-law, but he realised that Anne was right and he could not put that forward as an excuse. Nevertheless, he still had to relieve Harvey of $250,000. To think he could have done it with one sentence at Oxford. That was another thing he could not tell the rest of the Team.

As Oxford had been Stephen's victory, the Team dinner was at Magdalen College and James travelled out of London just after the rush hour, past the White City Stadium and on down the M40 to Oxford.

'You're always last, James,' said Stephen.

'Sorry, I've been up to my eyes . . .'

'Preparing a good plan, I hope,' said Jean-Pierre.

James didn't answer. How well they all knew each other now, he thought. In twelve weeks James felt he had come to know more about these three men than any of the so-called friends he'd known for twenty years. For the first time he understood why his father continually referred back to friendships formed during the war with men he normally would never have met. He began to realise how much he was going to miss Stephen when he returned to America. Success was, in fact, going to split them up.

James would have been the last to go through the agony of another Prospecta Oil, but it had certainly had its compensations.

Stephen could never treat any occasion as a celebration, and as soon as the servants had brought in the first course and left, he banged the table with a spoon and declared that the meeting was in progress.

'Make me a promise,' said Jean-Pierre.

'What's that?' asked Stephen.

'When we have every last penny back, I can sit at the top of the table and you won't speak until you're spoken to.'

'Agreed,' said Stephen, 'but not until we do have every last penny. The position at the moment is that we've received $777,560. Expenses on this operation have totalled $5,178, making a grand total of $27,661.24. Therefore, Metcalfe still owes us $250,101.24.'

Stephen handed round a copy of the current balance sheet.

'These sheets are to be added to your own folders as pages 63C. Any questions?'

'Yes, why were the expenses so high for this operation?' asked Robin.

'Well, over and above the obvious things,' said Stephen, 'the truth is that we've been hit by the floating exchange rate of sterling against the dollar. At the beginning of this operation you could get $2.44 to the pound. This morning I could only get $2.32. I'm spending in pounds but charging Metcalfe in dollars at the going rate.'

'Not going to let him off with one penny, are you?' said James.

'Not one penny. Now, before we go on I should like to place on record . . .'

'This gets more like a meeting of the House of Commons every time,' said Jean-Pierre.

'Stop croaking, frog,' said Robin.

'Listen, you Harley Street pimp.'

Uproar broke out. The college scouts, who had seen

some rowdy gatherings in their time, wondered if they would have to be called in to help before the evening was completed.

'Quiet,' the sharp, senatorial voice of Stephen brought them all back to order. 'I know you're in high spirits, but we still have to get $250,101.24.'

'We must on no account forget the 24 cents, Stephen.'

'You weren't as noisy the first time you had dinner here, Jean-Pierre:

The man that once did sell the lion's skin
While the beast liv'd, was killed with hunting him.'

The table was silent.

'Harvey still owes the Team money and it'll be just as hard to acquire the last quarter as it was with the first three-quarters. Before I hand over to James, I'd like to place on record that his performance at the Clarendon was nothing less than brilliant.'

Robin and Jean-Pierre banged the table in appreciation and agreement.

'Now, James, we're all ears.'

Once again the room fell into silence.

'My plan is nearly complete,' began James.

The others looked disbelieving.

'But I have something to tell you, which I hope will allow me a short respite before we carry it out.'

'You're going to get married.'

'Quite right, Jean-Pierre, as usual.'

'I could tell the moment you walked in. When do we meet her, James?'

'Not until it's too late for her to change her mind, Jean-Pierre.'

Stephen consulted his diary.

'How much reprieve are you asking for?'

'Well, Anne and I are getting married on August 3rd, in Boston. Anne's mother is American,' explained James, 'and although Anne lives in England, it would please her mother if she was married at home. Then there'll be the honeymoon and after that we anticipate returning to England on August 25th. My plan for Mr Metcalfe ought to be carried out on September 15th, the closing day of the Stock Exchange account.'

'I'm sure that's acceptable, James. All agreed?'

Robin and Jean-Pierre nodded.

James launched into his plan.

'I shall require a telex and seven telephones. They'll need to be installed in my flat. Jean-Pierre will have to be in Paris at the Bourse, Stephen in Chicago on the commodity market and Robin in London at Lloyds. I will present a full blue dossier as soon as I return from my honeymoon.'

They were all struck dumb with admiration and James paused for dramatic effect.

'Very good, James,' said Stephen. 'We'll await the details with interest. What further instructions do you have?'

'First, Stephen, you must know the opening and closing price of gold in Johannesburg, Zürich, New York and London each day for the next month. Jean-Pierre, you must know the price of the Deutschmark, the French franc and the pound against the dollar every day during the same period, and Robin must master a telex machine and PBX 8-line switchboard by September 2nd. You must be as competent as an international operator.'

'Always get the easy jobs, Robin, don't you?' said Jean-Pierre.

'You can . . .'

'Shut up, both of you,' said James.

Their faces registered surprise and respect.

'I've made notes for all of you to work on.'

James handed two typewritten sheets to each member of the Team.

'You add these to your dossiers as pages 74 and 75 and they should keep you occupied for at least a month. Finally, you're all invited to the wedding of Miss Anne Summerton to James Brigsley. I shan't bother issuing you with formal invitations at such short notice, but I've reserved seats for us on a 747 on the afternoon of August 2nd and we're all booked in at the Ritz in Boston for the night. I hope you'll honour me by being ushers.'

Even James was impressed by his own efficiency. The others received the plane tickets and instructions with astonishment.

'We'll meet at the airport at 3 pm and during the flight I shall test you on your dossier notes.'

'Yes, sir,' said Jean-Pierre.

'Your test, Jean-Pierre, will be in both French and English, as you'll be required to converse in two languages over a trans-Atlantic telephone, and appear expert on foreign currency exchange.'

There were no more jokes about James that evening, and as he travelled back up the motorway he felt a new man. Not only had he been the star of the Oxford plan; now he had the other three on the run. He would come out on top and do his old pa yet.

19

For a change James was the first to arrive at a meeting and the others joined him at Heathrow. He had gained the upper hand and was determined not to lose it. Robin arrived last, clutching an armful of newspapers.

'We're only going to be away for two days,' said Stephen.

'I know, but I always miss the English papers, so I've brought enough for tomorrow as well.'

Jean-Pierre threw his arms up in Gallic despair.

They checked their luggage through the No. 3 Terminal and boarded the British Airways 747 flight to Logan International Airport.

'It's more like a football ground,' said Robin, stepping for the first time inside a jumbo jet.

'It holds 350 people. About the size of the crowds most of your English clubs deserve,' said Jean-Pierre.

'Cut it out,' said James sternly, not realising that they were both nervous passengers and were only trying to relieve the tension. Later, during take-off, they both pretended to read, but as soon as the plane reached 3,000 feet and the little white light that says 'fasten seat-belts' switched off, they were back in top form.

The Team chewed its way stolidly through a plastic dinner of cold chicken and Algerian red wine.

'I do hope, James,' said Jean-Pierre, 'that your father-in-law will feed us a little better.'

After the meal James allowed them to watch the film, but insisted that as soon as it was over they must prepare to be tested one by one. Robin and Jean-Pierre moved back fifteen rows to watch *The Sting*. Stephen stayed in his seat to be grilled by James.

James handed Stephen a typewritten sheet of forty questions on the price of gold all over the world and the market movements during the past four weeks. Stephen completed it in twenty-two minutes, and it came as no surprise to James to find that every answer was correct: Stephen had always been the backbone of the Team, and it was his logical brain that had really defeated Harvey Metcalfe.

Stephen and James dozed intermittently until Robin and Jean-Pierre returned, when they were given their forty questions. Robin took thirty minutes over his and scored 38 out of 40. Jean-Pierre took twenty-seven minutes and scored 37.

'Stephen got 40 out of 40,' said James.

'He would,' said Jean-Pierre.

Robin looked a little sheepish.

'And so will you by September 2nd. Understood?'

They both nodded.

'Have you seen *The Sting*?' asked Robin,

'No,' replied Stephen. 'I rarely go to the cinema.'

'They're not in our league. One big operation, and they don't even keep the money.'

'Go to sleep, Robin.'

The meal, the film and James's quizzes had taken up most of the six-hour flight and they all nodded off in the last hour, to be woken by suddenly by:

'This is your captain speaking. We are approaching Logan International Airport and our flight is running twenty minutes late. We expect to land at 7.15 in approximately ten minutes. We hope you have enjoyed your flight and will travel again with British Airways.'

Customs took a little longer than usual as they all three had brought presents for the wedding and did not want James to know what they were. They had considerable trouble in explaining to the customs officer why one of the two Piaget watches had inscribed on the back: 'Part of the illicit profits from Prospecta Oil – the three who had plans.'

239

When they finally escaped the customs official, they found Anne standing at the entrance by a large Cadillac waiting to chauffeur them to the hotel.

'Now we know why it took you so long to come up with something: you were genuinely distracted. Congratulations, James, you're entirely forgiven,' said Jean-Pierre, and threw his arms round Anne as only a Frenchman could. Robin introduced himself and kissed her gently on the cheek. Stephen shook hands with her rather formally. They bustled into the car, Jean-Pierre sitting next to Anne.

'Miss Summerton,' stuttered Stephen.

'Do call me Anne.'

'Will the reception be at the hotel?'

'No,' replied Anne, 'at my parents' house, but there'll be a car to pick you up and take you there after the wedding. Your only responsibility is to see that James gets to the church by 3.30. Other than that you have nothing to worry about. While I think of it, James, your father and mother arrived yesterday and they're staying with my parents. We thought it might not be a good idea for you to spend this evening at home because Mother's flapping about everything.'

'Anything you say, darling.'

'If you should change your mind between now and tomorrow,' said Jean-Pierre, 'I find myself available. I may not be blessed with noble blood, but there are one or two compensations we French can always offer.'

Anne smiled to herself. 'You're a little late, Jean-Pierre. In any case, I don't like beards.'

'But I only . . .' began Jean-Pierre.

The others glared at him.

At the hotel they left Anne and James alone while they went to unpack.

'Do they know, darling?'

'They haven't the slightest idea,' replied James. 'They're going to get the surprise of their life tomorrow.'

'Is your plan ready?'

'Wait and see.'

'Well, I have one,' said Anne. 'When's yours scheduled for?'

'September 13th.'

'I win then – mine's for tomorrow.'

'What, you weren't meant to . . . '

'Don't worry. You just concentrate on getting married . . . to me.'

'Can't we go somewhere?'

'No, you terrible man. You can wait until tomorrow.'

'I do love you.'

'Go to bed, you silly thing. I love you too, but I must go home, otherwise nothing'll be ready.'

James took the lift to the seventh floor and joined the others for coffee.

'Anyone for blackjack?'

'Not with you, you pirate,' said Robin 'You've been tutored by the biggest crook alive.'

The Team were in top form and looking forward to the wedding. In spite of the transatlantic time dislocation they didn't depart for their separate rooms until well after midnight. Even then, James lay awake for some time, turning over the same question in his mind:

'I wonder what's she's up to this time?'

20

Boston in August is as beautiful a city as any in America, and the Team enjoyed a large breakfast in James's room.

'I don't think he looks up to it,' said Jean-Pierre. 'You're the captain of the Team, Stephen. I volunteer to take his place.'

'It'll cost you $250,000.'

'Agreed,' said Jean-Pierre.

'You don't have $250,000,' said Stephen. 'You have $187,474.69, being one quarter of what's been raised so far, so my decision is that James must be the bridegroom.'

'It's an Anglo-Saxon plot,' said Jean-Pierre, 'and when James has successfully completed his plan and we have the full amount, I shall re-open negotiations.'

They sat talking and laughing for a long time over the toast and coffee. Stephen regarded them fondly, regretting how rarely they would meet once, *if*, he corrected himself sternly, James's operation were accomplished successfully. If Harvey Metcalfe had ever had a team like this on his side instead of against him, he would have been the richest man in the world.

'You're dreaming, Stephen.'

'Yes, I'm sorry. I mustn't·forget that Anne has put me in charge.'

'Here we go again,' said Jean-Pierre. 'What time shall we report, Professor?'

'One hour from now, fully dressed to inspect James and take him to the church. Jean-Pierre, you will go and buy four carnations – three red ones and one white. Robin, you will arrange for the taxi and I shall take care of James.'

Robin and Jean-Pierre left, singing the *Marseillaise* lustily in two different keys. James and Stephen watched them depart.

'How are you feeling, James?'

'Great. I'm only sorry that I didn't complete my plan before today.'

'Doesn't matter at all. September 13th will be quite early enough. In any case, the break will do us no harm.'

'We'd never have managed it without you. You know that, don't you, Stephen? We'd all be facing ruin and I wouldn't even have met Anne. We all owe you so much.'

Stephen stared fixedly out of the window, unable to reply.

'Three red and one white,' said Jean-Pierre, 'as instructed, and I presume the white one is for me.'

'Pin it on James. Not behind his ear, Jean-Pierre.'

'You look fantastic, but I still fail to see what the lady sees in you,' said Jean-Pierre. Although the four of them were ready to leave, they still had half an hour to kill before the taxi was due. Jean-Pierre opened a bottle of champagne and they toasted James's health, the Team's health, Her Majesty The Queen, the President of the United States, and finally, with simulated reluctance, the President of France. Having finished the bottle, Stephen thought it wise for them to leave immediately and dragged the other three down to the waiting taxi.

'Keep smiling, James. We're with you.'

And they bundled him into the back.

The taxi took only a few minutes to reach Trinity Church, Copley Square, and the driver was not unhappy to be rid of the four of them.

'3.15 pm. Anne will be very pleased with me,' said Stephen.

He escorted the bridegroom to the front pew on the right-hand side of the church, while Jean-Pierre made eyes at the prettiest of the girls. Robin helped hand out the wedding sheets while one thousand overdressed guests waited for the bride.

Stephen had just come to Robin's aid on the steps of the church and Jean-Pierre had joined them, suggesting they took their seats, when the Rolls Royce arrived. They were riveted to the steps by the beauty of Anne in her Balenciaga wedding gown. Her father stepped out behind her. She took his arm and proceeded to climb the steps.

The three stood motionless, like sheep in the stare of a python.

'The bastard.'

'Who's been conning who?'

'She must have known all along.'

Harvey beamed vaguely at them as he walked past with Anne on his arm. They proceeded down the aisle.

'Good God,' thought Stephen. 'He didn't recognise any of us.'

They took their places at the back of the church, out of earshot of the vast congregation The organist stopped playing when Anne reached the altar.

'Harvey can't know,' said Stephen.

'How do you work that out?' asked Jean-Pierre.

'Because James would never have put us through this unless he'd passed the test himself at some earlier date.'

'Good thinking,' whispered Robin.

'I require and charge you both, as ye will answer at the dreadful day of judgment when the secrets of all hearts shall be disclosed . . .'

'I'd like to know one or two secrets right now,' said Jean-Pierre. 'To start with, how long has she known?'

'James Clarence Spencer, wilt thou have this woman to thy wedded wife, to live together after God's ordinance in the Holy estate of Matrimony? Wilt thou love her, comfort her, honour and keep her in sickness and in health and, forsaking all other, keep thee only unto her, so long as ye both shall live?'

'I will.'

'Rosalie Arlene, wilt thou have this man to thy wedded husband, to live . . . '

'I think,' said Stephen, 'we can be sure that she's a fully fledged member of the Team; otherwise we could never have succeeded at Monte Carlo or Oxford.'

'. . . so long as ye both shall live?'

'I will.'

'Who giveth this woman to be married to this man?'

Harvey bustled forward and took Anne's hand and gave it to the priest.

'I, James Clarence Spencer, take thee, Rosalie Arlene, to my wedded wife . . .'

'And what's more, why should he recognise us when he's only seen each of us once, and not as we really are,' continued Stephen.

'And thereto I plight thee my troth.'

'I, Rosalie Arlene, take thee, James Clarence Spencer, to my wedded husband . . .'

'But he must have a chance of working it out if we hang around,' said Robin.

'Not necessarily,' said Stephen. 'No need to panic. Our secret has always been to catch him off home ground.'

'But now he's on home ground,' said Jean-Pierre.

'No, he isn't. It's his daughter's wedding day and it's totally strange to the man. Naturally, we avoid him at the reception, but we don't make it too obvious.'

'You'll have to hold my hand,' said Robin.

'I will,' volunteered Jean-Pierre.

'Just remember to act naturally.'

'. . . and thereto I give thee my troth.'

Anne was quiet and shy, her voice only just reaching the astonished three at the back. James's was clear and firm:

'With this ring I thee wed, with my body I thee worship, and with all my worldly goods I thee endow . . .'

'And with some of ours too,' said Jean-Pierre.

'In the name of the Father, and of the Son and of the Holy Spirit. Amen.'

'Let us pray,' intoned the priest.

'I know what I'm going to pray,' said Robin. 'To be delivered out of the power of our enemy and from the hands of all that hate us.'

'O Eternal God, Creator and Preserver of all mankind . . .'

'We're near the end now,' said Stephen.

'An unfortunate turn of phrase,' offered Robin.

'Silence,' said Jean-Pierre. 'I agree with Stephen. We've got the measure of Metcalfe, just relax.'

'Those whom God hath joined together let no man put asunder.'

Jean-Pierre continued mumbling to himself, but it didn't sound like a prayer.

The blast of Handel's Wedding March from the organ brought them all back to the occasion. The ceremony was over and Lord and Lady Brigsley walked down the aisle watched by two thousand smiling eyes. Stephen looked amused, Jean-Pierre envious, and Robin nervous. James smiled beatifically as he passed them.

After a ten-minute session for the photographers on the steps of the church, the Rolls Royce carried the newly married couple back to the Metcalfes' house in Lincoln. Harvey and the Countess of Louth took the second car, and the Earl and Arlene, Anne's mother, took the third. Stephen, Robin and Jean-Pierre followed some twenty minutes later, still arguing the pros and cons of bearding the lion in his own den.

Harvey Metcalfe's Georgian house was magnificent, with an oriental garden leading down to a lake, great beds of roses and in the conservatory his pride and joy, his collection of rare orchids.

'I never thought I'd see this,' said Jean-Pierre.

'Nor me,' said Robin, 'and now that I have, I'm not too happy.'

'Let's run the gauntlet,' said Stephen. 'I suggest that we join the receiving line at well-separated intervals. I'll go first. Robin, you come second, at least twenty places

246

behind, and Jean-Pierre, you come third, at least twenty places behind Robin, and *act naturally*. We're just friends of James's from England. Now, when you take your places in the queue, listen to the conversation. Try and find someone who's a close friend of Harvey's and jump immediately in front of them. When it comes to your turn to shake hands, Harvey's eyes will already be on the next person because he won't know you and will want to talk to them. That way we should escape.'

'Brilliant, Professor,' said Jean-Pierre.

The queue seemed interminably long. A thousand people shuffled past the outstretched hands of Mr and Mrs Metcalfe, the Earl and Countess of Louth, and Anne and James. Stephen eventually made it and passed with flying colours.

'So glad you could come,' said Anne.

Stephen did not reply.

'Good to see you, Stephen.'

'We all admire your plan, James.'

Stephen slipped into the main ballroom and hid behind a pillar on the other side of the room, as far as he could be from the multi-storey wedding cake in the centre.

Robin was next and avoided looking Harvey in the eyes.

'How kind of you to come all this way,' said Anne.

Robin mumbled something under his breath.

'Hope you've enjoyed yourself today, Robin?'

James was obviously having the time of his life. After being put through it in the same way by Anne, he was relishing the Team's discomfiture.

'You're a bastard, James.'

'Not too loud, old fellow. My mother and father might hear you.'

Robin slipped through to the ballroom and, after a search behind all the pillars, found Stephen.

'Did you get through all right?'

'I think so, but I don't want to see him ever again. What time is the plane back?'

'8 pm. Now don't panic. Keep your eye out for Jean-Pierre.'

'Bloody good thing he kept his beard,' said Robin.

Jean-Pierre shook hands with Harvey, who was already intent on the next guest as Jean-Pierre had, by shameless queue-barging, managed to secure a place in front of a Boston banker who was obviously a close friend of Harvey's.

'Good to see you, Marvin.'

Jean-Pierre had escaped. He kissed Anne on both cheeks, whispered in her ear, 'Game, set and match to James,' and went off in search of Stephen and Robin. He forgot his original instructions when he found himself face to face with the chief bridesmaid.

'Did you enjoy the wedding?' she asked.

'Of course. I always judge weddings by the bridesmaids, not the bride.'

She blushed with pleasure.

'This must have cost a fortune,' she continued.

'Yes, my dear, and I know whose,' said Jean-Pierre, slipping his arm around her waist.

Four hands grabbed a protesting Jean-Pierre and unceremoniously dragged him behind the pillar.

'For God's sake, Jean-Pierre. She's not a day over seventeen. We don't want to go to jail for rape of a juvenile as well as theft. Drink this and behave yourself.' Robin thrust a glass of champagne into his hand.

The champagne flowed and even Stephen had a little too much. They were all clinging to their pillar for support by the time the toast-master called for silence.

'My lords, ladies and gentlemen. Pray silence for the Viscount Brigsley, the bridegroom.'

James made an impressive speech. The actor in him took over and the Americans adored it. Even his father had a look of admiration on his face. The toast-master then introduced Harvey, who spoke long and loud. He cracked his favourite joke about marrying off his daughter to Prince Charles, at which the assembled guests roared heartily as they always do at weddings, even for the weakest joke. He ended by calling the toast for the bride and groom.

When the applause had died down, and the hubbub of chatter had struck up again, Harvey took an envelope from his pocket and kissed his daughter on the cheek.

'Rosalie, here's a little wedding present for you, to make up for letting me keep the Van Gogh. I know you'll put it to good use.'

Harvey passed her the white envelope. Inside there was a cheque for $250,000. Anne kissed her father with genuine affection.

'Thank you, Daddy, I promise you James and I will use it wisely.'

She hurried off in pursuit of James, whom she found besieged by a group of American matrons:

'Is it true you're related to the Queen . . .?'

'I never met a real live lord . . .'

'I do hope you'll invite us over to see your castle . . .?'

'There are no castles in the King's Road,' said James, relieved to be rescued by Anne.

'Darling, can you spare me a minute?'

James excused himself and followed Anne, but they found it almost impossible to escape the crowd.

'Look,' she said. 'Quickly.'

James took the cheque.

'Good God – $250,000.'

'You know what I'm going to do with it, don't you?'

'Yes, darling.'

Anne hunted for Stephen, Robin and Jean-Pierre, which was not an easy task as they were still hidden behind a pillar in the far corner. She was eventually guided to the spot by the subdued but spirited rendering of 'Who Wants to be a Millionaire?' issuing from behind it.

'Can you lend me a pen, Stephen?'

Three pens shot out for her use.

She took the cheque from the middle of her bouquet

249

and wrote on its back, 'Rosalie Brigsley – pay Stephen Bradley'. She handed it to him.

'Yours, I believe.'

The three of them stared at the cheque. She was gone before they could even comment.

'What a girl our James has gone and married,' said Jean-Pierre.

'You're drunk, you frog,' said Robin.

'How dare you, sir, suggest that a Frenchman could get drunk on champagne. I demand satisfaction. Choose your weapons.'

'Champagne corks.'

'Quiet,' said Stephen. 'You'll give yourselves away.'

'Well now, tell me, Professor, what's the latest financial position?'

'I'm just working it out now,' said Stephen.

'What?' said Robin and Jean-Pierre together, but they were too happy to argue.

'He still owes us $101 and 24 cents.'

'DISGRACEFUL,' said Jean-Pierre. 'Burn the place down.'

Anne and James left to change, while Stephen, Robin and Jean-Pierre forced down some more champagne. The toast-master announced that the bride and groom would be leaving in approximately fifteen minutes and requested the guests to gather in the main hall and courtyard.

'Come on, we must watch them go,' said Stephen. The drink had given them new confidence and they took their places near the car.

It was Stephen who heard Harvey say, 'God damn it. Do I have to think of everything?' and watched him look round his guests until his eyes fell on the trio. Stephen's legs turned to jelly as Harvey's finger beckoned him.

'Hey, you, weren't you an usher?'

'Yes, sir.'

'Rosalie is going to leave at any moment and there are no flowers for her. God knows what's happened to them, but there are no flowers. Grab a car. There's a florist half a mile down the road, but hurry.'

'Yes, sir.'

'Say, don't I know you from somewhere?'

'Yes, sir, I mean, no sir. I'll go and get the flowers.'

Stephen turned and fled. Robin and Jean-Pierre, who had been watching horrified, thinking that Harvey had at last rumbled them, ran after him. When he reached the back of the house, Stephen came to a halt and stared at the most beautiful bed of roses. Robin and Jean-Pierre shot straight past him, stopped, turned round and staggered back.

'What the hell are you up to – picking flowers for your own funeral?'

'It's only Metcalfe's wishes. Somebody forgot the flowers for Anne and I have five minutes to get them, so start picking.'

'*Mes enfants*, do you see what I see?'

The others looked up. Jean-Pierre was staring rapturously at the conservatory.

Stephen rushed back to the front of the house, the prize orchids in his arms, followed by Robin and Jean-Pierre. He was just in time to pass them over to Harvey before James and Anne came out of the house.

'Magnificent. They're my favourite flowers. How much were they?'

'$100,' replied Stephen, without thinking.

Harvey handed over two $50 bills. Stephen retreated, sweating, to join Robin and Jean-Pierre.

James and Anne fought their way through the crowd. No man in the gathering could take his eyes off her.

'Oh Daddy, orchids, how beautiful.' Anne kissed Harvey. 'You've made this the most wonderful day in my life . . .'

The Rolls Royce moved slowly down the drive away from the large crowd on its way to the airport, where James and Anne were to catch the flight to San Francisco, their first stop on the way to Hawaii. As the car glided round the house, Anne stared at the empty conservatory and then at the flowers in her arms. James did not notice. He was thinking of other things.

'Do you think they'll ever forgive me?' he said.

'I'm sure they'll find a way, darling. But do let me into a secret. Did you really have a plan?'

'I knew you wouldn't be able to resist asking me that, and the truth is . . .'

The car purred effortlessly along the highway and only the chauffeur heard his reply.

Stephen, Robin and Jean-Pierre watched the guests dispersing, most of them saying their goodbyes to the Metcalfes.

'Don't let's risk it,' said Robin.

'Agreed,' said Stephen.

'Let's invite him out to dinner,' said Jean-Pierre.

The other two grabbed him and threw him into a taxi.

'What's that you have under your morning coat, Jean-Pierre?'

'Two bottles of Krug dix-neuf cent soixante-quatre. It seemed such a shame to leave them there on their own. I thought they might get lonely.'

Stephen instructed the driver to take them back to the hotel.

'What a wedding. Do you think James ever had a plan?' asked Robin.

'I don't know, but if he has it will only have to bring in $1.24.'

'We should have retrieved the money he made from his win on Rosalie at Ascot,' mused Jean-Pierre.

After packing and signing out of the hotel, they took another taxi to Logan International Airport and, with considerable help from the British Airways staff, managed to board the plane.

'Damn,' said Stephen. 'I wish we hadn't left without the $1.24.'

21

Once on board, they drank the champagne Jean-Pierre had captured at the wedding. Even Stephen seemed content, although he did occasionally revert to the theme of the missing $1.24.

'How much do you imagine this champagne cost?' teased Jean-Pierre.

'That's not the point. Not a penny more, not a penny less.'

Jean-Pierre decided he would never understand academics.

'Don't worry, Stephen. I've every confidence that James's plan will bring in $1.24.'

Stephen would have laughed, but it gave him a headache.

'To think that girl knew everything.'

On arrival at Heathrow, they had little trouble in clearing customs. The purpose of the trip had never been to bring back gifts. Robin made a detour to W. H. Smiths and picked up *The Times* and the *Evening Standard*. Jean-Pierre bargained with a taxi-driver about the fare to central London.

'We're not some bloody Americans who don't know the rate or the route and can be easily fleeced,' he was saying, still not yet sober.

The taxi-driver grumbled to himself as he nosed his black Austin towards the motorway. It was not going to be his day.

Robin read the papers happily, one of those rare people who could read in a moving car. Stephen and Jean-Pierre satisfied themselves with watching the passing traffic.

'Jesus Christ.'

Stephen and Jean-Pierre were startled. They had rarely heard Robin swear. It seemed out of character.

'God Almighty.'

This was too much for them, but before they could enquire, he began to read out loud:

'"BP announced a strike in the North Sea which is likely to produce 200,000 barrels of oil a day. The strike is described by their Chairman, Sir Eric Drake, as a major find. The British Petroleum Forties Field is one mile from the so far unexplored Prospecta Oil field and rumours of a bid by BP have sent Prospecta Oil shares to a record high of $12.25 at the close of business."'

'Nom de Dieu,' said Jean-Pierre. 'What do we do now?'

'Oh well,' said Stephen. 'I suppose we'll have to work out a plan for how to give it all back.'

JEFFREY ARCHER

SHALL WE TELL THE PRESIDENT?

To Adrian and Anne

Author's Note to Revised Edition

When I first wrote *Shall We Tell the President?* I set the story six or seven years in the future. Now that that future date lies in the past, some of the story's credibility becomes impaired.

Since that time too I have written *The Prodigal Daughter* in which the chief character, Florentyna Kane, becomes the first woman President of the United States. It therefore seems logical to me, in recasting *Shall We Tell the President?*, to introduce my fictional president rather than keep the real-life name of Edward M. Kennedy who was the focus of the original novel. This gives it a natural link to *The Prodigal Daughter* and also to *Kane and Abel*.

I have not altered the essential story of *Shall We Tell the President?* but a number of significant changes as well as minor ones, have been made in this revised, re-set edition.

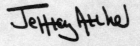

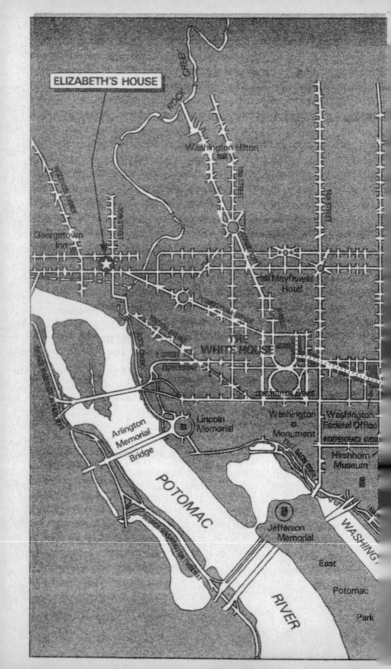

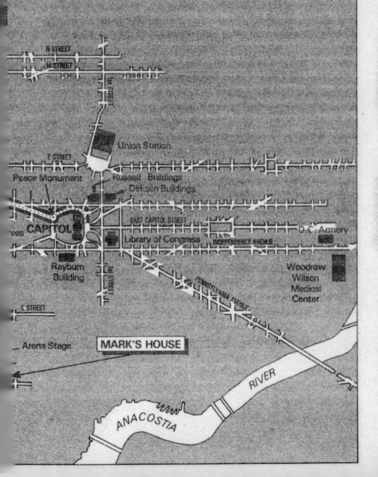

Tuesday afternoon, 20 January

12:26 pm

"I, Florentyna Kane, do solemnly swear . . ."
"I, Florentyna Kane, do solemnly swear . . ."
". . . that I will faithfully execute the office of the President of the United States . . ."
". . . that I will faithfully execute the office of the President of the United States . . ."
". . . and will to the best of my ability, preserve, protect and defend the Constitution of the United States. So help me God."
". . . and will to the best of my ability, preserve, protect and defend the Constitution of the United States. So help me God."

Her hand still resting on the Douay Bible, the forty-third President smiled at the First Gentleman. It was the end of one struggle and the beginning of another. Florentyna Kane knew about struggles. Her first struggle had been to be elected to Congress, then the Senate and finally four years later when she had become the first woman Vice President of the United States. After a fierce primary campaign, she had only narrowly managed to defeat Senator Ralph Brooks on the fifth ballot at the Democratic National Convention in June. In November she survived an even fiercer battle with the Republican candidate, a former congressman from New York. Florentyna Kane was elected President by 105,000 votes, a mere one per cent, the smallest margin in American history, smaller even than the 118,000 that John F. Kennedy had gained over Richard Nixon back in 1960.

While the applause died down, the President waited for the twenty-one-gun salute to come to an end. Florentyna Kane cleared her throat and faced fifty thousand attentive citizens on the Capitol Plaza and two hundred million more somewhere out there beyond the television transmitters. There was no need today for the blankets and heavy coats which normally accompanied these occasions. The weather was unusually mild for late January, and the crowded grassy area facing the east front of the Capitol, although soggy, was no longer white from the Christmas snow.

"Vice President Bradley, Mr Chief Justice, President Carter, President Reagan, Reverend clergy, fellow citizens."

The First Gentleman looked on, smiling occasionally to himself as he recognised some of the words and phrases he had contributed to his wife's speech.

Their day had begun at about 6:30 am. Neither had slept very well after the splendid pre-Inaugural concert given in their honour the previous evening. Florentyna Kane had gone over her presidential address for the final time, underlining the salient words in red, making only minor changes.

When she rose that morning, Florentyna wasted no time in selecting a blue dress from her wardrobe. She pinned on the tiny brooch her first husband, Richard, had given her just before he had died.

Every time Florentyna wore that brooch she remembered him; how he had been unable to catch the plane that day because of a strike by maintenance workers but still hired a car to be sure he could be by Florentyna's side when she addressed the Harvard commencement.

Richard never did hear that speech, the one *Newsweek* described as a launching pad for the Presidency – because by the time she had reached the hospital he was dead.

She snapped back into the real world of which she was the most powerful leader on earth. But still without enough power to bring Richard back. Florentyna checked herself in the mirror. She felt confident. After all, she had already been President for nearly two years since the unexpected death of President Parkin. Historians would be surprised to discover that she had learned of the President's death while trying to sink a four-foot putt against her oldest friend and future husband, Edward Winchester.

They had both stopped their match when the helicopters had circled overhead. When one of them had landed a Marines Captain had jumped out and run towards her, saluted and said, "Madam President, the President is dead." Now the American people had confirmed that they were willing to continue living with a woman in the White House. For the first time in its history, the United States had elected a woman to the most coveted position in its political life in her own right. She glanced out of the bedroom window at the broad placid expanse of the Potomac River, glinting in the early-morning sunlight.

She left the bedroom and went straight to the private dining-room where her husband Edward was chatting to her children William and Annabel. Florentyna kissed all three of them before they sat down to breakfast.

They laughed about the past and talked about the future but when the clock struck eight the President left them to go to the Oval Office. Her Chief of Staff, Janet Brown, was sitting outside in the corridor waiting for her.

"Good morning, Madam President."

"Good morning, Janet. Everything under control?" She smiled at her.

"I think so, Madam."

"Good. Why don't you run my day as usual? Don't worry about me, I'll just follow your instructions. What do you want me to do first?"

"There are 842 telegrams and 2,412 letters but they

3

will have to wait, except for the Heads of State. I'll have replies ready for them by twelve o'clock."

"Date them today, they'll like that, and I'll sign every one of them as soon as they are ready."

"Yes, Madam. I also have your schedule. You start the official day with coffee at eleven with the former Presidents Reagan and Carter, then you will be driven to the Inauguration. After the Inauguration, you'll attend a luncheon at the Senate before reviewing the Inaugural Parade in front of the White House."

Janet Brown passed her a sheaf of three-by-five index cards, stapled together, as she had done for fifteen years since she joined her staff when Florentyna had first been elected to Congress. They summarised the President's hour-by-hour schedule; there was rather less on them than usual. Florentyna glanced over the cards, and thanked her Chief of Staff. Edward Winchester appeared at the door. He smiled as he always did, with a mixture of love and admiration, when she turned towards him. She had never once regretted her almost impulsive decision to marry him after the eighteenth hole on that extraordinary day she was told of President Parkin's death, and she felt for certain that Richard would have approved.

"I'll be working on my papers until eleven," she told him. He nodded and left to prepare himself for the day ahead.

A crowd of well-wishers was already gathering outside the White House.

"I wish it would rain," confided H. Stuart Knight, the head of the Secret Service, to his aide; it was also one of the most important days of his life. "I know the vast majority of people are harmless, but these occasions give me the jitters."

The crowd numbered about one hundred and fifty; fifty of them belonged to Mr Knight. The advance car that always goes five minutes ahead of a President was already meticulously checking the route to the White

House; Secret Service men were watching small gatherings of people along the way, some waving flags; they were there to witness the Inauguration, and would one day tell their grandchildren how they had seen Florentyna Kane being inaugurated as President of the United States.

At 10:59 the butler opened the front door and the crowds began to cheer.

The President and her husband waved to the smiling eyes and only sensed by experience and professional instinct that fifty people were not looking towards them.

Two black limousines came to a noiseless stop at the North Entrance of the White House at 11:00 am. The Marine Honour Guard stood at attention and saluted the two ex-Presidents and their wives as they were greeted by President Kane on the Portico, a privilege normally accorded only to visiting Heads of State. The President herself guided them through to the library for coffee with Edward, William and Annabel.

The older of the ex-Presidents was grumbling that if he were frail it was because he had had to rely on his wife's cooking for the past eight years. "She hasn't dirtied a frying pan in ages, but she's improving every day. To make sure, I've given her a copy of *The New York Times Cook Book*; it's about the only one of their publications that didn't criticise me." Florentyna laughed nervously. She wanted to get on with the official proceedings, but she was conscious that the ex-Presidents were enjoying being back in the White House so she pretended to listen attentively, donning a mask that was second nature to her after nearly twenty years in politics.

"Madam President . . ." Florentyna had to think quickly to prevent anyone noticing her instinctive response to the words. "It's one minute past midday." She looked up at her press secretary, rose from her chair, and led the ex-Presidents and their wives to the steps of the White House. The Marine band struck up "Hail to the Chief" for the last time. At one o'clock they would play it again for the first time.

5

The two former Presidents were escorted to the first car of the motorcade, a black, bubble-topped, bullet-proof limousine. The Speaker of the House, Jim Wright, and the Senate Majority Leader, Robert Byrd, representing the Congress, were already seated in the second car. Directly behind the limousine there were two cars filled with Secret Service men. Florentyna and Edward occupied the fifth car in line. Vice President Bradley of New Jersey and his wife rode in the next car.

H. Stuart Knight was going through one more routine check. His fifty men had now grown to a hundred. By noon, counting the local police and the FBI contingent, there would be five hundred. Not forgetting the boys from the CIA, Knight thought ruefully. They certainly didn't tell him whether they were going to be there or not, and even he could not always spot them in a crowd. He listened to the cheering of the onlookers reaching a crescendo as the presidential limousine pulled out, on its way to the Capitol.

Edward chatted amiably but Florentyna's thoughts were elsewhere. She waved mechanically at the crowds lining Pennsylvania Avenue, but her mind was once again going over her speech. The renovated Willard Hotel, seven office buildings under construction, the tiered housing units that resembled an Indian cliff-dwelling, the new shops and restaurants and the wide landscaped sidewalks passed by. The J. Edgar Hoover Building, which housed the FBI, still named after its first Director, despite several efforts by certain senators to have the name changed. How this street had been transformed in fifteen years.

They approached the Capitol and Edward interrupted the President's reverie. "May God be with you, darling." She smiled and gripped his hand. The six cars came to a stop.

President Kane entered the Capitol on the ground floor. Edward waited behind for a moment as he thanked the chauffeur. Those who stepped out of the other cars were quickly surrounded by Secret Service agents and,

6

waving to the crowd, they made their way separately to their seats on the platform. Meanwhile the chief usher was taking President Kane quietly through the tunnel into the reception area, Marines saluting at every ten paces. There she was greeted by Vice President Bradley. The two of them stood talking of nothing, neither of them taking in the other's reply.

The two ex-Presidents came through the tunnel smiling. For the first time the older President was looking his age, his hair seemed to have turned grey overnight. Once again, he and Florentyna went through the formality of shaking hands with one another; they were to do it seven times that day. The chief usher guided them through a small reception room on to the platform. For this, as for all Presidential inaugurations, a temporary platform had been erected on the east steps of the Capitol. The crowds rose and cheered for over a minute as the President and the ex-Presidents waved; finally they sat in silence and waited for the ceremony to begin.

"My fellow Americans, as I take office the problems facing the United States across the world are vast and threatening. In South Africa, pitiless civil war rages between black and white; in the Middle East the ravages of last year's battles are being repaired, but both sides are rebuilding their armaments rather than their schools, their hospitals or their farms. On the borders between China and India, and between Russia and Pakistan, there is the potential for war among four of the most populous nations on earth. South America veers between extreme right and extreme left, but neither extreme seems to be able to improve the living conditions of their peoples. Two of the original signatories of the North Atlantic Treaty Organisation, France and Italy, are on the verge of withdrawing from that pact.

"In 1949, President Harry S. Truman announced that the United States stood ready with all its might and resources to defend the forces of freedom wherever they

7

might be endangered. Today, some would say that this act of magnanimity has resulted in failure, that America was, and is, too weak to assume the full burden of world leadership. In the face of repeated international crises, any American citizen might well ask why he should care about events so far from home, and why he should feel any responsibility for the defence of freedom outside the United States.

"I do not have to answer these doubts in my own words. 'No man is an island,' John Donne wrote more than three and a half centuries ago. 'Every man is a piece of the continent.' The United States stretches from the Atlantic to the Pacific and from the Arctic to the Equator. 'I am involved in mankind; and therefore never send to know for whom the bell tolls; it tolls for thee.'"

Edward liked that part of the speech. It expressed so well his own feelings. He had wondered, though, whether the audience would respond with the same enthusiasm as they had greeted Florentyna's flights of rhetoric in the past. The thunderous applause assaulting his ears in wave after wave reassured him. The magic was still working.

"At home, we will create a medical service that will be the envy of the free world. It will allow all citizens an equal opportunity for the finest medical advice and help. No American must be allowed to die because he cannot afford to live."

Many Democrats had voted against Florentyna Kane because of her attitude towards Medicare. As one hoary old G.P. had said to her, "Americans must learn to stand on their own two feet." "How can they if they're already flat on their backs?" retorted Florentyna. "God deliver us from a woman President," replied the doctor, and voted Republican.

"But the main platform of this administration will be in the field of law and order, and to this end I intend to present to Congress a bill that will make the sale of firearms without a licence illegal."

8

The applause from the crowd was not quite so spontaneous.

Florentyna raised her head. "And so I say to you, my fellow citizens, let the end of this century be an era in which the United States leads the world in justice as well as in power, in care as well as enterprise, an era in which the United States declares war – war on disease, war on discrimination, and war on poverty."

The President sat down; in a single motion, the entire audience rose to its feet.

The sixteen-minute speech had been interrupted by applause on ten occasions. But as the nation's Chief Executive turned from the microphone, now assured that the crowd was with her, her eyes were no longer on the cheering mass. She scanned the dignitaries on the platform for the one person she wanted to see. She walked over to her husband, kissed him on the cheek, and then took his arm before they were accompanied from the platform by the briskly efficient usher.

H. Stuart Knight hated things that didn't run on schedule, and today nothing had been on time. Everybody was going to be at least thirty minutes late for the lunch.

Seventy-six guests stood as the President entered the room. These were the men and women who now controlled the Democratic party. The Northern establishment who had decided to back the lady were now present, with the exception of those who had supported Senator Ralph Brooks.

Some of those at the luncheon were already members of her cabinet, and everyone present had played some part in returning her to the White House.

The President had neither the opportunity nor the inclination to eat her lunch; everyone wanted to talk to her at once. The menu had been specially made up of her favourite dishes, starting with lobster bisque and going on to roast beef. Finally, the chef's *pièce de résistance* was produced, an iced chocolate cake, in the form of the White House. Edward watched his wife ignore the neat

9

wedge of the Oval Office placed in front of her. "That's why she never needs to slim," commented Marian Edelman, who was the surprise appointment as Attorney General. Marian had been telling Edward about the importance of children's rights. Edward tried to listen; perhaps another day.

By the time the last wing of the White House had been demolished and the last hand pumped, the President and her party were forty-five minutes late for the Inaugural Parade. When they did arrive at the reviewing stand in front of the White House, the most relieved to see them, among the crowd of two hundred thousand, was the Presidential Guard of Honour, who had been standing at attention for just over an hour. Once the President had taken her seat the parade began. The State contingent in the military unit marched past, and the United States Marine Band played everything from Sousa to "God Bless America". Floats from each state, some, like that of Illinois, commemorating events from Florentyna's Polish background, added colour and a lighter touch to what for her was not only a serious occasion but a solemn one.

She still felt this was the only nation on earth that could entrust its highest office to the daughter of an immigrant.

When the three-hour-long parade was finally over and the last float had disappeared down the avenue, Janet Brown, Florentyna Kane's Chief of Staff, leaned over and asked the President what she would like to do between now and the first Inaugural Ball.

"Sign all those cabinet appointments, the letters to the Heads of State, and clear my desk for tomorrow," was the immediate reply. "That should take care of the first four years."

The President returned directly into the White House. As she walked through the South Portico, the Marine band struck up "Hail to the Chief". The President had taken off her coat even before she reached the Oval Office. She sat herself firmly behind the imposing oak and leather desk. She paused for a moment, looking around the room. Everything was as she wanted it; behind her there was the picture of Richard and William playing touch football. In front of her, a paperweight with the quotation from George Bernard Shaw which Annabel quoted so often: "Some men see things as they are and say, why; I dream things that never were and say, why not." On Florentyna's left was the Presidential flag, on her right the flag of the United States. Dominating the middle of the desk was a replica of the Baron Hotel, Warsaw, made out of papier mâché by William when he was fourteen. Coal was burning in the fireplace. A portrait of Abraham Lincoln stared down at the newly sworn-in President while outside the bay windows, the green lawns swept in an unbroken stretch to the Washington Monument. The President smiled. She was back at home.

Florentyna Kane reached for a pile of official papers and glanced over the names of those who would serve in her cabinet; there were over thirty appointments to be made. The President signed each one with a flourish. The final one was Janet Brown as Chief of Staff. The President ordered that they be sent down to the Congress immediately. Her press secretary picked up the pieces of paper that would dictate the next four years in the history of America and said, "Thank you, Madam President," and then added, "What would you like to tackle next?"

"Always start with the biggest problem is what Lincoln advised, so let's go over the draft legislation for the Gun Control bill."

The President's press secretary shuddered, for she knew only too well that the battle in the House over the next two years was likely to be every bit as vicious and hard-fought as the Civil War Lincoln had faced. So many people still regarded the possession of arms as their inalienable birthright. She only prayed that it all would not end the same way, as a House Divided.

Thursday evening, 3 March
(two years later)

5:45 pm

Nick Stames wanted to go home. He had been at work since seven that morning and it was already 5:45 pm. He couldn't remember if he had eaten lunch; his wife, Norma, had been grumbling again that he never got home in time for dinner, or, if he did, it was so late that her dinner was no longer worth eating. Come to think of it, when did he last find time to finish a meal? Norma stayed in bed when he left for the office at 6:30 am. Now that the children were away at school, her only real task was to cook dinner for him. He couldn't win; if he had been a failure, she would have complained about that, too, and he was, goddamn it, by anybody's standards, a success; the youngest special agent in charge of a Field Office in the FBI and you don't get a job like that at the age of forty-one by being at home on time for dinner every night. In any case, Nick loved the job. It was his mistress; at least his wife could be thankful for that.

Nick Stames had been head of the Washington Field Office for nine years. The third largest Field Office in America, although it covered the smallest territory – only sixty-one square miles of Washington, D.C. – it had twenty-two squads; twelve criminal, ten security. Hell, he was policing the capital of the world. Of course, he must be expected to be late sometimes. Still, tonight he intended to make a special effort. When he had the time to do so, he adored his wife. He was going to be home on time this evening. He picked up his internal phone and called his Criminal Co-ordinator, Grant Nanna.

"Grant."

"Boss."

"I'm going home."

"I didn't know you had one."

"Not you, too."

Nick Stames put the phone down, and pushed his hand through his long dark hair. He would have made a better movie criminal than FBI agent, since everything about him was dark – dark eyes, dark skin, dark hair, even a dark suit and dark shoes, but the last two were true of any special agent. On his lapel he wore a pin depicting the flags of the United States and of Greece.

Once, a few years ago, he had been offered promotion and a chance to cross the street to the Bureau Head-quarters and join the Director as one of his thirteen assistants. Being an assistant chained to a desk wasn't his style, so he stayed put. The move would have taken him from a slum to a palace; the Washington Field Office is housed on floors four, five, and eight of the Old Post Office Building on Pennsylvania Avenue, and the rooms are a little like railroad coaches. They would have been condemned as slums if they had been sited in the ghetto.

As the sun began to disappear behind the tall buildings, Nick's gloomy office grew darker. He walked over to the light switch. "Don't Be Fuelish," commented a fluorescent label glued to the switch. Just as the constant move-ment of men and women in dark sober suits in and out of the Old Post Office Building revealed the location of the FBI Washington Field Office, so this government graffito served notice that the czars of the Federal Energy Administration inhabited two floors of the cavernous building on Pennsylvania Avenue.

Nick stared out of his window across the street at the new FBI Headquarters, which had been completed in

1976, a great ugly monster with elevators that were larger than his office. He didn't let it bother him. He'd reached Grade 18 in the service, and only the Director was paid more than he was. In any case, he was not going to sit behind a desk until they retired him with a pair of gold handcuffs. He wanted to be in constant touch with the agent in the street, feel the pulse of the Bureau. He would stay put at the Washington Field Office and die standing up, not sitting down. Once again, he touched the intercom. "Julie, I'm on my way home."

Julie Bayers looked up and glanced at her watch as if it were lunchtime.

"Yes, sir," she said, sounding disbelieving.

As he passed through the office he grinned at her. "Moussaka, rice pilaf, and the wife; don't tell the Mafia." Nick managed to get one foot out of the door before his private phone rang. One more step and he would have made it to the open lift, but Nick never could resist the ring of a phone. Julie rose and began to walk towards his office. As she did so Nick admired, as he always did, the quick flash of leg. "It's all right, Julie. I'll get it." He strode back into his room and picked up the ringing telephone.

"Stames."

"Good evening, sir. Lieutenant Blake, Metropolitan Police."

"Hey, Dave, congratulations on your promotion. I haven't seen you in . . ." he paused, ". . . it must be five years, you were only a sergeant. How are you?"

"Thank you, sir, I'm doing just fine."

"Well, Lieutenant, moved into big-time crime, now have you? Picked up a fourteen-year-old stealing a pack of chewing gum and need my best men to find where the suspect has hidden the goods?"

Blake laughed. "Not quite that bad, Mr Stames. I have a guy in Woodrow Wilson Medical Center who wants to meet the head of the FBI, says he has something vitally important to tell him."

"I know the feeling, I'd love to meet him myself. Do you know whether he's one of our usual informers, Dave?"

"No, sir."

"What's his name?"

"Angelo Casefikis." Blake spelled out the name for Stames.

"Any description?" asked Stames.

"No. I only spoke to him on the phone. All he would say is it will be worse for America if the FBI doesn't listen."

"Did he now? Hold on while I check the name. He could be a nut."

Nick Stames pressed a button to connect him with the Duty Officer. "Who's on duty?"

"Paul Fredericks, boss."

"Paul, get out the nut box."

The nut box, as it was affectionately known in the Bureau, was a collection of white index cards containing the names of all the people who liked to call up in the middle of the night and claim that the Martians had landed in their back yards, or that they had discovered a CIA plot to take over the world.

Special Agent Fredericks was back on the line, the nut box in front of him.

"Right, boss. What's his name?"

"Angelo Casefikis," said Stames.

"A crazy Greek," said Fredericks. "You never know with these foreigners."

"Greeks aren't foreigners," snapped Stames. His name, before it was shortened, had been Nick Stamatakis. He never did forgive his father, God rest his soul, for anglicising a magnificent Hellenic surname.

"Sorry, sir. No name like that in the nut box or the informants' file. Did this guy mention any agent's name that he knows?"

"No, he just wanted the head of the FBI."

"Don't we all?"

"No more cracks from you, Paul, or you'll be on complaint duty for more than the statutory week."

Each agent in the Field Office did one week a year on the nut box, answering the phone all night, fending off canny Martians, foiling dastardly CIA coups, and, above all, never embarrassing the Bureau. Every agent dreaded it. Paul Fredericks put the phone down quickly. Two weeks on this job and you could write out one of the little white cards with your own name on it.

"Well, have you formed any view?" said Stames to Blake as he wearily took a cigarette out of his left desk drawer. "How did he sound?"

"Frantic and incoherent. I sent one of my rookies to see him, but he couldn't get anything out of him other than that America ought to listen to what he's got to say. He seemed genuinely frightened. He's got a gunshot wound in his leg and there may be complications. It's infected; apparently he left it for some days before he went to the hospital."

"How did he get himself shot?"

"Don't know yet. We're still trying to locate witnesses, but we haven't come up with anything so far, and Casefikis won't give us the time of day."

"Wants the FBI, does he? Only the best, eh?" said Stames. He regretted the remark the moment he said it; but it was too late. He didn't attempt to cover himself. "Thank you, Lieutenant," he said. "I'll put someone on it immediately and brief you in the morning." Stames put the telephone down. Six o'clock already – why had he turned back? Damn the phone. Grant Nanna would have handled the job just as well and he wouldn't have made that thoughtless remark about wanting the best. There was enough friction between the FBI and the Metropolitan Police without his adding to it. Nick picked up his intercom phone and buzzed the head of the Criminal Section.

"Grant."

"I thought you said you had to be home."

16

"Come into my office for a moment, will you?"

"Sure, be right there, boss."

Grant Nanna appeared a few seconds later along with his trademark cigar. He had put on his jacket which he only did when he saw Nick in his office.

Nanna's career had a storybook quality. He was born in El Campo, Texas, and received a BA from Baylor. From there, he went on to get a law degree at SMU. As a young agent assigned to the Pittsburgh Field Office, Nanna met his future wife, Betty, an FBI stenographer. They had four sons, all of whom had attended Virginia Polytechnic Institute: two engineers, a doctor, and a dentist. Nanna had been an agent for over thirty years. Twelve more than Nick. In fact, Nick had been a rookie agent under him. Nanna held no grudge, since he was head of the Criminal Section, and greatly respected Nick – as he called him in private.

"What's the problem, boss?"

Stames looked up as Nanna entered the office. He noted that his five-feet-nine, fifty-five-year-old, robust, cigar-chewing Criminal Co-ordinator was certainly not "desirable", as Bureau weight requirements demanded. A man of five-feet-nine was required to keep his weight between a hundred and fifty-four and a hundred and sixty-one pounds. Nanna had always cringed when the quarterly weigh-in of all FBI agents came due. Many times he had been forced to purge his body of excess pounds for that most serious transgression of Bureau rules, especially during the Hoover era, when "desirability" meant lean and mean.

Who cares, thought Stames. Grant's knowledge and experience were worth a dozen slender, young athletic agents who can be found in the Washington Field Office halls every day. As he had done a hundred times before, he told himself he would deal with Nanna's weight problem another day.

Nick repeated the story of the strange Greek in Woodrow Wilson Medical Center as it had been relayed to him by Lieutenant Blake. "I want you to send down two men. Who's on duty tonight?"

"Aspirin, but if you suspect it might be an informer, boss, I certainly can't send him."

"Aspirin" was the nickname of the oldest agent still employed in the WFO. After his early years under Hoover, he played everything by the book, which gave most people a headache. He was due to retire at the end of the year and exasperation was now being replaced by nostalgia.

"No, don't send Aspirin. Send two youngsters."

"How about Calvert and Andrews?"

"Agreed," replied Stames. "If you brief them right away, I can still make it in time for dinner. Call me at home if it turns out to be anything special."

Grant Nanna left the office, and Nick smiled a second flirtatious goodbye to his secretary. She was the only attractive thing in the WFO. Julie looked up and smiled nonchalantly. "I don't mind working for an FBI agent, but there is no way I would ever marry one," she told her little mirror in the top drawer.

Grant Nanna returned to his office and picked up the extension phone to the Criminal Room.

"Send in Calvert and Andrews."

"Yes, sir."

There was a firm knock on the door. Two special agents entered. Barry Calvert was big by anybody's standards, six-feet-six in his stockinged feet and not many people had seen him that way. At thirty-two, he was thought to be one of the most ambitious young men in the Criminal Section. He was wearing a dark green jacket, dark nondescript trousers, and clumpy black leather brogues. His brown hair was cut short and parted neatly on the right. His tear-drop aviator glasses had been his sign of nonconformity. He was always on duty long after the official check-out time of 5:30 and not just because he was fighting his way up the ladder. He loved the job. He didn't love anybody else, so far as his colleagues knew, or at least not on more than a temporary basis. Calvert was a Midwesterner by birth and he had entered the FBI after leaving college with a BA in sociology from Indiana University and then took the fifteen-week course at Quantico, the FBI Academy. From every angle, he was the archetypal FBI man.

By contrast, Mark Andrews had been one of the more unusual FBI entrants. After majoring in history at Yale he finished his education at Yale Law School, and then decided he wanted some adventure for a few years before he joined a law firm. He felt it would be useful to learn about criminals and the police from the inside. He didn't give this as his reason for applying to the Bureau – no one is supposed to regard the Bureau as an academic experiment. In fact, Hoover had regarded it so much as a career that he did not allow agents who left the service ever to return. At six feet Mark Andrews looked small next to Calvert. He had a fresh, open face with clear blue eyes and a mop of curly fair hair long enough to skim his shirt collar. At twenty-eight he was one of the youngest agents in the department. His clothes were always smartly fashionable and sometimes not quite regulation. Nick Stames had once caught him in a red sports jacket and brown trousers and relieved him from duty so that he could return home and dress properly. Never embarrass the Bureau. Mark's charm got him out of a lot of trouble in the Criminal Section, but he had a steadiness of purpose which more than made up for the Ivy League education and manner. He was self-confident, but never pushy or concerned about his own advancement. He didn't let anyone in the Bureau know about his career plan.

Grant Nanna went over the story of the frightened man waiting for them in Woodrow Wilson.

"Black?" queried Calvert.

"No, Greek."

Calvert's surprise showed in his face. Eighty per cent of the inhabitants of Washington were black, and ninety-eight per cent of those arrested on criminal charges were black. One of the reasons the infamous break-in at the Watergate had been suspicious from the beginning to those who knew Washington at all well was the fact that no blacks were involved, though no agents had admitted it.

"Okay, Barry, think you can handle it?"

"Sure, you want a report on your desk by tomorrow morning?"

"No, the boss wants you to contact him direct if it turns out to be anything special, otherwise just file a report overnight." Nanna's telephone rang. "Mr Stames on the radio line from his car for you, sir," said Polly, the night switchboard operator.

"He never lets up, does he?" Grant confided to the two junior agents, covering the mouthpiece of the phone with his palm.

"Hi, boss."

"Grant, did I say that the Greek had a bullet wound in his leg, and it was infected?"

"Yes, boss."

"Right, do me a favour will you? Call Father Gregory at my church, Saint Constantine and Saint Helen, and ask him to go over to the hospital and see him."

"Anything you say."

"And get yourself home, Grant. Aspirin can handle the office tonight."

"I was just going, boss."

The line went dead.

"Okay, you two – on your way." The two special agents headed down the dirty grey corridor and into the service elevator. It looked, as always, as if it required a crank to start it. Finally outside on Pennsylvania Avenue, they picked up a Bureau car.

Mark guided the dark blue Ford sedan down Pennsylvania Avenue past the National Archives and the Mellon Gallery. He circled around the lush Capitol grounds and picked up Independence Avenue going towards the south-east section of Washington. As the two agents waited for a light to change at 1st Street, near the Library of Congress, Barry scowled at the rush-hour traffic and looked at his watch.

"Why didn't they put Aspirin on this damn assignment?"

"Who'd send Aspirin to a hospital?" replied Mark.

Mark smiled. The two men had established an immediate rapport when they first met at the FBI Academy at Quantico. On the first day of the training course, every trainee received a telegram confirming his appointment. Each new agent was then asked to check the telegram of the person on his right and his left for authenticity. The manoeuvre was intended to emphasise the need for extreme caution. Mark had glanced at Barry's telegram and handed it back with a grin. "I guess you're legit," he said, "if FBI regulations allow King Kong in the ranks."

"Listen," Calvert had replied, reading Mark's telegram intently. "You may just need King Kong one day, Mr Andrews."

The light turned green, but a car ahead of Mark and Barry in the inside lane wanted to make a left turn on 1st Street. For the moment, the two impatient FBI men were trapped in a line of traffic.

"What do you imagine this guy could tell us?"

"I hope he has something on the downtown bank job," replied Barry. "I'm still the case agent, and I still don't have any leads after three weeks. Stames is beginning to get uptight about it."

"No, can't be that, not with a bullet in his leg. He's more likely to be another candidate for the nut box. Wife probably shot him for not being home on time for his stuffed vine leaves."

"You know, the boss would only send a priest to a fellow Greek. You and I could wallow in hell as far as he's concerned."

They both laughed. They knew if either of them were to

land in trouble, Nick Stames would move the Washington Monument stone by stone if he thought it would help. As the car continued down Independence Avenue into the heart of south-east Washington, the traffic gradually diminished. A few minutes later, they passed 19th Street and the D.C. Armory and reached Woodrow Wilson Medical Center. They found the visitors' parking lot and Calvert double-checked the lock on every door. Nothing is more embarrassing for an agent than to have his car stolen and then for the Metropolitan Police to call and ask if he could come and collect it. It was the quickest way to a month on the nut box.

The entrance to the hospital was old and dingy, and the corridors grey and bleak. The girl on night duty at the reception desk told them that Casefikis was on the fourth floor, in Room 4308. Both agents were surprised by the lack of security. They didn't have to show their credentials, and they were allowed to wander around the building as if they were a couple of interns. No one gave them a second look. Perhaps, as agents, they had become too security conscious.

The elevator took them gradually, grudgingly, to the fourth floor. A man on crutches and a woman in a wheelchair shared the elevator, chatting to one another as though they had a lot of time to spare, oblivious to the slowness of the elevator. When they arrived at the fourth floor, Calvert walked over to a nurse and asked for the doctor on duty.

"I think Dr Dexter has gone off duty, but I'll check," the staff nurse said and bustled away. She didn't get a visit from the FBI every day and the shorter one with the clear blue eyes was so good-looking. The nurse and the doctor returned together down the corridor. Dr Dexter came as a surprise to both Calvert and Andrews. They introduced themselves. It must have been the legs, Mark decided. The last time he had seen legs like that was when the Yale Cinema Club had shown a re-run of Anne Bancroft in *The Graduate*. It was the first time he had ever really looked at a woman's legs, and he hadn't stopped looking since.

"Elizabeth Dexter, MD" was stamped in black on a piece of red plastic that adorned her starched white coat. Underneath it, Mark could see a red silk shirt and a stylish skirt of black crepe that fell below her knees. Dr Dexter was of medium height and slender to the point of fragility. She wore no make-up, so far as Mark could tell; certainly her clear skin and dark eyes were in no need of any help. This trip was turning out to be worthwhile, after all. Barry, on the other hand, showed no interest whatever in the pretty doctor and asked to see the file on Casefikis. Mark thought quickly for an opening gambit.

"Are you related to Senator Dexter?" he asked, slightly emphasising the word Senator.

"Yes, he's my father," she said flatly, obviously used to the question and rather bored by it – and by those who imagined it was important.

"I heard him lecture in my final year at Yale Law," said Mark, forging ahead, realising he was now showing off, but he realised that Calvert would finish that damn report in a matter of moments.

"Oh, were you at Yale, too?" she asked. "When did you graduate?"

"Three years ago, Law School," replied Mark.

"We might even have met. I left Yale Med last year."

"If I had met you before, Dr Dexter, I would not have forgotten."

"When you two Ivy Leaguers have finished swapping life histories," Barry Calvert interrupted, "this Midwesterner would like to get on with his job."

Yes, thought Mark, Barry will end up as Director one day.

"What can you tell us about this man, Dr Dexter?" asked Calvert.

"Very little, I'm afraid," the doctor replied, taking back the file on Casefikis. "He came in of his own volition and reported a gun wound. The wound was septic and looked as if it had been exposed for about a week; I wish he had come in earlier. I removed the bullet this morning. As you know, Mr Calvert, it is our duty to inform the police immediately when a patient comes in with a gunshot wound, and so we phoned your boys at the Metropolitan Police."

"Not our boys," corrected Mark.

"I'm sorry," replied Dr Dexter rather formally. "To a doctor, a policeman is a policeman."

"And to a policeman, an MD is an MD, but you also have specialties – orthopaedics, gynaecology, neurology – don't you? You don't mean to tell me I look like one of those flatfoots from the Met Police?"

Dr Dexter was not to be beguiled into a flattering response. She opened the manilla folder. "All we know is that he is Greek by origin and his name is Angelo Casefikis. He has never been registered in this hospital before. He gave his age as thirty-eight . . . Not a lot to go on, I'm afraid."

"Fine, it's as much as we usually get. Thank you, Dr Dexter," said Calvert. "Can we see him now?"

"Of course. Please follow me." Elizabeth Dexter turned and led them down the corridor.

The two men followed her, Barry looking for the door marked 4308, Mark looking at her legs. When they arrived, they peered through the small window and saw two men in the room, Angelo Casefikis and a cheerful-looking black, who was staring at a television set which emitted no sound. Calvert turned to Dr Dexter.

"Would it be possible to see him alone, Dr Dexter?"

"Why?" she asked.

"We don't know what he is going to tell us, and he may not wish to be overheard."

"Well, don't worry yourself," said Dr Dexter, and laughed. "My favourite mailman, Benjamin Reynolds, who is in the next bed is as deaf as a post, and until we operate on him next week, he won't be able to hear

24

Gabriel's horn on the Day of Judgement, let alone a state secret."

Calvert smiled for the first time. "He'd make a hell of a witness."

The doctor ushered Calvert and Andrews into the room, then turned and left them. See you soon, lovely lady, Mark promised himself. Calvert looked at Benjamin Reynolds suspiciously, but the black mailman merely gave him a big happy smile, waved, and continued to watch the soundless *$25,000 Pyramid*; nonetheless, Barry Calvert stood on that side of the bed and blocked his view of Casefikis in case he could lip-read. Barry thought of everything.

"Mr Casefikis?"

"Yes."

Casefikis was a grey, sick-looking individual of medium build, with a prominent nose, bushy eyebrows, and an anxious expression that never left his face. His hair was thick, dark, and unkempt. His hands seemed particularly large on the white bedspread, and the veins stood out prominently. His face was darkened by several days of unshaven beard. One leg was heavily bandaged and rested on the cover of the bed. His eyes darted nervously from one man to the other.

"I am Special Agent Calvert and this is Special Agent Andrews. We are officers with the Federal Bureau of Investigation. We understand you wanted to see us."

Both men withdrew their FBI credentials from their right inside coat pockets, and displayed them to Casefikis while holding the credentials in their left hands. Even such a seemingly insignificant manoeuvre was carefully taught to all new FBI agents so that their "strong hand" would be free to withdraw and fire when necessary.

Casefikis studied their credentials with a puzzled frown, pressing his tongue over his lips, obviously not knowing what to look for. The agent's signature must pass partly over the seal of the Department of Justice to insure authenticity. He looked at Mark's card number,

3302, and his badge number, 1721. He didn't speak, as if wondering where to start, or perhaps whether to change his mind and say nothing at all. He stared at Mark, clearly the more sympathetic, and began his tale.

"I never been in any trouble with police before," he said. "Not with any of police."

Neither agent smiled or spoke.

"But I in big mess now and, by God, I need help."

Calvert stepped in. "Why do you need our help?"

"I am illegal immigrant and so is wife. We both Greek nationals, we came in Baltimore on ship and we been working here two years. We've nothing to go back to."

It came out in spurts and dashes.

"I have information to trade if we not deported."

"We can't make that sort –" began Mark.

Barry touched Mark's arm. "If it's important and you are able to help us solve a crime, we will speak to the Immigration authorities. We can promise no more than that."

Mark mused; with six million illegal immigrants in the United States, another couple was not going to sink the boat.

Casefikis looked desperate. "I needed job, I needed money, you understand?"

Both men understood. They faced the same problem a dozen times a week behind a dozen different faces.

"When I offered this job as waiter in restaurant, my wife very pleased. On second week I was given special job to serve lunch in a hotel room for big man. The only trouble that the man wanted waiter who not speak English. My English very bad so bossman tell me I could go, keep my mouth shut, speak only Greek. For twenty dollars I say yes. We go in back of van to hotel – I think in Georgetown. When we arrive I sent to kitchen, join staff in basement. I dress and start taking food to private dining-room. There five-six men and I heard big man say I no speak English. So they talk on. I don't listen. Very last cup of coffee, when start talking about President

26

Kane, I like Kane, I listen. I heard say, 'We have to blow her away.' Another man say: 'The best day would still be 10 March, the way we planned it.' And then I heard: 'I agree with Senator, let's get rid of the bitch.' Someone was staring at me, so I left room. When I downstairs washing up, one man came in and shouted, 'Hey, you, catch this.' I looked around put arms up. All at once he start come for me. I run for door and down street. He shoot gun at me, I feel bit pain in leg but I able to get away because he older, big and slower than me. I hear him shout but I knew he couldn't catch me. I scared. I get home pretty damn quick, and wife and I move out that night and hide out of town with friend from Greece. Hoped all would be okay, but my leg got bad after few days so Ariana made me come to hospital and call for you because my friend tell they come around to my place look for me because if they find me they kill me." He stopped, breathed deeply, his unshaven face covered in sweat, and looked at the two men imploringly.

"What's your full name?" said Calvert, sounding about as excited as he would if he were issuing a traffic ticket.

"Angelo Mexis Casefikis."

Calvert made him spell it in full.

"Where do you live?"

"Now at Blue Ridge Manor Apartments, 11501 Elkin Street, Wheaton. Home of my friend, good man, please don't give trouble."

"When did this incident take place?"

"Last Thursday," Casefikis said instantly.

Calvert checked the date. "24 February?"

The Greek shrugged. "Last Thursday," he repeated.

"Where is the restaurant you were working in?"

"A few streets from me. It called Golden Duck."

Calvert continued taking notes. "And where was this hotel you were taken to?"

"Don't know, in Georgetown. Maybe could take you there when out of hospital."

"Now, Mr Casefikis, please be careful about this. Was

27

there anyone else working at this luncheon who might have overheard the conversation in that room?"

"No, sir. I only waiter attend in room."

"Have you told anyone what you overheard? Your wife? The friend whose house you're staying at? Anyone?"

"No, sir. Only you. No tell wife what I hear. No tell no one, too scared."

Calvert continued to interview, asking for descriptions of the other men in the room and making the Greek repeat everything to see if the story remained the same. It did. Mark looked on silently.

"Okay, Mr Casefikis, that's all we can do for this evening. We'll return in the morning and have you sign a written statement."

"But they going to kill me. They going to kill me."

"No need to worry, Mr Casefikis. We'll put a police guard on your room as soon as possible; no one is going to kill you."

Casefikis dropped his eyes, not reassured.

"We'll see you again in the morning," said Calvert, closing his notebook. "You just get some rest. Good night, Mr Casefikis."

Calvert glanced back at a happy Benjamin, still deeply absorbed in *$25,000 Pyramid* with no words, just money. He waved again at them and smiled, showing all three of his teeth, two black and one gold. Calvert and Andrews returned to the corridor.

"I don't believe a word of it," Barry said immediately. "With his English, he could easily have got hold of the wrong end of the stick. It was probably quite innocent. People curse the President all the time. My father does, but that doesn't mean he would kill her."

"Maybe, but what about that gunshot wound? That's for real," said Mark.

"I know. I guess that's the one thing that worries me," Barry said. "It could just be a cover for something completely different. I think I'll speak to the boss to be on the safe side."

Calvert headed for the pay phone by the side of the elevator and took out two quarters. All agents carry a pocketful of quarters; there are no special telephone privileges for members of the Bureau.

"Well, was he hoping to rob Fort Knox?" Elizabeth Dexter's voice startled Mark, although he had half-expected her to return. She was obviously on her way home: the white coat had been replaced by a red jacket.

"Not exactly," replied Mark. "We'll have to come around tomorrow morning to tidy things up; probably get him to sign a written statement and take his finger-prints, then we'll pick up the gold."

"Fine," she said. "Dr Delgado will be on duty tomorrow." She smiled sweetly. "You'll like her, too."

"Is this hospital entirely staffed by beautiful lady doctors?" said Mark. "How does one get to stay the night?"

"Well," she said, "the flu is the fashionable disease this month. Even President Kane has had it."

Calvert looked around sharply at the mention of the President's name. Elizabeth Dexter glanced at her watch.

"I've just completed two hours' unpaid overtime," she said. "If you don't have any more questions, Mr Andrews, I ought to get home now." She smiled and turned to go, her heels tapping sharply against the tiled floor.

"Just one more question, Dr Dexter," said Mark, fol-lowing her around the corner beyond the range of Barry Calvert's disapproving eyes and ears. "What would you say to having dinner with me later tonight?"

"What would I say?" she said teasingly. "Let me see, I think I'd accept gracefully and not too eagerly. It might be interesting to find out what G-men are really like."

"We bite," said Mark. They smiled at each other. "Okay, it's 7:15 now. If you're willing to take a chance on it, I could probably pick you up by 8:30."

Elizabeth jotted her address and phone number on a page of his diary.

"So you're a left-hander, are you, Liz?"

The dark eyes flashed momentarily up to meet his. "Only my lovers call me Liz," she said, and was gone.

"It's Calvert, boss. I can't make my mind up about this one. I don't know if he's a jerk or for real so I'd like to run it past you."

"Fine, Barry. Shoot."

"Well, it could be serious, or just a hoax. He may even be nothing more than a small-time thief trying to get off the hook for something bigger. But I can't be sure. And if every word he said turned out to be true, I figured you ought to know immediately." Barry relayed the salient parts of the interview without mentioning the Senator, stressing that there was an added factor he did not want to discuss over the phone.

"What are you trying to do, get me in the divorce courts — I suppose I'll have to come back to the office," said Nick Stames, avoiding his wife's expression of annoyance. "Okay, okay. Thank God I got to eat at least some of the moussaka. I'll see you in thirty minutes, Barry."

"Right, boss."

Calvert depressed the telephone cradle with his hand momentarily and then dialled the Metropolitan Police. Two more quarters, leaving sixteen in his pockets. He often thought the quickest way to check out an FBI agent would be to make him turn his pockets inside out; if he produced twenty quarters, he was a genuine member of the Bureau.

"Lieutenant Blake is on the front desk. I'll put you right through."

"Lieutenant Blake."

"Special Agent Calvert. We've seen your Greek and we'd like you to put a guard on his room. He's scared to hell about something so we don't want to take any chances."

"He's not my Greek, damn it," said Blake. "Can't you use one of your own fancy guys?"

"There's no one we can spare at the moment, Lieutenant."

"I'm not exactly overstaffed myself, for God's sake. What do you think we're running, the Shoreham Hotel? Oh hell, I'll do what I can. But they won't be able to get there for a couple of hours."

"Fine. Thanks for your help, Lieutenant. I'll brief my office." Barry replaced the receiver.

Mark Andrews and Barry Calvert waited for the elevator, which was just as slow and reluctant to take them down as it had been to take them up. Neither of them spoke until they were inside the dark blue Ford.

"Stames is coming back to hear the story," said Calvert. "I can't imagine he'll want to take it any further, but we'd better keep him informed. Then maybe we can call it a day."

Mark glanced at his watch; another hour and forty-five minutes' overtime, technically the maximum allowed an agent on any one day.

"I hope so," said Mark. "I just got myself a date."

"Anyone we know?"

"The beautiful Dr Dexter."

Barry raised his eyebrows. "Don't let the boss know. If he thought you picked up someone while you were on duty, he'd send you for a spell in the salt mines in Butte, Montana."

"I didn't realise that they had salt mines in Butte, Montana."

"Only FBI agents who really screw it up know there are salt mines in Butte."

Mark drove back to downtown Washington while Barry wrote up his report of the interview. It was 7:40 by the time they had returned to the Old Post Office Building, and Mark found the parking lot almost empty. By this time at night most civilised people were at home doing civilised things, like eating moussaka. Stames's car was already there. Goddamn him. They took the elevator to the fifth floor and went into Stames's reception room.

31

It looked empty without Julie. Calvert knocked quietly on the chief's door and the two agents walked in. Stames looked up. He had already found a hundred and one things to do since he'd been back, almost as if he had forgotten that he had specifically come back to see them.

"Right, Barry. Let's have it from the top, slowly and accurately."

Calvert recounted exactly what had happened from the moment they had arrived at Woodrow Wilson to the moment he had asked the Metropolitan Police to put a guard on the room to protect the Greek. Mark was impressed by Barry's total recall. At no point had he exaggerated or revealed any personal prejudice. Stames lowered his head for a few moments and then suddenly turned to Mark.

"Do you want to add anything?" he asked.

"Not really, sir. It was all a bit melodramatic. Although he didn't come over as a liar, he was certainly frightened. Also there's no trace of him in any of our files. I radioed the Night Super for a name check. Negative on Casefikis."

Nick picked up the phone and asked to be put through to Bureau Headquarters. "Give me the National Computer Information Center, Polly." He was put straight through. A young woman answered the phone.

"Stames, Washington Field Office. Would you please have the following suspect checked out on the computer immediately? – Angelo Casefikis: Caucasian; male; Greek ancestry; height, five feet nine inches; weight, about a hundred and sixty-five pounds; hair, dark brown; eyes, brown; age; thirty-eight; no distinguishing marks or scars known; no identifying numbers known." He was reading from the report Calvert had placed in front of him. He waited silently.

"If his story is true," Mark said, "we should have no listing for him at all."

"If it's true," said Calvert.

Stames continued to wait. The days of waiting to find

out who was in the FBI files and who wasn't had long gone. The girl came back on the line.

"We have nothing on a Casefikis, Angelo. We don't even have a Casefikis. The best the computer can offer is a Casegikis who was born in 1901. Sorry I can't help, Mr Stames."

"Thanks very much." Stames put the phone down. "Okay boys, for the moment let's give Casefikis the benefit of the doubt. Let's assume he is telling the truth and that this is a serious investigation. We have no trace of him in any of our files, so we'd better start believing his story until it's disproved; he just might be on to something, and if he is, then it goes way above me. Tomorrow morning, Barry, I want you back at the hospital with a fingerprint expert; take his prints in case he is giving a false name, put them through the identification computer right away and make sure you get a full written statement, signed. Then check the Met files for any shooting incidents on 24 February he could have been involved in. As soon as we can get him out, I want him in an ambulance showing us where that luncheon took place. Push the hospital into agreeing to that tomorrow morning, if possible. To date, he's not under arrest or wanted for any crime we know about, so don't go too far, not that he strikes me as a man who would know much about his rights.

"Mark," Stames said, turning his head, "I want you to go back to the hospital immediately and make sure the Met are there. If not, stay with Casefikis until they do arrive. In the morning, go round to the Golden Duck and check him out. I'm going to make a provisional appointment for us to see the Director tomorrow morning, at 10:00 am, which will give you enough time to report back to me. And if, when we check the fingerprints through the identification computer, nothing comes up at all, and the hotel and the restaurant exist, we may be in a whole heap of trouble. If that's the case, I'm not taking it one inch further without the Director knowing.

33

For the moment, I want nothing in writing. Don't hand in your official memorandum until tomorrow morning. Above all, don't mention that a senator could be involved to anybody – and that includes Grant Nanna. It's possible tomorrow, after we have seen the Director, that we will do no more than make a full report and hand the whole thing over to the Secret Service. Don't forget the clear division of responsibility – the Secret Service guards the President, we cover federal crime. If a senator is involved, it's us; if the President's involved, it's them. We'll let the Director decide the finer points – I'm not getting involved in Capitol Hill, that's the Director's baby, and with only seven days to play with, we don't have time to sit and discuss the academic niceties."

Stames picked up the red phone which put him straight through to the Director's office.

"Nick Stames, WFO."

"Good evening," said a low, quiet voice. Mrs McGregor, a dedicated servant of the Director of the Federal Bureau of Investigation, was still on duty. It was said that even Hoover had been slightly frightened of her.

"Mrs McGregor, I'd like to make a provisional appointment for myself and Special Agents Calvert and Andrews to see the Director for fifteen minutes, if that's possible. Anytime between 9:00 am and 11.00 am tomorrow. It's likely that after further investigation tonight and early tomorrow, I won't need to bother him."

Mrs McGregor consulted the Director's desk diary. "The Director is going to a meeting of police chiefs at eleven but he is expected in the office at 8:30 and he has nothing marked in his diary before eleven. I'll pencil you in for 10:30, Mr Stames. Do you want me to tell the Director what the subject of your discussion will be?"

"I'd prefer not to."

Mrs McGregor never pressed or asked a second question. She knew if Stames called, it was important. He saw the Director ten times a year on a social basis, but only

three or four times a year on a professional basis, and he was not in the habit of wasting the Director's time.

"Thank you, Mr Stames. 10:30 tomorrow morning, unless you cancel beforehand."

Nick put the phone down and looked at his two men.

"Okay, we're fixed to see the Director at 10:30. Barry, why don't you give me a lift home, then you can take yourself off afterwards, and pick me up again first thing in the morning. That'll give us another chance to go over the details again." Barry nodded. "Mark, you get straight back to the hospital."

Mark had allowed his mind to slip away to visualise Elizabeth Dexter walking down the corridor of Woodrow Wilson towards him, red silk collar over the white medical coat, black skirt swinging. He was doing this with his eyes open and the result was quite pleasant. He smiled.

"Andrews, what the hell is so amusing about a reported threat on the President's life?" Stames demanded.

"Sorry, sir. You just shot my social life down in flames. Would it be okay if I use my own car? I was hoping to go directly from the hospital to dinner."

"Yes, that's fine. We'll use the duty car and see you first thing in the morning. Get your tail in gear, Mark, and hope the Met makes it before breakfast." Mark looked at his watch. "Christ, it's already 8:00 pm."

Mark left the office slightly annoyed. Even if the Met were there when he arrived, he would still be late for Elizabeth Dexter. Still, he could always call her from the hospital.

"Like a plate of warmed-up moussaka, Barry, and a bottle of retsina?"

"It was more than I was expecting, boss."

The two men left the office. Stames mentally checked off the items on his nightly routine.

"Barry, will you double-check that Aspirin is on duty, as you go out, and tell him we won't be back again tonight."

Calvert made a detour to the Criminal Room and

delivered the message to Aspirin. He was doing the crossword from *The Washington Star*. He had finished three clues; it was going to be a long night. Barry caught up with Nick Stames as he stepped into the blue Ford.

"Yes, boss, he's working away."

They looked at each other, a night of headaches. Barry got in the driver's seat, slid it back as far as it would go, and adjusted the seat belt. They moved quietly up Constitution Avenue, then past the White House on to the E Street Expressway, and on towards Memorial Bridge.

"If Casefikis is on to something, we've got one hell of a week ahead of us," said Nick Stames. "Did he seem sure of the date for the assassination attempt?"

"When I questioned him a second time about the details, he repeated 10 March, in Washington."

"Hum-uh, seven days, not very long. Wonder what the Director will make of it," said Stames.

"Hand it over to the Secret Police, if he's got any sense," Barry said.

"Ah, let's forget it for the moment. Let's concentrate on warmed-over moussaka and deal with tomorrow when tomorrow comes."

The car came to a halt at a traffic light, just beyond the White House, where a bearded, long-haired, dirty youth, who had been picketing the home of the President, stood with a large poster advising the world: BEWARE THE END IS NIGH. Stames glanced at it and nodded to Barry.

"That's all we need tonight."

They passed under Virginia Avenue on the Expressway and sped across Memorial Bridge. A black 3.5 Lincoln passed them at about seventy miles an hour.

"Bet the Met pick him up," said Stames.

"Probably late for Dulles Airport," replied Barry.

The traffic was light, the rush-hour well behind them and when they turned on to George Washington Parkway they managed to stay in top gear. The Parkway, which follows the Potomac along the wooded Virginia shore, was dark and winding. Barry's reflexes were as fast as any man's in the service and Stames, although older, saw exactly what happened at the same time. A Buick, large and black, started to overtake them on their left. Calvert glanced towards it and when he looked forward again an instant later, another car, a black Lincoln, had swung in front of them on the wrong side of the highway. He thought he heard a rifle shot. Barry wrenched the wheel towards the centre of the road but it didn't respond. Both cars hit him at once, but he still managed to take one of them with him down the rocky slope. They gathered speed until they hit the surface of the river with a thud. Nick thought as he struggled in vain to open the door that the sinking seemed grotesquely slow, but inevitable.

The black Buick continued down the highway as if nothing had happened; past a car skidding to a halt, carrying a young couple, two terrified witnesses to the accident. They leapt out of their car and ran to the edge of the slope. There was nothing they could do but watch helplessly for the few seconds it took the blue Ford sedan and the Lincoln to sink out of sight.

"Jee-sus, did you see what happened ahead?" said the young man.

"Not really. I just saw the two cars go over the top. What do we do now, Jim?"

"Get the police fast."

Man and wife ran back to their car.

Thursday evening, 3 March

8:15 pm

"Hello, Liz."

There was a moment's pause at the other end of the phone.

"Hello, G-man. Aren't you getting a little ahead of yourself?"

"Only wishful thinking. Listen, Elizabeth, I've had to come back to the hospital and keep an eye on your Mr Casefikis until the police arrive. It's just possible that he could be in some danger, so we're having to put a guard on him which means I'm bound to be late for our date. Do you mind waiting?"

"No, I won't starve. I always have lunch with my father on Thursdays, and he's a big eater."

"That's good. Because I think you need to be fed. You look as though you might be hard to find in the dark. I'm still trying to get the flu, incidentally."

She laughed warmly. "See you later."

Mark put the telephone back on the hook and walked over to the elevator, and pressed the arrow on the Up-button.

He only hoped the Met policeman had arrived and was already on duty. Christ. How long was the elevator going to take to return to the ground floor? Patients must have died just waiting for it. Eventually the doors slid open and a burly Greek Orthodox priest hurried out and past him. He could have sworn it was a Greek Orthodox priest, from the high dark hat and long trailing veil and the Orthodox Cross around his neck, although something about the priest struck Mark as strange, but he couldn't put his finger on it. He stood, puzzling for a moment, staring at his retreating back and only just managing to jump into the elevator before the doors closed. He pressed the fourth-floor button several times. Come on, come on. Get going, you bastard, but it had no ears for Mark, and proceeded upward at the same stately pace as it had earlier in the afternoon. It cared nothing for his date with Elizabeth Dexter. The door opened slowly, and he went through the widening gap sideways and ran down the corridor to Room 4308 but there was no sign of any policeman. In fact, the corridor was deserted. It looked as if he were going to be stuck there for some time. He peered through the little window in the door at the two men, asleep in their beds, the voiceless television set was still on giving out a square of light. Mark left to look for the staff nurse and eventually found her tucked away in the head nurse's office enjoying a cup of coffee. She was pleased to see that it was the better-looking of the two FBI men who had returned.

"Has anyone come from the Metropolitan Police to keep an eye on Room 4308?"

"No, no one's been anywhere near the place tonight. Silent as the grave. Were you expecting someone?"

"Yes, damn it. Guess I'll have to wait. Do you think I could take a chair? I'm going to have to stick around till an officer from the Metropolitan Police comes. I hope I won't be in your way."

"You won't be in my way. You can stay as long as you like. I'll see if I can find you a nice comfortable chair." She put her mug down. "Would you like some coffee?"

"I certainly would." Mark looked at her more carefully. It might be an evening with the nurse rather than the doctor. Mark decided he had better go back and check the room first, reassure Casefikis, if he were still awake, and then call the Met and ask where the hell their man was. He walked slowly to the door a second time; he felt no need to hurry now. He opened the door quietly. It was pitch black except for the light from the TV, and his eyes were not quite focused. He glanced at the two of them in bed. They were quite still. He wouldn't have bothered to look any further if it hadn't been for the dripping.

Drip, drip, drip.

It sounded like tap water but he couldn't remember a tap.

Drip, drip.

He moved quietly to the bedside of Angelo Casefikis, and glanced down.

Drip, drip.

Warm fresh blood was flowing over the bottom sheet, trickling from Casefikis's mouth, his dark eyes bulged from their sockets, his tongue was hanging loose and swollen. His throat had been cut, ear to ear, just below the chin line. The blood was starting to make a pool on the floor. Mark was standing in it. He felt his legs sink, and he was barely able to grip the side of the bed and stop himself falling. He lurched over towards the deaf man. Mark's eyes were now focused, and he retched loudly. The postman's head was hanging loose from the rest of his body; only the colour of his skin showed that they were once connected. Mark managed to scramble out of the door and get to the pay phone, his heartbeat thudding madly in his ears. He could feel his shirt clinging to his body. His hands were covered with blood. He fumbled ineffectually for a couple of quarters. He dialled Homicide and gave the bare outline of what had happened. This time they wouldn't be casual about sending someone. The nurse on duty returned with a cup of coffee.

"Are you okay? You look a bit pale," she said, and then she saw his hands and screamed.

"Don't go into Room 4308 whatever you do. Don't let

anyone into that room unless I say so. Send me a doctor immediately."

The nurse thrust the cup of coffee at him, forcing him to take it, and ran down the corridor. Mark made himself go back into Room 4308, although his presence was irrelevant. There was nothing he could do except wait. He switched on the lights and went over to the bathroom; he tried to remove the worst of the blood and vomit from himself and his clothes. Mark heard the swinging door and rushed back into the room. Another young, white-coated female doctor . . . "Alicia Delgado, MD" said her plastic label.

"Don't touch anything," said Mark.

Dr Delgado stared at him and then the bodies, and groaned.

"Don't touch anything," repeated Mark, "until Homicide arrive; they will be here shortly."

"Who are you?" she asked.

"Special Agent Mark Andrews, FBI." He instinctively took out his wallet and showed his credentials.

"Do we just stand here staring at each other or are you going to allow me to do something about this mess?"

"Nothing until Homicide has completed their investigation and given clearance. Let's get out of here." He passed her and pushed the door with his shoulder, not touching anything.

They were back in the corridor.

Mark instructed Dr Delgado to wait outside the door and to allow no one else inside while he phoned the Metropolitan Police again.

She nodded reluctantly.

He went over to the pay phone, two more quarters; he dialled the Metropolitan Police and asked for Lieutenant Blake.

"Lieutenant Blake went home about an hour ago. Can I help you?"

"When had you been planning to send someone over to guard Room 4308 at Woodrow Wilson Medical Center?"

"Who's speaking?"

"Andrews, FBI, Washington Field Office." Mark repeated the details of the double murder.

"Well, our man should be with you now. He left the office over half an hour ago. I'll inform Homicide immediately."

"I've already done that," snapped Mark.

He put the phone down and collapsed into a nearby chair. The corridor was now full of white coats. Two gurneys were being wheeled up to Room 4308. They were all waiting. What was the right thing to do?

Two more quarters, he dialled Nick Stames's home. The phone seemed to ring for a long time. Why didn't he answer? Eventually a female voice came on.

Mustn't show panic, he thought, holding on to the phone box. "Good evening, Mrs Stames. It's Mark Andrews. Can I speak to your husband?" An even tone, no sign of stress.

"I'm afraid Nick is not home, Mark. He went back to the office about two hours ago. Funny, he said he was going to see you and Barry Calvert."

"Yes, we saw him, but he left the office to go back home about forty minutes ago."

"Well, he hasn't arrived yet. He only managed to finish the first course of his dinner and said he would come straight back. No sign of him. Maybe he returned to the office. Why don't you try him there?"

"Yes, of course. Sorry to have bothered you." Mark hung up, looked over to check that no one had gone into Room 4308. No one had. He put two more quarters in and phoned the office. Polly was on duty.

"Mark Andrews. Put me through to Mr Stames, quickly, please."

"Mr Stames and Special Agent Calvert left about forty-five minutes ago – on their way home, I think, Mr Andrews."

"That can't be right. It can't be right."

"Yes, they did leave, sir. I saw them go."

"Could you double-check?"

"If you say so, Mr Andrews."

Mark waited, it seemed to him, for an interminable time. What should he be doing? He was only one man, where was everyone else? What was he supposed to do? Christ, nothing in his training covered this – the FBI are meant to arrive twenty-four hours after a crime, not during it.

"There's no answer, Mr Andrews."

"Thanks, Polly."

Mark looked desperately at the ceiling for inspiration. He had been briefed not to tell anybody about the earlier events of the evening, not to say a word whatever the circumstances until after Stames's meeting with the Director. He must find Stames; he must find Calvert. He must find somebody he could talk to. Two more quarters. He tried Barry Calvert. The phone rang and rang. No reply from the bachelor apartment. Same two quarters. He called Norma Stames again. "Mrs Stames, Mark Andrews. Sorry to trouble you again. The moment your husband and Mr Calvert arrive, please have them call me at Woodrow Wilson."

"Yes, I'll tell Nick as soon as he comes in. They probably stopped off on the way."

"Yes, of course, I hadn't thought of that. Maybe the best thing will be for me to go back downtown as soon as the relief arrives. So perhaps they could contact me there. Thank you, Mrs Stames." He hung up the receiver.

As he put the phone down Mark saw the Met policeman jauntily walking towards him down the middle of the now crowded corridor, an Ed McBain novel under his arm. Mark thought of bawling him out for his late arrival, but what was the point. No use crying over spilt blood he thought, morbidly, and began to feel sick again. He took the young officer aside, and briefed him on the killings, giving no details of why the two men were important, only of what had happened. He asked him to inform his chief and added that the Homicide Squad were on their way, again adding no details. The policeman called his own duty officer, and reported all he had been told, matter-of-factly. The Washington Metropolitan Police handled over six hundred murders a year.

The medical personnel were all waiting impatiently; it was going to be a long wait. Professional bustle seemed to have replaced the early panic. Mark still wasn't sure where to turn, what to do. Where was Stames? Where was Calvert? Where the hell was anybody?

He went over to the policeman again, who was explaining in detail why no one must enter the room ... they were not convinced but waited; Mark told him he was leaving for the Field Office. He still gave him no clue why Casefikis had been important. The Metropolitan policeman felt he had things under control. Homicide would be there at any moment. He told Mark they'd want to talk to him later that night. Mark nodded and left him.

When he arrived back at his car, he took the flashing red light out of the side compartment and fixed it to the roof, placing the switch into its special slot. He was going to get back to the office, at top speed, to people he knew, to reality, to men who would make some sense out of his nightmare.

Mark flicked on the car radio. "WFO 180 in service. Please try and locate Mr Stames and Mr Calvert. Urgent. I am returning to Field Office immediately."

"Yes, Mr Andrews."

"WFO 180 out of service."

Twelve minutes later, he arrived at the Washington Field Office and parked his car. He ran to the elevator. The operator took him up. He rushed out.

"Aspirin, Aspirin. Who the hell's on duty tonight?"

"I'm the only one on tonight, boy, I'm here on my own," said Aspirin, looking over his glasses, rather bored. "What's the matter?"

"Where's Stames? Where's Calvert?" Mark demanded.

"They went home just over an hour ago."

Oh hell, what should he do now? Aspirin was not a man to confide in, but he was the only person Mark could seek any advice from. And although Stames had carefully instructed him not to speak to anyone about the details until they had seen the Director, this was an emergency. He wouldn't give away any of the details, he would just find out what a Hoover man would have done.

"I have to find Stames and Calvert, wherever they are. Any suggestions?"

"Well, first of all, have you tried the car radio stations?" asked Aspirin.

"I asked Polly to check. I'll try her again."

Mark picked up the nearest phone. "Polly, did you locate Mr Stames or Mr Calvert on the car radio?"

"Still trying, sir."

He seemed to wait endlessly, endlessly; and nothing happened. "What's going on, Polly, what's going on?"

"I'm trying as hard as I can, sir. All I can get is a buzzing sound."

"Try One, Two, Three, or Four. Doesn't matter what you try. Try every station."

"Yes, sir. I can only do one at a time. There are four stations and I can only do one at a time."

Mark realised he was panicking. It was time to sit down and think things through. The end of the world hadn't come – or had it?

"They're not on One, sir. Not on Two. Why would they be on Three or Four at this time of night? They're only on their way home."

"I don't care where they're going. Just find them. Try again."

"Okay, okay." She tried Three. She tried Four. She had to have authorisation to break the code for Five and Six. Mark looked at Aspirin. The duty officer was authorised to break the code.

"This is an emergency – I swear to you it's an emergency."

Aspirin told Polly to try Five and Six. Five and Six are Federal Communications Commission to the FBI. They are known by the initial KGB: it always amused FBI men to have KGB as their network call code. But at that moment it didn't seem particularly funny. There was no reply to be had on KGB 5. Then KGB 6 was raised; likewise nothing. Now what, dear God, now what? Where did he turn next? Aspirin looked at him inquiringly, not really wanting to get involved.

"Always remember, son, C-Y-A. That's the ticket. C-Y-A."

"Covering your ass will not help me to locate Mr Stames," said Mark, forcing himself to speak calmly. "It doesn't matter, Aspirin, you get back to your crossword puzzle."

Mark left him and went into the men's room, cupped his hands under the tap and washed his mouth out; he still smelled of vomit and blood. He cleaned up as best he could. He returned to the Criminal Room, sat down, and counted to ten very slowly. He had to make up his mind what to do, and then to carry it out, come what may. Something had probably happened to Stames and Calvert, he knew something had happened to the black postman and the Greek. Perhaps he should try and get in touch with the Director, although it was an extreme course. A man of Mark's rank, two years out of training, didn't just pick up a phone and call the Director. In any case he could still keep Stames's appointment with the Director at 10:30 the next morning. 10:30 the next morning. That was half a day away. More than twelve hours of not knowing what to do. Nursing a secret that he had been told not to discuss with anyone. Holding information he couldn't impart to anybody else.

The phone rang and he heard Polly's voice. He prayed it would be Stames, but his prayer was not answered.

"Hey, Mr Andrews, are you still there? I've got Homicide on the line. Captain Hogan wants to talk to you."

"Andrews?"

"Yes, Captain."

"What can you tell me?"

Mark reported truthfully that Casefikis was an illegal immigrant who had delayed seeking treatment for his leg, and untruthfully that he alleged he had been shot by a crook who had subjected him to blackmail, threatening exposure of his illegal entry into the States. A full written report would be sent around to his office by tomorrow morning.

The detective sounded disbelieving.

"Are you holding out on me, son? What was the FBI doing there in the first place? There's going to be one hell of a scene if I find out you're withholding information. I wouldn't hesitate to roast your ass over the hottest coals in Washington."

Mark thought of Stames's repeated injunctions about secrecy.

"No, I'm not withholding information," he said in a raised voice; he knew he was trembling and could hardly have sounded less convincing. The Homicide detective grumbled to himself, asked a few more questions, and hung up. Mark put the phone down. The receiver was clammy with sweat, his clothes still stuck to him. He tried Norma Stames again; still the boss hadn't reached home. He called Polly again, and asked her to go through the whole routine with the radio channels again; still nothing except a buzzing sound on Channel One. Finally, Mark abandoned the telephone and told Aspirin he was leaving. Aspirin didn't seem interested.

Mark headed for the elevator and walked quickly to his car. Must get on to home ground. Then call the Director. Once again he was speeding through the streets towards his home.

It wasn't the most luxurious part of town, but the renovated south-west section of Washington was home for many young, single professionals. It was on the waterfront near the Arena Stage, conveniently located next to a

Metro station. Pleasant, lively, not too expensive – the place suited Mark perfectly.

As soon as he reached his apartment, he ran up the stairs, burst through the door and picked up the phone. After several rings, the Bureau answered. "Director's office. Duty officer speaking."

Mark drew a deep breath.

"My name is Special Agent Andrews, Washington Field Office," Mark began slowly. "I want to speak to the Director, priority and immediate."

The Director, it seemed, was dining with the Attorney General at her home. Mark asked for the telephone number. Did he have special authority to contact the Director at this time of night? He had special authority, he had an appointment with him at 10:30 tomorrow morning and, for God's sake, he had special authority.

The man must have sensed Andrews was desperate.

"I'll call you right back, if you'll give me your number."

Andrews knew that this was simply to check that he was an FBI agent and that he was scheduled to see the Director in the morning. The phone rang after one minute and the duty officer was back.

"The Director is still with the Attorney General. Her private number is 761-4386."

Mark dialled the number.

"Mrs Edelman's residence," said a deferential voice.

"This is Special Agent Mark Andrews," he began. "I need to speak to the Director of the Federal Bureau of Investigation."

He said it slowly, he said it clearly, although he was still trembling. The reply came back from a man whose biggest worry that night had been that the potatoes had taken longer than expected.

"Will you hold the line one moment please, sir?"

He waited, he waited, he waited.

A new voice said: "Tyson here."

Mark drew a deep breath and plunged in.

"My name is Special Agent Mark Andrews. I have an

appointment to see you with SAC Stames and Special Agent Calvert at 10:30 tomorrow morning. You don't know the details, sir, because it was made through Mrs McGregor after you had left your office. I have to see you immediately, you may wish to call me back. I'm at home."

"Yes, Andrews," said Tyson. "I'll call you back. What is your number?"

Mark gave it.

"Young man," Tyson said, "this had better be a priority."

"It is, sir."

Mark waited again. One minute passed, and then another. Had Tyson dismissed him as a fool? What was going on? Three minutes passed. Four minutes passed; he was obviously checking more thoroughly than his duty officer had done.

The phone rang. Mark jumped.

"Hi, Mark, it's Roger. Want to come out for a beer?"

"Not now, Roger, not now." He slammed the phone down.

It rang again immediately.

"Right, Andrews, what do you have to tell me? Make it quick and to the point."

"I want to see you now, sir. I need fifteen minutes of your time and I need you to tell me what the hell to do."

He regretted "hell" the moment he had said it.

"Very well, if it's that urgent. Do you know where the Attorney General lives?"

"No, sir."

"Take this down: 2942 Edgewood Street, Arlington."

Mark put the phone down, wrote the address carefully in block capitals on the inside of a matchbook advertising life insurance, and called Aspirin, who just couldn't get 7-across.

"If anything happens, I'll be on my car radio; you can get me there, I'll leave the line on Channel Two open the whole time. Something's wrong with Channel One."

Aspirin sniffed: the young agents took themselves far too seriously nowadays. It wouldn't have happened under J. Edgar Hoover, shouldn't be allowed to happen now. Still, he only had one more year and then retirement. He returned to the crossword. 7-across, ten letters: gathering of those in favour of buccaneering. Aspirin started to think.

Mark Andrews was thinking too as he rushed into the elevator, into the street, into his car, and moved off at speed to Arlington. He raced up East Basin Drive to Independence Avenue, past the Lincoln Memorial to get on to Memorial Bridge. He drove as fast as possible through the early night, cursing the people calmly strolling across the road on this mild, pleasant evening, casually on their way to nowhere in particular, cursing the people who took no notice of the flashing red light he had affixed to the car roof, cursing all the way. Where was Stames? Where was Barry? What the hell was going on? Would the Director think he was crazy?

He crossed Memorial Bridge and took the G.W. Parkway exit. A tie-up. He couldn't move an inch. Probably an accident. A goddamn accident right now. That was all he needed. He pulled into the centre lane and leaned on his horn. Most people assumed he was connected with the police rescue team: most people let him by. Eventually he made it to the group of police cars and rescue-squad ambulances. A young Metropolitan policeman approached the car. "Are you on this detail?"

"No. FBI. I've got to get to Arlington. Emergency."

He flashed his credentials. The policeman ushered him through. He raced away from the accident. Goddamn accident. Once he was clear of it, the traffic became light. Fifteen minutes later, he arrived at 2942 Edgewood Street, Arlington. One last check with Polly at the Washington Field Office on the car phone. No, neither Stames nor Calvert had called in.

Mark jumped out of the car. Before he had taken a step, a Secret Service man stopped him. Mark showed his credentials and said that he had an appointment with the Director. The Secret Service man courteously asked him to wait by his car. After consultation at the door, Mark was shown into a small room just on the right of the hall which was obviously used as a study. The Director came in. Mark stood up.

"Good evening, Director."

"Good evening, Andrews. You've interrupted a very important dinner. I hope you know what you are doing."

The Director was cold and abrupt, clearly displeased at being summoned to a meeting by an unknown junior agent.

Mark went through the whole story from the first meeting with Stames through to his decision to go over everybody's head. The Director's face remained impassive throughout the long recital. It was still impassive when Mark had finished. Mark's only thought was: I've done the wrong thing. He should have gone on trying to reach Stames and Calvert. They were probably home by now. He waited, a little sweat appearing on his forehead. Perhaps this was his last day in the FBI. The Director's first words took him by surprise.

"You did exactly the right thing, Andrews. I'd have made the same decision in your place. It must have taken guts to bring the whole thing to me." He looked hard at Mark. "You're absolutely certain only Stames, Calvert, you, and I know all the details of what happened this evening? No one from the Secret Service, and no one from the Metropolitan Police Department?"

"That's correct, sir, just the four of us."

"And the three of you already have an appointment with me at 10:30 tomorrow morning?"

"Yes, sir."

"Good. Take this down."

Mark took out a pad from his inside coat pocket.

"You have the Attorney General's number here?"

"Yes, sir."

"And my number at home is 721-4069. Learn them

and then destroy them. Now I'll tell you exactly what you do next. Go back to the Washington Field Office. Check on Stames and Calvert again. Call the morgue, call the hospitals, call the highway police. If nothing turns up, I'll see you in my office at 8:30 tomorrow morning, not 10:30. That's your first job. Second, get me the names of the Homicide officers working on this detail with the Metropolitan Police. Now tell me if I have this right – you told them nothing about the reason you went to see Casefikis?"

"Nothing, sir."

"Good."

The Attorney General put her head around the door.

"Everything under control, Halt?"

"Fine, thanks, Marian. I don't think you've met Special Agent Andrews of the Washington Field Office."

"No. Nice to meet you, Mr Andrews."

"Good evening, ma'am."

"Will you be long, Halt?"

"No, I'll be back as soon as I've finished briefing Andrews."

"Anything special?"

"No, nothing to worry about."

The Director had obviously decided nobody was going to be told the story until he got to the bottom of it himself.

"Where was I?"

"You told me to return to the Washington Field Office, sir, and check on Stames and Calvert."

"Yes."

"And then to call the morgue, the hospitals, and the highway police."

"Right."

"And you told me to check on the Homicide officers, get their names."

"Right. Take down the following: check the names of all hospital employees and visitors, as well as any other persons who can be identified as having been in the vicinity of Room 4308 between the time the two occupants were known to be alive and the time you found them dead. Check the names of the two dead men through NCIC and Bureau indexes for any background information we may have. Get fingerprints of all persons on duty and all visitors and all others who can be identified as having been near Room 4308, as well as fingerprints of the two dead men. We will need all these prints both for elimination purposes and possible suspect identification. If you don't find Stames and Calvert, as I said, see me at 8:30 in my office tomorrow morning. If anything else arises tonight, you call me here or at home. Don't hesitate. If it's after 11:30, I'll be home. If you call me on the phone, use a code name – now let me think – Julius – let's hope it's not prophetic, and give me your number. Make sure you use a pay phone and I'll call you back immediately. Don't bother me before 7:15 in the morning, unless it's really important. Have you understood all that?"

"Yes, sir."

"Right. I think I'll get back to dinner."

Mark stood up, ready to leave. The Director put a hand on his shoulder.

"Don't worry, young man. These things happen from time to time and you made the right decision. You showed a lot of self-possession in a lousy situation. Now get on with the job."

"Yes, sir."

Mark was relieved that someone else knew what he was going through; someone else with far bigger shoulders was there to share it.

On his way back to the FBI office, he picked up the car microphone. "WFO 180 in service. Any word from Mr Stames?"

"Nothing yet, WFO 180, but I'll keep trying."

Aspirin was still there when he arrived, unaware that Mark had just been talking with the Director of the FBI. Aspirin had met all four directors at cocktail parties, though none of them would have remembered his name.

"Emergency over, son?"

"Yes," Mark said, lying. "Have we heard from Stames or Calvert?" He tried not to sound anxious.

"No, must have dropped in somewhere on the way home. Never you worry. The little sheep will find their way back without you to hold their tails."

Mark did worry. He went to his office and picked up the phone. Polly had still heard nothing. Just a buzz that continued on Channel One. He called Norma Stames, still no news. Mrs Stames asked if there might be anything to worry about.

"Nothing at all." Another lie. Was he sounding too unconcerned? "We just can't find out which bar he's ended up in."

She laughed, but she knew Nick never frequented bars.

Mark tried Calvert; still no reply from the bachelor apartment. He knew in his bones something was wrong. He just didn't know what. At least the Director was there, and the Director knew everything now. He glanced at his watch: 11:15. Where had the night gone? And where was it going? 11:15. What was he supposed to have done tonight? Hell. He had persuaded a beautiful girl to have dinner with him. Yet again, he picked up the telephone. At least she would be safely at home, where she ought to be.

"Hello."

"Hello, Elizabeth, it's Mark Andrews. I'm really sorry about not making it tonight. Something happened that got way out of my control."

The tension in his voice was apparent.

"Don't worry," she said lightly. "You warned me you were unreliable."

"I hope you'll let me take a raincheck. Hopefully, in the morning, I can sort things out. I'll probably see you then."

"In the morning?" she said. "If you're thinking of the hospital, I'm off duty tomorrow."

Mark hesitated, thinking quickly of what he could

54

prudently say. "Well, that may be best. I am afraid it's not good news. Casefikis and the other man in his room were brutally murdered tonight. The Met is following it up, but we have nothing to go on."

"Murdered? Both of them? Why? Who? Casefikis wasn't killed without reason, was he?" The words came out in a torrent. "What's going on, for heaven's sake? No, don't answer that. You wouldn't tell me the truth in any case."

"I wouldn't waste my time lying to you, Elizabeth. Look, I've had it for tonight, and I owe you a big steak for messing up your evening. Can I call you some time soon?"

"I'd like that. Murder isn't food for the appetite, though. I hope you catch the men responsible. We see the results of a great deal of violence at Woodrow Wilson, but it isn't usually inflicted within our walls."

"I know. I'm sorry it involves you. Good night, Elizabeth. Sleep well."

"And you, Mark. If you can."

Mark put the phone down, and immediately the burden of the day's events returned. What now? There was nothing practicable he could do before 8:30, except keep in touch on the radio phone until he was home. There was no point just sitting there looking out of the window, feeling helpless, sick, and alone. He went in to Aspirin, told him he was going home, and that he'd call in every fifteen minutes because he was still anxious to speak to Stames and Calvert. Aspirin didn't even look up.

"Fine," he said, his mind fully occupied by the crossword puzzle. He had completed eleven clues, a sure sign it was a quiet evening.

Mark drove down Pennsylvania Avenue towards his apartment. At the first traffic circle, a tourist who didn't know he had the right of way was holding up traffic. Damn him, thought Mark. Visitors to Washington who hadn't mastered the knack of cutting out at the right turn-off could end up circling round and round many more times than originally planned. Eventually, Mark managed to get around the circle and back on Pennsylvania Avenue. He continued to drive slowly towards his home, at the Tiber Island Apartments, his thoughts heavy and anxious. He turned on the car radio for the midnight news; must take his mind off it somehow. There were no big stories that night and the newscaster sounded rather bored; the President had held a press conference about the Gun Control bill, and the situation in South Africa seemed to be getting worse. Then the local news; there had been an automobile accident on the G.W. Parkway and it involved two cars, both of which were being hauled out of the river by cranes, under floodlights. One of the cars was a black Lincoln, the other a blue Ford sedan, according to eyewitnesses, a married couple from Jacksonville vacationing in the Washington area. No other details as yet.

A blue Ford sedan. Although he had not really been concentrating, it kept repeating itself in his brain – a blue Ford sedan? Oh no, God, please no. He veered right off 9th Street on to Maine Avenue, narrowly missing a fire hydrant, and raced back towards Memorial Bridge, where he had been only two hours before. The roads were clearer now and he was back in a few minutes. At the scene of the accident the Metropolitan Police were still thick on the ground and one lane of the G.W. was closed off by barriers. Mark parked the car on the grassy verge and ran up to the barrier. He showed his FBI credentials and was taken to the officer in charge; he explained that he feared one of the cars involved might have been driven by an agent from the FBI. Any details yet?

"Still haven't got them out," the inspector replied. "We only have two witnesses to the accident, if it was an accident. Apparently there was some very funny driving going on. They should be up in about thirty minutes. All you can do is wait."

Mark went over to the side of the road to watch the vast cranes and tiny frogmen groping around in the river

56

under vast klieg lights. The thirty minutes wasn't thirty minutes; he shivered in the cold, waiting and watching. It was forty minutes, it was fifty minutes, it was over an hour before the black Lincoln came out. Inside the car was one body. Cautious man, he was wearing a seat belt. The police moved in immediately. Mark went back to the officer in charge and asked how long before the second car.

"Not long. That Lincoln wasn't your car, then?"

"No," said Mark.

Ten minutes, twenty minutes, he saw the top of the second car, a dark blue car; he saw the side of the car, one of the windows fractionally opened; he saw the whole of the car. Two men were in it. He saw the licence plate. For a second time that night, Mark felt sick. Almost crying, he ran back to the officer in charge and gave the names of the two men in the car, and then ran on to a pay phone at the side of the road. It was a long way. He dialled the number, checking his watch as he did so; it was nearly one o'clock. After one ring he heard a tired voice say, "Yes."

Mark said, "Julius."

The voice said, "What is your number?"

He gave it. Thirty seconds later, the telephone rang.

"Well, Andrews. It's one o'clock in the morning."

"I know, sir, it's Stames and Calvert, they're dead."

There was a moment's hesitation, the voice was awake now.

"Are you certain?"

"Yes, sir."

Mark gave the details of the car crash, trying to keep the weariness and emotion out of his voice.

"Call your office immediately, Andrews," Tyson said, "without releasing any of the details that you gave me this evening. Only tell them about the car crash – nothing more. Then get any further information about it you can from the police. See me in my office at 7:30, not 8:30;

come through the wide entrance on the far side of the building; there will be a man waiting there for you. He'll be expecting you; don't be late. Go home now and try to get some sleep and keep yourself out of sight until tomorrow. Don't worry, Andrews. Two of us know, and I'll put agents on the routine checks that I gave you to do earlier."

The phone clicked. Mark called Aspirin, what a night for him to have to be on duty, told him about Stames and Calvert, hanging up abruptly before Aspirin could ask any questions. He returned to his car and drove home slowly through the night. There was hardly another car on the streets and the early-morning mist gave everything an unearthly look.

At the entrance to his apartment garage he saw Simon, the young black attendant, who liked Mark and, even more, Mark's Mercedes. Mark had blown a small legacy from his aunt on the car just after graduating from college, but never regretted his extravagance. Simon knew Mark had no assigned spot in the garage and always offered to park his car for him – anything for a chance to drive the magnificent silver Mercedes SLC 580. Mark usually exchanged a few bantering words with Simon; tonight he passed him the keys without even looking at him.

"I'll need it at seven in the morning," he said, already walking away. "Okay, man," came back the reply.

Mark heard Simon restart the car with a soft whoosh before the elevator door closed behind him. He arrived at his apartment; three rooms, all empty. He locked the door, and then bolted it, something he had never done before. He walked around the room slowly, undressed, throwing his sour-smelling shirt into the laundry hamper. He washed for the third time that night and then went to bed, to stare up at the white ceiling. He tried to make some sense out of the night's events; he tried to sleep. Six hours passed, and if he slept it was never for more than a few minutes.

*

Someone else who didn't sleep that night for more than a few minutes was tossing and turning in her bed at the White House.

Abraham Lincoln, John F. Kennedy, Martin Luther King, John Lennon and Robert Kennedy. How many citizens distinguished and unknown needed to sacrifice their lives before the House would pass a bill to outlaw such self-destruction?

"Who else must die?" she remarked. "If I myself there is no hour so fit as . . ."

She turned over and looked at Edward whose expression left no doubt that such morbid thoughts were not on his mind.

Friday morning, 4 March

6:27 am

Eventually Mark could stand it no longer and at 6:30 am
he rose, showered, and put on a clean shirt and a fresh
suit. From his apartment window, he looked out across
the Washington Channel to East Potomac Park and went
over in his mind all that had happened yesterday. In
a few weeks the cherry trees would bloom. In a few
weeks . . .

He closed the apartment door behind him, glad simply
to be on the move again. Simon gave him the car keys;
he had managed to find a space for the Mercedes in one
of the private parking lots.

Mark drove the car slowly up 6th Street, turned left
on G and right on 7th. No traffic at this time of morning
except trucks. He passed the Hirshhorn Museum as he
crossed into Independence Avenue. At the intersection of
7th and Pennsylvania, next to the National Archives,
Mark came to a halt at a red light. He felt an eerie sense
of nothing being out of the ordinary, as though the
previous day had been a bad dream. He would arrive at
the office and Nick Stames and Barry Calvert would be
there as usual. The vision evaporated as he looked to his
left. At one end of the deserted avenue, he could see the
White House grounds and patches of the white building
through the trees. To his right, at the other end of the
avenue, stood the Capitol, gleaming in the early morning

sunshine. And between the two, between Caesar and Cassius, thought Mark, stood the FBI Building. Alone in the middle, he mused, the Director and himself, playing with destiny.

Mark drove the car down the ramp at the back of FBI Headquarters and parked. A young man in a dark blue blazer, grey flannels, dark shoes, and a smart blue tie, the regulation uniform of the Bureau, awaited him. An anonymous man, thought Mark, who looked far too neat to have just got up. Mark Andrews showed him his identification. The young man led him towards the elevator without saying a word; it took them to the seventh floor, where Mark was noiselessly escorted to a small room and asked to wait.

He sat in the reception room, next to the Director's office, with the inevitable out-of-date copies of *Time* and *Newsweek*; he might have been at the dentist's. It was the first time in his life that he would rather have been at his dentist's. He pondered the events of the last fourteen hours. He'd gone from being a man with no responsibility enjoying the second of five eventful years in the FBI to one who was staring into the jaws of a tiger. His only previous trip to the Bureau itself had been for his interview; they hadn't told him that this could happen. They had talked of salaries, bonuses, holidays, a worthwhile and fulfilling job, serving the nation, nothing about immigrant Greeks and black postmen with their throats cut, nothing about friends being drowned in the Potomac. He paced around the room trying to compose his thoughts; yesterday should have been his day off, but he had decided he could do with the overtime pay. Perhaps another agent would have got back to the hospital more quickly and forestalled the double murder. Perhaps if he had driven the Ford sedan last night, it would have been he, not Stames and Calvert, in the Potomac. Perhaps . . . Mark closed his eyes and felt an involuntary shiver run down his spine. He made an effort to disregard the panicky fear that had kept him awake all night – perhaps it would be his turn next.

His eyes came to rest on a plaque on the wall, which stated that, in over sixty years of the FBI's history, only thirty-four people had been killed while on duty; on only one occasion had two officers died on the same day. Yesterday made that out-of-date. Mark's eyes continued moving around the wall and settled on a large picture of the Supreme Court; government and the law hand-in-hand. On his left were the five directors, Hoover, Gray, Ruckelshaus, Kelley, and now the redoubtable H. A. L. Tyson, known to everyone in the Bureau by the acronym Halt. Apparently, no one except his secretary, Mrs McGregor, knew his first name. It had become a long-standing joke in the Bureau. When you joined the FBI, you paid one dollar to Mrs McGregor, who had served the Director for twenty-seven years, and told her what you thought the Director's first name was. If you got it right, you won the pool. The kitty had now reached $3,516. Mark had guessed Hector. Mrs McGregor had laughed and the pool was one dollar the richer. If you wanted a second guess, that cost you another dollar, but if you got it wrong, you paid a ten-dollar fine. Quite a few people tried the second time and the kitty grew larger as each new victim arrived.

Mark had had what he thought was the bright idea of checking the Criminal Fingerprints File. The FBI fingerprints records fall into three categories – military, civil, and criminal, and all FBI agents have their prints in the criminal file. This insures that they are able to trace any FBI agent who turns criminal, or to eliminate an agent's prints at the scene of a crime; these records are very rarely used. Mark had considered himself very clever as he asked to see Tyson's card. The Director's card was handed to him by an assistant from the Fingerprints Department. It read – "Height: 6′1″; Weight: 180 lbs; Hair; brown; Occupation: Director of FBI; Name: Tyson, H. A. L." No forename given. The assistant, another anonymous man in a blue suit, had smiled sourly at Mark and had said, loud enough for Mark to hear, as he returned the card to its file, "One more sucker who thought he was going to make a quick three thousand bucks."

Because the Bureau had become more political during the last decade the appointment of a professional law enforcement officer was a figure whom Congress found very easy to endorse. Law enforcement was in Tyson's blood. His great-grandfather had been a Wells Fargo man, riding shotgun on the stage between San Francisco and Seattle in the other Washington. His grandfather had been mayor of Boston and its chief of police, a rare combination, and his father before his retirement had been a distinguished Massachusetts attorney. That the great-grandson had followed family tradition, and ended up as Director of the Federal Bureau of Investigation, surprised no one. The anecdotes about him were legion and Mark wondered just how many of them were apocryphal.

There was no doubt that Tyson had scored the winning touchdown in his final Harvard–Yale game because it was there on record, as indeed was the fact that he was the only white man to box on the 1956 American Olympic team in Melbourne. Whether he had actually said to the late President Nixon that he would rather serve the devil than direct the FBI under his presidency, no one could be sure, but it was certainly a story the Kane camp made no effort to suppress.

His wife had died five years earlier of multiple sclerosis. He had nursed her for twenty years with a fierce loyalty.

He feared no man and his reputation for honesty and straight talking had raised him above most government employees in the eyes of the nation. After a period of malaise, following Hoover's death, Halt Tyson had restored the Bureau to the prestige it had enjoyed in the 1930s and 1940s. Tyson was one of the reasons Mark had been happy to commit five years of his life to the FBI.

Mark began to fidget with the middle button of his jacket, as all FBI agents tend to do. It had been drummed into him in the fifteen-week course at Quantico that jacket buttons should always be undone, allowing access to the gun, on the hip holster, never on a shoulder strap. It annoyed Mark that the television series about the FBI always got that wrong. Whenever an FBI man sensed danger, he would fiddle with that middle button to make sure his coat was open. Mark sensed fear, fear of the unknown, fear of H. A. L. Tyson, fear which an accessible Smith and Wesson could not cure.

The anonymous young man with the vigilant look and the dark blue blazer returned.

"The Director will see you now."

Mark rose, felt unsteady, braced himself, rubbed his hands against his trousers to remove the sweat from his palms and followed the anonymous man through the outer office and into the Director's inner sanctum. The Director glanced up, waved him to a chair, and waited for the anonymous man to leave the room and close the door. Even seated, the Director was a bull of a man with a large head placed squarely on massive shoulders. Bushy eyebrows matched his careless, wiry brown hair; it was so curly you might have thought it was a wig if it hadn't been H. A. L. Tyson. His big hands remained splayed on the surface as though the desk might try to get away. The delicate Queen Anne desk was quite subdued by the grip of the Director. His cheeks were red, not the red of alcohol, but the red of good and bad weather. Slightly back from the Director's chair stood another man, muscular, clean-shaven, and silent, a policeman's policeman.

The Director spoke. "Andrews, this is Assistant Director Matthew Rogers. I have briefed him on the events following Casefikis's death: we will be putting several agents on the investigation with you." The Director's grey eyes were piercing – piercing Mark. "I lost two of my best men yesterday, Andrews, and nothing – I repeat, nothing – will stop me from finding out who was responsible, even if it was the President herself, you understand."

"Yes, sir," Mark said very quietly.

"You will have gathered from the press releases we gave that the public is under the impression that what happened yesterday evening was just another automobile accident. No journalist has connected the murders in Woodrow Wilson Medical Center with the deaths of my agents. Why should they, with a murder every twenty-six minutes in America?"

A Metropolitan Police file marked "Chief of Metropolitan Police" was by his side; even they were under control.

"We, Mr Andrews . . ."

It made Mark feel slightly royal.

". . . we are not going to disillusion them. I have been going over carefully what you told me last night. I'll summarise the situation as I see it. Please feel free to interrupt me whenever you want to."

Under normal circumstances, Mark would have laughed.

The Director was looking at the file.

"The Greek immigrant wanted to see the head of the FBI," he continued. "Perhaps I should have granted his request, had I known about it." He looked up. "Still, the facts: Casefikis made an oral statement to you at Woodrow Wilson, and the gist of it was that he believed that there was a plot in motion to assassinate the President of the United States on 10 March; he overheard this information while waiting on a private lunch in a Georgetown hotel, at which he thought a US senator was present. Is that correct so far, Andrews?"

"Yes, sir".

Once more the Director looked down at the file.

"The police took prints of the dead man, and he hasn't shown up in our files or in the Metropolitan Police files. So for the moment we must act on the assumption, after last night's four killings, that everything the Greek immigrant told us was in good faith. He may not have got the story entirely accurately, but he certainly was on to something big enough to cause four murders in one night. I think we may also assume that whoever the people are behind these diabolical events, they believe they are now in the clear and that they have killed anyone who might have known of their plans. You may consider yourself lucky, young man."

"Yes, sir."

"I suppose it had crossed your mind that they thought it was you in the blue Ford sedan?"

Mark nodded. He had thought of little else for the past ten hours; he hoped Norma Stames would never think of it.

"I want these conspirators to think they are now in the clear and for that reason, I am going to allow the President's schedule for the week to continue as planned, at least for the moment."

Mark ventured a question. "But, sir, won't that put her in grave danger?"

"Andrews, somebody, somewhere, and it may be a United States senator, is planning to assassinate the President; so far, he has been prepared to murder two of my best agents, a Greek who might have recognised him, and a deaf postman whose only connection with the matter was that he may have been able to identify Casefikis's killer. If we rush in now with the heavy artillery, then we will scare them off. We have almost nothing to go on; we would be unlikely to discover their identities. And if we did, we certainly wouldn't be able to nail them. Our only hope of catching them is to let the bastards think they are in the clear – right up to the last moment. That way, we just might get them. It's possible they have already been frightened off, but I think not. They have used such violent means to keep their intentions secret they must have some overriding reason for wanting the President out of the way within seven days. We must find out what the reason is."

66

"Shall we tell the President?"

"No, no, not yet. God knows, over the past two years she's had enough problems with the Gun Control bill without having to look over her shoulder trying to figure out which senator is Mark Antony and which is Brutus."

"So what do we do for the next six days?"

"You and I will have to find Cassius. And he may not be the one with the lean and hungry look."

"What if we don't find him?" asked Mark.

"God help America."

"And if we do?"

"You may have to kill him."

Mark thought for a moment. He'd never killed anybody in his life; come to think of it, he hadn't knowingly killed anything at all. He didn't like stepping on insects. And the thought that the first person he might kill could be a US senator was, to say the least, daunting.

"Don't look so worried, Andrews. It probably won't come to that. Now let me tell you exactly what I intend to do. I'm going to brief Stuart Knight, the head of the Secret Service, that two of my officers were investigating a man claiming that the President of the United States was going to be assassinated some time within the next month. However, I have no intention of letting him know that a senator may be involved; and I won't tell him that two of our men died because of it; that's not his problem. It may actually have nothing to do with a senator, and I'm not having a whole bunch of people staring at their elected representatives wondering which one of them is a criminal."

The Assistant Director cleared his throat and spoke for the first time. "Some of us think that anyway."

The Director continued unswervingly. "This morning, Andrews, you will write a report on Casefikis's information and the circumstances of his murder, and you will hand it in to Grant Nanna. Do not include the subsequent murders of Stames and Calvert: no one must connect these two events. Report the threat on the President's life but not the possibility that a senator is involved. Is that how you would play it, Matt?"

"Yes, sir," said Rogers. "If we voice our suspicions to people who don't need to know them, we will run the risk of provoking a security operation that will make the assassins run for cover; then we would simply have to pick up our marbles and start over – if we were lucky enough to get a second chance."

"Right," said the Director. "So this is how we'll proceed, Andrews. There are one hundred senators. One of them provides our only link with the conspirators. It's going to be your task to pinpoint that man. The Assistant Director will have a couple of junior men follow up the few other leads that we have. No need for them to know the details, Matt. To start with, check out the Golden Duck Restaurant."

"And every hotel in Georgetown, to see which one put on a private luncheon party on 24 February," said Rogers. "And the hospital. Maybe someone saw suspicious characters hanging around the parking lot or the corridors; the assassins must have seen our Ford there while Calvert and you, Andrews, were interviewing Casefikis. I think that's about all we can do for the moment."

"I agree," said the Director. "Okay, thanks, Matt, I won't take up any more of your time. Please let me have anything you turn up immediately."

"Sure," said the Assistant Director. He nodded at Mark and left the room.

Mark had sat silently, impressed by the clarity with which the Director had grasped the details of the case; his mind must be like a filing cabinet.

The Director pressed a button on his intercom.

"Coffee for two, please, Mrs McGregor."

"Yes, sir."

"Now, Andrews, you come into the Bureau at seven o'clock every morning and report to me. Should any emergency arise, call me, using the code name Julius. I will use the same code name when calling you. When you hear the word 'Julius', break off whatever you are doing. Do you understand?"

"Yes, sir."

"Now, a most important point. If, in any circumstances, I die or disappear, you brief only the Attorney General, and Rogers will take care of the rest. If you die, young man, you can leave the decision to me." He smiled for the first time – it was not Mark's idea of a joke. "I see from the files that you're entitled to two weeks' leave. Well take it, starting at noon today. I don't want you to exist officially for at least a week. Grant Nanna has already been briefed that you have been seconded to me," continued the Director. "You may have to tolerate me night and day for six days, young man, and no one other than my late wife has had that problem before."

"And you me, sir," was Mark's quick and unthinking reply.

He waited for his head to be bitten off; instead the Director smiled again.

Mrs McGregor appeared with the coffee, served them, and left. The Director drank his coffee in one swallow and began to pace around the room as if it were a cage; Mark did not move, though his eyes never left Tyson. His massive frame and great shoulders heaved up and down, his large head with its bushy hair rocking from side to side. He was going through what the boys called the thought process.

"The first thing you're to do, Andrews, is find out which senators were in Washington on 24 February. As it was near the weekend, most of those dummies would have been floating all over the country, making speeches or vacationing with their pampered children."

What endeared the Director to everyone was not that he said it behind their backs but that he said it even more explicitly to their faces. Mark smiled and began to relax.

"When we have that list, we'll try and figure out what they have in common. Separate the Republicans from the Democrats, and then put them under party headings as to interests, public and private. After that, we have to find out which ones have any connection with President Kane, past or present, friendly or unfriendly. Your report will cover all these details and be ready for our meeting tomorrow morning. Understood?"

"Yes, sir."

"Now there's something else I want you to understand, Andrews. As I am sure you know, for the past decade, the FBI has been in a very sensitive political position. Those watchdogs in Congress are just waiting for us to exceed our legitimate authority. If we in any way cast suspicion upon a member of Congress, without indisputable evidence of his guilt, they will hang, draw and quarter the Bureau. And rightly so, in my opinion. Police agencies in a democracy must prove that they can be trusted not to subvert the political process. Purer than Caesar's wife. Understood?"

"Yes, sir."

"From today we have six days, from tomorrow five, and I want to catch this man and his friends red-handed. So neither of us will be on statutory overtime."

"No, sir."

The Director returned to his desk and summoned Mrs McGregor.

"Mrs McGregor, this is Special Agent Andrews, who'll be working closely with me on an extremely sensitive investigation for the next six days. Whenever he wants to see me, let him come right in; if I'm with anybody but Mr Rogers, notify me immediately – no red tape, no waiting."

"Yes, sir."

"And I'd appreciate it if you didn't mention this to anybody else."

"Of course not, Mr Tyson."

The Director turned to Mark. "Now you go back to the WFO and start working. I'll see you in this office at seven o'clock tomorrow morning."

Mark stood up. He didn't finish his coffee; perhaps by

the sixth day he would feel free to say so. He shook hands with the Director and headed towards the door. Just as he reached it, the Director added: "Andrews, I hope you'll be very careful. Keep looking over both shoulders at once."

Mark shivered and moved quickly out of the room, down the corridor, keeping his back firmly to the wall when he reached the elevator, and walking along the sides of the passage on the ground floor, where he ran into a group of tourists who were studying pictures of the Ten Most Wanted Criminals in America. Next week, would one of them be a senator?

When he reached the street, he dodged the traffic until he arrived at the Washington Field Office, on the other side of Pennsylvania Avenue. It wouldn't quite be like home this morning. Two men were missing, and they weren't going to be able to replace them with a training manual. The flag on top of the FBI Building and the flag on top of the Old Post Office Building were at half-mast; two of their agents were dead.

Mark went straight into Grant Nanna's office; he had aged ten years overnight. For him, two friends had died, one who worked under him and one who worked above him.

"Sit down, Mark."

"Thank you, sir."

"The Director has already spoken to me this morning. I didn't ask any questions. I understand you're taking a two-week leave as of noon today, and that you are writing me a memorandum on what happened at the hospital. I have to pass it on to higher authorities and that will be the end of it as far as the WFO is concerned, because Homicide will take over. They are also trying to tell me Nick and Barry died in a car accident."

"Yes, sir," said Mark.

"I don't believe a goddamn word of it," said Nanna. "Now you're in the middle of this, somehow, and maybe you can nail the bastards who did it. When you find them, grind their balls into powder and then call me so that I can come help you, because if I lay my hands on those bastards . . ."

Mark looked at Grant Nanna, and then tactfully away again, waiting until his superior had regained control of his face and voice.

"Now, you're not allowed to contact me once you leave this office, but if I can help at any time, just call me. Don't let the Director know, he'd kill us both if he found out. Get going, Mark."

Mark left quickly and went to his office. He sat down and wrote out his report exactly as the Director had instructed, bland and brief. He took it back to Nanna, who flicked through it and tossed it into the out-box. "Neat little whitewash job you've done there, Mark."

Mark didn't speak. He signed out of the Washington Field Office, the one place in which he felt secure. He'd be on his own for six days. Ambitious men always wanted to see a few years ahead, to know the shape of their careers; Mark would have settled for a week.

The Director pressed a button. The anonymous man in the dark blue blazer and light grey trousers entered the room.

"Yes, sir."

"I want a full surveillance on Andrews, night and day; six men on three shifts reporting to me every morning. I want detailed background on him, his education, girl friends, associates, habits, hobbies, religion, organisational affiliations, everything by tomorrow morning, 6:45. Understood?"

"Yes, sir."

Aware that Senate staff members would be suspicious of an FBI agent who asked for information about their employers, Mark began his research at the Library of Congress. As he climbed the long flight of steps, he remembered a scene from *All the President's Men*, in which

Woodward and Bernstein had spent innumerable fruitless hours searching for a few slips of paper in the bowels of the building. They had been trying to find proof that E. Howard Hunt had checked out materials on Edward M. Kennedy. And for an FBI agent on the trail of a killer, just as for the investigative reporters, it would be tedious research, not glamorous assignments, that would make the difference between success and failure.

Mark opened the door marked "Readers Only" and strolled into the Main Reading Room, a huge, circular, domed room decorated in muted tones of gold, beige, rust, and bronze. The ground floor was filled with rows of dark, curved wooden desks, arranged in concentric circles around the reference area in the centre of the room. On the second floor, visible from the reading area through graceful arches, were thousands of books. Mark approached the reference desk and, in the hushed tones appropriate to all libraries, asked the Clerk where he could find current issues of the *Congressional Record*.

"Room 244. Law Library Reading Room."

"How do I get there?"

"Go back past the card catalogue to the other side of the building and take an elevator to the second floor."

Mark managed to find the Law Library, a white, rectangular room with three tiers of bookshelves on the left-hand side. After questioning another clerk, he located the *Congressional Record* on one of the dark brown reference shelves along the right-hand wall. He carried the unbound volume marked 24 February, to a long, deserted table and began the tedious weeding-out process.

After leafing through the digest of Senate business for half an hour, Mark realised that he was in luck. Many senators had apparently left Washington for the weekend, because a check of the roll calls on 24 February revealed that, of the one hundred senators, the number present on the floor never exceeded sixty. And the bills which were voted on were sufficiently important to command the presence of those senators who might have been hiding in the nooks and crannies of the Senate or the city. When he had eliminated those senators who were listed by the Whips of each party as "absent because of illness" or "necessarily absent", and added those who were merely "detained on official business", Mark was left with sixty-two senators who were definitely in Washington on 24 February. He then double-checked the other thirty-eight senators, one by one, a long and tiresome task. All of them had for some reason been out of Washington that day.

He glanced at his watch: 12:15. He couldn't afford to take time off for lunch.

Friday afternoon, 4 March

12:30 pm

Three men had arrived. None of them liked one another; only the common bond of financial reward could have got them into the same room. The first went by the name of Tony; he'd had so many names that nobody could be sure what his real name was, except perhaps his mother, and she hadn't seen him in the twenty years since he had left Sicily to join his father, her husband, in the States. Her husband had left twenty years before that; the cycle repeated itself.

Tony's FBI criminal file described him as five-feet-eight, a hundred and forty-six pounds, medium build, black hair, straight nose, brown eyes, no distinguishing features, arrested and charged once in connection with a bank robbery; first offence, two-year jail sentence. What the rap sheet did not reveal was that Tony was a brilliant driver; he had proved that yesterday and if that fool of a German had kept his head, there would have been four people in the room now instead of three. He had told the boss, "If you're going to employ a German, have him build the damn car, never let him drive it." The boss hadn't listened and the German had been dragged out of the bottom of the Potomac. Next time they'd use Tony's cousin Mario. At least then there would be another human on the team; you couldn't count the ex-cop and the little Jap who never said a word.

Tony glanced at Xan Tho Huc, who only spoke when asked a direct question. He was actually Vietnamese, but he had finally escaped to Japan in 1979. Everyone would have known his name if he had entered the Los Angeles Olympics, because nobody could have stopped him from getting the gold medal for rifle shooting, but Xan had decided, with his chosen career in mind, he had better keep a low profile and withdraw from the Japanese Olympic trials. His coach tried to get him to change his mind, but without success. To Tony, Xan remained a goddamn Jap, though he grudgingly admitted to himself he knew no other man who could fire ten shots into a three-inch square at eight hundred yards. The size of Florentyna Kane's forehead.

The Nip sat staring at him, motionless. Xan's appearance helped him in his work. No one expected that the slight frame, only about five-feet-two and a hundred and ten pounds, was that of a superlative marksman. Most people still associated marksmanship with hulking cowboys and lantern-jawed Caucasians. If you had been told this man was a ruthless killer, you would have assumed he worked with his hands, with a garrote or nunchaki, or even with poison. Among the three, Xan was the only one who carried a personal grudge. As a child he had seen his parents butchered by the Americans in Vietnam. They had spoken warmly of the Yanks and had supported them until the bullets tore into their bodies. They had left him for dead. A target almost too small to hit. From that moment he had vowed in silent torment to avenge his loss. He escaped to Japan and there, for two years after the fall of Saigon, he had lain low, getting a job in a Chinese restaurant, and participating in the US Government Program for Vietnamese refugees. Then he had gone with the offer of practical assistance to some of his old contacts in the Vietnamese intelligence community. With the US presence so scaled down in Asia, and the Communists needing fewer killers, and more lawyers, they had been sorry but they had no work for him. So Xan had begun freelancing in Japan. In 1981, he obtained Japanese citizenship, a passport, and started his new career.

Unlike Tony, Xan did not resent the others he was working with. He simply didn't think about them. He had been hired, willingly, to perform a professional task, a task for which he would be well paid and that would at last avenge, at least in part, the outraged bodies of his parents. The others had limited roles to play in support of his operation. Provided they played them with a minimum of foolish error, he would perform his part flawlessly, and within a few days, he would be back in the Orient. Bangkok or Manila, perhaps, Singapore. Xan hadn't decided yet. When this one was over, he would need – and would be able to afford – a long rest.

The third man in the room, Ralph Matson, was perhaps the most dangerous of the three. Six-feet-two tall and broad, with a big nose and heavy chin, he was the most dangerous because he was highly intelligent. After five years as a special agent with the Federal Bureau of Investigation, he found an easy way out after Hoover's death; loyalty to the Chief and all that garbage. By then, he had learned enough to take advantage of everything the Bureau had taught him about criminology. He had started with a little blackmail, men who had not wanted their FBI records made public, but now he had moved on to bigger things. He trusted no man – the Bureau had also taught him that – certainly not the stupid wop, who under pressure might drive backward rather than forward, or the silent slant-eyed yellow hit man.

Still nobody spoke.

The door swung open. Three heads turned, three heads that were used to danger and did not care for surprises; they relaxed again immediately when they saw the two men enter.

The younger of the two was smoking. He took the seat at the head of the table as befits a chairman; the other

77

man sat down next to Matson, keeping the Chairman on his right. They nodded acknowledgment, no more. The younger man, Peter Nicholson on his voter-registration card, Pyotr Nicolaivich by birth certificate, looked for all the world like the reputable head of a successful cosmetics company. His suit revealed that he went to Chester Barrie. His shoes were Loeb's. His tie Ted Lapidus. His criminal record revealed nothing. That was why he was at the head of the table. He didn't look upon himself as a criminal; he looked upon himself as a man who wished to maintain the status quo.

He was one of a small group of Southern millionaires who had made their money in the small-arms trade. Theirs was a giant business: it was the right of every American citizen under Amendment Two of the Constitution to bear arms, and one in every four American males exercised that right. A regular pistol or revolver could be had for as little as $100 but the fancy shotguns and rifles that were a status symbol to many patriots could fetch as much as $10,000. The Chairman and his ilk sold handguns by the millions and shotguns by the tens of thousands. It had not been hard to persuade Ronald Reagan to leave the arms trade alone, but they knew they were never going to convince Florentyna Kane. The Gun Control bill had already squeaked through the House, and unless some drastic action were taken, there was undoubtedly going to be the same result in the Senate. To preserve the status quo, therefore, the Chairman sat at the head of their table.

He opened the meeting formally, as any regular chairman would, by asking for reports from his men in the field. First Matson.

The big nose bobbed, the heavy jaw moved.

"I was tuned into the FBI's Channel One." During his years as an FBI agent, preparing for a career in crime, Matson had stolen one of the Bureau's special portable walkie-talkies. He had signed it out for some routine purpose and then reported that it was lost. He was reprimanded and had to reimburse the Bureau; it had been a small price to pay for the privilege of listening to FBI communications. "I knew the Greek waiter was hiding somewhere in Washington, and I suspected that because of his leg injury, he would eventually have to go to one of D.C.'s five hospitals. I guessed he wouldn't end up with a private doctor, too expensive. Then I heard that bastard Stames come up on Channel One."

"Cut out the profanity, if you please," said the Chairman.

Stames had given Matson four reprimands during his service with the FBI. Matson did not mourn his death. He started again.

"I heard Stames come up on Channel One, on his way to Woodrow Wilson Medical Center, to ask a Father Gregory to go to the Greek. It was a long shot, of course, but I remembered that Stames was a Greek himself, and it wasn't hard to trace Father Gregory. I just caught him as he was about to leave. I told him the Greek had been discharged from the hospital and that his services would no longer be needed. And thanked him. With Stames dead, no one is likely to follow that one up and, if they do, they won't be any the wiser. I then went to the nearest Greek Orthodox church and stole the vestments, a hat, a veil, and a cross and I drove to Woodrow Wilson. By the time I arrived, Stames and Calvert had already left. I learned from the receptionist on duty that the two men from the FBI had returned to their office. I didn't ask for too much detail as I didn't want to be remembered. I discovered which room Casefikis was in and it was simple to reach there unnoticed. I slipped in. He was sound asleep. I cut his throat."

The Senator winced.

"There was a nigger in the bed next to him, we couldn't take the risk. He might have overheard everything, and he might have given a description of me, so I cut his throat too."

The Senator felt sick. He hadn't wanted these men to

79

die. The Chairman had showed no emotion, the difference between a professional and an amateur.

"Then I called Tony in the car. He drove to the Washington Field Office and saw Stames and Calvert coming out of the building together. I then contacted you, boss, and Tony carried out your orders."

The Chairman passed over a packet. It was one hundred one-hundred-dollar bills. All American employees are paid by seniority and achievement; it was no different in the criminal world.

"Tony."

"When the two men left the Old Post Office Building, we followed them as instructed. They went over Memorial Bridge. The German passed them and managed to get well ahead of them. As soon as I realised they were turning up on to the G.W. Parkway, as we thought they would, I informed Gerbach on the walkie-talkie. He was waiting in a clump of trees on the middle strip, with his lights off, about a mile ahead. He turned on his lights and came down from the top of the hill on the wrong side of the divided highway. He swung in front of the Feds' car just after it crossed Windy Run Bridge. I accelerated and overtook on the left-hand side of the car. I hit them with a glancing sideways blow at about seventy miles an hour, just as that damn-fool German hit them head-on. You know the rest, boss. If he had kept his cool," Tony finished contemptuously, "the German would be here today to make his report in person."

"What did you do with the car?"

"I went to Mario's workshop, changed the engine block and the licence plates, repaired the damage to the fender, sprayed it, and dumped it. The owner probably wouldn't recognise his own car if he saw it."

"Where did you dump it?"

"New York. The Bronx."

"Good. With a murder there every four hours, they don't have a lot of time to check on missing cars."

The Chairman flicked a packet over the table. Three

thousand dollars in used fifties. "Stay sober, Tony, we'll be needing you again." He refrained from saying what assignment number two would be; he simply said, "Xan". He stubbed out his cigarette and lit another one. All eyes turned to the silent Vietnamese. His English was good, though heavily accentuated. He tended, like so many educated Orientals, to omit the definite article, giving his speech a curious staccato effect.

"I was in car with Tony whole evening when we got your orders to eliminate two men in Ford sedan. We followed them over bridge and up freeway and when German swung across path of Ford, I blew both back tyres in under three seconds, just before Tony bounced them. They had no chance of controlling car after that."

"How can you be so sure it was under three seconds?"

"I'd been averaging two-point-eight in practice all day."

Silence. The Chairman passed yet another packet. Another one hundred fifties, twenty-five hundred dollars for each shot.

"Do you have any questions, Senator?"

The Senator did not look up, but shook his head slightly.

The Chairman spoke. "From the press reports and from our further investigation, it looks as if nobody has connected the two incidents, but the FBI just aren't that stupid. We have to hope that we eliminated everybody who heard anything Casefikis might have said, if he had anything to say in the first place. We may just be oversensitive. One thing's for certain, we eliminated everybody connected with that hospital. But we still can't be sure if the Greek knew anything worth repeating."

"May I say something, boss?"

The Chairman looked up. Nobody spoke unless it was relevant, most unusual for an American board meeting. The Chairman let Matson have the floor.

"One thing worries me, boss. Why would Nick Stames be going to Woodrow Wilson?"

They all stared at him, not quite sure what he meant.

"We know from my inquiries and my contacts that Calvert was there, but we don't actually know that Stames was there. All we know is that two agents went and that Stames asked Father Gregory to go. We know Stames was on his way home with Calvert, but my experience tells me that Stames wouldn't go to the hospital himself; he'd send somebody else —"

"Even if he thought it were a serious matter?" interrupted the Chairman.

"He wouldn't know it was a serious matter, boss. He wouldn't have known until the agents had reported back to him."

The Chairman shrugged. "The facts point to Stames going to the hospital with Calvert. He left the Washington Field Office with Calvert driving the same car that left the hospital."

"I know, boss, but I don't like it; I know that we've covered all the angles, but it's possible that three or more men left the Washington Field Office and that there is still at least one agent running around who knows what actually happened."

"It seems unlikely," said the Senator. "As you will discover when you hear my report."

The lips compressed in the heavy jaw.

"You're not happy are you, Matson?"

"No, sir."

"Very well, check it out. If you come up with anything report back to me."

The Chairman never left a stone unturned. He looked at the Senator.

The Senator despised these men. They were so small-minded, so greedy. They only understood money, and Kane was going to take it away from them. How their violence had frightened and sickened him. He should never have allowed that smooth-talking plausible bastard Nicholson to pump so much into his secret campaign funds, although God knows he would never have been elected without the money. Lots of money, and such a small price to pay at the time: steadfast opposition to any gun control proposals. Hell, he was genuinely opposed to gun control anyway. But assassinating the President to stop the bill, by God, it was lunacy, but the Chairman had him by the balls. "Co-operate, or be exposed, my friend," he had said silkily. The Senator had spent half a lifetime sweating to reach the Senate and what's more, he did a damned good job there. If they stopped him now he would be finished. A public scandal. He couldn't face it. "Co-operate, my friend, for your own good. All we need is some inside information, and your presence at the Capitol on 10 March. Be reasonable, my friend, why ruin your whole life for a Polish woman?" The Senator cleared his throat.

"It is highly unlikely that the FBI knows any details about our plans. As Mr Matson knows, if the Bureau had anything to go on, any reason to think that this supposed threat is any different from a thousand others the President has received, the Secret Service would have been informed immediately. And my secretary has ascertained that the President's schedule for this week remains unchanged. All her appointments will be kept. She will go to the Capitol on the morning of 10 March for a special address to the Senate –"

"But that's exactly the point," Matson interrupted with a contemptuous sneer. "All threats against the President, no matter how far-fetched, are routinely reported to the Secret Service. If they haven't reported anything, it must mean that –"

"It may mean that they don't know a thing, Matson," said the Chairman firmly. "I told you to look into it. Now let the Senator answer a more important question: If the FBI knew the details, would they tell the President?"

The Senator hesitated. "No, I don't think so, or only if they were absolutely certain of danger on a particular day; otherwise they'd go ahead as planned. If every threat or suggestion of a threat were taken seriously, the

President would never be able to leave the White House. The Secret Service report to Congress last year showed that there were 1,572 threats against the President's life, but thorough investigations revealed that there were no actual known attempts."

The Chairman nodded. "Either they know everything or they know nothing."

Matson persisted. "I am still a member of the Society of Former Special Agents and I attended a meeting yesterday, and no one there knew a damn thing. Someone would have heard something by now. Later, I had a drink with Grant Nanna, who was my old boss at the Washington Field Office, and he seemed almost uninterested, which I found strange. I thought Stames was a friend of his, but I obviously couldn't push it too far, since Stames was no friend of mine. I'm still worried. It doesn't make sense that Stames went to the hospital and no one in the Bureau is saying anything about his death."

"Okay, okay," said the Chairman. "If we don't get her on 10 March, we may as well quit now. We go ahead as if nothing had happened, unless we hear any rumbles – and that's in your hands, Matson. We'll be there on the day, unless you stop us. Now let's plan ahead. First I'll go over Kane's schedule for that day. Kane" – no one in that room except for the Senator ever called her the President – "leaves the White House at 10 am. She passes the FBI Building at three minutes past, she passes the Peace Monument at the north-west corner of the Capitol grounds at five minutes past. She gets out of her car at the east front of the Capitol at six minutes past. Normally, she would go in the private entrance, but the Senator has assured us that she will milk this visit for all it's worth. It takes her forty-five seconds to walk from the car to the top of the Capitol steps. We know that Xan can easily complete the job in forty-five seconds. I will be watching at the corner of Pennsylvania Avenue when Kane passes the FBI Building. Tony will be there with a car, in case of an emergency, and the Senator will be on the Capitol steps to stall her, if we need more time. The most important part of the operation is Xan's, which we have worked out to a split second. So listen and listen carefully. I have arranged for Xan to be on the construction crew working on the renovation of the front of the Capitol. And, believe me, with that union it was no mean feat to place an Oriental. Take over, Xan."

Xan looked up. He had said nothing since his last invitation to speak.

"Construction on west front of Capitol has been going on for nearly six months. No one is more enthusiastic about it than Kane. She wants it finished in time for her second Inaugural." He grinned. All eyes were upon the little man, intent on his every word. "I have been part of work force now for just over four weeks. I am in charge of checking all supplies that come on to site, which means I am in site office. From there, it has not been hard to discover movements of everybody connected with construction. The guards are not from FBI, Secret Service, or from CIA, but from Government Building Security Service. They are usually a lot older than normal agents, often retired from one of services. There are sixteen in all, and they work in fours on four shifts. I know where they drink, smoke, play cards, everything; no one is very interested in site because at moment it overlooks nothing and it's on least-used side of Capitol. A little petty theft from site but not much else to excite guards." Xan had total silence. "Right in middle of site is biggest American Hoist Co. crane in world, number 11-3-10, specially designed for lifting new parts of Capitol into place. Fully extended, it is 322 feet, almost double regulation height allowed in Washington buildings. Nobody expect us on west side, and nobody figure we can see that far. On top is small covered platform for general maintenance of pulleys, used only when it is flat and parallel to ground, but platform becomes like a small box in effect. It is four feet long, two feet three inches in width, and one foot five inches in height. I have slept there for last three nights.

I see everything, no one can see me, not even White House helicopter."

There was a stunned silence.

"How do you get up there?" asked the Senator.

"Like cat, Senator. I climb. An advantage of being very small. I go up just after midnight and come down at five. I overlook all Washington and no one see me."

"Do you have a good view of the Capitol steps from such a small platform?" asked the Chairman.

"Perhaps it will take four seconds," Xan replied. "View allows me to see Whte House as no one has ever seen it. I could have killed Kane twice last week. When she make official visits, it will be easy. I can't miss –"

"What about the other workers on Thursday? They may want to use the crane," the Senator interrupted.

This time the Chairman smiled. "There will be a strike next Thursday, my friend. Something to do with unfair rates for overtime, no work while Kane is visiting the Capitol to emphasise their point. One thing is certain, with no one on the site other than some ageing guards, nobody will be eager to climb to the top of a crane that is all but open to the world. From the ground it doesn't look as if a mouse could hide up there, let alone a human being." The Chairman paused. "Xan flies to Vienna tomorrow and will be back in time to report the results of his trip at our final meeting next Wednesday. By the way, Xan, have you got your can of yellow paint?"

"Yes, stole one from site."

The Chairman looked around the table – silence. "Good, we seem to be well organised. Thank you, Xan."

"I don't like it," mumbled Matson. "Something's wrong. It's all too easy, it's all too clever."

"The FBI has taught you to be overly suspicious, Matson. You'll discover that we're better prepared than they are, because we know what we're going to do and they don't. Fear not, you'll be able to attend Kane's funeral."

86

Matson's big chin moved up and down. "You're the guy that wants her dead," he said sourly.

"And you're being paid to see it happens," said the Chairman. "Right, we meet again in five days to go over the final plan. You will be told where to report on Wednesday morning. Xan will have returned from Austria long before then."

The Chairman smiled and lit another cigarette. The Senator slipped out. Five minutes later, Matson left. Five minutes later, Tony left. Five minutes later, Xan left. Five minutes later, the Chairman ordered lunch.

Friday afternoon, 4 March

4:00 pm

Mark was too hungry to work efficiently any longer, so he left the Library in search of some food. When the elevator stopped, the opening doors provided a view of the card catalogue: "Harrison-Health" confronted him. Some sub-conscious word association triggered in his mind the welcome vision of the beautiful, witty girl he had met the previous day, walking along the corridor in her black skirt and red shirt, heels tapping on the tiles. A big grin spread across Mark's face. It was amazing the pleasure it gave him just to know he could call her and rearrange the date, unusual for him to find just how much he wanted to.

Mark found the snack bar and munched his way through a hamburger, letting his mind recall all the things she had said, and the way she had looked while she was saying them. He decided to call Woodrow Wilson.

"I'm sorry, Dr Dexter is not on duty today," said a nurse. "Can Dr Delgado help?"

"No thank you," said Mark. "I'm afraid she can't." He took out his diary, and dialled Elizabeth Dexter's home number. He was delighted to find her in.

"Hello, Elizabeth. It's Mark Andrews. Any hope of givng you dinner tonight?"

"Promises, promises. I continue to live in the hope of a real meal."

"Not a laughing matter," said Mark, almost to himself.

"You sound a bit low, Mark. Perhaps you really do have a touch of flu."

"No, I don't think it's flu, just thinking of you makes it hard to breathe. I'd better hang up now, before I turn blue."

It was good to hear her laugh.

"Why don't you come by about eight?"

"Fine. See you around eight, Elizabeth."

"Take care, Mark."

He put the telephone down, suddenly conscious that once again he was smiling from ear to ear. He glanced at his watch: 4:30. Good. Three more hours in the Library, then he could go in pursuit of her. He returned to his reference books and continued to make biographical notes on the sixty-two senators.

His mind drifted for a moment to the President. This wasn't just any President. This was the first woman President. But what could he learn from the last presidential assassination of John F. Kennedy. Were there any senators involved with those deaths? Or was this another lunatic working on his own? All the evidence on this inquiry so far pointed to teamwork. Lee Harvey Oswald, long since dead, and still there was no convincing explanation of his assassination or, for that matter, of Robert Kennedy's.

Some people still claimed the CIA was behind President Kennedy's death because he had threatened to hang them out to dry in 1961, after the Bay of Pigs fiasco. Others said Castro had arranged the murder in revenge; it was known that Oswald had an interview with the Cuban ambassador in Mexico two weeks before the assassination, and the CIA had known about that all along. Thirty years after the event, and still no one could be certain.

A smart guy from L.A., Jay Sandberg, who had roomed with Mark at law school, had maintained that the conspiracy reached the top, even the top of the FBI: they knew the truth but said nothing.

Maybe Tyson and Rogers were two of those who knew the truth and had sent him out on useless errands to keep him occupied: he hadn't been able to tell anyone the details of yesterday's events, not even Grant Nanna.

If there were a conspiracy, whom could he turn to? Only one person might listen and that was the President, and there was no way of getting to her. He'd have to call Jay Sandberg, who had made a study of presidential assassinations. If anyone would have a theory, it would be Sandberg. Mark retraced his steps to the pay phone, checked Sandberg's home number in New York, and dialled the ten digits. A woman's voice answered the telephone.

"Hello," she said coolly. Mark could visualise the cloud of cocaine smoke that went with the voice.

"Hello, I'm trying to reach Jay Sandberg."

"Oh." More cocaine smoke. "He's still at work."

"Can you tell me his number?" asked Mark.

After more smoke, she gave it to him, and the phone clicked.

Sheeesh, Mark said to himself, Upper East Side women.

A very different voice, warm Irish-American, answered the phone next.

"Sullivan and Cromwell."

Mark recognised the prestigious New York law firm. Other people were getting ahead in the world.

"Can I speak to Jay Sandberg?"

"I'll connect you, sir."

"Sandberg."

"Hi, Jay, it's Mark Andrews. Glad I caught you. I'm calling from Washington."

"Hello, Mark, nice to hear from you. How's life for a G-man? Rat-a-tat-tat and all that."

"It can be," said Mark, "sometimes. Jay, I need some advice on where to find the facts on political assassination

90

attempts, particularly the one in Massachusetts in 1979; do you remember it?"

"Sure do. Three people arrested; let me think." Sandberg paused. "All released as harmless. One died in an auto accident in 1980, another was knifed in a brawl in San Francisco, later died in 1981, and the third disappeared mysteriously last year. I tell you it was another conspiracy."

"Who this time?"

"Mafia wanted Edward Kennedy out of the way in '76 so they could avoid an inquiry he was pressing for into the death of those two hoodlums, Sam Giancana and John Rosselli; they don't love President Kane now with the way she is running the Gun Control bill."

"Mafia? Gun Control bill? Where do I start looking for the facts?" asked Mark.

"I can tell you it's not in the Warren Commission Report or any of the later inquiries. Your best bet is *The Yankee and Cowboy Wars* by Carl Oglesby – you'll find it all there."

Mark made a note.

"Thanks for your help, Jay. I'll get back to you if it doesn't cover everything. How are things in New York?"

"Oh, fine, just fine. I'm one of about a million lawyers interpreting the constitution at an exorbitant fee. Let's get together soon, Mark."

"Sure, next time I'm in New York."

Mark went back to the Library thoughtfully. It could be CIA, it could be Mafia, it could be a nut, it could be anyone – even Halt Tyson. He asked the girl for the Carl Oglesby book. A well-thumbed volume beginning to come apart was supplied. Sheed Andrews & McMeel, Inc., 6700 Squibb Road, Mission, Kansas. It was going to make good reading, but for now it was back to the senators' life histories. Mark spent two more hours trying to eliminate senators or find motives for any of them wanting President Kane out of the way: he wasn't getting very far.

"You'll have to leave now, sir," said the young librarian, her arms full of books, looking as if she would like to go home. "I'm afraid we lock up at 7:30."

"Can you give me two more minutes? I'm very nearly through."

"I guess so," she said, staggering away under a load of Senate Reports, 1971–73, which few but herself would ever handle.

Mark glanced over his notes. There were some very prominent names among the sixty-two "suspects", men like Alan Cranston of California, often described as the "liberal whip" of the Senate; Ralph Brooks of Massachusetts, whom Florentyna Kane had defeated at the Democratic Convention. Majority Leader Robert C. Byrd of West Virginia. Henry Dexter of Connecticut. Elizabeth's father, he shuddered at the thought. Sam Nunn, the respected senator for Georgia, Robert Harrison of South Carolina, an urbane, educated man with a reputation for parliamentary skill; Marvin Thornton, who occupied the seat vacated by Edward Kennedy in 1980; Mark O. Hatfield, the liberal and devout Republican from Oregon; Hayden Woodson of Arkansas, one of the new breed of Southern Republicans; William Cain of Nebraska, a staunch conservative who had run as an independent in the 1980 election; and Birch Bayh of Indiana, the man who had pulled Ted Kennedy from a plane wreck in 1967, and probably saved his life. Sixty-two men under suspicion, thought Mark. And six days to go. And the evidence must be iron-clad. There was little more he could do that day.

Every government building was closing. He just hoped the Director had covered as much and could bring the sixty-two names down to a sensible number quickly. Sixty-two names; six days.

He returned to his car in the public parking lot. Six dollars a day for the privilege of being on vacation. He paid the attendant, eased the car out on Pennsylvania Avenue, and headed down 9th Street back towards his apartment in N Street, SW, the worst of the rush-hour behind him. Simon was there, and Mark tossed him the car keys. "I'm going out again as soon as I've changed," Mark called over his shoulder as he went up to his eighth-floor apartment.

He showered and shaved quickly and put on a more casual suit than the one he had worn for the Director. Now for the good part of the day.

When he came back down, the car was turned around so that Mark could, to quote Simon, make a quick get-away. He drove to Georgetown, turned right on 30th, and parked outside Elizabeth Dexter's house. A small red-brick town house, very chic. Either she was doing well for herself or her father had bought it for her. Her father, he couldn't help remembering . . .

She looked even more beautiful on the doorstep than she had in his imagination. That was good. She wore a long red dress with a high collar. It set off her dark hair and deep brown eyes.

"Are you going to come in, or are you just going to stand there looking like a delivery boy?"

"I'm just going to stand here and admire you," he said. "You know, Doctor, I've always been attracted to beautiful, clever women. Do you think that says something about me?"

She laughed and led him into the pretty house.

"Come and sit down. You look as though you could do with a drink." She poured him the beer he asked for. When she sat down, her eyes were serious.

"I don't suppose you want to talk about the horrible thing that happened to my mailman."

"No," said Mark. "I'd prefer not to, for a number of reasons."

Her face showed understanding.

"I hope you'll catch the bastard who killed him." Again, those dark eyes flashed to meet his. She got up to turn over the record on the stereo. "How do you like this kind of music?" she asked lightly.

"I'm not much on Haydn," he said. "I'm a Mahler freak. And Beethoven, Aznavour. And you?"

She blushed slightly.

"When you didn't turn up last night, I called your office to see if you were there."

Mark was surprised and pleased.

"Finally I got through to a girl in your department. You were out at the time, and besides she said you were very busy, so I didn't leave a message."

"That's Polly," said Mark. "She's very protective."

"And pretty?" She smiled with the confidence of one who knows she is good-looking.

"Good from far but far from good," said Mark. "Let's forget Polly. Come on, you ought to be hungry by now, and I'm not going to give you that steak I keep promising you. I've booked a table for nine o'clock at Tio Pepe."

"Lovely," she said. "Since you managed to get your car parked, why don't we walk?"

"Great."

It was a clear, cool evening and Mark enjoyed the fresh air. What he didn't enjoy was the continual urge to look over his shoulder.

"Looking for another woman already?" she teased.

"No," said Mark. "Why should I look any further?" He spoke lightly, but he knew he hadn't fooled her. He changed the subject abruptly. "How do you like your work?"

"My work?" Elizabeth seemed surprised, as though she never thought of it in those terms. "My life, you mean? It's just about my entire life. Or has been so far."

She glanced up at Mark with a sombre expression on her face. "I hate the hospital. It's a big bureaucracy, old and dirty and a lot of the people there, petty administrative types, don't really care about helping people. To them it's just another way of earning a living. Only yesterday I had to threaten to resign in order to convince the Utilisation Committee to let an old man remain in the hospital. He had no home to go back to."

They walked down 30th Street, and Elizabeth continued to tell him about her work. She spoke with spirit, and Mark listened to her with pleasure. She showed a pleasant self-assurance, as she told him about a soulful Yugoslav who would sing incomprehensible Slavic songs of love and of longing as she inspected his ulcerated armpit and who had finally, in a misplaced gesture of passion, seized her left ear and licked it.

Mark laughed and took her arm as he guided her into the restuarant. "You ought to demand combat pay," he said.

"Oh, I wouldn't have complained, other than to tell him that his singing was always out of tune."

The hostess led them upstairs to a table in the centre of the room, near where the floor show would be performed. Mark rejected it in favour of a table in the far corner. He did not ask Elizabeth which seat she would prefer. He sat down with his back to the wall, making a lame excuse about wanting to be away from the noise so he could talk to her. Mark was sure that this girl would not fall too easily for that sort of blarney; she knew something was wrong and she sensed his edginess, but she did not pry.

A young waiter asked them if they would like a cocktail. Elizabeth asked for a Margarita, Mark for a spritzer.

"What's a spritzer?" asked Elizabeth.

"Not very Spanish, half white wine, half soda, lots of ice. Stirred but not shaken. Sort of a poor man's James Bond."

The pleasant atmosphere of the restaurant helped to dispel some of Mark's tension; he relaxed slightly for the first time in twenty-four hours. They chatted about movies, music, and books, and then about Yale. Her face, often animated, was sometimes serene but always lovely in the candlelight. Mark was enchanted by her. For all her intelligence and self-sufficiency, she had a touching fragility and femininity.

As they ate their paella Mark asked Elizabeth why her father had become a senator, about his career, and her childhood in Connecticut. The subject seemed to make her uneasy. Mark couldn't help remembering that her father was still on the list. He tried to shift the conversation to her mother. Elizabeth avoided his eyes and even, he thought, turned pale. For the first time, a tiny ripple of suspicion disturbed his affectionate vision of Elizabeth, and made him worry momentarily. She was the first beautiful thing that had happened for quite a while, and he didn't want to distrust her. Was it possible? Could she be involved? No, of course not. He tried to put it out of his mind.

The Spanish floor show came on and was performed with enthusiasm. Mark and Elizabeth listened and watched, unable to speak to each other above the noise. Mark was happy enough just to sit and be with her; her face was turned away as she looked at the dancers. When the floor show eventually ended, they had both long finished the paella. They ordered dessert and coffee.

"Would you like a cigar?"

Elizabeth smiled. "No, thanks. We don't have to ape men's vile habits as well as their good ones."

"Like that," said Mark. "You're going to be the first woman Surgeon General, I suppose?"

"No, I'm not," she said demurely. "I'll probably be the second or third."

Mark laughed. "I'd better get back to the Bureau, and do great things. Just to keep up with you."

"And it may well be a woman who stops you becoming Director of the FBI," Elizabeth added.

"No, it won't be a woman that stops me becoming Director of the FBI," said Mark, but he didn't explain.

"Your coffee, señorita, señor."

If Mark had ever wanted to sleep with a woman on the first date, this was the occasion, but he knew it wasn't going to happen.

He paid the bill, left a generous tip for the waiter, and congratulated the girl from the floor show, who was sitting in a corner drinking coffee.

When they left the restaurant Mark found the night had a chill edge. Once again he began looking nervously around him, trying not to make it too obvious to Elizabeth. He took her hand as they crossed the street, and didn't let it go when they reached the other side. They walked on, chatting intermittently, both aware of what was happening. He wanted to hold on to her. Lately, he had been seeing a lot of women, but with none of them had he held their hand either before or afterwards. Gradually his mood darkened again. Perhaps fear was making him excessively sentimental.

A car was driving up behind them. Mark stiffened with anticipation. Elizabeth didn't appear to notice. It slowed down. It was going slower as it neared them. It stopped just beside them. Mark undid his middle button and fidgeted, more worried for Elizabeth than for himself. The doors of the car opened suddenly and out jumped four teenagers, two girls, two boys. They darted into a Hamburger Haven. Sweat appeared on Mark's forehead. He shook free of Elizabeth's touch. She stared at him. "Something's very wrong, isn't it?"

"Yes," he said. "Just don't ask me about it."

She sought his hand again, held it firmly, and they walked on. The oppression of the horrible events of the previous day bore down on Mark and he did not speak again. When they arrived at her front door, he was back in the world which was shared only by him and the hulking, shadowy figure of Halt Tyson.

"Well, you have been most charming this evening, when you've actually been here," she said smilingly.

Mark shook himself. "I'm really sorry."

"Would you like to come in for coffee?"

"Yes and no. Can I take another raincheck on that? I don't feel like good company right now."

He still had several things to do before he saw the Director at 7:00 am and it was already midnight. Also he hadn't slept properly for a day and a half.

"Can I call you tomorrow?"

"I'd like that," she said. "Be sure to keep in touch, whatever happens."

Mark would carry those few words around with him like a talisman for the next few days. He could recall her every word and its accompanying gesture. Were they said in fun, were they said seriously, were they said teasingly? Lately, it hadn't been fashionable to fall in love; very few people seemed to be getting married and a lot of people who had were getting divorced. Was he really going to fall madly in love in the middle of all this?

He kissed her on the cheek and turned to leave, his eyes darting up and down the road again. She whispered after him:

"I hope you find the man who killed my mailman and your Greek."

Your Greek, your Greek, Greek Orthodox priest, Father Gregory. God in heaven, why hadn't he thought of it before? He'd forgotten Elizabeth for a moment as he started to run towards his car. He turned to wave; she was staring at him with a puzzled expression, wondering what she had said. Mark leaped into the car and drove as fast as he could to his apartment. He must find Father Gregory's number. Greek Orthodox priest, what did he look like, the one who came out of the elevator, what did he look like; it was all coming back, there had been something unusual with him: what the hell was it? His clothes? No, they were fine, or was it his face? His face was wrong somehow. Of course. Of course. How could he have been so stupid. When he arrived home, he called the Washington Field Office immediately. Polly, on the switchboard, was surprised to hear him.

"Aren't you on leave?"

"Yes, sort of. Do you have Father Gregory's number?"

"Who is Father Gregory?"

"A Greek Orthodox priest whom Mr Stames used to contact occasionally; I think he was his local priest."

"Yes, you're right. Now I remember."

Mark waited.

She checked Stames's Rolodex and gave him the number. Mark wrote it down, and replaced the phone. Of course, of course, of course. How stupid of him. It was so obvious. Well past midnight, but he had to call. He dialled the number. The telephone rang several times before it was answered.

"Father Gregory?"

"Yes."

"Do all Greek Orthodox priests have beards?"

"Yes, as a rule. Who is this asking such a damn silly question in the middle of the night?"

Mark apologised. "My name is Special Agent Mark Andrews. I worked under Nick Stames."

The man at the other end, who had sounded sleepy, immediately woke up. "I understand, young man. What can I do for you?"

"Father Gregory, last night Mr Stames's secretary called you and asked you to go to Woodrow Wilson to check a Greek who had a bullet wound in his leg?"

"Yes, that's right – I remember, Mr Andrews. But somebody else called about thirty minutes later, just as I was leaving, in fact, to tell me I needn't bother because Mr Casefikis had been discharged from the hospital."

"He'd been what?" Mark's voice rose with each word.

"Discharged from the hospital."

"Did the caller say who he was?"

"No, the man gave no other details. I assumed he was from your office."

"Father Gregory, can I see you tomorrow morning at eight o'clock?"

"Yes, of course, my son."

"And can you be sure you don't talk to anybody else about this phone call, whoever they say they are?"

"If that is your wish, my son."

"Thank you, Father."

Mark dropped the telephone and tried to concentrate. He was taller than I was, so he was over six feet. He was dark, or was that just his priest's robes? No, he had dark hair, he had a big nose, I remember he had a big nose, eyes, no I can't remember his eyes, he had a big nose, a heavy chin, a heavy chin. Mark wrote everything down he could remember. A big heavy man, taller than me, big nose, heavy chin, big nose, heavy . . . he collapsed. His head fell on the desk and he slept.

Saturday morning, 5 March

6:32 am

Mark had awoken, but he wasn't awake. His head was swimming with incoherent thoughts. The first vision to flash across his mind was Elizabeth; he smiled. The second was Nick Stames; he frowned. The third was the Director. Mark woke with a start and sat up, trying to focus his eyes on his watch. All he could see was the second hand moving: 6:35. Hell. He shot up from the chair, his stiff neck and back hurting him; he was still dressed. He threw off his clothes and rushed into the bathroom and showered, without taking time to adjust the water temperature. Goddamn freezing. At least it woke him up and made him forget Elizabeth. He jumped out of the shower and grabbed a towel: 6:40. After throwing the lather on his face, he shaved too quickly, mowing down the stubble on his chain. Damn it, three nicks; the aftershave lotion stung viciously: 6:43. He dressed: clean shirt, same cuff links, clean socks, same shoes, clean suit, same tie. A quick look in the mirror: two nicks still bleeding slightly, the hell with it. He bundled the papers on his desk into his briefcase and ran for the elevator. First piece of luck, it was on the top floor. Downstairs: 6:46.

"Hi, Simon."

The young black garage attendant didn't move. He was dozing in his little cubbyhole at the garage entrance.

"Morning Mark. Hell, man, is it eight o'clock already?"

"No, thirteen minutes to seven."

"What are you up to? Moonlighting?" asked Simon, rubbing his eyes and handing over the car keys. Mark smiled, but didn't have time to answer. Simon dozed off again.

Car starts first time. Reliable Mercedes. Moves on to the road: 6:48. Must stay below speed limit. Never embarrass the Bureau. At 6th Street, held up by lights: 6:50. Cut across G Street, up 7th, more lights. Cross Independence Avenue: 6:53. Corner of 7th and Pennsylvania. Can see FBI Building: 6:55. Down ramp, park, show FBI pass to garage guard, run for elevator: 6:57; elevator to seventh floor: 6:58. Along the corridor, turn right, Room 7074, straight in, past Mrs McGregor as instructed. She barely glances up; knock on door of Director's office; no reply; go in as instructed. No Director: 6:59; sink into easy chair. Director going to be late; smile of satisfaction. Thirty seconds to seven: glance around room, casually, as if been waiting for hours. Eyes land on grandfather clock. Strikes: one, two, three, four, five, six, seven.

The door opened, and the Director marched in. "Good morning, Andrews." He did not look at Mark, but at the clock on the wall. "It's always a little fast." Silence. The Old Post Office Tower clock struck seven.

The Director settled into his chair, and once again the large hands took possession of the desk.

"We'll start with my news first, Andrews. We have just received some identification on the Lincoln that went into the Potomac with Stames and Calvert."

The Director opened a new manilla file marked "Eyes only" and glanced at its contents. What was in the file that Mark didn't know about and ought to know about?

"Nothing solid to go on. Hans-Dieter Gerbach, German. Bonn has reported that he was a minor figure in the Munich rackets until five years ago, then they lost track of him. There is some evidence to suggest he was in Rhodesia and even hitched up with the CIA for a while. The White-Lightning Brigade. The CIA is not being helpful on him. I can't see much information coming from them before Thursday. Sometimes I wonder whose side they're on. In 1980, Gerbach turned up in New York, but there's nothing there except rumours and street talk, no record to go on. It would have helped if he'd lived."

Mark thought of the slit throats in Woodrow Wilson Medical Center and wondered.

"The interesting fact to emerge from the car crash is that both back tyres of Stames's and Calvert's car have small holes in them. They could have been the result of the fall down the bank, but our laboratory boys think they are bullet holes. If they are, whoever did the shooting makes Wyatt Earp look like a boy scout."

The Director spoke into his intercom. "Have Assistant Director Rogers join us please, Mrs McGregor."

"Yes, sir."

"Mr Rogers's men have found the catering outfit Casefikis was working for, for what that's worth."

The Assistant Director knocked and entered. The Director indicated a chair. Rogers smiled at Mark and sat down.

"Let's have the details, Matt."

"Well, sir, the owner of the Golden Duck wasn't exactly co-operative. Seemed to think I was after him for contravening employers' regulations. I threatened to shut him down if he didn't talk. Finally he admitted to employing a man matching Casefikis's description on 24 February. He sent Casefikis to serve at a small luncheon party in one of the rooms at the Georgetown Inn on Wisconsin Avenue. The man who made the arrangement was a Lorenzo Rossi. He insisted on a waiter who couldn't speak English. Paid in cash. We've run Rossi through all the computers – nothing. Obviously a false name. Same story at the Georgetown Inn. The proprietor said the room had been hired for the day of 24 February by a Mr Rossi, food to be supplied, but no service, cash paid in advance. Rossi was about five-feet-eight, dark complexion, no distinguishing features, dark hair, sunglasses. The proprietor thought he "seemed Italian". No one at the hotel knows or cares who the hell went to lunch in that room that day. I'm afraid it doesn't get us very far."

"I agree. I suppose we could pull every Italian answering that description off the street," said the Director. "If we had five years, not five days. Did you turn up anything new at the hospital, Matt?"

"It's a hell of a mess, sir. The place is full of people coming and going, all day and most of the night. The staff all work shifts. They don't even know their own colleagues, let alone outsiders. You could wander around there all day with a torchlight in your hand and no one would stop you unless they wanted a light."

"That figures," said Tyson. "Right, Andrews, what have you been up to for the past twenty-four hours?"

Mark opened his regulation blue plastic portfolio. He reported that there were sixty-two senators left, the other thirty-eight accounted for, most of them having been a long way from Washington on 24 February. He passed the list of names over to the Director, who glanced through them.

"Some pretty big fish still left in the muddy pond, Andrews. Go on."

Mark proceeded to outline his encounter with the Greek Orthodox priest. He expected a sharp reprimand for failing to remember the matter of the beard immediately. He was not disappointed. Chastened, he continued: "I am seeing Father Gregory at eight o'clock this morning, and I thought I would go on to see Casefikis's widow afterwards. I don't think either will have much to offer, but I imagine you want those leads followed up, sir. After that I intended to return to the Library of Congress to try and figure out why any of those sixty-two senators might wish to see an end of President Kane."

"Well, to start with, put them in categories," said the Director. "First political party, then committees, then outside interests, then their personal knowledge of the President. Don't forget, Andrews, we do know that our man had lunch in Georgetown on 24 February and that should bring the numbers down."

"But sir, presumably they all had lunch on 24 February."

"Exactly, Andrews, but not all in private. Many of them would have been seen in a public place or lunched officially, with constituents or federal employees or lobbyists. You have to find out who did what, without letting the senator we're after get suspicious."

"How do you suggest I go about doing that, sir?"

"Simple," replied the Director. "You call each of the senators' secretaries and ask if the boss would be free to attend a luncheon on –" he paused "– 'The Problems of Urban Environment'. Yes, I like that. Give them a date, say 5 May, then ask if they attended either the one given on," the Director glanced at his calendar, "17 January or 24 February, as some senators who had accepted didn't attend, and one or two turned up without invitations. Then say a written invitation will follow. All the secretaries will put it out of their minds unless you write, and if any of them does remember on 5 May, it will be too late for us to care. One thing is certain: no senator will be letting his secretary know that he is planning to kill the President."

The Assistant Director grimaced slightly. "If he gets caught, sir, all hell will break loose. We'll be back in the dirty-tricks department."

"No, Matt, if I tell the President one of her precious brethren is going to knife her in the back, she won't see anything particularly pleasant in that trick."

"We haven't got any real proof, sir," said Mark.

"Then you had better find it, Andrews, or we'll all be looking for a new job, trust my judgement."

Trust my judgement, Mark thought.

105

"All we have is one strong lead," the Director continued. "That a senator may be involved, but we have only five days left. If we fail next Thursday, there will be enough time during the next twenty years to study the inquiry and you, Andrews, will be able to make a fortune writing a book about it."

Mark looked apprehensive.

"Andrews, don't get too worried. I have briefed the head of the Secret Service. I told him no more and no less than was in your report, as we agreed yesterday, so that gives us a clear run right through to 10 March. I'm working on a contingency plan, in case we don't know who Cassius is before then; but I won't bore you with it now. I have also talked to the boys from Homicide; they have come up with very little that can help us. It may interest you to know that they have seen Casefikis's wife already. Their brains seem to work a little faster than yours, Andrews."

"Perhaps they don't have as much on their minds," said the Assistant Director.

"Maybe not. Okay, go see her if you think it might help. You may pick up something they missed. Cheer up, you've covered a lot of ground. Perhaps this morning's investigation will give us some new leads to work on. I think that covers everything for now. Right, Andrews, don't let me waste any more of your time."

"No, sir."

Mark rose.

"I'm sorry, I forgot to offer you coffee, Andrews."

I didn't manage to drink it the last time, Mark wanted to say. He left as the Director ordered coffee for himself and the Assistant Director. He decided that he too could do with some breakfast and a chance to collect his thoughts. He went in search of the Bureau cafeteria.

The Director drank his coffee and asked Mrs McGregor to send in his personal assistant. The anonymous man appeared almost instantly, a grey folder under his arm.

He didn't have to ask the Director what it was that he wanted. He placed the folder on the table in front of him, and left without speaking.

"Thank you," said the Director to the closing door.

He turned the cover of the folder and browsed through it for twenty minutes, a chuckle here, and a grunt there, the odd comment to Matthew Rogers. There were facts in it about Mark Andrews of which Mark himself would have been unaware. The Director finished his second cup of coffee, closed the file, and locked it in the personal drawer of the Queen Anne desk. Queen Anne had never held as many secrets as that desk.

Mark finished a much better breakfast than he could have hoped for at the Washington Field Office. There, you had to go across the street to the Lunch Connection, because the snack bar downstairs was so abominable, much in keeping with the rest of the building. Not that he wouldn't have liked to return to it now instead of the underground garage to pick up his car. He didn't notice the man across the street who watched him leave, but he did wonder whether the blue Ford sedan that stayed in his rear-view mirror so long was there by chance. If it wasn't, who was watching whom, who was trying to protect whom?

He arrived at Father Gregory's church just before 8:00 am and they walked together to the priest's house. The priest's half-rim glasses squatted on the end of a stubby nose. His large, red cheeks and even larger basketball belly led the uncharitable to conclude that Father Gregory had found much to solace him on earth while he waited for the eternal kingdom of heaven. Mark told him that he had already breakfasted, but it didn't stop the Father from frying two eggs and bacon, plus toast, marmalade, and a cup of coffee. Father Gregory could add very little to what he had told Mark on the telephone the previous night, and he sighed deeply when he was reminded of the two deaths at the hospital.

"Yes, I read the details in the *Post*." When they talked about Nick Stames, a light came into his grey eyes; it was clear that priest and policeman had shared a few secrets, this was no jolly old Jesus freak.

"Is there any connection between Nick's death and the accident in the hospital?" Father Gregory asked suddenly.

The question took Mark by surprise. There was a shrewd brain behind the half-rim glasses. Lying to a priest, Greek Orthodox or otherwise, seemed somehow worse than the usual lies which were intended to protect the Bureau from the general public.

"Absolutely none," said Mark. "Just one of those horrible auto accidents."

"Just one of those weird coincidences?" said Father Gregory quizzically, peering at Mark over the top of his glasses. "Is that right?" he sounded almost as unconvinced as Grant Nanna. He continued: "There's one more thing I would like to mention. Although it's hard to remember exactly what the man said when he called me and told me not to bother to go to the hospital, I'm fairly certain he was a well-educated man. I feel sure by the way he carried it off that he was a professional man, and I am not sure what I mean by that; it's just the strange feeling that he had made that sort of call before; there was something professional about him."

Father Gregory repeated the phrase to himself – "Something professional about him" – and so did Mark, while he was in the car on the way to the house in which Mrs Casefikis was staying. It was the home of the friend who had harboured her wounded husband.

Mark drove down Connecticut Avenue, past the Washington Hilton and the National Zoo, into Maryland. Patches of bright, yellow forsythia had begun to appear along the road. Connecticut Avenue turned into University Boulevard, and Mark found himself in Wheaton, a suburban satellite of stores, restaurants, gas stations, and a few apartment buildings. Stopped by a red light near

Wheaton Plaza, Mark checked his notes. 11501 Elkin Street. He was looking for the Blue Ridge Manor Apartments. Fancy name for a group of squat, three-storey faded-brick buildings lining Blue Ridge and Elkin streets. As he approached 11501, Mark looked for a parking space. No luck. He hovered for a moment, then decided to park in front of a fire hydrant. He draped the radio microphone carefully over his rear-view mirror, so that any observant meter maid or policeman would know that this was an official car on official business.

Ariana Casefikis burst into tears at the mere sight of Mark's badge. She looked frail; only twenty-nine, her clothes unkempt, her hair all over the place, her eyes grey and still full of tears. The lines on her face showed where the tears had been running, running for two days. She and Mark were about the same age. She didn't have a country, and now she didn't have a husband. What was going to happen to her? If Mark had felt alone, he was certainly better off than this poor woman.

Mrs Casefikis's English turned out to be rather better than her husband's. She had already seen two policemen. She told them that she knew nothing. First the nice man from the Metropolitan Police who had broken the news to her and been so understanding, then the Homicide lieutenant who had come a little later and been much firmer, wanting to know things she hadn't the faintest clue about, and now a visit from the FBI. Her husband had never been in trouble before and she didn't know who shot him or why anybody would want to. He was a gentle, kind man. Mark believed her.

He also assured her that she had no immediate cause for worry and that he would deal personally with the Immigration Office and the Welfare people about getting her some income. It seemed to cheer her up and make her a little more responsive.

"Now please try to think carefully, Mrs Casefikis. Have you any idea where your husband was working on 23 or

24 February, the Wednesday and Thursday of last week, and did he tell you anything about his work?"

She had no idea. Angelo never told her what he was up to and half the jobs were casual and only for the day, because he couldn't risk staying on without a work permit, being an illegal immigrant. Mark was getting nowhere, but it wasn't her fault.

"Will I be able to stay in America?"

"I'll do everything I can to help, Mrs Casefikis. That I promise you. I'll talk to a Greek Orthodox priest I know about finding some money to tide you over till I've seen the Welfare people."

Mark opened the door, despondent about the lack of any hard information either from Father Grègory or from Ariana Casefikis.

"The priest already give me money."

Mark stopped in his tracks, turned slowly, and faced her. He tried to show no particular interest.

"Which priest was that?" he asked casually.

"He said he help. Man who came to visit yesterday. Nice man, very nice, very kind. He give me fifty dollars."

Mark turned cold. The man had been ahead of him again. Father Gregory was right, there was something professional·about him.

"Can you describe him, Mrs Casefikis?"

"What do you mean?"

"What did he look like?"

"Oh, he was a big man, very dark, I think," she began.

Mark tried to remain offhand. It must have been the man who had passed him in the elevator, the man who had earlier kept Father Gregory from going to the hospital and who, if Mrs Casefikis had known anything at all about the plot, would no doubt have dispatched her to join her husband.

"Did he have a beard, Mrs Casefikis?"

"Of course he did," she hesitated, "but I can't remember him having one."

Mark asked her to stay in the house, not to leave under

any circumstances. He made an excuse that he was going to check on the Welfare situation and talk to the Immigration officials. He was learning how to lie. The clean-shaven Greek Orthodox priest was teaching him.

He jumped into the car and drove a few hundred yards to the nearest pay phone on Georgia Avenue. He dialled the Director's private line. The Director picked up the phone.

"Julius."

"What is your number?" asked the Director.

Thirty seconds later the phone rang. Mark went over the story carefully.

"I'll send an Identikit man down to you immediately. You go back there and hold her hand. And, Andrews, try to think on your feet. I'd like that fifty dollars. Was it one bill, or several? There may just be a fingerprint on them." The telephone clicked. Mark frowned. If the phony Greek Orthodox priest weren't always two steps ahead of him, the Director was.

Mark returned to Mrs Casefikis and told her that her case would be dealt with at the highest level; he must remember to speak to the Director about it at the next meeting, he made a note about it on his pad. Back to the casual voice again.

"Are you sure it was fifty dollars, Mrs Casefikis?"

"Oh, yes, I don't see a fifty-dollar bill every day, and I was most thankful at the time."

"Can you remember what you did with it?"

"Yes, I went and bought food from the supermarket just before they closed."

"Which supermarket, Mrs Casefikis?"

"Wheaton Supermarket. Up the street."

"When was that?"

"Yesterday evening about six o'clock."

Mark realised that there wasn't a moment to lose. If it weren't already too late.

"Mrs Casefikis, a man will be coming, a colleague of

mine, a friend, from the FBI, to ask you to describe the kind Father who gave you the money. It will help us greatly if you can remember as much about him as possible. You have nothing to worry about because we're doing everything we can to help you."

Mark hesitated, took out his wallet and gave her fifty dollars. She smiled for the first time.

"Now, Mrs Casefikis, I want you to do just one last thing for me. If the Greek priest ever comes to visit again, don't tell him about our conversation, just call me at this number."

Mark handed her a card. Ariana Casefikis nodded, but her lacklustre grey eyes followed Mark to his car. She didn't understand, or know which man to trust: hadn't they both given her fifty dollars?

Mark pulled into a parking space in front of the Wheaton Supermarket. A huge sign in the window announced that cases of cold beer were sold inside. Above the window was a blue and white cardboard representation of the dome of the Capitol. Five days, thought Mark. He went into the store. It was a small family enterprise, privately owned, not part of a chain. Beer lined one wall, wine the other, and in between were four rows of canned and frozen foods. A meat counter stretched the length of the rear wall. The butcher seemed to be minding the store alone. Mark hurried towards him, starting to ask the question before he reached the counter.

"Could I please see the manager?"

The butcher eyed him suspiciously. "What for?"

Mark showed his credentials.

The butcher shrugged and yelled over his shoulder, "Hey, Flavio. FBI. Wants to see you."

Several seconds later, the manager, a large red-faced Italian, appeared in the doorway to the left of the meat counter. "Yeah? What can I do for you, Mr, uh . . ."

"Andrews, FBI." Mark showed his credentials once again.

"Yeah, okay. What do you want, Mr Andrews? I'm

Flavio Guida. This is my place. I run a good, honest place."

"Yes, of course, Mr Guida. I'm simply hoping you can help me. I'm investigating a case of stolen money, and we have reason to believe that a stolen fifty-dollar bill was spent in this supermarket yesterday and we wonder now if there is any way of tracing it."

"Well, my money is collected every night," said the manager. "It's put into the safe and deposited in the bank first thing in the morning. It would have gone to the bank about an hour ago, and I think –"

"But it's Saturday," Mark said.

"No problem. My bank is open till noon on Saturday. It's just a few doors down."

Mark thought on his feet.

"Would you please accompany me to the bank immediately, Mr Guida?"

Guida looked at his watch and then at Mark Andrews. "Okay. Give me just half a minute."

He shouted to an invisible woman in the back of the store to keep an eye on the cash register. Together he and Mark walked to the corner of Georgia and Hickers. Guida was obviously getting quite excited by the whole episode.

At the bank Mark went immediately to the chief cashier. The money had been handed over thirty minutes before to one of his tellers, a Mrs Townsend. She still had it in piles ready for sorting. It was next on her list. She hadn't had time to do so yet, she said rather apologetically. No need to feel sorry, thought Mark. The supermarket's take for the day had been just over five thousand dollars. There were twenty-eight fifty-dollar bills. Christ Almighty, the Director was going to tear him apart, or to be more exact, the fingerprint experts were. Mark counted the fifty-dollar notes using gloves supplied by Mrs Townsend and put them on one side – he agreed there were twenty-eight. He signed for them, gave the receipt to the chief cashier, and assured him they would be returned in the very near future. The bank manager came over and took charge of the receipt and the situation.

"Don't FBI men usually work in pairs?"

Mark blushed. "Yes, sir, but this is a special assignment."

"I would like to check," said the manager. "You are asking me to release one thousand four hundred dollars on your word."

"Of course, sir, please do check."

Mark had to think quickly. He couldn't ask the manager of a local bank to ring the Director of the FBI. It would be like charging your gasoline to the account of Henry Ford.

"Why don't you ring the FBI's Washington Field Office, sir, ask for the head of the Criminal Section. Mr Grant Nanna."

"I'll do just that."

Mark gave him the number, but he ignored it and looked it up for himself in the Washington directory. He got right through to Nanna. Thank God he was there.

"I have a young man from your Field Office with me. His name is Mark Andrews. He says he has the authority to take away twenty-eight fifty-dollar bills. Something to do with stolen money."

Nanna also had to think quickly. Deny the allegation, defy the alligator – Nick Stames's old motto.

Mark, meanwhile, offered up a little prayer.

"That's correct, sir," said Nanna. "He has been instructed by me to pick up those notes. I hope you will release them immediately. They will be returned as soon as possible."

"Thank you, Mr Nanna. I'm sorry to have bothered you. I just felt I ought just to check; you never can be sure nowadays."

"No bother, sir, a wise precaution. We wish everybody were as careful." The first truth he'd uttered, thought Grant Nanna.

The bank manager replaced the receiver, put the pile

of fifty-dollar bills in a brown envelope, accepted the receipt, and shook hands with Mark apologetically.

"You understand I had to check?"

"Of course," said Mark. "I would have done the same myself."

He thanked Mr Guida and the manager and asked them both not to mention the matter to anybody. They nodded with the air of those who know their duty.

Mark returned to the FBI Building immediately and went straight to the Director's office. Mrs McGregor nodded at him. A quiet knock on the door, and he went in.

"Sorry to interrupt you, sir."

"Not at all, Andrews. Have a seat. We were just finishing."

Matthew Rogers rose and looked carefully at Andrews and smiled.

"I'll try and have the answers for you by lunch, Director," he said, and left.

"Well, young man, do you have our Senator in the car downstairs?"

"No, sir, but I do have these."

Mark opened the brown envelope and put twenty-eight fifty-dollar bills on the table.

"Been robbing a bank, have you? A federal charge, Andrews."

"Almost, sir. One of these notes, as you know, was given to Mrs Casefikis by the man posing as the Greek Orthodox priest."

"Well, that will be a nice little conundrum for our fingerprint boys; fifty-six sides with hundreds, perhaps thousands of prints on them. It's a long shot and it will take a considerable time, but it's worth a try." He was careful not to touch the notes. "I'll have Sommerton deal with it immediately. We'll also need Mrs Casefikis's prints. I'll also put one of our agents on her house in case the big man returns." The Director was writing and talking at the same time. "It's just like the old days when I ran a field office. I do believe I'd enjoy it if it weren't so serious."

"Can I mention just one other thing while I'm here, sir?"

"Yes, say whatever you want to, Andrews." Tyson didn't look up, just continued writing.

"Mrs Casefikis is worried about her status in this country. She has no money, no job, and now no husband. She may well have given us a vital lead and she has certainly been as co-operative as possible. I think we might help."

The Director pressed a button.

"Ask Sommerton from Fingerprints to come up immediately, and send Elliott in."

Ah, thought Mark, the anonymous man has a name.

"I'll do what I can. I'll see you Monday at seven, Andrews. I'll be home all weekend if you need me. Don't stop working."

"Yes, sir."

Mark left. He stopped at the Riggs Bank and changed fifteen dollars into quarters. The teller looked at him curiously.

"Have your own pinball machine, do you?"

Mark smiled.

He spent the rest of the morning and most of the afternoon with a diminishing pile of quarters, calling the weekend-duty secretaries of the sixty-two senators who had been in Washington on 24 February. All of them were most gratified that their senator should be invited to an Environmental Conference; the Director was no fool. At the end of sixty-two phone calls, his ears were numb. Mark studied the results . . . thirty senators had eaten in the office or with constituents, fifteen had not told their secretaries where they were having lunch or had mentioned some vague "appointment", and seventeen had attended luncheons hosted by groups as varied as the National Press Club, Common Cause, and the NAACP. One secretary even thought her boss had been at that particular Environmental Luncheon on 24 February. Mark hadn't been able to think of a reply to that.

With the Director's help he was now down to fifteen senators.

He returned to the Library of Congress, and once again made for the quiet reference room. The librarian did not seem the least bit suspicious of all his questions about particular senators and committees and procedure in the Senate; she was used to graduate students who were just as demanding and far less courteous.

Mark went back to the shelf that held the *Congressional Record*. It was easy to find 24 February: it was the only thumbed number in the pile of unbound latest issues. He checked through the fifteen remaining names. On that day, there had been one committee in session, the Foreign Relations Committee; three senators on his list of fifteen were members of that committee, and all three had spoken in committee that morning, according to the *Record*. The Senate itself had debated two issues that day: the allocation of funds in the Energy Department for solar-energy research, and the Gun Control bill. Some of the remaining twelve had spoken on one or both issues on the floor of the Senate: there was no way of eliminating any of the fifteen, damn it. He listed the fifteen names on fifteen sheets of paper, and read through the *Congressional Record* for every day from 24 February to 3 March. By each name he noted the senator's presence or absence from the Senate on each working day. Painstakingly, he built up each senator's schedule; there were many gaps. It was evident that senators do not spend all their time in the Senate.

The young librarian was at his elbow. Mark glanced at the clock: 7:30. Throwing-out time. Time to forget the senators and to see Elizabeth. He called her at home.

"Hello, lovely lady. I think it must be time to eat again.

I haven't had anything since breakfast. Will you take pity on my debilitated state, Doctor, and eat with me?"

"And do what with you, Mark? I've just washed my hair. I think I must have soap in my ears."

"Eat with me, I said. That will do for the moment. I just might think of something else later."

"I just might say no later," she said sweetly. "How's the breathing?"

"Coming on nicely, thank you, but if I go on thinking what I am thinking right now, I may break out in pimples."

"What do you want me to do, pour cold water in the phone?"

"No, just eat with me. I'll pick you up in half an hour, hair wet or dry."

They found a small restaurant called Mr Smith's in Georgetown. Mark was more familiar with it in the summer, when one could sit at a table in the garden at the back. It was crowded with people in their twenties. The perfect place to sit for hours and talk.

"God," said Elizabeth. "This is just like being back at college; I thought we had grown out of that."

"I'm glad you appreciate it," Mark smiled.

"It's all so predictable. Folksy wooden floors, butcher-block tables, plants. Bach flute sonatas. Next time we'll try McDonald's."

Mark couldn't think of a reply, and was saved only by the appearance of a menu.

"Can you imagine, four years at Yale, and I still don't know what *ratatouille* is," said Elizabeth.

"I know what it is, but I wasn't sure how to pronounce it."

They both ordered chicken, baked potato, and salad.

"Look, Mark, there, that ghastly Senator Thornton with a girl young enough to be his daughter."

"Perhaps she is his daughter."

"No civilised man would bring his daughter here." She smiled at him.

"He's a friend of your father's, isn't he?"

"Yes, how do you know that?" asked Elizabeth.

"Common knowledge." Mark already regretted his question.

"Well, I'd describe him as more of a business associate. He makes his money manufacturing guns. Not the most attractive occupation."

"But your father owns part of a gun company."

"Daddy? Yes, I don't approve of that either, but he blames it on my grandfather who founded the firm. I used to argue with him about it when I was at school. Told him to sell his stock and invest it in something socially useful, saw myself as a sort Major Barbara."

"How is your dinner?" a hovering waiter asked.

"Um, just great, thanks," said Elizabeth looking up. "You know, Mark, I once called my father a war criminal."

"But he was against the war, I thought."

"You seem to know an awful lot about my father," said Elizabeth looking at him suspiciously.

Not enough, thought Mark, and how much could you really tell me? If Elizabeth picked up any sign of his anxiety, she didn't register it but simply continued.

"He voted to approve the MX missile, and I didn't sit at the same table with him for almost a month. I don't think he even noticed."

"How about your mother?" asked Mark.

"She died when I was fourteen, which may be why I'm so close to my father," Elizabeth said. She looked down at her hands in her lap, evidently wanting to drop the subject. Her dark hair shone as it fell across her forehead.

"You have very beautiful hair," Mark said softly. "I wanted to touch it when I first saw you. I still do."

She smiled. "I like curly hair better." She leaned her chin on her cupped hands and looked at him mischievously. "You'll look fantastic when you're forty and fashionably grey at the temples. Provided you don't lose it all first, of course. Did you know that men who lose their hair at the crown are sexy, those who lose it at the temples, think, and those who lose it all over, think they are sexy?"

"If I go bald at the crown, will you accept that as a declaration of intent?"

"I'm willing to wait but not that long."

On the way back to her house he stopped, put his arm around her and kissed her, hesitantly at first, unsure of how she would respond.

"You know, my knees are feeling weak, Elizabeth," he murmured into her soft, warm hair. "What are you going to do with your latest victim?"

She walked on without speaking for a little way.

"Get you some knee pads," she said.

They walked on hand in hand, silently, happily, slowly. Three not very romantic men were following them.

In the pretty living-room, on the cream-coloured sofa, he kissed her again.

The three unromantic men waited in the shadows outside.

She sat alone in the Oval Office going over the clauses in the bill one by one, searching for any line that still might trip her up when the bill was voted on tomorrow.

She looked up suddenly startled to see her husband standing in front of her, a mug of steaming cocoa in his hand.

"An early night won't harm your chances of influencing that lot," he said pointing towards the Capitol.

She smiled, "Darling Edward, where would I be without your common sense?"

Sunday morning, 6 March

9:00 am

Mark spent Sunday morning putting the finishing touches to his report for the Director. He began by tidying his desk; he could never think clearly unless everything was in place. Mark gathered all his notes together and put them in a logical sequence. He completed the task by two o'clock, without noticing that he had missed lunch. Slowly he wrote down the names of the fifteen senators who were left, six under the heading Foreign Relations Committee, nine under Gun Control bill – Judiciary Committee. He stared at the lists, hoping for inspiration but none came. One of these men was a killer and there were only four days left to find out which one. He put the papers into his briefcase, which he locked in his desk.

He went into the kitchen and made himself a sandwich. He looked at his watch. What could he do that would be useful for the rest of the day? Elizabeth was on duty at the hospital. He picked up the phone and dialled the number. She could only spare a minute, due in the operating theatre at three o'clock.

"Okay, Doctor, this won't take long and it shouldn't hurt. I can't call you every day just to tell you that you are lovely and intelligent and that you drive me crazy, so listen carefully."

"I'm listening, Mark."

"Okay. You are beautiful and bright and I'm crazy about you . . . What, no reply?"

"Oh, I thought there might be more. I'll say something nice in return when I'm three inches away from you, not three miles."

"Better make it soon, or I am going to crack up. Off you go, and cut out someone else's heart."

She laughed. "It's an ingrown toenail actually . . ."

She hung up. Mark roamed about the room, his mind jumping from fifteen senators, to Elizabeth, back to one Senator. Wasn't it going just a little too well with Elizabeth? Was one Senator looking for him, rather than the other way around? He cursed and poured himself a Michelob. His mind switched to Barry Calvert; on Sunday afternoons they usually played squash. Then to Nick Stames, Stames who had unknowingly taken his place. If Stames were alive now, what would he do? . . . A remark that Stames had made at the office party last Christmas came flashing across Mark's mind: "If I'm not available, the second best crime man in this goddamn country is George Stampouzis of *The New York Times*" – another Greek, naturally. "He must know more about the Mafia and the CIA than almost anyone on either side of the law."

Mark dialled Information in New York, and asked for the number, not quite sure where it was leading him. The operator gave it to him.

"Thank you."

"You're very welcome."

He dialled it.

"Crime desk, George Stampouzis, please." They put him through.

"Stampouzis," said a voice. They don't waste words on *The New York Times*.

"Good afternoon. My name is Mark Andrews. I'm calling from Washington. I was a friend of Nick Stames; in fact, he was my boss."

The voice changed. "Yes, I heard about the terrible accident, if it was an accident. What can I do for you?"

"I need some inside information. Can I fly up and see you immediately?"

"Does it concern Nick?"

"Yes."

"Then yes. Meet me at eight o'clock, north-east corner of Twenty-first and Park Avenue South?"

"I'll be there," said Mark looking at his watch.

"And I'll be waiting for you."

The Eastern Airlines shuttle flight arrived a few minutes after seven. Mark made his way through the crowd milling around the baggage pickup and headed for the taxi stand. A potbellied, middle-aged, unshaven New Yorker with an unlit cigar stub bobbing up and down in his mouth drove him towards Manhattan. He never stopped talking the whole way, a monologue that required few replies. Mark could have used the time to compose his thoughts.

"This country's full of shit," said the bobbing cigar.

"Yes," said Mark.

"And this city is nothing more than a garbage hole."

"Yes," said Mark.

"And that daughter of a bitch Kane's to blame. They ought to string her up."

Mark froze. It was probably said a thousand times a day; someone in Washington was saying it and meaning it.

The cab driver pulled up to the curb.

"Eighteen dollars even," said the bobbing cigar.

Mark put a ten and two fives into the little plastic drawer in the protective screen that divided driver from passenger, and climbed out. A heavy-set man in his mid-fifties and wearing a tweed overcoat, headed towards him. Mark shivered. He had forgotten how cold New York could be in March.

"Andrews?"

"Yes. Good guess."

"When you spend your life studying criminals, you

begin to think like them." He was taking in Mark's suit. "G-men are certainly dressing better than they did in my day."

Mark looked embarrassed. Stampouzis must know that an FBI agent was paid almost double the salary of a New York cop.

"You like Italian food?" He didn't wait for Mark's reply. "I'll take you to one of Nick's old favourites." He was already on the move. They walked the long block in silence, Mark's step hesitating as he passed each restaurant entrance. Suddenly, Stampouzis disappeared into a doorway. Mark followed him through a run-down bar full of men who were leaning on the counter and drinking heavily. Men who had no wives to go home to, or if they did, didn't want to.

Once through the bar, they entered a pleasant, brick-walled dining area. A tall, thin Italian guided them to a corner table: obviously Stampouzis was a favoured customer. Stampouzis didn't bother with the menu.

"I recommend the shrimp marinara. After that, you're on your own."

Mark took his advice and added a *piccata al limone* and half a carafe of Chianti. Stampouzis drank Colt 45. They talked of trivia while they ate. Mark knew the residual Mediterranean creed after two years with Nick Stames – never let business interfere with the enjoyment of good food. In any case, Stampouzis was still sizing him up, and Mark needed his confidence. When Stampouzis had finished an enormous portion of zabaglione and settled down to a double espresso with Sambuca on the side, he looked up at Mark and spoke in a different tone.

"You worked for a great man, a rare lawman. If one tenth of the FBI were as conscientious and intelligent as Nick Stames, you would have something to be pleased about in that brick coliseum of yours."

Mark looked at him, about to speak.

"No, don't add anything about Nick; that's why you're here, and don't ask me to change my opinion of the

Bureau. I've been a crime reporter for over thirty years and the only change I've seen in the FBI and the Mafia is that they are both bigger and stronger." He poured the Sambuca into his coffee, and took a noisy gulp. "Okay. How can I help?"

"Everything off the record," said Mark.

"Agreed," said Stampouzis. "For both our sakes."

"I need two pieces of information. First, are there any senators with close connections in organised crime and second, what is the attitude of the mob to the Gun Control bill?"

"You don't want much, do you?" said the Greek sarcastically. "Where shall I begin? The first is easier to answer directly, because the truth is that half the senators have loose connections with organised crime, by which I mean the Mafia, however out-of-date that is. Some don't even realise it but if you include accepting campaign contributions from businessmen and large corporations directly or indirectly associated with crime, then every President is a criminal. But when the Mafia needs a senator they do it through a third party, and even that's rare."

"Why?" queried Mark.

"The Mafia needs clout at the state level, in courts, with deals, local by-laws, all that. They're just not interested in foreign treaties and the approval of Supreme Court justices. In a more general way, there are some senators who owe their success to links with the Mafia, the ones who have started as civil court judges or state assemblymen and received direct financial backing from the Mafia. It's possible they didn't even realise it; some people don't check too carefully when they are trying to get elected. Added to this are cases like Arizona and Nevada, where the Mafia runs a legit business, but God help any outsiders who try to join in. Finally, in the case of the Democratic party, there's organised labour, especially the Teamsters Union. There you are, Mark, thirty years' experience in ten minutes."

"Great background. Now can I ask you some specifics.

If I name fifteen senators, will you indicate if they could fall into any of the categories you have mentioned?" Mark asked.

"Maybe. Try me. I'll go as far as I feel I can. Just don't push me."

"Bradley."

"Never," said Stampouzis.

"Thornton."

He didn't move a muscle.

"Bayh."

"Not that I have ever heard."

"Harrison."

"No idea. I don't know much about South Carolina politics."

"Nunn."

'Sam Sunday-School? Scout's Honour Nunn? You've got to be kidding."

"Brooks."

"Hates the President but I don't think he'd go that far."

Mark went down the list. Stevenson, Biden, Moynihan, Woodson, Clark, Mathias. Stampouzis shook his head silently.

"Dexter."

He hesitated. Mark tried not to tense.

"Trouble, yes," Stampouzis began. "But Mafia, no."

He must have heard Mark sigh. Mark was anxious to know what the trouble was; he waited but Stampouzis didn't add anything.

"Byrd."

"Majority leader. Not his style."

"Pearson."

"You're joking."

"Thank you," said Mark. He paused. "Now to the Mafia's attitude towards the Gun Control bill."

"I'm not certain at the moment," began Stampouzis. "The Mafia is no longer monolithic. It's too big for that and there has been a lot of internal disagreement lately.

The old-timers are dead set against it because of the obvious difficulty of getting guns legally in the future, but they are more frightened by the riders to the bill, like mandatory sentences for carrying an unregistered gun. The Feds will love that; for them it's the best thing since tax evasion. They will be able to stop any known criminal, search him, and if he is carrying an unregistered gun, which he is almost certain to be, wham, he's in the court-house. On the other hand, some of the young Turks are looking forward to it, a modern-day Prohibition for them. They will supply unregistered guns to unorganised hoodlums and any mad radical who wants one, another source of income for the mob. They also believe the police won't be able to enforce the law and the cleaning-up period will take a decade. Does that get near to answering the question?"

"Yes, very near," said Mark.

"Now, my turn to ask you a question, Mark."

"Same rules?"

"Same rules. Are these questions directly connected with Nick's death?"

"Yes," said Mark.

"I won't ask any more then, because I know what to ask and you're going to have to lie. Let's just make a deal. If this breaks into something big, you'll see I get an exclusive over those bastards from the *Post*."

"Agreed," said Mark.

Stampouzis smiled and signed the check; the last comment had made Mark Andrews a legitimate expense.

Mark looked at his watch; with luck he would make the last shuttle from La Guardia. Stampouzis rose and walked to the door; the bar was still full of men drinking heavily, the same men with the same wives. Once on the street, Mark hailed a cab. This time, a young black pulled up beside him.

"I'm halfway there," said Stampouzis, puzzling Mark. "If I pick up anything that I think might help, I'll call you."

Mark thanked him and climbed into the cab.

"La Guardia, please."

Mark rolled down the window, Stampouzis stared in briefly.

"It's not for you, it's for Nick." He was gone.

The journey back to the airport was silent.

When Mark eventually reached his own apartment, he tried to put the pieces together in his mind ready for the Director the following morning. He glanced at his watch. Christ, it was already the following morning.

Monday morning, 7 March

7:00 am

The Director listened to the results of Mark's research in attentive silence and then added his own unexpected piece of information.

"Andrews, we may be able to narrow your list of fifteen senators even further. Last Thursday morning a couple of agents picked up an unauthorised transmission on one of our KGB channels. Either temporary interference from some commercial station caused us to tune in a different frequency momentarily or else some guy is in possession of an illegal transmitter for our frequency. The only thing our boys heard was: 'Come in, Tony. I just dropped the Senator back for his committee meeting and I'm . . .' The voice stopped transmitting abruptly and we couldn't find it again. Perhaps the conspirators had been listening in on our conversations, and this time one of them without thinking started to transmit on our frequency as well; it's easy enough to do. The agents who heard it filed a report concerning the illegal use of our frequency without realising its particular significance."

Mark was leaning forward in his chair.

"Yes, Andrews," said the Director. "I know what's going through your mind: 10:30 am. The message was sent at 10:30 am."

"10:30 am, 3 March," said Mark urgently. "Let me just check . . . which committees were already in progress

. . ." He opened his file. "Dirksen Building . . . that hour
. . . I have the details at hand somewhere, I know,"
he continued as he flicked through his papers. "Three
possibilities, sir. The Foreign Relations and Government
Operations committees were in session that morning. On
the floor of the Senate they were debating the Gun Control
bill: that seems to be taking up a lot of their time right
now."

"Now we may be getting somewhere," said the Director. "Can you tell from your records how many of your
fifteen were in the Capitol on 3 March and what they
were up to?"

Mark leafed through the fifteen sheets of paper and
slowly divided them into two piles. "Well, it isn't conclusive, sir, but I have no record of these eight" – he placed
his hand on one of the piles – "being in the Senate
that morning. The remaining seven were definitely there.
None on the Government Operations Committee. Two
on Foreign Relations – Pearson and Nunn, sir. The
other five are Brooks, Byrd, Dexter, Harrison and
Thornton. They were all on the floor. And they were
all on the Judiciary Committee, Gun Control bill, as
well."

The Director grimaced. "Well, as you say, Andrews,
it's hardly conclusive. But it's all we have, so you concentrate on those seven. With only four days, it's a chance
we will have to take. Don't get too excited just because
we had one lucky break, and double-check that those
eight could not have been in Dirksen that morning. Now,
I am not going to risk putting seven senators under
surveillance. Those folks on the Hill are suspicious
enough of the FBI as it is. We'll have to use different
tactics. Politically, we can't take a chance on a full-scale
investigation. I'm afraid we'll have to find our man by
using the only clues we're certain of – where he was on
Thursday, 24 February at lunchtime, and this 10:30
Judiciary Committee meeting last week. So don't bother
with the motive – we needn't waste time second-guessing

that, Andrews. Just keep looking for ways of narrowing the list, and spend the rest of the day at the Foreign Relations Committee and the floor of the Senate. Talk to the staff directors. There is nothing they don't know – public or private – about the senators."

"Yes, sir."

"And one more thing. I'm having dinner with the President tonight so I may be able to glean some information from her which could help us reduce the number of suspects."

"Will you tell the President, sir?"

The Director of the FBI paused. "No, I don't think so. I still believe we have the problem under control. I see no reason for worrying her at this stage, certainly not before I'm convinced we're likely to fail."

Finally the Director passed over an Identikit picture of the Greek priest. "Mrs Casefikis's version," he said. "What do you think of it?"

"It's not a bad likeness at all," said Mark. "Maybe a little fleshier around the jaws than that. Those men really know their job."

"What worries me," said the Director, "is that I've seen that damn face before. So many criminals have come across my path that to remember one of them is almost impossible. Maybe it will come to me."

"I do hope it comes before Thursday, sir," said Mark, without thinking.

"So do I," Tyson replied grimly.

"And to think I was only twenty-four hours behind him. It hurts."

"Think yourself lucky, young man. If you had been ahead of him, I think Ariana Casefikis would now be dead and so might you. I've still got a man on Mrs Casefikis's home just in case he returns, but I think he is far too professional a bastard to risk that."

Mark agreed. "Professional bastard," he repeated.

The red light on the internal telephone winked.

"Yes, Mrs McGregor?"

"You'll be late for your appointment with Senator Hart."

"Thank you, Mrs McGregor." He put the phone down. "I'll see you at the same time tomorrow, Mark." It was the first time he called him Mark. "Leave no stone unturned; only four days left."

Mark took the elevator down and left the building by his usual route. He didn't notice he was being followed from the other side of the street. He went to the Senate Office Building and made appointments to see the staff directors of the Foreign Relations and Judiciary committees. The earliest either could manage was the following morning. Mark returned to the Library of Congress to research more thoroughly the personal histories of the seven senators left on his list. They were a rather varied bunch, from all over the country, with little in common; one of them had nothing in common with the other six, but which one? Nunn – it didn't add up. Thornton – Stampouzis obviously didn't care for him but what did that prove. Byrd – surely not the majority leader? Harrison – Stampouzis said he was against the Gun Control bill, but so was almost half the Senate. Dexter – what was the trouble Stampouzis wouldn't tell him about? Perhaps Elizabeth would enlighten him tonight. Ralph Brooks, a strangely intense, driven man and certainly lacking any affection for Kane, that was for sure. Pearson – if he turned out to be the villain, no one would believe it: thirty-three years in the Senate, and always playing honest Casca in public and private.

Mark sighed – the long weary sigh of a man who has come to an impasse. He glanced at his watch: 10:45; he must leave immediately if he were to be on time. He returned the various periodicals, *Congressional Records*, and Ralph Nader reports to the librarian, and hurried across the street to the parking lot to pick up his car. He drove quickly down Constitution Avenue and over Memorial Bridge – how many times had he done that this week? Mark glanced in his rear-view mirror and thought he recognised the car behind him, or was it just the memory of last Thursday?

Mark parked his car at the side of the road. Two Secret Service men stopped him. He produced his credentials and walked slowly down the path just in time to join a hundred and fifty other mourners standing around two graves, freshly dug to receive two men who a week ago were more alive than most of the people attending their burial. The Vice President, former Senator Bill Bradley, was representing the President. He stood next to Norma Stames, a frail figure in black, being supported by her two sons. Hank, the eldest, stood next to a giant of a man, who must have been Barry Calvert's father. Next was the Director, who glanced around and saw Mark, but didn't acknowledge him. The game was being played out even at the graveside.

Father Gregory's vestments fluttered slightly in the cold breeze. The hem was muddy, for it had rained all night. A young chaplain in white surplice and black cassock stood silently at his side.

"I am the image of Thine inexpressible glory, even though I bear the wounds of sin," Father Gregory intoned.

His weeping wife bent forward and kissed Nick Stames's pale cheek and the coffin was closed. As Father Gregory prayed, Stames's and Calvert's coffins were lowered slowly, slowly into their graves. Mark watched sadly: it might have been him going down, down; it should have been him.

"With the saints give rest, O Christ, to the souls of Thy servants, where there is neither sickness nor sorrow, nor sighing, but Life everlasting."

The final blessing was given, the Orthodox made the sign of the cross and the mourners began to disperse.

After the service Father Gregory was speaking warmly of his friend Nick Stames and expressed the hope that he and his colleague Barry Calvert had not died without purpose; he seemed to be looking at Mark as he said it.

Mark saw Nanna, Aspirin, Julie, and the anonymous man, but realised he mustn't speak to them. He slipped quietly away. Let the others mourn the dead: his job was to find their living murderers.

Mark drove back to the Senate, more determined than ever to find out which senator should have been present at the poignant double funeral. Had he stayed a little longer, he would have seen Matson talking casually to Grant Nanna, saying what a good man Stames was and what a loss he would be to law enforcement.

Mark spent the afternoon at the Foreign Relations Committee listening to Pearson and Nunn. If it were either of them, they were cool customers, going about their job without any outward signs of anxiety. Mark wanted to cross their names off the list but he needed one more fact confirmed before he could. When Pearson finally sat down, Mark felt limp. He also needed to relax tonight if he were going to survive the next three days. He left the committee room and called Elizabeth to confirm their dinner date. He then called the Director's office and gave Mrs McGregor the telephone numbers at which he could be reached: the restaurant, his home, Elizabeth's home. Mrs McGregor took the numbers down without comment.

Two cars tailed him on his way back: a blue Ford sedan and a black Buick. When he arrived home, he tossed the car keys to Simon, dismissed the oppressive but familiar sensation of being continually watched, and started thinking of more pleasant things, an evening with Elizabeth.

6:30 pm

Mark walked down the street thinking about the evening ahead of him. Already I adore that girl. That's the one thing I am certain of at the moment. If only I could get rid of the nagging doubt about her father – even about her.

He went into Blackistone's and ordered a dozen roses, eleven red, one white. The girl handed him a card and an envelope. Quickly, he wrote Elizabeth's name and address on the envelope, and he pondered the blank card, fragments of sentences and poems flashing through his mind. Finally, he smiled. He wrote, carefully:

Happly I think on thee, and then my state,
Like to the lark at break of day arising
From sullen earth, sings hymns at heaven's gate.
   P.S. Modern version. Is it at long last love?

"Have them sent at once, please."
"Yes, sir."
Good. Back home. What to wear? A dark suit? Too formal. The light blue suit? Too much like a gay, should never have bought it in the first place. The double-breasted suit – latest thing. Shirt. White, casual, no tie. Blue, formal, tie. White wins. Too virginal? Blue wins. Shoes: black slip-on or laces? Slip-on wins. Socks: simple choice, dark blue. Summing up: denim suit, blue shirt, dark blue tie, dark blue socks, black slip-on shoes. Leave clothes neatly on bed. Shower and wash hair – I like curly hair better. Damn, soap in eyes. Grope for towel, soap out, drop towel, out of shower. Towel around waist. Shave; twice in one day. Shave very carefully. No blood. Aftershave. Dry hair madly with towel. Curls all over the place. Back to bedroom. Dress carefully. Get tie exactly – that won't do, tie again. Better, this time. Pull up zipper – could stand to lose inch around waist. Check in mirror. Seen worse. To hell with modesty, have seen a whole lot worse. Check money, credit cards. No gun. All set. Bolt door. Press button for elevator.

"Can I have my keys, please, Simon?"

"Well, goddamn." Simon's eyes opened very wide. "Found yourself a new fox!"

"You better not wait up, because if I fail, Simon, I'll probably jump on top of you."

"Thanks for the warning, Mark. Tough it out, man."

Beautiful evening, climb into car, check watch: 7:34.

The Director checked his dinner jacket again.

I miss Ruth. Housekeeper does a great job, but not the same thing at all. Pour a scotch, check clothes. Tuxedo just pressed – a little out of fashion. Dress shirt back from the cleaners. Black tie to be tied. Black shoes, black socks, white handkerchief – all in order. Turn on shower. Ah, how to get something useful out of the President? Damn, where's the soap? Have to get out of shower and soak bathmat and towel. Only one towel. Grab soap, revolting smell. Nowadays, they must only make it for gays. Wish I could still get army surplus. Out of the shower. Overweight; I need to lose about fifteen pounds. Body too white. Hide it quickly and forget. Shave. Good old trusty cutthroat. Never shave twice a day except when dining with the President. Good. No damage. Get dressed. Fly buttons; hate zippers. Now to tie black tie. Damn it. Ruth could always do it the first time, perfectly. Try again. At last. Check wallet. Don't really need money, credit cards, or anything else. Unless the President's going through hard times. Tell housekeeper I'll be back about eleven. Put on overcoat. Special agent there with car, as always.

"Good evening, Sam, beautiful evening."

The only chauffeur in the employ of the FBI opened the back door of the Ford sedan.

Climb into car, check watch: 7:45.

Drive slowly – lots of time – don't want to be there early – never seems to be any traffic when you have all the time in the world – hope roses have arrived – take longer route to Georgetown, past Lincoln Memorial and up Rock Creek and Potomac Parkway – it's prettier – at least con yourself that's why you're doing it. Don't run yellow lights, even though man behind you is obviously late and gesticulating. Obey the law – con yourself again – you'd shoot through the lights if you were running late for her. Never embarrass the Bureau. Careful of trolley lines in Georgetown, so easy to skid on them. Turn right at end of street and find parking space. Circle slowly looking for perfect spot – no such thing. Double-park and hope no traffic cop's around. Stroll nonchalantly towards house – bet she's still in the tub. Check watch: 8:04. Perfect. Ring doorbell.

"We're running a bit late, Sam." Perhaps unwise to say that because he'll break the speed limit and might embarrass the Bureau. Why is there so much traffic when you're in a hurry? Damn Mercedes in front of us at the circle, stopping even before the lights turned red. Why have a car that can do 120 mph if you don't even want to do thirty? Good, the Mercedes has turned off towards Georgetown. Probably one of the beautiful people. Down Pennsylvania Avenue. At last the White House in sight. Turn on to West Executive Avenue. Waved on by guard at gate. Pull up to West Portico. Met by Secret Service man in dinner jacket. His tie looks better than mine. Bet it's a clip-on. No, come to think of it, it's regulation to have to tie them in the White House. Damn it, the man must be married. Didn't do it himself. Follow him through foyer to West Wing Reception Room past Remington sculpture. Met by another Secret Service man also in dinner jacket. Also better tie. I give up. Escorted to elevator. Check watch: 8:06. Not bad. Enter West Sitting Hall.

"Good evening, Madam President."

"Hello, lovely lady."

She looks beautiful in that blue dress. Fantastic creature. How could I have any suspicions about her?

"Hello, Mark."

"That's a terrific dress you're wearing."

"Thank you. Would you like to come in for a minute?"

"No, I think we'd better go, I'm double-parked."

"Fine, I'll just grab my coat."

Open car door for her. Why didn't I just take her by the hand into the bedroom and make mad passionate love to her? I would have happily settled for a sandwich. That way we could do what we both want to do and save a lot of time and trouble.

"Did you have a good day?"

"Very busy. How about you, Mark?"

Oh, managed to think about you for a few hours while I got some work done, but it wasn't easy.

"Busy as all hell. I wasn't sure I was going to be able to make it."

Start car, right on M Street to Wisconsin. No parking spaces. Past Roy Rogers' Family Restaurant. Let's just get some chicken legs and head back home.

"Aah, success."

Hell, where did that Volkswagen come from?

"What lousy luck. You'll find another one."

"Yes, but four hundred yards away from the restaurant."

"The walk will do us good."

Did the roses come? I'll put that florist's girl in jail in the morning if she forgot to send them.

"Oh, Mark, how thoughtless of me not to mention it before; thank you for those glorious roses. Are you the white one? And the Shakespeare?"

"Think nothing of it, lovely lady."

Liar. So you liked the Shakespeare, but what was your answer to the Cole Porter? Enter supersmooth French restaurant. Rive Gauche. Gauche is right. A Fed in a place like this? Bet it'll cost an arm and a leg. Full of snotty waiters with their hands out. What the hell, it's only money.

"Did you know that this place is responsible for making Washington the French-restaurant capital of America?"

Trying to impress her with a little inside dope.

"No, why?"

"Well, the owner keeps bringing his chefs over from France. One by one they quit and go off to start their own restaurants."

"You G-men really do carry around a store of useless information."

Look for the maître d'.

"Table in the name of Andrews."

"Good evening, Mr Andrews. How nice to see you."

Damn man's never seen me before and probably will never see me again. Which table is he going to give me? Not too bad. She might even believe I've been here before. Slip him a five-dollar bill.

"Thank you, sir. Enjoy your dinner."

They settled back in the deep red leather chairs. The restaurant was crowded.

"Good evening. Would you care for an aperitif, sir?"

"What will you have, Elizabeth?"

"Campari and soda, please."

"One Campari and soda and I'll have a spritzer."

Glance at menu. Chef Michel Laudier. The restaurant motto: *Fluctuat nec mergitur*. Oh, I'll *mergitur*, all right, cover charges, service charges. Ouch. And she has no way of knowing. This is one of those sexy places where the man is given a menu with the prices.

"I'll have a first course, but only if you'll join me."

"Of course, I'm going to have one, lovely lady."

"Good, I'll have the avocado . . ."

Without prawns?

". . . with prawns, and then . . ."

. . . Caesar salad?

". . . the filet mignon Henri IV – rare, please."

$20.50. To hell with it, she's worth every penny. I think I'll have the same.

"Have you decided, sir?"

"Yes, we'll both have the avocado with prawns and the fillet mignon Henri IV, rare."

"Would you care to look at the wine list?"

No, thank you, I'll have a beer.

"Would you like some wine, Elizabeth?"

"That would be lovely, Mark."

"A bottle of Hospice de Beaune, *soixante-dix-huit*, please."

I bet he can tell the only damn French I learned at school was the numbers.

"Very good, sir."

The first course arrived and so did the sommelier with the wine.

If you think you're going to sell us two bottles, you damn frog, think again.

"Shall I serve the wine, sir?"

"Not yet, thank you. Open it and then serve it with the main course."

"Certainly, sir."

"Your avocado, Mademoiselle."

Prawns go before the fall.

"Good evening, Halt. How's life at the Bureau?"

"We're surviving, Madam."

What banal remarks the mighty make to each other.

The Director glanced around the pleasant blue and gold room. H. Stuart Knight, the head of the Secret Service, stood alone at the far end. On the sofa, by the window overlooking the West Wing and the Executive Office Building, sat the Attorney General, Marian Edelman, talking to Senator Birch Bayh, the man who had succeeded Ted Kennedy as chairman of the Judiciary Committee. The hackneyed phrase "boyish good looks", which had been applied to Bayh constantly during his campaigning in the 1976 Democratic presidential primaries, was still an accurate description. The thin, gaunt senator from Texas, Marvin Thornton, hovered over his colleague and Marian Edelman.

My God, let me have men about me that are fat . . .

"You see I've invited Thornton."

"Yes, Madam."

"We must try and talk him round on the Gun Control bill."

The West Sitting Hall was a comfortable room on the family floor of the White House, adjacent to the First Gentleman's dressing-room. It was an honour to be entertained in this part of the White House. And to eat in the small dining-room, rather than the President's dining-room downstairs, was a special privilege, since the former was usually reserved for strictly family dining. The fact that the President's husband was absent only confirmed how private this occasion had to be.

"What will you drink, Halt?"

"Scotch on the rocks."

"Scotch on the rocks for the Director and an orange juice for me. I'm watching my weight."

Doesn't she know orange juice is the last thing to drink if you're dieting?

"How are the votes stacking up, Madam?"

"Well, the numbers are forty-eight for and forty-seven against at the moment, but it's got to go through on the tenth or I'll have to forget the whole thing until the next session. That's my biggest worry at the moment, what with my European tour and the New Hampshire primary less than a year off. I would have to drop the bill until I was re-elected and I can't afford it to be the main election issue. I want it out of the way and seen to be working before then."

"Then let's hope it passes on the tenth, because it would certainly make my job easier, Madam President."

"Marian's too. Another drink, Halt?"

"No, thank you, Madam."

"Shall we go in to dinner?"

The President led her five guests into the dining-room. The wallpaper in the room depicted scenes from the American Revolution. It was furnished in the Federal style of the early nineteenth century.

I never get bored with the beauty of the White House.

The Director gazed at the plaster-composition mantel designed by Robert Welford of Philadelphia in 1815. It bore the famous report of Commodore Oliver Hazard Perry after the Battle of Lake Erie during the War of 1812: "We have met the enemy, and they are ours."

"Five thousand people passed through this building today," H. Stuart Knight was saying. "Nobody really grasps the security problems. This building may be the home of the President, but it still belongs to the people and that makes one continuous democratic headache."

If he knew everything . . .

The President sat at the head of the table, the Attorney General at the other end, Bayh and Thornton on one side, the Director and Knight on the other. The first course was avocado with prawns.

I always get sick when I eat prawns.

"It's good to see my law officers together," said the President. "I want to take this opportunity to discuss the Gun Control bill, which I remain determined will pass on 10 March. That's why I invited Birch and Marvin here tonight, because their support will influence the fate of this bill."

10 March again. Perhaps Cassius has to keep to a deadline. Seem to remember Thornton being firmly against this bill, and he's on Andrews' list of seven.

"The rural states are going to be a problem, Madam President," Marian Edelman was saying. "They won't be willing to hand over their guns all that readily."

"A long amnesty period, say about six months, might be the answer," the Director offered. "So the law remains unaffected for a statutory period. It's what always happens after a war. And the public relations boys can keep announcing that hundreds of weapons have been handed in to local police stations."

"Good thinking, Halt," said the President.

"It's going to be a hell of an operation," said the

Attorney General, "with seven million members of the National Rifle Association and probably fifty million firearms in America."

No one disagreed with that conclusion.

The second course arrived.

Dover sole. Obviously the President is serious about her diet.

"Coffee or brandy, sir?"

"Don't let's bother," said Elizabeth, touching Mark's hand gently. "Let's have it at home."

"Nice idea."

He smiled into her eyes and tried to guess what was going on in her mind . . .

"No, thank you. Just the check."

The waiter scurried away obediently.

They always scurry away obediently when you ask for the check. She hasn't let go of my hand.

"A delicious meal, Mark. Thank you very much."

"Yes, we must come here again sometime."

The check arrived. Mark glanced at it in rueful bemusement.

$87.20, plus tax. If you can understand how a restaurant gets to its final figure you deserve to be Secretary of the Treasury. Hand over the American Express Card. The little piece of blue paper comes back to sign. Make it up to $100.00 and forget it until the envelope marked American Express arrives in the mail.

"Good night, Mr Andrews." Much bowing and scraping. "I hope we will see you and Mademoiselle again soon."

"Yes, indeed."

You'll need a very good memory to recognise me next time I come. Open car door for Elizabeth. Will I do this when we're married? Christ, I'm thinking about marriage.

"I think I must have eaten too much. I'm rather sleepy."

Now what does that mean? You could take that about twenty different ways.

"Oh, really, I feel ready for anything."

A bit clumsy, maybe. Look for parking space again. Good. There's one right in front of the house and no Volkswagen to stop me grabbing it. Open car door for Elizabeth. She fumbles with front door keys. Into kitchen. Kettle on.

"What a nice kitchen."

Silly remark.

"I'm glad you like it."

Equally silly.

Into living-room.

Good, there are the roses.

"Hello, Samantha. Come and meet Mark."

Christ Almighty, she has a roommate.

Samantha rubbed up against Mark's leg and purred.

Relief. Samantha is Siamese, not American.

"Where shall I sit?"

"Anywhere."

She's no help at all.

"Black or with cream, darling?"

"Darling." The odds must be better than 50–50.

"Black, please, with one sugar."

"Amuse yourself till the water boils. I'll only be a few minutes."

"More coffee, Halt?"

"No thank you, Madam, I have to be getting home, if you'll excuse me."

"I'll walk you to the door. There are one or two things I'd like to discuss with you."

"Yes, of course, Madam President."

The Marines at the West Entrance came to attention. A man in a dinner jacket hovered in the shadows behind the pillars.

"I'll need your backing a hundred per cent for this Gun Control bill, Halt. The committee is bound to be

144

pushing for your views. And although the numbers are just with us on the floor of the House, I don't want any last-minute hiccups; I'm running out of time."

"I'll be with you, Madam. I've wanted it ever since the death of John F. Kennedy."

"Have you any particular worries about it, Halt?"

"No, Madam. You deal with the politics and sign the bill, and I'll see that the law is enforced."

"Any advice, perhaps?"

"No, I don't think so . . ."

Beware the ides of March.

". . . although it's always puzzled me, Madam President, why in the end you left the bill this late. If something goes wrong on 10 March and if you were to lose next year's election, we would all be back at square one."

"I know, Halt, but I had to decide between my Medicare bill, which was a controversial enough way to start an administration, and pushing a Gun Control bill through at the same time; I might have ended up losing both. To tell you the truth, it had been my intention to start the bill in committee a year earlier, but no one could have anticipated Nigeria attacking South Africa without warning, and America finally having to decide where she stood on that continent."

"You sure stuck your neck out on that one, Madam President, and I confess at the time I thought you were wrong."

"I know, Halt. I had a few sleepless nights myself. But, getting back to the Gun Control bill: don't ever forget that Dexter and Thornton have run the most successful two-man filibuster in the history of the Senate. By 10 March, this damn bill will have been going the rounds for nearly two years despite the tacit support of Senator Byrd as Majority Leader. But I'm not too worried. I still believe we'll pull it off. I can't foresee anything that can stop it now, can you, Halt?"

The Director hesitated. "No, Madam."

The first lie I have ever told the Chief. Would an

investigating commission believe my reasons if the President is assassinated in three days' time?

"Good night, Halt, and thank you."

"Good night, Madam President, and thank you for an excellent dinner."

The Director stepped out, and into his car. The special agent in the driver's seat looked around at him.

"An important message has just come in for you, sir. Could you return to the Bureau immediately?"

Not again.

"All right, but it might be simpler to keep a bed in the place, except someone would accuse me of trying to live rent-free on taxpayers' money."

The driver laughed; the Director had obviously had a good dinner, which was more than he had.

Elizabeth brought the coffee in and sat down by him.

Only the brave deserve the fair. Lift arm casually, place at the back of the couch, touch her hair lightly.

Elizabeth rose. "Oh, I nearly forgot. Would you like a brandy?"

No, I don't want a brandy. I want you to come back.

"No, thank you."

She settled back into Mark's shoulder.

Can't kiss her while she's got the coffee cup in her hand. Ah, she's put the cup down. Hell, she's up again.

"Let's have some music."

No thank you.

"Great idea."

"How about 'In Memory of Sinatra'?"

"Great."

. . . "This time we almost made the pieces fit . . . didn't we . . . gal?"

It's got to be absolutely the wrong song. Ah, she's back. Try the kiss again. Damn, still more coffee. The cup's down at last. Gentle. Yes, very nice. Christ, she's beautiful. Long kiss – are her eyes open? – no, closed. She's enjoying it – good – longer and even better.

"Would you like some more coffee, Mark?"

No no no no no no no.

"No, thank you."

Another long kiss. Start moving hand across back – I've been this far before with her – can't possibly be any objection – move hand to leg – pause – what fabulous legs and she's got two of them. Take hand off leg and concentrate on kissing.

"Mark, there's something I have to tell you."

Oh, Christ! It's the wrong time of the month. That's all I need now.

"Uh-mh?"

"I adore you."

"I adore you too, darling."

He unzipped her skirt, and began to caress her gently. She began to move her hand up his leg.

Heaven is about to happen.

Ring, ring, ring, ring.

Jee-sus!

"It's for you, Mark."

"Andrews?"

"Sir."

"Julius."

Shit.

"I'm coming."

Tuesday morning, 8 March

1:00 am

The man standing at the corner of the churchyard was trying to keep warm in the chill of the early March morning by slapping himself on the back. He had once seen Gene Hackman do it in a movie and it had worked. It wasn't working. Perhaps he needed the big Warner Brothers arc light Hackman had had to help him. He considered the matter, while he continued slapping.

There were actually two men on surveillance, Special Agent Kevin O'Malley and Assistant Field Supervisor Pierce Thompson, both selected by Tyson for their ability and discretion. Neither had shown any sign of surprise when the Director had instructed them to tail a fellow FBI man and report back to Elliott. It had been a long wait for Mark to emerge from Elizabeth's house, and O'Malley didn't blame him. Pierce left the churchyard and joined his colleague.

"Hey, Kevin, have you noticed that someone else is tailing Andrews for us?"

"Yeah. Matson. Why?"

"I thought he was retired."

"He is. I just assumed old Halt was making sure."

"I guess you're right but I wonder why Tyson didn't tell us."

"Because the whole operation's pretty irregular. No one seems to be telling anyone anything. You could always ask Elliott."

"You ask Elliott. You might as well ask the Lincoln Memorial."

"Or you could ask the Director."

"No, thank you."

A few minutes passed by.

"Think we should talk to Matson?"

"You remember the special orders. No contact with anyone. He probably has the same orders, and he would report us without thinking about it. He's that sort of bastard."

O'Malley was the first to see Mark leaving the house and could have sworn he was carrying one shoe. He was right and Mark was running, so he began to follow him. Must avoid getting burned, thought O'Malley. Mark stopped at the pay phone; his pursuer disappeared into some new shadows, to continue his vain attempts to keep warm. He was thankful for the brisk walk, which had helped a little.

Mark had only two quarters; the others were all lying uselessly on the floor by the side of Elizabeth's couch. Where had the Director phoned from? Could it have been the Bureau? That didn't make sense, what would he be doing there at this time of night? Wasn't he supposed to be with the President? Mark looked at his watch. Hell, 1:15. He must be at home; if he isn't I'll be out of quarters. Mark put on his other shoe. Easy slip-on. He cursed, and tossed one of the quarters; George Washington, I call the Bureau. *E pluribus unum*, then I call him at home. The coin landed – George Washington. Mark dialled the Director's private number at the Bureau.

"Yes."

God bless George Washington.

"Julius?"

"Come in immediately."

That didn't sound very friendly. Perhaps he had just returned from the President with some important new information, or maybe something at the dinner had given him indigestion.

149

Mark walked quickly to his car, checking his shirt buttons and tie as he went. His socks felt uncomfortable, as if one of the heels were in the arch of his foot. He passed the man in the shadows, who watched as Mark returned to his car and hesitated. Should he return to Elizabeth and say, say what? He looked up at the light in the window, took a deep breath, cursed again, and fell into the bucket seat of the Mercedes. There hadn't even been time for a cold shower.

It took only a few minutes to reach the Bureau. There was very little traffic, and with the streets so quiet, the computerised lights meant no stopping.

Mark parked the car in the basement garage of the FBI and immediately there was the anonymous man, the anonymous man who obviously was waiting for him. Didn't he ever go to bed? A harbinger of bad tidings, probably, but he didn't let him know, because as usual he didn't speak. Perhaps he's a eunuch, Mark thought. Lucky man. They shared the elevator to the seventh floor. The anonymous man led him noiselessly to the Director's office; wonder what he does for a hobby, thought Mark. Probably a prompter at the National Theater for the Deaf.

"Mr Andrews, sir."

The Director offered no greeting. He was still in evening clothes and looked as black as thunder.

"Sit down, Andrews."

Back to Andrews, thought Mark.

"If I could take you out into the parking lot, stick you up against the wall, and shoot you, I would."

Mark tried to look innocent; it had usually worked with Nick Stames. It didn't seem to cut any ice with the Director.

"You stupid, unthinking, irresponsible, reckless idiot."

Mark decided he was more frightened of the Director than he was of those who might be trying to kill him.

"You've compromised me, the Bureau, and the President," continued the Director. Mark could hear his heart pounding. If he could have counted it, it would have been a hundred and twenty. Tyson was still in full cry. "If I could suspend you or just dismiss you, if only I could do something as simple as that. How many senators are there left, Andrews?"

"Seven, sir."

"Name them."

"Brooks, Harrison, Thornton, Byrd, Nunn, Dex . . . Dexter, and . . . " Mark went white.

"Summa cum laude at Yale, and you have the naïvete of a boy scout. When we first saw you with Dr Elizabeth Dexter, we, in our stupidity, knowing she was the doctor on duty on the evening of 3 March at Woodrow Wilson, assumed in our stupidity" – he repeated it even more pointedly – "that you were on to a lead, but now we discover that not only is she the daughter of one of the seven senators whom we suspect of wanting to murder the President but, as if that's not enough, we find out you're having an affair with her."

Mark wanted to protest but couldn't get his lips to move.

"Can you deny you've slept with her, Andrews?"

"Yes, sir, I can," Mark said very quietly.

The Director was momentarily dumbfounded. "Young man, we wired the place; we know exactly what went on."

Mark leaped out of his chair, stunned dismay yielding to fierce anger. "I couldn't have denied it," he cried, "if you hadn't interrupted me. Have you forgotten what it feels like to love someone, if you ever knew? Fuck your Bureau, and I don't use that word that often, and fuck you. I've been working sixteen hours a day and I'm not getting any sleep at night. Someone may be trying to murder me and I find that you, the only man I've trusted, have ordered your anonymous pimps to play Peeping Tom at my expense. I hope you all roast in hell. I'd rather join the Mafia because I'm sure they let their people have it off occasionally."

Mark was angrier than he had ever been in his life. He collapsed back into the chair, and waited for the consequences. His only strength was that he no longer cared. The Director was equally silent. He walked to the window and stared out. Then he turned slowly; the heavy shoulders, the large head were turning towards him. This is it, thought Mark.

The Director stopped about a yard away from him, looking him square in the eyes, the way he had done from the first moment they had met.

"Forgive me," said the Director. "I've been thoughtless but I'm becoming paranoid about the whole problem. I've just left the President, healthy, fit, full of plans for the future of this country, only to be told that her one hope of carrying out those dreams is sleeping with the daughter of one of the seven men who might at this very moment be planning to assassinate her. I didn't think much further than that."

A big man, thought Mark.

The Director's eyes hadn't left him .

"Let's pray it's not Dexter. Because if it is, Mark, you may well be in considerable danger." He paused again. "By the way, those anonymous pimps have been guarding you night and day, also on a sixteen-hour day, without a break. Some of them even have wives and children. Now we both know the truth. Let's get back to work, Mark, and let's try and stay sane for three more days. Just remember to tell me everything."

Mark had won. No, Mark had lost.

"There are seven senators left." The words were slow and tired, the man was still on edge. Mark had never seen him like this and doubted that many members of the Bureau had.

"My discussions with the President have confirmed my suspicion that the link between 10 March and the Senator is the Gun Control bill. The chairman of the Judiciary Committee, who handled the planning stages of the bill, was there – Senator Bayh. He's still on the list. You had better see what he and our other suspects on that committee had to say about the bill – but keep your eye on Pearson and Nunn at Foreign Relations as well." He paused. "Only three days to go. I intend to stick to my original plan and let things run just as they are for the moment. I'm still in a position to cancel the President's schedule for the tenth at the very last minute. Do you wish to add anything, Mark?"

"No, sir."

"What are your plans?"

"I am seeing the staff directors of both the Foreign Relations and Judiciary committees tomorrow, sir. I may have a clearer idea then on how to approach the problem and what to be looking for."

"Good. Follow them both up meticulously, just in case I've missed something."

"Yes, sir."

"We've had our fingerprint men working overtime on those twenty-eight bills; at the moment, they are only looking for the prints of Mrs Casefikis. That way at least we will know which one might have our man's on it. They have found over a thousand prints, so far, but none fit Mrs Casefikis's. I'll brief you the moment I hear anything. Now let's call it a day, we're both bushed. Don't bother to come in at seven tomorrow" – the Director looked at his watch – "I mean today. Make it 7:00 am on Wednesday and make it on time because then we'll have only one full day left."

Mark knew he was being invited to leave but there was something he wanted to say. The Director looked up and sensed it immediately.

"Save it, Mark. Go home and get some rest. I'm a tired old man, but I would like those bastards, each and every one of them, behind bars on Thursday night. For your sake, I hope to God Dexter isn't involved. But don't close your eyes to anything, Mark. Love may be blind, but let's hope it's not deaf and dumb."

A very big man, thought Mark.

"Thank you, sir. I'll see you on Wednesday morning."

Mark drove his car quietly out of the FBI's garage. He was drained. There was no sign of the anonymous man. He stared in the rear-view mirror. A blue Ford sedan was following him, and this time it seemed obvious. How could he ever be sure whose side they were on? In three more days, he might know. This time next week he'd know everything or nothing. Would the President be alive or dead?

Simon, still on duty at the entrance to the apartment house, gave Mark a cheerful grin. "Make it, man?"

"Not exactly," he replied.

"I could always call up my sister, if you're desperate." Mark tried to laugh.

"A generous offer, but not tonight, Simon." He tossed the car keys over and headed for the elevator. Once locked and bolted into his apartment, he strode into his bedroom, pulled off his shirt and tie, picked up the phone and dialled seven digits slowly. A gentle voice answered.

"You still awake?"

"Very much so."

"I love you." He put the phone down and slept.

Tuesday morning, 8 March

8:04 am

The phone was ringing, but Mark was still in a deep
sleep. It continued to ring. Eventually he awoke, focused
on his watch: 8:05. Damn, probably the Director asking
where the hell he was; no, he hadn't wanted to see him
this morning, isn't that what they agreed? He grabbed
the phone.

"You're awake?"

"Yes."

"I love you, too."

He heard the phone click. A good way to start the day,
though if she knew he was going to spend it investigating
her father . . . And almost certainly the Director was
investigating her.

Mark let the cold shower run on and on until he was
fully awake. Whenever he was awakened suddenly, he
always wanted to go back to sleep. Next week, he promised himself he would. There was one hell of a lot of
things he was going to do next week. He glanced at his
watch: 8:25. No Wheaties this morning. He flicked on the
television to see if he had missed anything going on in
the rest of the world; he was sitting on a news story that
would make Barbara Walters fall off her CBS chair. What
was the man saying?

". . . and now one of the greatest achievements of
mankind, the first pictures ever taken from the planet

155

Jupiter by an American spacecraft. History in the making, but first, this message from Jell-O, the special food for special children."

Mark turned it off, laughing. Jupiter, along with Jell-O, would have to wait until next week.

Because he was running late, he decided to return to taking the Metro from the Waterfront Station next to his apartment. It was different when he had been going in early and had the roads to himself, but at 8:30, the cars would be bumper to bumper the whole way.

The entrance to the subway was marked with a bronze pylon sporting an illuminated M. Mark stepped on to the escalator, which took him from street level down to the Metro station. The tunnel-like station reminded him of a Roman bath, grey and dark with a honeycombed, curved ceiling. One dollar. Rush-hour fare. And he needed a transfer. Another dollar. Mark fumbled in his pockets for the exact fare. Must remember to stock up on quarters when I get to the centre of town, he thought, as he stepped on to another escalator and was deposited at track level. During rush-hour, 6:30–9:00 am, the trains drew in every five minutes. Round lights on the side of the platform began to flash to indicate the train was approaching. The doors opened automatically. Mark joined the crowd in a colourful, brightly lit car, and five minutes later heard his destination announced on the public address system: Gallery Place. He stepped out on to the platform and waited for a red line train. The green line worked perfectly on mornings when he was going to the Washington Field Office, but to get to Capitol Hill, he had to switch. Four minutes later, he emerged into the sunshine at Union Station Visitors' Center, the bustling command post for bus, train, and subway travel in and out of Washington. The Dirksen Senate Office Building was three blocks away, down 1st Street, at the corner of Constitution. That was quick and painless, thought Mark, as he went in the Constitution Avenue entrance. Why do I ever bother with a car at all?

He walked past two members of the Capitol police who were inspecting briefcases and packages at the door, and pressed the Up-button at the public elevator.

"Four, please," he said to the elevator operator.

The Foreign Relations Committee hearing was scheduled to begin shortly. Mark pulled the list of "Today's Activities in the House and Senate", which he had torn out of *The Washington Post*, from his coat pocket. "Foreign Relations: 9:30 am. Open. Hearing on US policy towards the Common Market; administration representatives. 4229 DOB." As Mark walked down the hall, Senator Ralph Brooks of Massachusetts stepped into Suite 4229, and Mark followed him into the hearing room.

The senator, a tall man with rugged, almost film star good looks, had dogged every step of President Kane's political career until finally she had replaced him as Secretary of State when she took over after President Parkin's death.

He had quickly won her seat back in the Senate and then stood against Florentyna Kane as the Democratic candidate and only lost on the seventh ballot. He had gone on to be chairman of the Senate Foreign Relations Committee.

Did he now intend to kill the President in order to reach the highest office himself? It didn't add up because if Kane were assassinated the Vice President Bill Bradley, who was younger than he was, would take her place and then Brooks would be left with no chance. No, the senator didn't look a serious threat but Mark still needed proof before he could cross him off the list.

The hearing room had light-coloured wood panelling, accented by green marble on the lower part of the wall and around the door. At the end of the chamber, there was a semi-circular desk of the same light wood, which was raised one step above the rest of the room. Fifteen burnt-orange chairs. Only about ten of them were occupied. Senator Brooks took his seat, but the assorted staff members, aides, newsmen, and administrative officials continued to mill around. On the wall behind the senators hung two large maps, one of the world, the other of Europe. At a desk immediately in front of and below the senators sat a stenotypist, poised to record the proceedings verbatim. In front, there were desks for witnesses.

More than half the room was given over to chairs for the general public, and these were nearly all full. An oil painting of George Washington dominated the scene. The man must have spent the last ten years of his life posing for portraits, thought Mark.

Senator Brooks whispered something to an aide, and rapped his gavel for silence. "Before we begin," he said, "I'd like to notify Senate staff members and the press of a change in schedule. Today and tomorrow, we will hear testimony from the State Department concerning the European Common Market. We will then postpone the continuation of these hearings until next week, so the committee may devote its attention to the pressing and controversial issue of arms sales to Africa."

By this time, almost everyone in the room had found a seat, and the government witnesses were glancing through their notes. Mark had worked on Capitol Hill one summer during college, but even now he could not help feeling annoyed at the small number of senators who showed up at these hearings. Because each senator served on three or more committees and innumerable sub- and special committees, they were forced to specialise, and to trust the expertise of fellow senators and staff members in areas outside their own speciality. So it was not at all unusual for committee hearings to be attended by three or two or sometimes even only one senator.

The subject under debate was a bill to dismantle the North Atlantic Treaty Organisation. Portugal and Spain had gone Communist and left the Common Market, like two well-behaved dominoes, at the turn of the decade. The Spanish bases went soon after; King Juan Carlos was living in exile in England. NATO had been prepared for the Communist takeover in Portugal, but when Italy finally installed a Fronto Popolare government in the Quirinal, things began to fall apart. The Papacy, trusting to tried and proven methods, locked itself behind its gates, and American Catholic opinion forced the United States to cut off financial aid to the new Italian government. The Italians retaliated by closing her NATO bases.

The economic ripples of the Italian collapse were thought to have influenced the French elections, which had led to a victory for Chirac and the Gaullists. The more extreme forms of socialism had recently been repudiated in Holland and some Scandinavian countries. The Germans were happy with their social democracy. But as the west entered the last decade of the twentieth century, Senator Pearson was declaring that America's only real ally in NATO was Britain, where a Tory government had recently won an upset victory in the February general election.

The British Foreign Secretary, Kenneth Clarke, had argued forcefully against the formal breakup of NATO. Such a move would sever Great Britain from her alliance with the United States, and commit her solely to the EEC, seven of whose fifteen members were not Communist or close to it. Senator Pearson thumped the table. "We should take the British view seriously in our considerations and not be interested only in immediate strategic gains."

After an hour of listening to Brooks and Pearson questioning State Department witnesses about the political situation in Spain, Mark slipped out of the door and went into the Foreign Relations Committee suite down the hall. The secretary informed him that Lester Kenneck, the committee staff director, was out of the office. Mark had telephoned him the day before, leaving the impression that he was a student doing research for his dissertation.

"Is there someone else who could give me some information about the committee?"

"I'll see if Paul Rowe, one of our staff members, might

be able to help you." She picked up the telephone and, several moments later, a thin bespectacled man emerged from one of the back rooms.

"What can I do for you?"

Mark explained that he would like to see other members of the committee in action, particularly Senator Nunn. Rowe smiled patiently. "No problem," he said. "Come back tomorrow afternoon or Thursday for the discussion about arms sales to Africa. Senator Nunn will be here, I guarantee. And you'll find it much more interesting than the Common Market stuff. In fact, the meeting may be closed to the public. But I'm sure if you come by here and talk to Mr Kenneck, he'll arrange for you to sit in."

"Thank you very much. Would you by any chance happen to know if Nunn and Pearson were present at the hearing on 24 February, or last Thursday?"

Rowe raised his eyebrows. "I have no idea. Kenneck might know."

Mark thanked him. "Oh, one more thing. Can you give me a pass for the Senate gallery?" The secretary stamped a card and wrote in his name. Mark headed for the elevator. Arms sales. Africa, he thought. Thursday's too late. Damn. How the hell am I supposed to know why one of these guys would want to kill President Kane? Could be some crazy military thing, or a severe case of racism. It doesn't make any sense. Not why, but who, he reminded himself. As he walked, Mark almost knocked over one of the Senate pages, who was running down the corridor clutching a package. The Congress operates a page school for boys and girls from across the nation who attend classes and work as "gophers" in the Capitol. They all wear dark blue and white and always give the impression of being in a hurry. Mark stopped just in time and the boy scooted around him without even breaking stride.

Mark took the elevator to the ground floor and walked out of the Dirksen Building on to Constitution Avenue.

He made his way across the Capitol grounds, entered the Capitol on the Senate side, underneath the long marble expanse of steps, and waited for the public elevator.

"Busy day," the guard informed him. "Lots of tourists here to watch the gun control debate."

Mark nodded. "Is there a long wait upstairs?"

"Yes, sir, I think so."

The elevator arrived, and on the gallery level a guard ushered Mark into line with a horde of gaping visitors. Mark was impatient. He beckoned to one of the guards.

"Listen, officer," he said, "I have a regular public pass for the gallery, but I'm a student from Yale doing research. Think there is any way you could get me in?"

The guard nodded sympathetically.

A few minutes later, Mark was seated in the chamber. He could see only part of the floor. The senators were seated at desks in semi-circular rows facing the Chair. Even while someone was speaking, staff members and senators wandered around, giving the impression that the really significant manoeuvring took place in hushed tones, not in dramatic debate.

The Judiciary Committee had reported out the bill two weeks before, after prolonged hearings and discussion. The House had already passed similar legislation, which would have to be reconciled with the stricter Senate version if it were to be approved.

Senator Dexter was speaking. My future father-in-law? Mark wondered. He certainly didn't look like a killer, but then which senator did? He had given his daughter her glorious dark hair, although there was a little white at his temples. Not as much as there ought to be, thought Mark – a politician's vanity. And he had also given her his dark eyes. He seemed fairly contemptuous of most of the people around him, tapping the desk with his long fingers to emphasise a point.

"In our discussion about this bill, we have side-stepped a critical, perhaps the most crucial, consideration. And that is the principle of Federalism. For the past fifty years, the federal government has usurped many of the powers once wielded by the states. We look to the President, the Congress, for answers to all our problems. The Founding Fathers never intended the central government to have so much power, and a country as wide and diverse as ours cannot be governed democratically or effectively on that basis. Yes, we all want to reduce crime. But crime differs from place to place. Our constitutional system wisely left the business of crime control to state and local jurisdiction, except for those federal criminal laws which deal with truly national matters. But crimes committed with guns are of a local nature. They ought to be legislated against and enforced at the local level. Only at the state and local levels can the attitudes of the people and the specific characteristics of the crime problem be understood and dealt with by public officials.

"I know that some of my colleagues will argue that, since we require registration of cars and drivers, we ought also to register guns. But gentlemen, we have no national car – or driver-registration law. These matters are left to the states to determine. Each state should be allowed to decide for itself, taking into account the interests of its people, what is reasonable and necessary."

Senator Dexter monopolised the floor for twenty minutes before yielding to the Chair, occupied today by Senator Kemp, who recognised Senator Brooks. When Brooks had finished his preliminary remarks, he launched into a prepared speech:

". . . have consistently decried the killing in the Middle East, in Africa, in Northern Ireland, in Chile. We ended the bloodshed in Vietnam. But when are we going to confront the killing that takes place in our own communities, our own streets, our own homes, every day of every year?" Brooks paused and looked at Senator Harrison from South Carolina, one of the leading opponents of the bill. "Are we waiting for another national tragedy to compel us to take action? Only after the assassination of John F. Kennedy was Senator Thomas Dodd's Handgun

Control bill taken seriously by a Senate committee. No legislation was passed. After the Watts riots of August 1965, in which purchased, not looted guns were used, the Senate held hearings about control of handguns. No action was taken. It took the slaying of Martin Luther King, before the Judiciary Committee passed legislation, controlling interstate sale of handguns as a rider to the omnibus Crime Control bill. The Senate approved the bill. The House concurred after Robert Kennedy was murdered too. In response to the violence of 1968, we enacted the Handgun Control act. But the act, gentlemen, contained a huge loophole – it did not regulate domestic production of these weapons, because at that time eighty per cent of available handguns were manufactured overseas. In 1972, after George Wallace was shot with a Saturday-Night Special, the Senate finally acted to close the loophole. But the bill died in a House Committee.

"Now, some twenty years or more later, having disregarded the fact that President Reagan was seriously wounded in 1981 by a man wielding a handgun in the streets of Washington, even with all that history someone in America is killed or injured by gunfire every two minutes, and we are still without an effective gun control law. What are we waiting for? Someone to try again to assassinate the President?" He paused for effect. "The American people favour gun control legislation. Every poll indicates that this is the case, and it has been true for a decade. Why do we allow the National Rifle Association to manipulate us, to persuade us that they and their views are compelling when in fact they are hollow? What has happened to our capacity for the clear weighing of alternatives, and for outrage at the violence in our society?"

Mark, along with many other observers, was astonished by this impassioned outburst. His impression from informed political journalists was that Brooks would not support the President as, quite apart from personal animosity, he had been a key figure on a number of constitutional issues and in the fight against two of Kane's Supreme Court appointees, Haynsworth and Carswell.

Senator Harrison of South Carolina, an urbane, quietly distinguished man, asked to be recognised. "Will the distinguished Senator from Massachusetts yield?"

Brooks nodded to the Chair.

Harrison addressed his colleagues in a soft, firm voice. "This bill completely negates the concept of self-defence. It asserts that the only legitimate reason for owning a handgun, a shotgun, or a rifle is for sporting purposes. But I would like to ask my distinguished colleagues from the urban states to consider for a moment – just a moment – the plight of a family on a farm in Iowa or on a homestead in Alaska which needs a gun in the house to protect itself. Not for sport, but for self-defence. In my estimation, they have a right to take that step. For what we face in this country, in urban as well as rural areas, is increasing lawlessness. That is the root problem – lawlessness – not the number of guns in circulation. Increased lawlessness means more crimes involving guns, to be sure. But guns do not cause crimes, people cause crimes. If we want to fight crime, we should investigate its root causes instead of trying to take guns away from people who would use them legally. As many a bumper sticker in this great land proclaims, 'If guns are outlawed, only outlaws will have guns'."

Senator Thornton of Texas, thin and gaunt, with greasy black hair, whom Mark remembered from Mr Smith's Restaurant, had only just begun to express his agreement with the views of Senator Dexter and Senator Harrison when six lights around the numbers on the clock at Mark's end of the chamber came alive. A buzzer sounded six times to signal that morning business was concluded. The "morning hour" on the floor of the Senate, from midday until no later than 2:00 pm, was set aside for the presentation of petitions and memorials, reports of standing and select committees, and introduction of bills and resolutions.

Senator Kemp looked at his watch. "Excuse me, Senator Thornton, but it is noon and now that morning business is over, a number of us are expected to appear in committee to debate the Clean Air bill which is on the calendar for this afternoon. Why don't we reconvene at 2:30? As many of us who can get away from the committee at that time can meet back here to discuss this bill. It's important that we move as quickly as possible on this legislation, as we are still hoping to vote on it in this session."

The Senate floor was cleared in a minute. The actors had said their lines and left the stage. Only those who had to get the theatre ready for the afternoon performance remained. Mark asked the guard which was Henry Lykham, the other staff director he had to see. The doorman in the official blue uniform of the Senate Security Staff pointed to a short fat man with a thin moustache and a jolly open face sitting firmly in a large seat at the far side of the gallery, making notes and checking papers. Mark strolled over to him, unaware that a pair of eyes behind dark glasses was following his every movement.

"My name is Mark Andrews, sir."

"Ah, yes, the graduate student. I'll be free in a moment, Mr Andrews."

Mark sat down and waited. The man in dark glasses left the chamber by the side door.

"All right, Mr Andrews, how about some lunch?"

"Great," replied Mark. He was taken to the ground floor, to G-211, the Senators' Dining-Room. They found a table at the side of the room. Mark chatted convincingly about the hard work a committee staff director must have to do, while others get the praise and publicity. Henry Lykham readily agreed. They both chose their meal from the fixed menu; so did the man three tables away, who was watching them both carefully. Mark told the committee staff director that he intended to write his thesis on the Gun Control bill if it became law, and that he wanted

165

some interesting inside information that the general public wouldn't get from the newspapers. "Therefore, Mr Lykham," he concluded, "I have been advised to speak to you."

The fat man beamed; he was duly flattered, as Mark had hoped, and he began.

"There is nothing I can't tell you about this bill or the bunch of politicians involved in it."

Mark smiled, he had studied the Watergate hearings in an elective seminar at Yale and he recalled a particular remark of Anthony Ulasewicz, a retired NYPD detective. "Why bother to bug the place? Politicians and officials will tell you anything you want to know, over the phone, they'll even want to send it to you in the mail, whoever you are."

Senator Sam Irvin of North Carolina, the committee chairman, had reprimanded him for treating the committee lightly and turning the matter into a joke. "It's no joke – it's the truth," was Ulasewicz's reply.

Mark asked which of the eleven senators on the committee were for the bill. Only four of them had been present at the morning discussion. From his research, Mark was fairly certain about the opinions of most of them but he wanted his assessments confirmed.

"Among the Democrats, Brooks, Burdick, Stevenson, and Glenn will vote for the measure. Abourezk, Byrd, and Moynihan are keeping their own counsel, but will probably come through in support of the Administration position. They voted for the bill in committee. Thornton is the only Democrat who may vote against it. You heard him start to speak in favour of Dexter's states' rights position. Well, for Thornton, young man, it's not a matter of principle. He wants it both ways. Texas has a strong state gun control measure, so he can claim that his stance means that states can take whatever action they deem necessary to protect their citizens. But Texas also has a number of firearms companies – Smith and Wesson,

GKN Powdermet, Harrington and Richardson – which would be seriously affected by a federal gun control act. The spectre of unemployment again. As long as those companies can sell their wares outside Texas, they're okay. So Thornton fools his constituents into thinking they can control guns and manufacture them at the same time. Strange games are being played by that particular man. As for the Republicans, Mathias of Maryland will vote for the bill. He's a very liberal guy – I'll never understand why he stays in the GOP. McCollister of Nebraska is against, along with Woodson of Arkansas. Harrison and Dexter you heard. No question where they stand.

"Harrison despite being a Democrat knows damn well that his constituents wouldn't tolerate gun control and will vote him out if he goes with it. Hard to tell if he's been brainwashed by the National Rifle Association, because he seems to be sincere when he talks about the idea of self-defence. He's a strange guy. Everyone in this place regards him as a dyed-in-the-wool conservative, but no one really knows him. He hasn't been here all that long. He succeeded Sparkman when he retired – bit of an unknown quantity."

Mark let him talk on. Lykham was enjoying the role of the expert, the man who knew everything. Normally, he sat for hours in the hearing room, unable to say a word, listening and making notes and occasionally whispering a suggestion in the ear of the chairman. Only his wife listened to his opinions and she never understood their significance. Lykham was delighted to have found an academic who had come to him for the facts.

"Dexter talks a good game – smooth character, that one. He beat the guy who was appointed to fill Ribicoff's term when Abe was picked by the President for a roving ambassadorship. Surprise winner. Wouldn't have thought that Connecticut would be represented by two Republicans. Guess all those rich New Yorkers moving to Stamford are making a difference. Anyway, just between the two of us, Mark, I have my suspicions about the purity of his principles. Do you know how many gun companies there are in Connecticut? Remington, Colt, Olin, Winchester, Marlin, Sturm-Ruger. Now, that never stopped Senator Ribicoff from voting for gun control, but Dexter . . . well, he owns a big slice of one of them, that's no secret. Something's biting him at the moment, he's as grouchy as hell, and he hasn't missed a session yet."

Mark had a sick feeling in his stomach. My God, Elizabeth's father? He just didn't want to believe it.

"So you think the bill will be passed?" said Mark in a conversational tone.

"No question, while the Democrats remain in control of both Houses. The minority report was vicious, but it'll get a majority on 10 March. There wasn't much doubt about that after the House put it through. By Thursday, nothing can stop it. The Majority Leader is only too aware of the importance the President attaches to this bill."

Byrd, thought Mark. He's on the list. "Could you tell me a little about the Majority Leader? He was on the Judiciary Committee, right? Where does he stand?"

"That's an interesting question, Andrews. Senator Byrd is a humourless, driven, ambitious individual. He has ulcers. He was born in poverty, always makes a point of emphasising his origins, so much so that some of his colleagues call him Uriah Heep. In the 1940s, when he was only nineteen, he belonged to the Ku Klux Klan; yet he managed to overcome that handicap and rise to the most powerful post in the Senate in a party dominated by liberals. He got where he is because he's a team player. He does favours for other senators, and always has. He's diligent, conscientious about meeting their needs. His attention to detail has paid off in spades. He had always supported the Democratic – with a capital D – position. And he's a very effective Majority Leader.

"No love lost in that relationship, but since Byrd has become Majority Leader he has fallen into line. With his background, it's unlikely that he's genuinely in favour of gun control, but he hasn't spoken out against the bill, naturally, because he has been shepherding it through the Senate for the President. He's done it very efficiently. He's scheduled it early, avoided recesses –"

"Sorry to interrupt you, Mr Lykham, but what do you mean he's avoided recesses? The committee didn't sit round the clock, surely?"

"No, young man, I was referring to a technical, procedural distinction between adjournment and recess. You see, the Senate usually recesses from one day to the next. The day after a recess, the unfinished business of the previous day is in order; the morning business can be dispensed with. Whenever the Majority Leader opts for a recess rather than adjournment, he thereby lengthens the 'legislative day'. And since bills reported from committee must lay over one legislative day before a motion to consider is in order, the recess can be used to delay action on a particular measure. The so-called legislative day can extend for days, weeks, conceivably even months now she only has two years left. This bill has been put through in the minimum possible time. If the President doesn't get support on 10 March, she will not have time to put it up again before she goes for re-election. It will be a victory for those against the bill. And she may not be re-elected if the polls are to be believed. Americans get sick of their presidents very quickly nowadays. So it's 10 March or forget it."

"What could stop it on 10 March?"

"Nothing I can think of offhand, except the death of the President, which could recess the Senate for seven days. Still the President looks pretty fit to me, perhaps a little tired, not that I'm one to comment."

Mark was about to question Lykham about Brooks, when the staff director glanced at his watch.

"Look at the time," Lykham expostulated, "I must get

back. I have to be the first, you know, get everything in order, so those senators think that we haven't been away at all."

Mark thanked him. Lykham picked up the check and signed it.

"Any time you want more help or information, don't hesitate to get in touch."

"I certainly will," said Mark.

The fat staff director waddled away at what for him was full speed. Mark pondered over his coffee. The man three tables away had finished his and was waiting for Mark's next move. Those damn bells were ringing again. Only one this time, indicating that the yeas and nays were being tallied on the Senate floor. As soon as the vote was over, the senators would be flocking back to committee meetings. The bell brought Mark sharply out of his thoughts.

Once again he returned to the Dirksen Building and the Foreign Relations Committee Suite, where he asked if he could see Mr Kenneck.

"Who shall I say is asking for him?" the receptionist inquired.

"Andrews, I'm a Yale student."

She picked a phone up and pressed two digits, informed the listener of what Mark had told her.

"He's in Room 4491."

Mark thanked her and left for Room 4491, which was only a few doors down the corridor.

"Well, Andrews, what can I do for you?" he asked, even before Mark had closed the door.

Mark was taken aback by the suddenness of his question; he recovered.

"I'm doing some research for a thesis, Mr Kenneck, on the work of senators, and Mr Lykham said you were the man to speak to. I wondered if Senators Nunn and Pearson were in the Senate on Thursday, 3 March, at 10:30, for the Foreign Relations Committee?"

Kenneck bent over a red leather-bound book. "Nunn – no," he paused. "Pearson – no. Anything else, Mr Andrews?" He obviously hadn't any time to waste.

"No, thank you," said Mark and left.

Mark headed for the Library. Suddenly he was down to five senators, if the Bureau were right about what they had overheard on the illegal radio transmission when their man must have been in the Senate on the morning of 3 March. He checked his notes: each one of the remaining suspects – Brooks, Byrd, Dexter, Harrison, and Thornton – had sat on the Judiciary Committee on the Gun Control bill and was in the Senate for the debate. Five men and a motive?

He was followed out of the room and into the elevator that took him to the ground floor. He used the pay phone across the hall from the elevator, near the Constitution Avenue entrance, to call the Director.

He dialled the Director's private number.

"Julius."

"What's your number?"

Mark gave it. A few seconds later the Director called him back.

"Nunn and Pearson are off. I'm down to five and the one thing they have in common is that all of them were on the committee of the Gun Control bill."

"Good," said the Director. "Much as I had expected. Getting better, Mark, but your time is running out, we've only about forty-eight hours left."

"Yes, sir."

The phone clicked.

He waited for a moment and then dialled Woodrow Wilson. There was the usual interminable wait while they found Elizabeth. What could he say about last night? What if the Director were right and her father –"

"Dr Dexter."

"When do you finish work tonight, Liz?"

"Five o'clock, lover," she said mockingly.

"May I pick you up?"

"If you like, now that I know your intentions are pure and honourable."

"Listen, one day, but not today, I'll be able to explain about that."

"See you at five, Mark."

"See you at five, Liz."

Mark put Elizabeth out of his mind by a conscious effort of will, and walked across the street to the Capitol grounds. He sat down under a tree on the grassy area between the Supreme Court and the Capitol. Protected, he thought, by law and legislature, bounded by Constitution and Independence. Who would dare to confront him here in front of the Capitol, the favoured haunt of Senate staff, law clerks, and the Capitol police? A blue and white sight-seeing tourmobile passed by on 1st Street, blocking his view of the fountains in front of the Supreme Court. Tourists gaped at Washington's white-marbled splendour. "And on your right, ladies and gentlemen, the United States Capitol. The cornerstone of the original building was laid in 1793. The British burned the Capitol building on 24 August, 1814 . . ."

And some crazy senator is going to defile it on 10 March, added Mark silently as the tourmobile moved on. Foreboding oppressed him; it really is going to happen, we can't stop it. Comes Caesar to the Capitol . . . Blood on the steps.

He forced himself to look at his notes. Brooks, Byrd, Dexter, Harrison, Thornton. He had two days to transform five into one. The conspirator he sought was Cassius, not Brutus. Brooks, Byrd, Dexter, Harrison, and Thornton. Where were they at lunchtime on 24 February? If he knew the answer, he would know which four men were innocent and which man was so desperate that he would plot to assassinate the President. Even if we find out which man is behind this, he thought, as he stood up and brushed the grass from his trousers, how do we stop the murder? Obviously, the Senator isn't going to commit the killing himself. We must keep the President away from the Capitol. The Director must have a plan, he surely wouldn't let it go that far. Mark closed his file and walked to the Metro.

Once home, he picked up his car and drove slowly to Woodrow Wilson. He looked in the rear-view mirror. A different car was following him today, a black Buick. Someone looking after me again, he thought. He arrived at the hospital at 4:45 but Elizabeth wasn't free yet, so he went back to his car and turned on the evening news. An earthquake in the Philippines that had killed 112 people was the lead story. President Kane was still confident of support for the Gun Control bill. The Dow-Jones index had moved up three points to 1,411. The Yankees beat the Dodgers in a spring training game, what's new?

Elizabeth came out of the hospital looking depressed and jumped in beside him.

"What can I say about last night?" Mark asked.

"Nothing," said Elizabeth. "It was like reading a book with the last chapter torn out. Who tore it out, Mark?"

"Perhaps I've brought the last chapter with me," said Mark, avoiding the question.

"Thanks, but I don't think I'll be in the mood for another bedtime story for a while," she replied. "The last one gave me a bad dream."

Elizabeth was very quiet and Mark could get little response from her. He turned right off Independence and stopped the car on one of the side streets on the Mall, facing the Jefferson Memorial and the sunset.

"Is it last night?" asked Mark.

"Partly," she said. "You made me feel pretty silly walking off like that. I don't suppose you're going to tell me what it was all about?"

"I can't do that," said Mark uneasily. "But believe me, it had nothing to do with you. At least that's almost –" He stopped abruptly.

Never embarrass the Bureau.

"'At least that's almost' what? Almost true? Why was that call so important?"

"Let's stop this and go eat."

Elizabeth didn't reply.

He started the car again. Two cars pulled out at the same time as he did. A blue Ford sedan and a black Buick. They're certainly making sure today, he thought. Perhaps one of them is just looking for a parking space. He glanced at Elizabeth to see if she'd noticed them too; no, why should she, only he could see in the rear-view mirror. He drove to a small, warm Japanese restaurant on Wisconsin Avenue. He couldn't take her home, while the damned Bureau had the place bugged. Deftly, the Oriental waiter sliced the fat shrimps, cooked them on the metal slab in the centre of their table. He flicked each shrimp as he finished it on to their plates, giving them small, delicious bowls of sauces in which to dip the pieces. Elizabeth brightened under the influence of the hot sake.

"I'm sorry to react so strongly. I have a lot on my mind at the moment."

"Like to tell me about it?"

"I can't, I'm afraid. It's personal and my father has asked me not to discuss it with anyone yet."

Mark froze. "Can't you tell me?"

"No. I guess we'll both have to be patient."

They went to a drive-in movie and sat in the comfortable semi-darkness, arms companionably intertwined. Mark sensed she didn't wish to be touched, and indeed he was in no mood to do so. They were both concerned about the same man, but for different reasons – or was it the same reason? And how would she react if she discovered that he had been investigating her father since the day after they met? Maybe she knew. Damn it, why couldn't he simply believe in her? Surely, she wasn't setting him up. He could remember very little about the film, and when it ended he took her home and left immediately. Two cars were still following him.

A figure jumped out of the shadows. "Hi, stud!" Mark swung around and checked his holster nervously.

"Oh, hi, Simon."

"Listen, man, I can show you some dirty postcards if you're still desperate, 'cause it seems that you're just not good enough, man. I had a black one last night, I'm having a white one tonight."

"How can you be so sure?" asked Mark.

"I check in advance, man, I ain't got time to waste with my pretty body." Simon burst out laughing. "Think about me when you go to bed tonight, all alone, Mark, 'cause I sure will have forgotten you. Cool your jets, man."

Mark threw him the keys and watched him as he walked towards the Mercedes swinging his hips, dancing and laughing.

"You ain't got it, baby, whatever it is."

"Bullshit! You're a jive-ass bastard," Mark said, and laughed.

"Now, you're just jealous, man, or prejudiced," said Simon, as he revved up the car and moved to a parking space. As he passed Mark, he shouted, "Either way, I'm the winner."

Mark wondered if he ought to apply for a job as a garage attendant at the apartment building. It seemed to have its compensations. He looked around; something moved; no, it was just his nerves or his imagination. Once in his room, he wrote his report for the morning session with the Director and fell into bed.

Two days to go.

Wednesday morning, 9 March

1:00 am

The phone rang. Mark was just falling asleep, still in that world between sleeping and waking. The phone insisted. Try to answer it, it could be Julius.

"Hello," he said, yawning.

"Mark Andrews?"

"Yes," he said wearily, shifting himself to a more comfortable position in the bed, fearing if he woke up fully he would never get back to sleep.

"It's George Stampouzis. Sorry to wake you, but I've come up with something I thought you would want to know about immediately."

Stampouzis's statement acted like cold water. Mark was wide awake instantly.

"Right, don't say anything else, I'll call you from a pay phone. What's your number?" Mark wrote it down on the back of a Kleenex box, the only thing he could reach. He threw on a bathrobe, forced his feet into a pair of tennis shoes, and started for the door. He opened the door, looked both ways. Hell, he was getting paranoid. There was no sound in the hall; there wouldn't be even if someone were waiting for him. He took the elevator down to the garage level, where there was a pay phone. Simon was asleep on the chair – how did he manage it? Mark had found it hard enough to sleep in bed.

He dialled the 212 area code.

"Hello, Stampouzis. Mark Andrews."

"Do you G-men always play games at one in the morning? I would have thought you'd figured out a better system by now."

Mark laughed; the sound echoed in the garage; Simon twitched.

"What can I do for you?"

"I traded some information today, now you owe me two stories." Stampouzis paused. "The Mafia had nothing to do with Stames's death, and they are not going overboard for the Gun Control bill, although they basically oppose it. So you can eliminate them. I wouldn't have gone this far for anyone but Nick, so make sure you handle it right."

"I'm doing my best," Mark replied. "Thanks for your help."

He put the phone on the hook and walked back to the elevator, thinking about the tousled bed which he hoped was still warm. Simon was still asleep.

Wednesday morning, 9 March

5:50 am

"It's for you, sir."

"What?" mumbled the Director, still half-asleep.

"The phone, sir, it's for you." His housekeeper was standing by the doorway in her dressing-gown.

"Ugh. What time is it?"

"Ten to six, sir."

"Who is it?"

"Mr Elliott, sir."

"Right, switch it through."

"Yes, sir."

Elliott had woken him up. A decision he would never have taken unless it was urgent.

"Good morning, Elliott, what is it?" He paused. "Can you be sure? That changes the whole situation. What time is he due in? 7:00, of course. I'll see you at 6:30."

The Director put the phone down, and sat on the edge of the bed, and said very loudly: " Damn," which by the Director's standards was extreme. His big feet placed firmly on the floor, his large hands splayed on his equally large thighs, he was deep in thought. Eventually he rose, put on a dressing-gown, and disappeared into the bathroom, repeating the expletive several times.

Mark also had a phone call, not from the anonymous man, but from Elizabeth. She needed to see him urgently.

They agreed to meet at eight o'clock in the lobby of the Mayflower. He felt sure no one would recognise him there, but he wondered why Elizabeth had chosen that particular meeting place.

Mark took off his dressing-gown and returned to the bathroom.

The Senator took an early-morning phone call as well, not from the anonymous man or from Elizabeth, but from the Chairman, who was confirming their midday meeting for the final briefing at the Sheraton Hotel in Silver Spring. The Senator agreed, replaced the phone, and roamed around the room in his dressing-gown thinking.

"Coffee for three, Mrs McGregor. Are they both here?" the Director asked as he passed her.

"Yes, sir."

Mrs McGregor looked very chic in a new turquoise, two-piece suit, but the Director didn't notice. He strolled into his office.

"Good morning, Matt. Good morning, Mark." When should he drop the bomb? He decided to let Andrews speak first. "Right, let's hear what you've found out."

"As I told you yesterday, sir, I think I've cut the list of senators down to five – Brooks of Massachusetts, Byrd of West Virginia, Dexter of Connecticut, Harrison of South Carolina, and Thornton of Texas. The only common factor is their interest in the Gun Control bill, which as we know, sir, is likely to become law on 10 March. Assassination of the President would now be about the only way of holding that bill up."

"I would have thought," said Rogers, "that that could be the one act that would make certain the bill passed through both Houses."

"You tell that to two Kennedys, Martin Luther King, George Wallace and Ronald Reagan and see what they all have to say," responded the Director. "Continue, Mark."

Mark summarised what Lykham and Stampouzis had briefed him on each man, and explained how he was able to eliminate two other men from the list of seven – namely Pearson and Nunn. "That completes my report, sir, unless, of course, we are approaching this thing in the wrong way and I'm heading down a blind alley. And as far as I'm concerned that is entirely possible, as I seem to be boxing with shadows."

The Director nodded and waited.

Mark continued: "I was going to spend today trying to hear each one of them in action in the Senate. I wish I could think of a good way of finding out where they were at lunchtime on 24 February, short of asking them outright, that is."

"Don't go anywhere near any of them. That would be the surest way to shut down the whole plot. Now, Mark, I must warn you my news is not good, so settle back and prepare for the worst. We are beginning to think the man we are after is Dexter,' said the Director.

Mark went cold. "Why, sir?" he managed to get out.

The Assistant Director leaned forward to speak. "I have had some men checking out the Georgetown Inn, very unobtrusively. We didn't expect to turn anything up. We questioned all the day staff but they couldn't help. Early this morning, just to be thorough, we interviewed the night staff. Turned out that one of the night porters, who was off duty during the day, of course, is pretty sure he saw Senator Dexter hurrying away from the hotel some time like 2:30 in the afternoon on 24 February."

Mark was stunned. "How did he know it was Senator Dexter?"

"The man was born and raised in Wilton, Connecticut; he knows his face well. I'm afraid there's something else, too; he was accompanied by a young woman whose rough description tallies with his daughter."

"That's not proof," said Mark. "It's all circumstantial. It wouldn't stand up in a court of law."

"I'm sure you're right," said the Director, "but it's an unfortunate coincidence for Senator Dexter. Remember his involvement in the arms business; it won't do his finances any good if the Gun Control bill goes through; in fact our inquiries show he stands to lose a personal fortune, so we have a motive as well."

"But, sir," Mark argued, carried away by the desire to believe in Elizabeth, "do you really think that a senator would plot to kill the President just to keep one of his companies afloat? There are so many less drastic ways to stall the bill. He could try to tie it up in committee. Or organise a filibuster . . ."

"He already has tried – and failed, Mark," Matthew Rogers interrupted.

"The other four senators may have more powerful motives we don't happen to know about. It doesn't have to be Dexter," continued Mark, sounding unconvinced.

"Mark, I understand what you're saying and you do have a point. Under ordinary circumstances I'd agree that it seems unlikely, but we have to go on the evidence we have, even if it's slim and at present no more than circumstantial. And there's something else. On the night of 3 March, when Casefikis and the postman were killed, Dr Dexter's name was not marked on the duty register. She should have finished work at five, but for some inexplicable reason she stayed an extra two hours, treated the Greek – who was not her patient – and then went home. Now it's possible that she was just conscientious and working overtime, or that she was filling in for a colleague, but there are a hell of a lot of coincidences here, Mark. I'm bound to say if one is dispassionate about it, the odds are stacked heavily against Senator Dexter – and his daughter."

Mark did not reply.

"Now listen and listen carefully," the Director went on. "I know you want to believe that all this is circumstantial and that it's one of the other four – but I only have twenty-six hours left before the President leaves the White

House, and I have to live with the facts as they present themselves. I want to catch the man involved, whoever he is, and I'm not willing to risk the life of the President to do it. When are you seeing the girl next?"

Mark looked up. "At eight, at the Mayflower."

"Why?"

"I have no idea, sir. She just said that it was important."

"Um, well I think you still ought to go but then report back to me immediately you're through."

"Yes, sir."

"I can't understand why, Andrews. Be careful."

"Yes, sir."

"It's twenty to eight now, you'd better be on your way. Incidentally, we're still having no luck with those fifty-dollar bills. We're down to the last eight, but still no prints from Mrs Casefikis. Better news on the German, Gerbach, however. We've established beyond a doubt that he had no connection with the CIA during his stay in Rhodesia or at the time of his death, so that's one more problem out of the way."

Mark didn't give a damn about the fifty-dollar bills, the German driver, the Mafia, or the CIA. All his hard work appeared to be leading them straight to Dexter. He left the office even more despondent than he had been when he came in.

Once back on the street, he decided to walk to the Mayflower in the hope of clearing his head. He didn't notice that two men followed him down Pennsylvania Avenue, past the White House, and on towards the hotel.

At the press of a button, Elliott entered the Director's office.

"Elliott, you were right about the Mayflower. What have you done about it?"

"There are two men already there, sir, and one following Andrews."

"It's the first time in thirty-six years that I've hated

my job,' said the Director. "You've done very well, Elliott, and all too soon I'll be able to tell you what this whole damn thing is about."

"Yes, sir."

"Follow up these five names. Leave no stone unturned."

"Yes, sir."

"Thank you."

Elliott slid out of the room.

Damn man has no heart. Can't have a right-hand man without a heart. Makes him damn useful in a strange situation like this though. When this operation's all over, I'll transfer him back to Idaho and –

"You said something, sir?"

"No, Mrs McGregor, I'm just going quietly mad. Don't worry about me. When the men in the white coats come to take me away, just sign the forms in triplicate and look relieved."

Mrs McGregor smiled.

"I like your new suit," the Director said.

She blushed. "Thank you, sir."

Mark pushed through the revolving doors of the Mayflower Hotel, his eyes searching the lobby for Elizabeth. How he wanted to see her and how he wanted to stop being devious and tell her the truth. It's all circumstantial, he continued to insist. He couldn't spot her so chose a comfortable seat which had a good view of the lobby.

On the far side of the lobby, a man was buying *The Washington Post* from the newspaper stand. Mark didn't notice that he made no attempt to read it. Suddenly he saw Elizabeth heading towards him with Senator Dexter by her side. Hell, that was all he needed.

"Hello, Mark." She kissed him gently on the cheek.

Judas showing the Pharisees which one was to be killed? The unkindest cut of all.

"Mark, I'd like you to meet my father."

"Good morning, sir."

"Good morning, Mark, it's good to meet you. Elizabeth has told me quite a bit about you."

And what should you be able to tell me, thought Mark. Where were you on 24 February? Where will you be tomorrow?

"Mark, are you all right?" Elizabeth inquired.

"Yes, fine. I'm sorry, Senator, it's good to meet you too."

The Senator was staring at him strangely.

"Well, I must be getting along, dear – I have a busy schedule. I look forward to our usual lunch tomorrow."

"See you then, Father. Thanks for the breakfast and the chat."

"Goodbye, Mark. See you again soon, I hope." Senator Dexter still looked at him quizzically.

"Perhaps," replied Mark quietly.

They watched him leave. So did three other people. One of them left to make a phone call.

"Mark, what's come over you? Why were you so brusque with my father? I especially wanted you to meet him."

"I'm sorry, I'm just tired."

"Or is there something you're not telling me?" said Elizabeth.

"I could ask you the same question."

"What are you talking about?"

"Oh, I don't know, let's forget it," said Mark. "Why did you want to see me so urgently?"

"Simply because I wanted you to meet my father. What's so strange about that? Why the hell did I bother?"

She began to walk away down the corridor, pushing her way quickly through the revolving door at the entrance to the hotel. Three men saw her leave. One followed her, two stuck with Mark. He walked slowly towards the doors. The doorman saluted him punctiliously.

"Cab, sir?"

"No, thanks. I'll walk."

*

The Director was on the phone when Mark returned and waved him into the large leather chair by his desk. He sank down in it, his mind fuzzy. The Director put the phone down and looked directly at him.

"So now you've met Senator Dexter, and I must tell you that either Dr Dexter knows nothing or she deserves an Oscar for her performance at the Mayflower."

"You saw everything," said Mark.

"Of course, and more. She was just involved in an automobile accident, two minutes ago. That phone call was the details."

Mark jumped out of his seat.

"She's all right. A couple of hundred dollars' worth of damage to the front of her little Fiat and not a mark on the bus she hit. Sensible girl. She's on her way to work now in a cab, or rather, she think it's a cab."

Mark sighed, resigned to whatever would happen next. "Where is Senator Dexter?" he asked.

"He's gone to the Capitol. Made one phone call when he got there, but it didn't turn out to be of any significance."

Mark was beginning to feel like a puppet. "What do you expect me to do now?"

There was a knock on the door and the anonymous man appeared. He handed a note to the Director, who read it quickly.

"Thank you."

The anonymous man left. Mark feared the worst. The Director placed the note on the desk and looked up.

"Senator Thornton has called a press conference at 10:30 in Senate Committee Room 2228. Better get down there immediately. Phone me as soon as he has said his piece. The questions from the press afterwards will be irrelevant; they always are."

Mark walked to the Senate, once again hoping it would clear his head. It didn't. He wanted to ring Elizabeth and ask if she were all right after the accident; he wanted to ask her a hundred questions, but he only wanted one answer. Three men also walked to the Senate, two of them taking a half of the route each, and the third walking the whole way. All three of them arrived eventually in Room 2228; none of them was interested in Senator Thornton's statement.

The room was already well lit by the large Idreg lights especially set up for the television cameras, and the members of the press were chatting among themselves. It was a packed house, even though Senator Thornton had not yet arrived. Mark wondered what he had to say, whether it would throw any light on his own questions. Point the guilty finger at Thornton perhaps, supply a motive he could return with to the Director. He thought, as he looked at the senior reporters, that they might have a shrewd idea or even a tip from one of Thornton's staff as to the contents of his statement. But he didn't want to ask them any questions for fear of being remembered. With an entrance that would have pleased Caesar himself, Senator Thornton came in, accompanied by three aides and a private secretary. He certainly was making the most of it. His dark hair was covered with grease, and he had put on what he obviously imagined to be his best suit, green with a blue pin-stripe. No one had briefed him on what to wear when facing colour television – only dark clothes, as plain as possible – or if he had been briefed, he hadn't listened.

He sat in a large throne of a chair at the far end of the room, his feet only just touching the ground. He was now surrounded by arc lights and the TV acoustics men put microphones all around him and in front of him. Suddenly, three more vast Idreg lights were switched on. Thornton was sweating already, but still smiling. The three television networks agreed that they were ready for the Senator. Thornton cleared his throat.

"Ladies and gentlemen of the press . . ."

"That's a pompous start," said a correspondent in front of Mark, writing every word down in shorthand.

Mark looked more closely, he thought he recognised the face. It was Bernstein of *The Washington Post*. Senator Thornton now had complete silence from the room.

"I have just left the White House after a private session with the President of the United States and because of that meeting, I wish to make a statement for press and television." He paused. "My criticisms of the Gun Control bill and my vote against it in committee were motivated by a desire to represent my constituents and their genuine fear of unemployment . . ."

". . . and *your* own genuine fear of unemployment," remarked Bernstein, *sotto voce*. "What bribe did the President offer you at dinner on Monday?"

The Senator cleared his throat again. "The President has assured me that if this piece of legislation is passed, and domestic production of guns is prohibited, she will sponsor legislation to give immediate financial assistance to gun manufacturers and their employees, in the hope that the facilities of the gun industry can be turned to other, less dangerous uses than the production of weapons of destruction. The President's concern has made it possible for me to vote in favour of the Gun Control bill. I have for some considerable time been in two minds . . ."

"True enough," said Bernstein.

". . . concerning this bill, because of my genuine fear of the freedom and ease with which criminals can obtain firearms."

"It didn't worry you yesterday. Just what contracts did the President promise," murmured the correspondent, "or did she say she would help you win re-election next year?"

"And the problem for me has always been in the balance . . ."

". . . and a little bribe tipped that balance."

Bernstein now had his own audience, which was enjoying his offerings far more than those of the Senator from Texas.

"Now that the President has shown such consideration, I feel able to announce with a clear conscience . . ."

". . . so clear we can see right through it," more Bernstein.

". . . that I am now able to support my party's position over gun control. I will, therefore, not be opposing the President on the floor of the Senate tomorrow."

Wild applause from scattered parts of the room, sounding – and looking – suspiciously like aides placed in strategic spots.

"I shall, ladies and gentlemen," Senator Thornton continued, "rest an easier man tonight . . ."

"And a re-elected one," added Bernstein.

"I should like to end by thanking the members of the press for attending . . ."

"We had to; it was the only show in town."

Laughter broke out around the *Post* correspondent, but it didn't reach Thornton.

"And I would like to say that I will be delighted to answer any questions. Thank you."

"Bet you don't answer any of mine."

Most of the other reporters left the room immediately, in order to catch the early editions of the afternoon papers, already going to press right across the country. Mark joined them but glanced over the famous journalist's shoulder. He had been scribbling in longhand.

"Friends, Romans, country bumpkins, lend me your jeers; I come to bury Kane, not to praise her." Not exactly front-page material.

Three other men who had attended the press conference followed Mark out of the room, as he ran to the nearest pay telephones, halfway down the hall. Mark found them all occupied by newspapermen anxious to get their copy in first, and there was a long line behind those already dictating. Another line had formed by the two phones at the other end of the hall. Mark took the elevator to the ground floor; same problem; his only chance would be the pay phone in the Russell Building across the street.

He ran all the way; so did three other men. When he reached there, a middle-aged woman stepped into the booth a pace ahead of him, and put her quarter in.

"Hello . . . it's me. I got the job . . . Yeah, pretty good . . . Mornings only. Start tomorrow . . . But I can't complain, money's not bad."

Mark paced up and down while the three men caught their breath. At last, the woman finished talking and, with a big smile all over her face, she walked away, oblivious of Mark or the nation's problems. At least someone is confident about tomorrow, thought Mark. He glanced around to be sure that there was no one near him, though he could have sworn he recognised a man standing by the Medicare poster; perhaps it was one of his colleagues from the FBI. He had seen that face behind the dark glasses somewhere. He was getting better protection than the President. He dialled the Director's private line and gave him his pay phone number. The phone rang back almost immediately.

"Thornton's off the list, sir, because he has –"

"I know, I know," said the Director. "I've just been briefed on what Thornton said. It's exactly what I would have expected him to say if he were involved. It certainly does not get him off my list; if anything, I'm a little more suspicious. Keep working on all five this afternoon and contact me the moment you come up with anything; don't bother to come in."

The phone clicked. Mark felt despondent. He depressed the cradle and waited for the dial tone, put in a quarter and dialled Woodrow Wilson. The nurse on duty went on a search for Elizabeth, but returned and said that no one had seen her all day. Mark hung up, forgetting to say thank you or goodbye. He took the elevator down to the basement cafeteria to have lunch. His decision gained the restaurant two more customers; the third man already had a lunch date, for which he was running late.

Wednesday afternoon, 9 March

1:00 pm

Only Tony and Xan were on time for the meeting at the Sheraton Hotel in Silver Spring. They had spent many hours together but seldom spoke; Tony wondered what the Nip thought about all the time. Tony had had a busy schedule checking the routes for the final day, getting the Buick perfectly tuned – and chauffeuring the Chairman and Matson; they all treated him like a damn cab driver. His skill was equal to theirs anytime, and where the hell would they be without him? Without him those FBI men would still be around their necks. Still, the whole damn thing would be over by tomorrow night and he could then get away and spend some of his hard-earned money. He couldn't make up his mind whether it would be Miami or Las Vegas. Tony always planned how to spend his money before he got it. The Chairman came in, a cigarette hanging from his mouth as always. He looked at them, and asked brusquely where Matson was. Both shook their heads. Matson always worked alone. He trusted no one. The Chairman was irritated and made no attempt to hide it. The Senator arrived, just a few moments later, looking equally annoyed, but he didn't even notice that Matson wasn't there.

"Why don't we start?" demanded the Senator. "I find this meeting inconvenient as it is, since it's the final day of debate on the bill."

The Chairman looked at him with contempt. "We're missing Matson and his report is vital."

"How long will you wait?"

"Two minutes."

They waited in silence. They had nothing to say to each other; each man knew why he was there. Exactly two minutes later, the Chairman lit another cigarette and asked Tony for his report.

"I've checked the routes, boss, and it takes a car going at twenty-two miles per hour three minutes to get from the south exit of the White House on to E Street and down Pennsylvania Avenue to the FBI Building and another three minutes to reach the Capitol. It takes forty-five seconds to climb the steps and be out of range. On average six minutes forty-five seconds in all. Never under five minutes thirty seconds, never over seven minutes. That's trying it at midnight, one o'clock, and two o'clock in the morning, remembering the routes are going to be even clearer for Kane."

"What about after the operation is over?" asked the Chairman.

"It's possible to get from the crane through basement passageways to the Rayburn Building and from there to the Capitol South Metro Station in two minutes at best and three minutes fifteen seconds at worst – depends on elevators and congestion. Once the VC –" He stopped himself. "Once Xan is in the Metro, they'll never find him; in a few minutes, he can be on the other side of Washington."

"How can you be sure they won't pick him up in under three minutes fifteen seconds?" asked the Senator, whose personal interest in Xan was non-existent, but he didn't trust the little man not to sing if he were caught.

"Assuming they know nothing, they also won't know which way to turn for at least the first five minutes," answered the Chairman.

Tony continued: "If it goes as planned, you won't even need the car so I'll just dump it and disappear."

"Agreed," said the Chairman. "But nevertheless I trust the car is in perfect condition?"

"Sure is, it's ready for Daytona."

The Senator mopped his brow, which was surprising, since it was a cold March day.

"Xan, your report," said the Chairman.

Xan went over his plan in detail; he had rehearsed it again and again during the last two days. He had slept at the head of the crane for the last two nights and the gun was already in place. The men would be going on a twenty-four-hour strike starting at six that evening. "By six tomorrow evening, I will be on other side of America and Kane will be dead."

"Good," said the Chairman, stubbing out his cigarette and lighting another one. "I shall be on the corner of 9th and Pennsylvania and will contact you on my watchband radio when I arrive at 9:30 and again when Kane's car passes me. When your watch starts vibrating, she will be three minutes away, giving you three minutes and forty-five seconds in all. How much warning do you need?"

"Two minutes and thirty seconds will be enough," said Xan.

"That's cutting it a bit close, isn't it?" inquired the Senator, still sweating.

"If that turns out to be the case you will have to delay her on the steps of the Capitol because we don't want to expose Xan more than necessary," said the Chairman. "The longer he is in view, the greater the chance the Secret Service helicopters will have of spotting him."

The Senator turned his head towards Xan. "You say you've been rehearsing every day?"

"Yes," replied Xan. He never saw any reason to use more words than necessary, even when addressing a United States Senator.

"Then why don't people notice you carrying a rifle or at least a gun box?"

"Because g n has been taped to platform on top of

crane three hundred and twenty feet out of harm's way ever since I returned from Vienna."

"What happens if the crane comes down? They'll spot it right away."

"No, I am in yellow overalls and rifle is in eight parts and has been painted yellow and is taped to underpart of platform. Even with strong field glasses, it looks like part of crane. When I picked up latest sniper rifle from Dr Schmidt of Helmut, Helmut, and Schmidt, even he was surprised by can of yellow paint."

They all laughed except the Senator.

"How long does it take you to assemble it?" continued the Senator, probing for a flaw, something he always did when questioning so-called experts in Senate committees.

"Two minutes to put rifle together and thirty seconds to get into perfect firing position; two more minutes to dismantle gun and retape it. It's a 5.6 by 61 millimetre Vomhofe Super Express rifle, and I'm using a .77 grain bullet with a muzzle speed of 3,480 feet per second, which is 2,000 foot-pounds of muzzle energy which, in layman's language, Senator, means if there is no wind, I will aim one and one half inches above Kane's forehead at two hundred yards."

"Are you satisfied?" the Chairman asked the Senator.

"Yes, I suppose so," he said, and sank into a brooding silence, still wiping his brow. Then he thought of something else and was about to start his questioning again, when the door flew open and Matson rushed in.

"Sorry, boss. I've been following something up."

"It'd better be good," snapped the Chairman.

"It could be bad, boss, very bad," said Matson between breaths.

They all looked anxiously at him.

"Okay, let's have it."

"His name is Mark Andrews," said Matson, as he fell into the unoccupied seat.

"And who is he?" asked the Chairman.

"The FBI man who went to the hospital with Calvert."

"Could we start at the beginning?" the Chairman asked calmly.

Matson took a deep breath. "You know I've always been bothered about Stames going to the hospital with Calvert – it never made sense, a man of his seniority."

"Yes, yes," said the Chairman impatiently.

"Well, Stames didn't go. His wife told me. I went by to visit her to offer my condolences, and she told me everything Stames had done that evening, right down to eating half his moussaka. The FBI told her not to say anything to anyone but she thinks that I'm still with the Bureau, and she doesn't remember, or maybe she never knew, that Stames and I were not exactly friends. I've checked up on Andrews and I've been following him for the last forty-eight hours. He's listed in the Washington Field Office as on leave for two weeks, but he's been spending his leave in a very strange way. I've seen him at FBI Headquarters, going around with a female doctor from Woodrow Wilson, and nosing around at the Capitol."

The Senator flinched.

"The good doctor was on duty the night that I got rid of the Greek and the black bastard."

"So if they know everything," said the Chairman quickly, "why are we still here?"

"Well, that's the strange part. I arranged to have a drink with an old buddy from the Secret Service; he's on duty detail tomorrow with Kane and nothing has been changed. It is painfully obvious that the Secret Service has no idea what we have planned for tomorrow, so either the FBI know one hell of a lot or nothing, but if they do know everything, they're not letting the Secret Service in on it."

"Did you learn anything from your contacts in the FBI?" asked the Chairman.

"Nothing. Nobody knows anything, even when they're blind drunk."

"How much do you think Andrews knows?" continued the Chairman.

"I think he's fallen for our friend the doctor and knows very little. He's running around in the dark," Matson replied. "It's possible he's picked up something from the Greek waiter. If so, he's working on his own, and that's not FBI policy."

"I don't follow," said the Chairman.

"Bureau policy is to work in pairs or threes, so why aren't there dozens of men on it? Even if there were only six or seven, I would have heard about it and so would at least one of my contacts in the FBI," said Matson. "I think they may believe there is going to be an attempt on the President, but I don't think they have a clue when – or where."

"Did anyone mention the date in front of the Greek?" asked the Senator nervously.

"I can't remember, but there's only one way of finding out if they know anything," said the Chairman.

"What's that, boss?" asked Matson.

The Chairman paused, lit another cigarette, and said dispassionately, "Kill Andrews."

There was silence for a few moments. Matson was the first to recover.

"Why, boss?"

"Simple logic. If he is connected with an FBI investigation, then they would immediately change tomorrow's schedule. They would never risk allowing Kane to leave the White House if they believed such a threat existed. Just think of the consequences involved; if the FBI knew of an assassination attempt on the President and they haven't made an arrest to date and they didn't bother to inform the Secret Service . . ."

"That's right," said Matson. "They would have to come up with some excuse and cancel at the last minute."

"Exactly, so if Kane comes out of those gates, we will still go ahead because they know nothing. If she doesn't, we're going to take a long holiday, because they know far too much for our health."

The Chairman turned to the Senator, who was now sweating profusely.

"Now, you just make sure that you're on the steps of the Capitol to stall her if necessary and we'll take care of the rest," he said harshly. "If we don't get her tomorrow, we have wasted one hell of a lot of time and money, and we sure aren't going to get another chance as good as this."

The Senator groaned. "I think you're insane, but I won't waste time arguing. I have to get back to the Senate before somebody notices that I'm missing."

"Settle down, Senator. We have it all under control; now we can't lose either way."

"Maybe you can't, but at the end of the day I might end up the fall guy."

The Senator left without another word. The Chairman waited in silence for the door to close.

"Now we've got that little funk out of the way, let's get down to business. Let's hear all about Mark Andrews and what he's been up to."

Matson gave a detailed description of Mark's movements during the past forty-eight hours. The Chairman took in every detail without writing down a word.

"Right, the time has come to blow away Mr Andrews, and then we'll sit back and monitor the FBI's reaction. Now listen carefully, Matson. This is the way it will be done: you will return to the Senate immediately and . . ."

Matson listened intently, taking notes and nodding from time to time.

"Any questions?" the Chairman asked when he had finished.

"None, boss."

"If they let the bitch out of the White House after that, they know nothing. One more thing before we finish. If anything does go wrong tomrrow, we all take care of ourselves. Understood? No one talks; compensation will be made at a later date, in the usual way."

They all nodded.

"And one final point: if there should be a foul-up, there's one man who certainly won't take care of us, so we must be prepared to take care of him. I propose we do it in the following way. Xan, when Kane . . ."

They all listened in silence; no one disagreed.

"Now I think it's time for lunch. No need to let that bitch in the White House spoil our eating habits. Sorry you'll be missing it, Matson; just make sure it's Andrews' last lunch."

Matson smiled. "It will give me a good appetite," he said, and left.

The Chairman picked up the phone. "We're ready for lunch now, thank you." He lit another cigarette.

Wednesday afternoon, 9 March

2:15 pm

Mark finished his lunch. Two other men finished their sandwiches and also rose to leave. Mark quickly returned to the Senate, as he wanted to catch Henry Lykham before the floor debate started. He hoped that Lykham would have something new to reveal after having had a night to sleep on it. He also needed copies of the Judiciary Committee Gun Control Hearings so that he could study the questions asked by Brooks, Byrd, Dexter, Harrison, and Thornton. Perhaps they would reveal another missing piece of the jigsaw. But somehow Mark doubted it. He was becoming convinced that politicians rarely revealed anything. He arrived a few minutes before the session was scheduled to begin, and asked a page if he could locate Lykham in the ante-chamber.

Lykham bustled out a few moments later. It was obvious he didn't want a chat ten minutes before a full session. So he had no real chance to tell him anything new even if he had thought of something. All Mark did manage to find out was where to obtain transcripts of the committee hearings and discussions.

"You can get them from the committee office at the end of the corridor."

Mark thanked him and walked upstairs to the gallery, where his new friend, the guard, had saved him a seat. The place was already packed. Senators were entering the chamber and taking their places, so he decided to pick up the transcripts later.

The Vice President, Bill Bradley, called for order and the tall figure of Senator Dexter looked around the room slowly and dramatically, sweeping the chamber with his eyes to be assured of everyone's attention. When his eyes alighted on Mark he looked a little surprised, but he quickly recovered and began his final arguments against the bill.

Mark was embarrassed and wished he had taken a seat nearer the back, beyond the range of Dexter's piercing glance. The debate dragged on. Brooks, Byrd, Dexter, Harrison, Thornton. They all wanted a final word before tomorrow's vote. Before tomorrow's death.

Mark listened to them all but he learned nothing new. He seemed to have come to a dead end. All that was left for him to do that day was to go and pick up transcripts of the hearings. He would have to read them through the night and he doubted, having listened to the five speak twice already, that they would reveal anything. But what other lead did he have left? Everything else was being covered by the Director. He walked down the hall to the elevator, left the Capitol by the ground-floor exit, and made his way across the Capitol grounds to the Dirksen Building.

"I would like the transcripts of the Gun Control Hearings, please."

"All of them?" asked the disbelieving secretary.

"Yes," replied Mark.

. "But there were six all-day sessions."

Oh, hell, he thought, it will be worse than all night; still, it would be only the questions and statements of Brooks, Byrd, Dexter, Harrison and Thornton.

"Sign or pay?"

"I wish I could sign," he said jokingly.

"Well, are you an official of any kind?"

Yes, thought Mark. But I can't admit it.

"No," said Mark, and took out his wallet.

"If you asked for these through one of the senators

from your state, you could probably get them for nothing. Otherwise that'll be ten dollars, sir."

"I'm in a hurry," said Mark. "Guess I'll have to pay."

He handed over the money. Senator Stevenson appeared in the doorway connecting the hearing room to the committee office.

"Good afternoon, Senator," said the secretary, turning away from Mark.

"Hi, Debbie. Would you happen to have a copy of the Clean Air bill as it was reported out of the sub-committee, before the committee markup?"

"Certainly, Senator, just a moment." She disappeared into a back room. "It's the only copy we have at the moment. Can I trust you with it, Senator?" She laughed. "Or should I make you sign for it?"

Even senators sign, thought Mark. Senators sign for everything. Henry Lykham signs for everything, even lunch. No wonder my taxes are so high. But I imagine they have to pay for the food later. The food. My God, why didn't I think of it before. Mark started running.

"Sir, sir, you've left your hearings," a voice shouted. But it was too late.

"Some kind of nut," said the secretary to Senator Stevenson.

"Anyone who wants to read all those hearings must be crazy to begin with," said Senator Stevenson, staring at the pile of paper Mark had left behind him.

Mark went straight to Room G-211, where he had lunched with Lykham the previous day. The door was marked "Officials' Dining-Room". There were only two or three attendants in evidence.

"Excuse me, I wonder if you could tell me, is this where the senators eat?"

"I'm sorry, I don't know. You'd have to talk to the hostess. We're just cleaning up."

"Where might I find the hostess?"

"She's not here. Gone for the day. If you come back tomorrow, maybe she can help you."

"Okay." Mark sighed. "Thanks. But can you tell me – is there another Senate dining-room?"

"Yeah, the big one in the Capitol. S-109, but you won't be able to get in there."

Mark ran back to the elevator and waited impatiently. When he reached the basement level, he jumped out and walked past the entrance to the labyrinthine tunnels which connect all the office buildings on Capitol Hill. Past the door marked "Tobacco Shop", he raced towards the large sign – "Subway Cars to Capitol". The subway car, actually just an open train with compartments, was about to leave. Mark stepped into the last compartment and sat down opposite a couple of Senate staffers who were jabbering away about some bill or other, with an air of "we belong".

A few moments later, a bell signalled their arrival and the train came to a stop at the Senate side of the Capitol. Easy life, thought Mark. These guys need never even wander out into the cold, cruel world. They just shuttle back and forth between votes and hearings. The basement on this side was a replica of the basement on the other side, a dull yellow, with exposed plumbing, and the inevitable Pepsi machine; it must have made Coca-Cola mad that Pepsi had the concession for the Senate. Mark bounded up the small escalator and waited for the public elevator, while a couple of men with a certain air of importance were ushered into the elevator marked "Senators Only".

Mark got off on the ground floor, and looked around, perplexed. Nothing but marble arches and corridors. Where was the Senate Dining-Room? he asked one of the Capitol policemen.

"Just walk straight ahead, take the first corridor on the left. It's the narrow one, the first entrance you get to." He pointed.

Mark tossed a thank-you over his shoulder and found the narrow corridor. He passed the kitchens and a sign which announced "Private – Press Only". Straight ahead, in large letters on a wooden sign, he saw another "Senators Only". An open door on the right led into the anteroom, decorated with a chandelier, a rose-coloured, patterned carpet, and green leather furniture, all dominated by the colourful, crowded painting on the ceiling. Through another door, Mark could see white tablecloths, flowers, the world of gracious dining. A matronly woman appeared in the doorway.

"What can I do for you?" she asked, raising her eyebrows inquisitively.

"I'm doing a thesis on the working life of a senator for my Ph.D." Mark took out his wallet and showed his Yale I.D. card, covering the expiration date with his thumb.

The lady was not visibly impressed.

"I really only want to look at the room. Just to get the atmosphere of the place."

"Well, there are no senators in here at the moment, sir. There almost never are this late on a Wednesday. They start going back to their home states on Thursdays for a long weekend. The only thing that is keeping them here this week is that Gun Control bill."

Mark had managed to edge himself into the centre of the room. A waitress was clearing a table. She smiled at him.

"Do senators sign for their meals? Or do they pay cash?"

"Almost all of them sign, and then they pay at the end of the month."

"How do you keep track?"

"No problem. We keep a daily record." She pointed to a large book marked *Accounts*. Mark knew that twenty-three senators had lunched that day because their secretaries had told him so. Had any other senator done so without bothering to inform his secretary? He was a yard away from finding out.

"Could I just see a typical day? Just out of interest," he asked with an innocent smile.

"I'm not sure I'm allowed to let you look."

"Only a glance. When I write my thesis, I want people

to think that I really know what I'm talking about, that I've seen for myself. Everyone's been so kind to me."

He looked at the woman pleadingly.

"Okay," she said grudgingly, "but please be quick."

"Thank you. Why don't you pick any old day, let's say 24 February."

She opened the book and thumbed through to 24 February. "A Thursday," she said. Stevenson, Nunn, Moynihan, Heinz, names rang one after the other. Dole, Hatfield, Byrd. So Byrd lunched at the Senate that day. He read on. Templeman, Brooks – Brooks as well. More names. Barnes, Reynolds, Thornton. So his statement this morning was for real. The hostess closed the book. No Harrison, no Dexter.

"Nothing very special about that, is there?" she said.

"No," said Mark. He thanked the woman and left quickly.

In the street he hailed a taxi. So did one of the three men following him; the other two went off to pick up their car.

Mark arrived at the Bureau a few moments later, paid the driver, showed his credentials at the entrance, and took the elevator to the seventh floor. Mrs McGregor smiled. The Director must be alone, thought Mark. He knocked and went in.

"Well, Mark?"

"Brooks, Byrd, and Thornton are not involved, sir."

"The first two don't surprise me," said the Director. "It never made any sense that they were, but I'd have put a side bet on Thornton. Anyway, how did you dispose of those three?"

Mark described his brainstorm about the Senate dining-room, and wondered what else he had overlooked.

"You should have worked all of that out three days ago, shouldn't you, Mark?"

"Yes, sir."

"So should I," said the Director. "So we're down to Dexter and Harrison. It will interest you to know that both men, along with almost all of the senators, intend to be in Washington tomorrow and both are down to attend the ceremony at the Capitol. Amazing," he mused, "even at that level, men like to watch their crimes enacted.

"Let's go over it once again, Andrews. The President leaves the south entrance of the White House at 10:00 am unless I stop her, so we have seventeen hours left and one last hope. The boys in Fingerprints have isolated the bill with Mrs Casefikis's prints on it. The twenty-second, we may be lucky – with still another half dozen to go we shouldn't have had a hope before ten o'clock tomorrow. There are several other prints on the bill, and they will be working on them all through the night. I expect to reach home by midnight. If you come up with anything before then, call me. I want you here in the office at 8:15 tomorrow. There's very little you can do now. But don't worry too much; I have twenty agents still working on it, though none of them knows all the details. And I'll only let the President into the danger zone if we have a fix on these villains."

"I'll report at 8:15 then, sir," said Mark.

"And, Mark, I strongly advise you not to see Dr Dexter. I don't want to blow this whole operation at the last moment, because of your love life. No offence intended."

"No, sir."

Mark left, feeling slightly superfluous. Twenty agents now assigned to the case. How long had the Director had them working round the clock without telling him? Twenty men trying to find out whether it was Dexter or Harrison, without knowing why. Still, only he and the Director knew the whole story, and he feared the Director knew more than he did. Perhaps it would be wiser to avoid Elizabeth until the following evening. He picked up his car, and drove back to the Dirksen Building and then remembered he had left the hearings' transcripts at the Committee Office. When he got there he found himself drawn towards the telephone booths. He had to call her, he had to find out how she was after her accident. He dialled Woodrow Wilson.

"Oh, she left the hospital – some time ago."

"Thank you," said Mark. He could feel his heart beat as he dialled her Georgetown number.

"Elizabeth?"

"Yes, Mark." She sounded – cold? frightened? tired? A hundred questions were racing through his mind.

"Can I come and see you right now?"

"Yes." The telephone clicked.

Mark left the booth, conscious of the sweat on the palms of his hands. One more job to do before he could drive off to Elizabeth, pick up those damned papers from the Senate Gun Control Hearings.

Mark walked towards the elevator and thought he could hear footsteps behind him. Of course he could hear footsteps behind him; there were several people behind him. When he reached the elevator, he pressed the Up-button and glanced around at the footsteps. Among the crowd of Senate staffers, congressmen, and sightseers, two men were watching him – or were they protecting him? There was a third man in dark glasses staring at a Medicare poster, even more obviously an agent, to Mark's quick eyes, than the other two.

The Director had said that he had put twenty agents on the case, and three of them must have been allocated to watch Mark. Hell. Soon they would be following him back to Elizabeth and Mark did not doubt that the Director would learn about it immediately. Mark resolved that no one was going to follow him back to Elizabeth's. It was none of their damned business. He'd shake the three of them off. He needed to see her in peace, without prying eyes and malicious tongues. He thought quickly as he waited to see which of the two elevators would arrive first. Two of the agents were now walking towards him, but the one by the Medicare poster remained motionless. Perhaps he wasn't an operative after all, but there certainly was something familiar about him. He had the aura of an agent; other agents can sense it with their eyes shut.

Mark concentrated on the elevator. The arrow on his

right lit up and the doors opened slowly. Mark shot in and stood facing the buttons and stared out at the corridor. The two operatives followed him into the elevator, and stood behind him. The man by the Medicare poster started walking towards the elevator. The doors were beginning to close. Mark pressed the Open-button, and the doors parted again. Must give him a chance to get in, and have all three of them together, Mark thought, but the third man did not respond. He just stood, staring, as if waiting for the next elevator. Perhaps he wanted to go down and wasn't an agent at all. Mark could have sworn . . . The doors began to close and at what Mark thought was the optimum point, he jumped back out. Wrong. O'Malley managed to squeeze himself out as well, while his partner was left to travel slowly but inevitably up to the eighth floor. Now Mark was down to two tails. The other elevator arrived. The third agent stepped into it immediately. Very clever or innocent, Mark thought, and waited outside. O'Malley was at his shoulder – which one next?

Mark strolled into the elevator and pressed the Down-button, but O'Malley was able to get in easily. Mark pressed the Open-button and sauntered back out. O'Malley followed him, face impassive. The third man remained motionless in the elevator. They must be working together. Mark jumped back in and jabbed the Close-button hard. The doors closed horribly slowly, but O'Malley had walked two paces away and was not going to make it. As the doors slammed together, Mark smiled. Two gone, one standing on the ground floor helpless, the other heading for the roof, while he was descending to the basement alone with the third.

O'Malley caught up with Pierce Thompson on the fifth floor. Both were out of breath.

"Where is he?" cried O'Malley.

"What do you mean, where is he? I thought he was with you."

"No, I lost him on the first floor."

"Shit, he could be anywhere," said Thompson. "Whose side does the smart-ass think we are on? Which one of us is going to tell the Director?"

"Not me," O'Malley said. "You're the senior officer, you tell him."

"No way I'm telling him," Thompson said. "And let that bastard Matson take all the credit – you can be sure he's still with him. No, we're going to find him. You take the first four floors and I'll take the top four. Bleep immediately when you spot him."

When Mark reached the basement, he stayed in the elevator. The third man walked out and seemed to hesitate. Mark's thumb was jammed on the Close-button again. The door responded. He was on his own. He tried to make the elevator bypass the ground floor but he couldn't; someone else wanted to get in. He prayed it was not one of the three men. He had to risk it. The doors opened and he walked out immediately. No agents in sight, no one studying the Medicare poster. He ran towards the revolving doors at the end of the corridor. The guard on duty looked at him suspiciously and fingered the holster of his gun. Through the revolving doors and out into the open, running hard. He glanced around. Everyone was walking, no one was running. He was safe.

Pennsylvania Avenue – he dodged in and out of the traffic amid screeching tyres and angry expletives. He reached the parking lot and jumped into his car, fumbling for some change. Why did they make trousers that you couldn't get your hands into when you sat down? He quickly paid for his ticket and drove towards Georgetown – and Elizabeth. He glanced in the rear-view mirror. No Ford sedan in sight. He'd done it. He was on his own. He smiled. For once he had beaten the Director. He drove past the lights at the corner of Pennsylvania and 14th just as they were changing. He began to relax.

A black Buick ran the lights. Lucky there were no traffic cops around.

When Mark arrived in Georgetown, his nervousness returned, a new nervousness associated with Elizabeth and her world, not with the Director and his world. When he pressed the bell on her front door, he could still hear his heart beating.

Elizabeth appeared. She looked drawn and tired and didn't speak. He followed her into the living-room.

"Have you recovered from your accident?"

"Yes, thank you. How did you know I'd had an accident?" she asked.

Mark thought quickly. "Called the hospital. They told me there."

"You're lying, Mark. I didn't tell them at the hospital, and I left early after a phone call from my father."

Mark couldn't look her in the eyes. He sat down and stared at the rug. "I . . . I don't want to lie to you, Elizabeth. Please don't."

"Why are you following my father?" she demanded. "He thought you looked familiar when he met you at the Mayflower. You've been haunting his committee meetings and you've been watching the debates in the Senate."

Mark didn't answer.

"Okay, don't explain. I'm not completely blind. I'll draw my own conclusions. I'm part of an FBI assignment. My, you've been working late hours, haven't you, Agent Andrews? For a man singled out to work a senators' daughters' beat, you're pretty goddamn inept. Just how many daughters have you seduced this week? Did you get any good dirt? Why don't you try the wives next? Your boyish charm might be more effective on them. Although, I must confess, you had me fooled, you lying bastard."

Despite a considerable effort to maintain the icy control with which she had launched her attack, Elizabeth bit her lip. Her voice caught. Mark still couldn't look at her.

He heard the anger and the tears in her voice. In a moment, the chilling frost had covered her emotion again.

"Please leave now, Mark. Now. I've said my piece and I hope I never lay eyes on you again. Perhaps then I can recover some of my self-respect. Just go; crawl back into the slime."

"You've misunderstood, Elizabeth."

"I know, you poor misunderstood agent, and you love me for myself. There's no other girl in your life," she said bitterly. "At least not until you're transferred to a new case. Well, this case has just finished. Go find somebody else's daughter to seduce with your lies about love."

He couldn't blame her for her reaction, and left without another word.

He drove home in a daze. The occupants of the car following him were fully alert. When he arrived, Mark left the car keys with Simon and took the elevator to his apartment.

The black Buick was parked a hundred yards from the building. The two men could see the light in Mark's apartment. He dialled six of the seven digits of her number, but then he put the phone back on the hook and turned off the light. One of the men in the Buick lit another cigarette, inhaled, and checked his watch.

After months of bargaining, bullying, cajoling and threatening the Gun Control bill was at last to be presented to the House for their final approval.

This was to be the day when Florentyna made an indelible mark on American history. If she achieved nothing else during her term of office she would live to be proud of this single act.

What could prevent it now? she asked for the thousandth time. And for the thousandth time the same dreadful thought flashed across her mind.

She dismissed it once again.

Thursday morning, 10 March

5:00 am

The Director woke suddenly. He lay there, frustrated; there was nothing he could do at this hour except look at the ceiling and think, and that didn't help much. He went over and over in his mind the events of the past six days, always leaving until last the thought of cancelling the whole operation, which would probably mean even now that the Senator and his cohorts would get away scot-free. Perhaps they already knew and had disappeared to lick their wounds and prepare for another day. Either way it would remain his problem.

The Senator woke at 5:35 in a cold sweat – not that he had really slept for more than a few minutes at any one time. It had been an evil night, thunder and lightning and sirens. It was the sirens that had made him sweat. He was even more nervous than he had expected to be; in fact just after he heard three chime he had nearly dialled the Chairman to say that he couldn't go through with it, despite the consequences that the Chairman had so delicately, but so frequently, adumbrated. But the vision of President Kane dead beside him reminded the Senator that everybody even now could remember exactly where he was when John F. Kennedy was assassinated, and he himself was never going to be able to forget where he was when Florentyna Kane died. Even that seemed less appalling than the thought of his own name in the headlines, his public image irreparably damaged, and his career ruined. Even so, he nearly called the Chairman, as much for reassurance as anything, despite their agreement that they had contacted each other for the last time until late the following morning, when the Chairman would be in Miami.

Five men had already died and that had caused only a ripple: President Kane's death would reverberate around the world.

The Senator stared out of the window for some time, focusing on nothing, then turned away. He kept looking at his watch, wishing he could stop time. The second hand moved relentlessly – relentlessly towards 10:56. He busied himself with breakfast and the morning paper. The *Post* informed him that many buildings had caught fire during the night in one of the worst storms in Washington's history, and the Lubber Run in Virginia had overflowed its banks, causing heavy property damage. There was little mention of President Kane. He wished he could read tomorrow's papers today.

The first call the Director received was from Elliott, who informed him that the recent activities of Senators Dexter and Harrison revealed nothing new about the situation – not that the anonymous man knew exactly what the situation was. The Director grumbled to himself, finished his egg – sunny-side up – and read the *Post*'s description of the demonic weather that had assailed Washington during the night. He glanced out of the window at the day, now clear and dry. A perfect day for an assassination, he thought. The bright day that brings fourth the adder. How late could he leave it before letting everyone know everything? The President was scheduled to leave the White House at 10:00 am. The Director would have to brief the head of the Secret Service, H. Stuart Knight, long before then and, if necessary, the President at least one hour before that. To hell with it, he would leave it to

the last minute and make a full explanation afterwards.
He was willing to risk his career to catch this pernicious
Senator red-handed. But risking the President's life . . .

He drove to the Bureau soon after 6:00. He wanted to
be there a full two hours before Andrews to study all the
reports he had ordered the evening before. Not many of
his senior aides would have had much sleep last night,
though they were probably still wondering why. They
would know soon enough. His deputy Associate Director
for Investigation, his Assistant Director for Planning and
Evaluation, and the head of the Criminal Section of that
division would help him decide if he should go ahead
or cancel. His Ford sedan slid down the ramp to the
underground parking lot and his reserved parking
place.

Elliott was there to meet him at the elevator – he was
always there, never late. He's not human, he'll have to
go, thought the Director, if I don't have to go first. He
suddenly realised that he could be handing his resignation
in to the President that night. Which President? He put
it out of his mind – that would all take care of itself in
its own time, he must now take care of the next five
hours.

Elliott had nothing useful to say. Dexter and Harrison
had both received and made phone calls during the night
and early morning, but nothing incriminating had been
picked up. No other information was forthcoming. The
Director asked where the two senators were at that
moment.

"Both eating breakfast at their homes. Dexter in
Kensington, Harrison in Alexandria. Six agents have
been watching them since five o'clock this morning and
have been detailed to follow them all day."

"Good. Report back to me immediately if anything
unusual happens."

"Of course, sir."

The fingerprint man was next. When he arrived, the
Director first apologised for keeping him up all night,

though the man's face and eyes looked more alight and alive than his own had been in the shaving mirror that morning.

Five feet four inches tall, slight and rather pale, Daniel Sommerton began his report. He was like a child with a toy. For him, working with prints had always been a passion as well as a job. The Director remained seated while Sommerton stood. If the Director had stood, he would not have been head and shoulders above him, but head, shoulders, and chest above him.

"We have found seventeen different fingers, and three different thumbs, Director," he said gleefully. "We're putting them through the Ninhydrin rather than the iodine-fume process, since we were unable to do them one at a time for technical reasons that I won't bother you with."

He waved his arm imperiously to imply that he would not waste a scientific explanation on the Director, who would have been the first to acknowledge such a pointless exercise.

"We think there are two more prints we might identify," Sommerton continued, "and we will have a read-out for you on all twenty-two of them within two, at the most three hours."

The Director glanced at his watch – already 6:45.

"Well done. That won't be a minute too soon. Get me the results – even if they are negative – as quickly as possible, and please thank all of your staff for working through the night."

The fingerprint expert left the Director, anxious to return to his seventeen fingers, three thumbs and two unidentified marks. The Director pressed a button and asked Mrs McGregor to send in the Assistant Director for Planning and Evaluation.

Two minutes later, Walter Williams was standing in front of him.

Five feet eleven, fair with a thin pallid face, dominated by a magnificent high-domed forehead, lined with amusement not grief, Williams was known in the Bureau either as the Brain or W.W. His primary responsibility was to head the Bureau's think tank of six lesser but still impressive brains. The Director often confronted him with hypothetical situations to which W.W. would later provide an answer which often proved, in retrospect, to be the right one. The Director placed great faith in his judgement, but he could not take any risks today. W.W. had better come up with a convincing answer to his hypothetical question of last night or his next call would be to the President.

"Good morning, Director."

"Good morning, W.W. What is your decision concerning my little problem?"

"Most interesting, Director . . . I feel, to be fair, the answer is simple, even when we look at the problem from every angle."

For the first time that morning a trace of a smile appeared on the Director's face.

"Assuming I haven't misunderstood you, Director."

The Director's smile broadened slightly; W.W. neither missed nor misunderstood anything, and was so formal that he didn't address the Director even in private as Halt. W.W. continued, his eyebrows moving up and down like the Dow-Jones index in an election year:

"You asked me to assume that the President would be leaving the White House at X hundred hours and then travelling by car to the Capitol. That would take her six minutes. I'm assuming her car is bullet-proof and well covered by the Secret Service. Under these conditions would it be possible to assassinate her. The answer is, it's possible but almost impossible, Director. Nevertheless, following the hypothesis through to its logical conclusion, the assassination team could use three methods: (a) explosives; (b) a handgun at close range; (c) a rifle."

W.W. always sounded like a textbook. "The bomb can be thrown at any point on the route, but it is never used by professionals, because professionals are paid for results, not attempts. If you study bombs as a method of removing a President, you will find there hasn't been a successful one yet, despite the fact that we have had four Presidents assassinated in office. Bombs inevitably end up killing innocent people and quite often the perpetrator of the crime as well. For that reason, since you have implied that the people involved would be professionals, I feel they must rely on the handgun or the rifle. Now the short-range gun, Director, is not a possible weapon on the route itself because it is unlikely that a pro would approach the President and shoot him at close range, thereby risking his own life. It would take an elephant gun or an anti-tank gun to pierce the President's limousine, and you can't carry those around in the middle of Washington without a permit."

With W.W., the Director could never be sure if it were meant to be a joke or just another fact. The eyebrows were still moving up and down, a sure signal not to interrupt him with foolish questions.

"When the President arrives at the steps of the Capitol, the crowd is too far away from her for a handgun to (a) be accurate and (b) give the assassin any hope of escape. So we must assume that it's the best-tested and most successful method of assassination of a Head of State – the rifle with telescopic sights for long range. Therefore, the only hope the assassin would have must be at the Capitol itself. The assassin can't see into the White House, and in any case the glass in the windows is four inches thick, so he must wait until the President actually leaves the limousine at the steps of the Capitol. This morning we timed a walk up the Capitol steps and it takes around fifty seconds. There are very few vantage points from which to make an assassination attempt, but we have studied the area carefully and you will find them all listed in my report. Also the conspirators must be convinced that we know nothing about the plot, because they know we can cover every possible shooting site. We think an assassination here in the heart of Washington unlikely, but nevertheless just possible by a man or team daring and skilful enough."

"Thank you, W.W. I'm sure you're right."

"A pleasure, sir. I do hope it's only hypothetical."

"Yes, W.W."

W.W. smiled like the only schoolboy in the class who can answer the teacher's questions. The Brain left the room to return to other problems. The Director paused and called for his other Assistant Director.

Matthew Rogers knocked and entered the room, waiting to be asked to take a seat. He understood authority. Like W.W. he would never become the Director, but no one who did would want to be without him.

"Well, Matt?" said the Director, pointing to the leather chair.

"I read Andrews' latest report last night, Director, and I really think the time has come for us to brief the Secret Service."

"I will be doing so in about an hour," said the Director. "Don't worry. Have you decided how you'll deploy your men?"

"It depends where the maximum risk is, sir."

"All right, Matt, let's assume that the point of maximum risk is the Capitol itself, at 10:06, right on the steps – what then?"

"First, I would surround the area for about a quarter of a mile in every direction. I'd close down the Metro, stop all traffic, public and private, pull aside for interrogation anyone who has a past record of making threats, anyone who's on the Security Index. I'd get assistance from the Met to provide perimeter security. We'd want as many eyes and ears in the area as possible. We could get two to four helicopters from Andrews Air Force Base for close scanning. In the immediate vicinity of the President, I'd use the full Secret Service Presidential detail in tight security."

"Very good, Matt. How many men do you need for such an operation, and how long would it take them to be ready if I declared an emergency procedure now?"

The Assistant Director looked at his watch – just after 7:00. He considered the matter for a moment. "I need three hundred special agents briefed and fully operational in two hours."

"Right, go ahead," said the Director crisply. "Report to me as soon as they're ready but leave the final briefing to the last possible moment, and, Matt, I want no helicopters until 10:01. I don't want there to be a chance of a leak of any sort; it's our one hope of catching the assassin."

"Why don't you simply cancel the President's visit, sir? We're in enough deep water as it is, and it's not entirely your responsibility in the first place."

"If we pull out now, we only have to start all over again tomorrow," said the Director, "and I may never get another chance like this."

"Yes, sir."

"Don't let me down, Matt, because I am going to leave the ground operations entirely in your hands."

"Thank you, sir."

Rogers left the room. The Director knew his job would be done as competently as it could be by any professional law-enforcement officer in America.

"Mrs McGregor."

"Yes, sir?"

"Get me the head of the Secret Service at the White House."

"Yes, sir."

The Director glanced at his watch: 7:10. Andrews was due at 8:15. The phone rang.

"Mr Knight on the line, sir."

"Stuart, can you call me on my private line and be sure you're not overheard?

H. Stuart Knight knew Halt well enough to realise that he meant what he said. He called back immediately on his special scrambler.

"Stuart, I'd like to see you immediately, usual place, take about thirty minutes, no more. Top priority."

Damned inconvenient, thought Knight, with the President leaving for the Capitol in two hours, but Halt only made this request two or three times a year, and he knew that other matters must be put to one side for the moment. Only the President and the Attorney General took priority over Halt.

The Director of the FBI and the head of the Secret Service met at a line of cabs in front of Union Station ten minutes later. They didn't take the first cab in the line, but the seventh. They climbed in the back without speaking or acknowledging each other. Elliott drove the Max's Yellow Cab off to circle the Capitol. The Director talked and the head of the Secret Service listened.

Mark's alarm woke him at 6:45. He showered and shaved and thought about those transcripts he had left in the Senate, trying to convince himself that they would have thrown no light on whether it was Dexter or Harrison. He silently thanked Senator Stevenson for indirectly disposing of Senators Brooks, Byrd, and Thornton. He would thank anybody who could dispose of Senator Dexter. He was beginning to agree with the Director's reasoning – it all pointed to Dexter. His motive was particularly compelling, but . . . Mark looked at his watch; he was a little early. He sat on the edge of his bed; he scratched his leg which was itching; something must have bitten him during the night. He continued trying to figure out if there was anything he had missed.

The Chairman got out of bed at 7:20 and lit his first cigarette. He couldn't remember exactly when he had woken. At 6:10 he had phoned Tony, who was already up and waiting for his call. They weren't to meet that day unless the Chairman needed the car in an emergency. The next time they would speak to each other would be on the dot of 9:30 for a check-in to confirm they were all in position.

When he had completed the call, the Chairman dialled room service and ordered a large breakfast. What he was about to do that morning was not the sort of work to be tackled on an empty stomach. Matson was due to ring him any time after 7:30. Perhaps he was still asleep. After that effort last night, Matson deserved some rest. The Chairman smiled to himself. He went into the bathroom and turned on the shower; a feeble trickle of cold water emerged. Goddamn hotels. One hundred dollars a night and no hot water. He splashed around ineffectively and began to think about the next five hours, going over the plan again carefully to be sure he had not overlooked even the smallest detail. Tonight, Kane would be dead and he would have $2,000,000 in the Union Bank of Switzerland, Zurich, account number AZL–376921–B, a small reward from his grateful friends in the gun trade. And to think Uncle Sam wouldn't even get the tax.

The phone rang. Damn. He dripped across the floor, his heartbeat quickened. It was Matson.

Matson and the Chairman had driven back from Mark's apartment at 2:35 that morning, their task completed. Matson had overslept by thirty minutes. The damned hotel had forgotten his wake-up call; you couldn't trust anyone nowdays. As soon as he had woken, he phoned the Chairman and reported in.

Xan was safely in the top of the crane and ready – probably the only one of them who was still asleep.

The Chairman, although dripping, was pleased. He put the phone down and returned to the shower. Damn, still cold.

Matson masturbated. He always did when he was nervous and had time to kill.

Florentyna Kane did not wake until 7:35. She rolled over, trying to recall the dream she had just had, but none of it would come back to her, so she let her mind wander. Today, she would be going to the Capitol to plead her case for the Gun Control bill before a special session of the Senate and then on to have lunch with all the key supporters and opponents of the bill. Since the bill had been approved in committee, as she had been confident it would be, she had concentrated on her strategy for the final day of floor battle; at least the odds now seemed to be with her. She smiled at Edward, although he had his back to her. It had been a busy session, and she was looking forward to going to Camp David and spending more time with her family. Better get moving, more than half of America is already up, she thought, and I am still lying in bed . . . Still, that waking half of America had not had to dine the previous evening with the four-hundred-pound King of Tonga, who wasn't going to leave the White House until he was virtually thrown out. The President wasn't absolutely certain she could pinpoint Tonga on the map. The Pacific was after all a large ocean. She had left her Secretary of State, Abe Chayes, to do the talking; he at least knew exactly where Tonga was.

She stopped thinking about the overweight king and put her feet on the floor – or to be more exact, on the Presidential Seal. The damned thing was on everything except the toilet paper. She knew that when she appeared for breakfast in the dining-room across the hall, she would find the third edition of the *New York Times*, the third edition of the *Washington Post*, the first editions of the *Los Angeles Times* and the *Boston Globe*, all ready for her to read, with the pieces referring to her marked in red, plus a prepared digest of yesterday's news. How did they get it all completed before she was even dressed? Florentyna went to the bathroom and turned on the shower; the water pressure was just right. She began to consider what she could say finally to convince the waverers in the Senate that the Gun Control bill must become law. Her train of thought was interrupted by her efforts to reach the middle of her back with the soap. Presidents still do that for themselves, she thought.

*

Mark was due to be with the Director in twenty minutes. He checked his mail – just an envelope from American Express, which he left on the kitchen table unopened.

A yawning O'Malley was sitting in the Ford sedan a hundred yards away. He was relieved to be able to report that Mark had left the apartment building and was talking to the black garage attendant. Neither O'Malley nor Thompson had admitted to anybody that they had lost Mark for several hours the previous evening.

Mark walked around the side of the building and disappeared from the view of the man in the blue Ford. It didn't worry him. O'Malley had checked the location of the Mercedes an hour earlier; there was only one way out.

Mark noticed a red Fiat as he came around the corner of the building. Looks like Elizabeth's, he thought to himself, except for the damage to a bumper. He stared at it again and was taken by surprise to see Elizabeth sitting in it. He opened the door. If he were to be Ragani and she were Mata Hari, he was now past caring. He climbed in beside her. Neither of them spoke until they both spoke at once and laughed nervously. She tried again. Mark sat in silence.

"I've come to say I'm sorry about being so touchy last night. I should have at least given you a chance to explain. I really don't want you to sleep with any other senator's daughter," she said, trying to force a smile.

"I'm the one who should be sorry, Liz. Trust me, as they say in Hollywood. Whatever happens, let's meet this evening and then I'll try to explain everything. Don't ask me anything before then and promise that whatever happens you will see me tonight. If after that you never want to see me again I promise I'll leave quietly."

Elizabeth nodded her agreement. "But not as abruptly as you left once before, I hope."

Mark put his arm around her and kissed her quickly. "No more nasty cracks about that night. I've spent every night since looking forward to a second chance."

They both laughed. He started to get out.

"Why don't I drive you to work, Mark? It's on my way to the hospital and we won't have to bother with two cars this evening."

Mark hesitated. "Why not?"

He wondered if this were the final set-up.

As she drove around the corner, Simon waved them down. "Apartment Seven's car won't be back until late this morning, Mark. I'll have to park the Mercedes on the street for now but don't worry, I'll keep an eye on it." Simon looked at Elizabeth and grinned. "You won't be needing my sister after all, man."

Elizabeth pulled out and joined the traffic on 6th Street. A hundred yards away, O'Malley was chewing gum.

"Where shall we have dinner tonight?"

"Let's go back to that French restaurant and try the whole evening again. This time we'll complete the final act of the play."

I hope it begins, "This was the noblest Roman of them all. All the conspirators, save only he . . ." Mark thought.

"This time it's my treat," said Elizabeth.

Mark accepted, remembering his unopened bill from American Express. The lights turned red at the corner of G Street. They stopped and waited. Mark started scratching his leg again, it really felt quite painful.

The cab was still circling the Capitol but Halt was coming to the end of his briefing for H. Stuart Knight.

"We believe that the attempt will be made when the President gets out of her car at the Capitol. We'll take care of the Capitol itself if you can manage to get her into the building unharmed. I'll have my men cover the buildings and roofs of buildings and every elevated vantage point from which it would be possible to shoot."

"It would make our job a lot easier if the President didn't insist on walking up the steps. Ever since Carter took his little stroll up Pennsylvania Avenue in '77 . . ." His voice trailed off in exasperation. "By the way, Halt, why didn't you tell me about this earlier?"

"There's a strange quirk to it, Stuart. I still can't give you all the details, but don't worry, they're not relevant to the task of protecting the President."

"Okay. I'll buy that. But are you sure my men can't help at your end?"

"No, I'm happy as long as I know you're keeping a close watch on the President. It will give me the freedom I need to catch the bastards red-handed. They mustn't be allowed to get suspicious. I want to catch the killer while he still has the weapon in his hand."

"Shall I tell the President?" asked Knight.

"No, just inform her that it's a new security measure you are putting into practice from time to time."

"She's had so many of those she's bound to believe it," said Knight.

"Stick to the same route and timetable and I'll leave the finer points to you, Stuart. And I don't want any leaks. I'll see you after the President's lunch. We can bring each other up-to-date then. By the way, what's today's code name for the President?"

"Julius."

"Good God, I don't believe it."

"You are telling me everything I need to know, aren't you, Halt?"

"No, of course I'm not, Stuart. You know me, Machiavelli's younger brother."

The Director tapped Elliott on the shoulder and the cab slipped back into the seventh place in line. The two passengers got out and walked in opposite directions, Knight to catch the Metro to the White House, the Director a cab to the Bureau. Neither looked back.

Lucky Stuart Knight, thought the Director, he's gone through the last seven days without the information I have. Now the meeting was over, the Director's confidence in his own stratagem was renewed, and he was resolved that only he and Andrews would ever know the full story – unless they had conclusive proof on which to secure the Senator's conviction. He had to catch the conspirators alive, get them to testify against the Senator. The Director checked his watch with the clock on the Old Post Office Tower over the Washington Field Office. It was 7:58. Andrews would be due in two minutes. He was saluted as he went through the revolving doors of the Bureau. Mrs McGregor was standing outside his office, looking agitated.

"It's Channel Four, sir, asking for you urgently."

"Put them through," said the Director. He moved quickly into his office and picked up the extension.

"It's Special Agent O'Malley from the patrol car, sir."

"Yes, O'Malley?"

"Andrews has been killed, sir, and there must have been another person in the car."

The Director couldn't speak.

"Are you there, Director?" O'Malley waited. "I repeat are you there, Director?"

Finally the Director said, "Come in immediately." He put the phone down, and his great hands gripped the Queen Anne desk like a throat he wanted to strangle. The fingers then curled and clenched slowly into the palms of his hands until they made massive fists, the nails digging into the skin. Blood trickled slowly down on to the leather-work on the desk, leaving a dark stain. Halt Tyson sat alone for several minutes. Then he instructed Mrs McGregor to get the President at the White House. He was going to cancel the whole damned thing; he'd already gone too far. He sat silently waiting. The bastards had beaten him. They must know everything.

It took Special Agent O'Malley ten minutes to reach the Bureau, where he was ushered straight into the Director.

My God, he looks eighty, thought O'Malley.

The Director stared at him. "How did it happen?" he asked quietly.

"He was blown up in a car; we think someone else was with him."

"Why? How?"

224

"Must have been a bomb attached to the ignition. It blew up right there in front of us. Made an unholy mess."

"I don't give a fuck for the mess," began the Director on a slowly rising note, when the door opened.

Mark Andrews walked in. "Good morning, sir. I hope I'm not interrupting something. I thought you said 8:15."

Both men stared at him.

"You're dead."

"Excuse me, sir?"

"Well, who the hell," said Special Agent O'Malley, "was driving your Mercedes?"

Mark stared at him uncomprehending.

"My Mercedes?" he said quickly. "What are you talking about?"

"Your Mercedes has just been blown to smithereens. I saw it with my own eyes. My colleague down there is trying to put the pieces together; he's already reported finding the hand of a black man."

Mark steadied himself against the wall. "The bastards have killed Simon," he cried in anger. "There will be no need to call Grant Nanna to screw their balls off. I'll do it myself."

"Please explain yourself," said the Director.

Mark steadied himself again, turned around and faced them both. "I came in with Elizabeth Dexter this morning; she came by to see me. I came in with her," he repeated, not yet coherent.

"Simon moved my car because it was occupying a reserved daytime parking space and now the bastards have killed him."

"Sit down, Andrews. You too, O'Malley."

The telephone rang. "The President's Chief of Staff, sir. The President will be with you in about two minutes."

"Cancel it and apologise. Explain to Janet Brown that it was nothing important, just wanted to wish the President luck on the Gun Control bill today."

"Yes, sir."

"So they think you're dead, Andrews, and they have now played their last card. So we must hold ours back. You're going to remain dead – for a little while longer."

Mark and O'Malley looked at each other, both puzzled.

"O'Malley, you return to your car. You say nothing, even to your partner. You have not seen Andrews alive, do you understand?"

"Yes, sir."

"Get going."

"Mrs McGregor, get me the head of External Affairs."

"Yes, sir."

The Director looked at Mark. "I was beginning to miss you."

"Thank you, sir."

"Don't thank me, I'm just about to kill you again."

A knock on the door, and Bill Gunn came in. He was the epitome of the public relations man, better dressed than anyone else in the building, with the biggest smile and a mop of fair hair that he washed every two days. His face as he entered was unusually grim.

"Have you heard about the death of one of our young agents, sir?"

"Yes, Bill. Put out a statement immediately that an unnamed special agent was killed this morning and that you will brief the press fully at eleven o'clock."

"They'll be hounding me long before then, sir."

"Let them hound you," said the Director sharply.

"Yes, sir."

"At eleven, you will put out another statement saying the agent is alive . . ."

Bill Gunn's face registered surprise.

". . . and that a mistake has been made, and the man who died was a young garage attendant who had no connection with the FBI."

"But sir, our agent?"

"No doubt you would like to meet the agent who is supposed to be dead. Bill Gunn – this is Special Agent Andrews. Now not a word, Bill. This man is dead for the

226

next three hours and if I find a leak, you can find a new job."

Bill Gun looked convincingly anxious. "Yes, sir."

"When you've written the press statement, call me and read it over to me."

"Yes, sir."

Bill Gunn left, dazed. He was a gentle, easy-going man and this was way above his head, but he like so many others trusted the Director.

The Director was becoming very aware just how many men did trust him and how much he was carrying on his own shoulders. He looked back at Mark, who had not recovered from the realisation that Simon had died instead of him – the second man to do so in eight days.

"Right, Mark, we have under two hours left, so we will mourn the dead later. Have you anything to add to yesterday's report?"

"Yes, sir. It's good to be alive."

"If you get past eleven o'clock, young man, I think you have a good chance for a long and healthy life, but we still don't know if it's Dexter or Harrison. You know I think it's Dexter." The Director looked at his watch again: 8:29 – ninety-seven minutes left. "Any new ideas?"

"Well, sir, Elizabeth Dexter certainly can't be involved, she saved my life by bringing me in this morning. If she wanted me dead, that sure was a funny way of going about it."

"I'll accept that," said the Director, "but it doesn't clear her father."

"Surely he wouldn't kill a man he thought might marry his daughter," said Mark.

"You're sentimental, Andrews. A man who plans to assassinate a President doesn't worry about his daughter's boy friends."

The phone rang. It was Bill Gunn from Public Relations.

"Right, read it over." The Director listened carefully.

"Good. Issue it immediately to radio, television, and the papers, and release the second statement at eleven o'clock, no earlier. Thank you, Bill." The Director put the phone down.

"Congratulations, Mark, you're the only dead man alive and, like Mark Twain, you will be able to read your own obituary. Now, to bring you quickly up-to-date. I have three hundred field agents already out covering the Capitol and the area immediately surrounding it. The whole place will be sealed off the moment the Presidential car arrives."

"You're letting her go to the Capitol?" said Mark in astonishment.

"Listen carefully, Mark. I'll have a minute-by-minute briefing on where the two senators are from 9:00 am on and six men are tailing both of them. At 9:15, we're going into the street ourselves. When it happens, we're going to be there. If I'm going to carry the ultimate responsibility, I may as well carry it in person."

"Yes, sir."

The intercom buzzed.

"It's Mr Sommerton. He wants to see you urgently, sir." The Director looked at his watch: 8:45. On the minute, as promised.

Daniel Sommerton rushed in, looking rather pleased with himself. He came straight to the point. "One of the prints has come up on the criminal file, it's a thumb, his name is Matson – Ralph Matson."

Somerton produced a photograph of Matson, an Identikit picture, and an enlarged thumbprint.

"And here's the part you're not going to like, sir. He's an ex-FBI agent." He passed Matson's card over for the Director to study. Mark looked at the photo. It was the Greek Orthodox priest, big nose, heavy chin.

"Something professional about him," said the Director and Mark simultaneously.

"Well done, Sommerton, make three hundred copies of the picture immediately and get them to the Assistant

Director in charge of the Investigation Division – and that means immediately."

"Yes, sir." The fingerprint expert scurried away, pleased with himself. They wanted his thumb.

"Mrs McGregor, get me Mr Rogers."

The Assistant Director was on the line; the Director briefed him.

"Shall I arrest him on sight?"

"No, Matt. Once you've spotted him, watch him and keep your boys well out of sight. He could still call everything off if he got suspicious. Keep me briefed all the time. Move in on him at 10:06. I'll let you know if anything changes."

"Yes, sir. Have you briefed the Secret Service?"

"Yes, I have." He slammed the phone down.

The Director looked at his watch: 9:05. He pressed a button and Elliott came in. "Where are the two senators?"

"Harrison's still in his Alexandria town house, Dexter has left Kensington and is heading towards the Capitol, sir."

"You stay here in this office, Elliott, and keep in radio contact with me and the Assistant Director on the street. Never leave this room. Understood?"

"Yes, sir."

"I'll be using my walkie-talkie on Channel Four. Let's go, Andrews." They left the anonymous man.

"If anybody calls me, Mrs McGregor, put them through to Special Agent Elliott in my office. He will know where to contact me."

"Yes, sir."

A few moments later, the Director and Mark were on the street walking up Pennsylvania Avenue towards the Capitol. Mark put on his dark glasses and pulled his collar up. They passed several agents on the way. None of them acknowledged the Director. On the corner of Pennsylvania Avenue and 9th Street, they passed the Chairman, who was lighting a cigarette and checking his watch: 9:30. He moved to the edge of the sidewalk, leaving a pile of cigarette butts behind him. The Director glanced at the cigarette butts: litter bug, ought to be fined a hundred dollars. They hurried on.

"Come in, Tony. Come in, Tony."

"Tony, boss. The Buick's ready. I've just heard it announced on the car radio that pretty boy Andrews bought it."

The Chairman smiled.

"Come in, Xan."

"Ready, await your signal."

"Come in, Matson."

"Everything's set, boss. There's a hell of a lot of agents around."

"Don't sweat, there's always a lot of Secret Service men around when the President is travelling. Don't call again unless there's a real problem. All three keep your lines open. When I next call, I will only activate the vibrators on the side of your watches. Then you have three minutes forty-five seconds, because Kane will be passing me. Understood?"

"Yes."

"Yes."

"Yes."

The Chairman broke the circuit and lit another cigarette: 9:40.

The Director spotted Matthew Rogers in a special squad car and went quickly over to him. "Everything under control, Matt?"

"Yes, sir. If anybody tries anything, no one will be able to move for half a mile."

"Good; what time do you have?"

"Nine-forty-five."

"Right, you control it from here. I'm going to the Capitol."

Halt and Mark left the Assistant Director and walked on.

"Elliott calling the Director."

"Come in, Elliott."

"They have spotted Matson at the junction of Maryland Avenue and 1st Street, other side of the Garfield statue, south-west corner of the Capitol grounds, near the west front renovation site."

"Good. Observe and post fifty men around the area, don't move in yet, brief Mr Rogers and tell him to keep his men out of Matson's field of vision."

"Yes, sir."

"What the hell is he doing on that side of the Capitol?" said Mark softly. "You couldn't shoot anyone on the Capitol steps from the north-west side unless you were in a chopper."

"I agree, it beats me," said the Director.

They reached the police cordon surrounding the Capitol. The Director showed his credentials to get himself and Andrews through. The young Capitol policeman double-checked them; he couldn't believe it; he was looking at the real live object. Yes, it was the Director of the FBI. H. A. L. Tyson himself.

"Sorry, sir. Please come through."

"Elliott to the Director."

"Yes, Elliott?"

"Head of the Secret Service for you, sir."

"Stuart."

"The advance car is leaving the front gate now. Julius will leave in five minutes."

"Thank you, Stuart. Keep your end up and surprise me.'

"Don't worry, Halt. We will."

Five minutes later, the Presidential car left the South Entrance and turned left on to E Street. The advance car passed the Chairman on the corner of Pennsylvania Avenue and 9th. He smiled, lit another cigarette and waited. Five minutes later, a large Lincoln, flags flying on both front fenders, the Presidential Seal on the doors, passed by the Chairman. Through the misty grey windows, he could see three figures in the back. A limousine known as the "gun car" and occupied by Secret Service agents and the President's personal physician, followed the President's car. The Chairman pressed a button on his watch. The vibrator began to tickle his wrist. After ten seconds, he stopped it, walked one block north and hailed a taxi.

"National Airport," he said to the cab driver, fingering the ticket in his inside pocket.

The vibrator on Matson's watch was touching his skin. After ten seconds, it stopped. Matson walked to the side of the construction site, bent down and tied his shoelace.

Xan started to take off the tape. He was glad to be moving; he had been bent double all night. First he screwed the barrel into the sight finder.

"Assistant Director to Director. Matson is approaching the construction site. Now he has stopped to tie his shoe. No one on the construction site but I'm asking a helicopter to check it out. There's a huge crane in the middle of the site which looks deserted."

"Good. Stay put until the last minute. I'll give you the timing the moment the President's car arrives. You must catch them red-handed. Alert all agents on the roof of the Capitol."

The Director turned to Mark, more relaxed. "I think it's going to be all right."

Mark's eyes were on the steps of the Capitol. "Have you noticed, sir, both Senator Dexter and Senator Harrison are in the welcoming party for the President?"

"Yes," said the Director. "The car is due to arrive in two minutes; we'll catch the others even if we can't figure out which Senator it is. We'll make them talk in due course. Wait a minute – that's odd."

The Director's finger was running down a couple of closely typed sheets he held in his hand.

"Yes, that's what I thought. The President's detailed

schedule shows that Dexter will be there for the special address to Congress but isn't attending the luncheon with the President. Very strange: I'm sure all the key leaders of the opposition were invited to lunch. Why won't Dexter be present?"

"Nothing strange about that, sir. He always has lunch with his daughter on Thursdays. Good God! 'I always have lunch with my father on Thursdays.'"

"Yes, Mark, I heard you the first time."

"No, sir, 'I always have lunch with my father on Thursdays.'"

"Mark, the car will be here in one minute."

"It's Harrison, sir. It's Harrison. I'm a fool – Thursday, 24 February, in Georgetown. I always thought of it as 24 February, not as Thursday. Dexter was having lunch with Elizabeth. 'I always have lunch with my father on Thursdays.' That's why he was seen in Georgetown that day, must be. They never miss it."

"Are you sure? Can you be certain? There's a hell of a lot riding on it."

"It's Harrison, sir. It can't be Dexter. I should have realised it on the first day. Christ, I'm stupid."

"Right, Mark. Up those steps quickly, watch Harrison's every move and be prepared to arrest him whatever the consequences."

"Yes, sir."

"Rogers."

The Assistant Director came in. "Sir?"

"The car is pulling up. Arrest Matson immediately; check the roof of the Capitol." The Director stared up into the sky. "Oh my God, it's not a helicopter, it's that damn crane. It has to be the crane."

Xan nestled the butt of the yellow rifle into his shoulder and watched the President's car. He had attached a feather to a piece of thread on the end of the gun barrel, a trick he had picked up when training for the Olympics – no wind. The hours of waiting were coming to an end.

Senator Harrison was standing there on the Capitol steps. Through the thirty-power Redfield scope he could even see the beads of sweat standing out on the man's forehead.

The President's car drew up on the north side of the Capitol. All was going according to plan. Xan levelled the telescopic sight on the car door and waited for Kane. Two Secret Service men climbed out, scanned the crowd, and waited for the third. Nothing happened. Xan put the sight on the Senator, who looked anxious and bemused. Back at the car, still no Kane. Where the hell was she, what was going on? He checked the feather; still no wind. He moved his sight back on the President's car. Good God, the crane was moving and Kane wasn't in the car. Matson had been right all along, they knew everything. Xan knew exactly what had to be done in these circumstances. Only one man could ditch them and he wouldn't hesitate to do it. Xan moved his sight up the Capitol steps. One and one-half inches above the forehead. A moment's hesitation before he squeezed the trigger once . . . twice, but the second time he didn't have a clear shot, and a fraction of a second later he could no longer see the Capitol steps. He looked down from the moving crane. He was surrounded by fifty men in dark suits, fifty guns were pointing up at him.

Mark was about a yard away from Senator Harrison when he heard him cry out and fall. Mark jumped on top of the Senator and the second bullet grazed his shoulder. There was a panic among the other senators and officials on the top steps. The welcoming party scurried inside. Thirty FBI men moved in quickly. The Director was the only man who remained on the Capitol steps, steady and motionless, staring up at the crane. They hadn't nicknamed him Halt by mistake.

"May I ask where I'm going, Stuart?"

"Certainly, Madam President. To the Capitol."

"But this isn't the normal route to the Capitol."

"No, Madam. We're going down Constitution Avenue

to the Russell Building. We hear there has been a little trouble at the Capitol. A demonstration of some kind. The National Rifle Association."

"So I'm avoiding it, am I? Like a coward, Stuart."

"No, Madam, I'm slipping you through the basement. Just as a safety precaution and for your own convenience."

"That means I'll have to go on that damned subway. Even when I was a senator, I preferred to walk outside."

"We've cleared the way for you, Madam. You'll still be there bang on time."

The President grumbled as she looked out of the window and saw an ambulance race in the opposite direction.

Senator Harrison died before he reached the hospital and Mark had his wound patched up by a house doctor. Mark checked his watch and laughed. It was 11:04 – he was going to live.

"Phone for you, Mr Andrews. The Director of the FBI."

"Sir?"

"Mark, I hear you're fine. Good. I am sorry to say the Senate went into recess out of respect for Senator Harrison. The President is shocked but feels this is precisely the moment to emphasise the significance of gun control, so we're all now going into lunch early. Sorry you can't join us. And we caught three of them – Matson, a Vietnamese sharpshooter, and a petty crook called Tony Loraido. There may still be more, I'll let you know later. Thank you, Mark."

The telephone clicked before Mark could offer any opinion.

Thursday evening, 10 March

7:00 pm

Mark arrived in Georgetown at seven that evening. He had gone to Simon's wake and paid his respects to the bewildered parents that afternoon. They had five other children, but that never helped. Their grief made Mark long for the warmth of the living.

Elizabeth was wearing the red silk shirt and black skirt in which he had first seen her. She greeted him with a cascade of words.

"I don't understand what's been going on. My father called earlier and told me you tried to save Senator Harrison's life. What were you doing there anyway? My father is very upset about the shooting. Why have you been following him around? Was he in any danger?"

Mark looked at her squarely. "No, he wasn't involved in any way so let's try and start over again."

Still she didn't understand.

When they arrived at the Rive Gauche, the maître d' welcomed them with open arms.

"Good evening, Mr Andrews, how nice to see you again. I don't remember your booking a table."

"No, it's in my name. Dr Dexter," said Elizabeth.

"Oh, yes, Doctor, of course. Will you come this way?"

They had baked clams, and, at last, a steak with no fancy trimmings and two bottles of wine.

Mark sang most of the way home. When they arrived,

he took her firmly by the hand and led her into the darkened living-room.

"I'm going to seduce you. No coffee, no brandy, no music, just straightforward seduction."

"I should be so lucky."

They fell on the couch.

"You're too drunk," Elizabeth added.

"Wait and see." He kissed her fully on the lips for a long time and started to unbutton her shirt.

"Are you sure you wouldn't like some coffee?" she asked.

"Yes, quite sure," he said as he pulled the shirt slowly free from her skirt and felt her back, his other hand moving on to her leg.

"What about some music?" she said lightly. "Something special." Elizabeth touched the start button on the hi-fi. It was Sinatra again, but this time it was the right song:

> Is it an earthquake or simply a shock
> Is it the real turtle soup or merely the mock,
> Is it a cocktail, this feeling of joy,
> Or is what I feel – the real – McCoy?
>
> Is it for all time or simply a lark,
> Is it Granada I see or only Asbury Park,
> Is it a fancy not worth thinking of,
> Or is it at . . . long . . . last . . . love?

She settled back into Mark's arms.

He unzipped her skirt. Her legs were slender and beautiful in the dim light. He caressed her gently.

"Are you going to tell me the truth about today, Mark?"

"Afterwards, darling."

"When you've had your way with me," she said.

He slipped his shirt off. Elizabeth stared at the bandage on his shoulder.

237

"Is that where you were wounded in the line of duty?"

"No, that's where my last lover bit me."

"She must have had more time than I did."

They moved closer together.

He took the phone off the hook – not tonight, Julius.

"I can't get through, sir," Elliott said, "just a continual busy signal."

"Try again, try again. I'm sure he's there."

"Shall I go through the operator?"

"Yes, yes," said the Director testily.

The Director waited, tapping his fingers on the Queen Anne desk, staring at the red stain and wondering how it had got there.

"The operator says the phone is off the hook, sir. Shall I ask her to bleep him; that'll certainly get his attention."

"No, Elliott, just leave it and go home. I'll have to call him in the morning."

"Yes, sir. Good night, sir."

He'll have to go – back to Idaho or wherever he came from, thought the Director, as he switched off the lights and made his own way home.

Friday morning, 11 March

7:00 am

Mark woke first; perhaps because he was in a strange bed. He turned over and looked at Elizabeth. She never wore make-up and was just as beautiful in the morning as she was on the other side of a dinner table. Her dark hair curled in towards the nape of her neck and he stroked the soft strands gently. She stirred, rolled over, and kissed him.

"Go and brush your teeth."

"What a romantic way to start the day," he said.

"I'll be awake by the time you get back." She groaned a little and stretched.

Mark picked up the Pepsodent – that was one thing that would have to change, he preferred Macleans – and tried to figure out which part of the bathroom he was going to be able to fit his things into. When he returned, he noticed the phone was still off the hook. He looked at his watch: 7:05. He climbed back into bed. Elizabeth slipped out.

"Only be a minute," she said.

It was never like this in the movies, thought Mark.

She returned and lay down beside him. After a moment she said, "Your chin is hurting my face. You're not as clean-shaven as you were the first time."

"I shaved very carefully that first evening," said Mark. "Funny, I was never so sure of anything. Didn't happen quite the way I intended."

"What did you intend?"

"It was never like this in the movies." This time he stated the sentiments clearly. "Do you know what the Frenchman said when accused of raping a dead woman?"

"No."

"I didn't realise she was dead; I thought she was English."

After she had proved she wasn't English Elizabeth asked Mark what he would like for breakfast.

After Mark had told her, he disappeared into the shower.

Mark turned on the shower, getting the temperature just right.

"Disappointing, I thought we would take a bath together," said Elizabeth.

"I never bathe with the domestic staff. Just give me a call when breakfast is ready," Mark replied from under the shower and started to sing "At Long Last Love" in several different keys.

A slim arm appeared through the falling water and turned off the hot water tap. The singing stopped abruptly. Elizabeth was nowhere to be seen.

Mark dressed quickly and put the phone back on the hook. It rang almost immediately. Elizabeth appeared in a brief slip.

Mark wanted to go back to bed.

She picked up the phone. "Good morning. Yes, he's here. It's for you. A jealous lover, I shouldn't wonder."

She put on a dress and returned to the kitchen.

"Mark Andrews."

"Good morning, Mark."

"Oh, good morning, sir."

"I've been trying to get you since eight o'clock last night."

"Oh, really, sir. I thought I was on vacation. If you look in the official book in the WFO, I think you'll find I've signed out."

"Yes, Mark, but you are going to have to interrupt that vacation because the President wants to see you."

"The President, sir?"

"Of the United States."

"Why would she want to see me, sir."

"Yesterday I killed you, but today I've made you a hero and she wants to congratulate you personally on trying to save Senator Harrison's life."

"What?"

"You'd better read the morning papers. Say nothing for now; I'll explain my actions later."

"Where do I go, what time, sir?"

"You'll be told." The line clicked.

Mark replaced the phone and thought about the conversation. He was just about to call Elizabeth to ask if the morning paper had come when the phone rang again.

"Answer it will you, Mark darling. Now that the lovers have found your whereabouts, it's bound to be for you."

Mark picked it up.

"Mr Andrews?"

"Speaking."

"Hold the line one moment, please. The President will be with you in one moment."

"Good morning. Florentyna Kane. I just wanted to know if you could find time to drop into the White House this morning at about ten o'clock. I'd like to meet you and have a chat."

"I'd be honoured, Madam."

"Then I'll look forward to it, Mr Andrews, and the chance to meet you and congratulate you personally. If you come to the West Entrance, Janet Brown will be there to meet you."

"Thank you, Madam."

One of those legendary phone calls that the press so often wrote about. The Director had only been checking where he was. Had the President been trying to reach him since eight last night?

"Who was it, darling?"

"The President of the United States."

"Tell her you'll call back; she's always on the line, usually calls collect."

"No, I'm serious."

"Yes, of course you are."

"She wants to see me."

"Yes, darling, your place or hers?"

Mark went into the kitchen and attacked some Wheaties. Elizabeth came in brandishing the *Post*.

"Look," she said. "It's official. You're not a villain, you're a hero."

The headline read: SENATOR HARRISON KILLED ON STEPS OF CAPITOL.

"It was the President, wasn't it?" she said.

"Yes, it was."

"Why didn't you tell me?"

"I did, but you didn't choose to listen."

"I'm sorry," said Elizabeth.

"I love you."

"I love you too, but let's not go through this every week."

She continued to read the paper. Mark munched his Wheaties.

"Why would someone want to kill Senator Harrison, Mark?"

"I don't know. What does the *Post* say?"

"They haven't figured out a reason yet; they say he was known to have many enemies both here and abroad." She began to read from the paper:

"Senator Robert Harrison (D-South Carolina) was shot by an assassin on the steps of the Capitol yesterday morning at 10:06.

"The assassination took place only moments before President Kane was due to arrive for her final assault on behalf of the Gun Control bill, which had been scheduled for a vote in the Senate yesterday. Because they had been warned of a demonstration on the steps of the Capitol, the Secret Service diverted the President's car to the Russell Senate Office Building.

"The bullet lodged in Senator Harrison's brain and he was pronounced dead on arrival at Woodrow Wilson Medical Center. A second bullet grazed the shoulder of FBI Agent Mark Andrews, 28, who threw himself on the Senator in an effort to save his life. Andrews was treated at the same hospital and later released.

"There was no immediate explanation of the fact that a second presidential motorcade did arrive at the Capitol steps a few moments before the assassination, without the President.

"Vice President Bradley ordered an immediate recess of the Senate out of respect for Senator Harrison. The House then voted unanimously to extend the recess for seven days.

"The President, who arrived at the Capitol via the congressional subway from the Russell Building, first learned the news of Harrison's assassination when she reached the Senate. Visibly shaken, she announced that the luncheon to discuss gun control would continue as planned but asked the assembled Senators to observe a minute of silence in honour of their dead colleague.

"The President went on to say, 'I know we are all shocked and saddened by the tragic and horrifying event which has just occurred. This senseless killing of a good and decent man must, however, only strengthen our determination to work together in making our country safe from the easy access of arms.'

"The President plans to address the nation at nine o'clock tonight."

"So now you know everything, Liz."

"I know nothing," she replied.

"I didn't know very much of that myself," Mark admitted.

"Living with you is going to be difficult."

"Who said I was going to live with you?"

"I took it for granted from the way you're eating my eggs."

At the Fontainebleau Hotel a man was sitting by the side of the swimming pool reading the *Miami Herald* and drinking coffee. At least Senator Harrison could cause no more trouble which made him feel a little safer. Xan had kept his part of the bargain.

He sipped the coffee, a little hot, it didn't matter, he was in no hurry. He had already given new orders; he couldn't afford any further risks. Xan would be dead by the evening; that had been arranged. Matson and Tony would be freed for lack of evidence, so his lawyer, who had never let him down yet, had assured him, and he would not be visiting Washington for a while. He relaxed and settled back in his beach chair to let the Miami sun warm him. He lit another cigarette.

At 9:45, the Director was met at the White House by Janet Brown, the President's Chief of Staff. They waited and chatted. The Director briefed her on Special Agent Andrews' background. Brown made careful notes.

Mark arrived just before 10:00. He had only just managed to get home and change into a new suit.

"Good morning, Director," he said nonchalantly.

"Good morning, Mark. Glad you could make it." Slightly quizzical but not disapproving. "This is the President's Chief of Staff, Janet Brown."

"Good morning, ma'am," said Mark.

Janet Brown took over. "Will you be kind enough to come through to my office, where we can wait. The President will be videotaping her address to the nation for this evening's television broadcast so that she can fly to Camp David at 11:15. I imagine you and the Director will have about fifteen minutes with her."

Janet Brown took them to her office, a large room in

the West Wing with a fine view of the Rose Garden through a bow window.

"I'll get us some coffee," she said.

"That'll be a change," murmured Mark.

"I'm sorry?" said Janet Brown.

"Nothing."

The Director and Mark settled down in comfortable chairs where they could watch a large liquid-crystal monitor screen on one of the walls, already alive with comings and goings in the Oval Office.

The President's forehead was being powdered in preparation for her speech and the cameramen were wheeling around her. Janet Brown was on the phone.

"CBS and NBC can roll, Janet, but ABC is still fixing things up with their OB unit," said an agitated female voice.

Janet Brown got the producer of ABC on the other line.

"Get a move on, Harry, the President doesn't have all day."

"Janet."

Florentyna Kane was on the middle of the screen.

She looked up. "Yes, Madam President?"

"Where's ABC?"

"I'm just chasing them, Madam President."

"Chasing them? They've had four hours' warning. They couldn't get a camera to the Second Coming."

"No, ma'am. They're on their way now."

Harry Nathan, ABC's producer, appeared on the screen. "We're all set now, Janet. Ready to record in five minutes."

"Fine," said Florentyna Kane and looked at her watch. It was 10:11. The digits changed – and were replaced by the rate of her heartbeat – 72; normal, she thought. They disappeared again, to be replaced by her blood pressure, 140/90; a little high; she'd get it checked by her doctor this weekend. The digits were replaced by the Dow-Jones index, showing an early fall of 1.5 to 1,409. This disappeared and the watch showed 10:12. The President rehearsed the opening line of her speech for the last time. She'd gone over the final draft with Edward that morning, and she was satisfied with it.

"Mark."

"Sir?"

"I want you to report back to Grant Nanna at the WFO this afternoon."

"Yes, sir."

"Then I want you to take a vacation. I mean a real vacation, some time in May. Mr Elliott is leaving me at the end of May to take up the post of Special Agent in Charge of the Columbus Field Office. I'm going to offer you his job, and enlarge it to your being my personal assistant."

Mark was stunned. "Thank you very much, sir. I would be delighted." Bang goes the five-year plan.

"You said something, Mark?"

"No, sir."

"In private, Mark, you must stop calling me 'sir', if we're going to work together all the time; it's more than I can stand. You can call me Halt or Horatio – I don't mind which."

Mark couldn't help laughing.

"You find my name amusing, Mark?"

"No, sir. But I just made $3,516."

"Testing: one, two, three. Loud and clear. Could you give us a voice test, please, Madam President?" asked the floor producer, now less agitated. "What did you have for breakfast?"

"Toast and coffee," said the President resonantly.

"Thank you, Madam. That's fine. Ready to roll."

All the cameras were focused on the President, who sat behind her desk, sombre and serious.

"When you're ready, Madam President."

The President looked into the lens of Camera One.

"My fellow Americans, I speak to you tonight from the Oval Office in the wake of the bloody assassination of Senator Harrison on the steps of the Capitol. Robert Everard Harrison was my friend and colleague, and I know we will all feel his loss greatly. Our sympathy goes out to his family in their distress. This evil deed only strengthens my determination to press for legislation early in the new session strictly limiting the sale and the unauthorised ownership of guns. I will do this in memory of Senator Robert Harrison, so that we may feel he did not die in vain."

The Director looked at Mark; neither of them spoke. The President continued, repeating her belief in the importance of gun control and why the measure deserved the full support of the American people.

"And so I leave you, my fellow citizens, thanking God that America can still produce men who are willing to risk their own lives for public service. Thank you and good night."

The camera panned to the Presidential Seal. Then the Outside Broadcast units took over and switched to a picture of the White House with the flag at half-mast.

"It's a wrap, Harry," said the female floor producer. "Let's do a re-run and see what it looks like."

The President in the Oval Office, and the Director and Mark in Janet Brown's room watched the re-run. It was good. The Gun Control bill will sail through, thought Mark.

The chief usher arrived at Janet Brown's door. He addressed the Director.

"The President wonders if you and Mr Andrews would be kind enough to join her in the Oval Office."

Both men rose from their chairs and followed in silence down the long marble corridor of the West Wing, passing pictures of former presidents, intermingled with oil paintings commemorating famous incidents in American history. They passed the bronze bust of Lincoln. When they reached the East Wing, they stopped at the massive white semi-circular doors of the Oval Office, dominated by the great Presidential Seal. A Secret Service man was sitting behind a desk in the hallway. He looked up at the chief usher, neither spoke. Mark watched the Secret Service agent's hand go under the desk, and he heard a click. The Seal split as the doors opened. The usher remained in the entrance.

Someone was unclipping a tiny microphone from under the President's collar, and the remnants of make-up were being removed by an attentive young woman. The television cameras had already gone. The usher announced, "The Director of the Federal Bureau of Investigation, Mr H. A. L. Tyson, and Special Agent Mark Andrews, Madam President."

The President rose from her seat at the far end of the room and waited to greet them. They walked towards her slowly.

"Sir," said Mark under his breath.

"Yes, Mark?"

"Shall we tell the President?"

The End